# GENO WASHINGTO

was born into a gospel-sin[...] bootlegging family in Eva[...] December, 1943. A stint in[...] him to East Anglia, and or[...] 1964, Geno settled in 'Swinging London', where he formed his own soul and R&B band.

Geno Washington and The Ram Jam Band quickly became the most popular live outfit on the circuit. Their classic *Hand Clappin', Foot Stompin', Funky Butt Live* was the third biggest selling album of 1967, only out-sold by the schmaltz of *The Sound of Music* and *Bridge Over Troubled Waters*. The Dexy's Midnight Runners' hit 'Geno' pays tribute to the man's legendary status as a power-house musician and performer.

Still leading a band – currently The Purple Aces – and selling-out clubs and theatres wherever he goes, Geno has recently notched up a string of hit TV appearances – including co-starring with Nick Berry in the TV movie *Paparazzo* and a show-stopping singing performance on *The White Room* .

Geno's latest album, 'Change Your Thoughts You Change Your Life' (CSA114) is currently available on Thunderbird Records.

*The Blood Brothers* is Geno Washington's first novel.

*First Published in Great Britain in 1998 by*
*The Do-Not Press*
*PO Box 4215*
*London SE23 2QD*

*Casebound: ISBN 1 899 344 44 6*

*British Library Cataloguing in Publication Data. A catalogue*
*record for this book is available from the British Library.*

*h  g  f  e  d  c  b  a*

*Printed and bound in Great Britain by The Guernsey Press Co Ltd.*

# The Blood Brothers

## Geno Washington

THE DO-NOT PRESS

*I would like to dedicate this book to my loving wife, Frenchie, who is always there when the storm comes and when it leaves.*

# 1

This story begins with me flat on my back at Cedar-Sinai Hospital in Los Angeles, California. I am waiting for an operation to repair nerve damage in the spinal area of my back. If the operation is a success, I will be able to walk and live again as a happy, fun loving good old boy. In the meantime, there is nothing to do but rest, look at the pretty nurses, and beat my meat on the sly.

Anyway, one day I heard footsteps walking past my door and then suddenly stop. I heard the name Robbie Jones mentioned, my ears pricked up. You see, I'm Robbie Jones and I can hear the nurse say to Dr McCoy, 'What a shame. Nobody comes to visit Mr Jones,' and she calls me a poor bastard.

Nurse Kay means well. You see, she's from London, England and takes her job very much to heart. She loves people and tries to make every patient feel that she loves you, the Almighty God loves you, and the coke-sniffing doctors love you. She'll do any damn thing to get your ass well, just to pay the bill, and get out. She knows I have lost the use of my legs temporarily, that I'm flat broke, and can't pay the hospital bill, the reason for which I will explain later if any gin arrives to make the day brighter. Anyway, nurse Kay came into my room with a big smile on her face. And with that English accent she said at the top of her voice, all common-like, 'What a lovely day, me-o mate.'

'Cut the bullshit Kay,' I said spitting into my bedpan. 'Can you get me a half pint of gin?' I asked. 'Don't be a silly-willy. You want me to lose my job?' she snapped back.

I didn't answer. I tried to look sad as I smiled back with a shit-eating grin. Nurse Kay strolled over to my bed all sexy like, kissed me on the cheek, and went on cleaning my room. Nurse Kay was very jolly, singing and dancing as she was cleaning under and around my bed, shaking that big ass of hers. She knew I was looking, watching, peeping spying , and getting hot as a firecracker. Moving over to my bed, she bent down near my head where I could see her tits hanging out of her dress, She had enough to fill Wilt Chamberlain's hands. She put her right hand on my pillow, sliding her left hand under the sheets, slowly up to my beautiful brown balls. I must admit this old lady's hand felt so warm and welcome. She smiled and gave a wink. Looking into my eyes, she whispered to me in a sexy voice 'You want a nice massage? My left hand will make you loose, and my right hand will catch the juice.'

'Fuck off bitch. Can that Shakespeare shit. Just get me some fucking gin, dammit to hell.' I replied, not appreciating her poetry.

Nurse Kay jumped back quickly from my bed feeling a little embarrassed and with a strange expression on her face. I began to laugh out loud and pulled the covers over my head. After a couple of seconds, Nurse Kay began to see the funny side of it also and began to laugh with me as she playfully pulled on my blanket. Boom! boom! boom! someone knocked on the wall and shouted, 'Not so loud asshole. I'm trying to get some sleep. Shit. If that nurse did as much working as she does fucking, we'd all be well by now. '

Nurse Kay ignored the Preacher's comments from the next room and began to whisper. 'Ok Robbie, I'll get you your damn gin.' She then picked up the phone and asked Toe Joe, a day medic, to bring up a bottle of gin. She walked over and kissed me and said sweetly, 'I'll see you Monday, after the weekend.' As she was walking out the door she said softly, 'Don't get drunk,' and closed the door.

Knock, knock. 'Who is it?' I asked. 'It's me Robbie, Toe Joe with the gin.'

'Come on in Toe Joe. Put it over here on the table near my bed. Would you like a drink?'

'No way man. I've got an appointment in the operating room in one hour, man. can you imagine me with all them fancy doctors and fucked up?' He began to laugh as he closed the door.

As I began to drink more and more of the gin, my mind rolled back over my whole life, and I began to weep and feel sorry for myself. I wouldn't tell anyone about my life because no on would believe me or could imagine the nightmare and horror of it all. But I'm gonna tell you as I drink this bottle of gin. I rather feel like talking, so I'll tell you the whole story from the beginning and maybe it will save you from the same fate. Please, I beg of you to take note of this story. It could save your life, or the life of some-one dear to you.

It all started my junior year at Stanford University. I was training to be a doctor and I was the star quarterback on the football team. I was having the time of my life. I had girls, a big Lincoln Continental car, and my pockets were full of money which my dad sent every month. I had all the votes of America's top football coaches and was selected All-American Quarterback that year.

As for training to be a doctor, my mom and dad were so pleased. I would be the first black doctor in my home town and in my family.The people from my home town would organise bus trips to see football games on the campus, or come over to my father's church on Tuesday nights and watch the games on film.

But I had a skeleton in my closet. I was hooked on cocaine. I was spitting blood and every time I'd get hit very hard in a football game, my nose would bleed. The coach would always ask if I was OK, I'd shake my head and assure him everything was cool. He never guessed the real problem was coke.

You see, I had two roommates. One named cheese and the other Kareem Kareem. Cheese was a pal, always. Every time there was a party, or getting together with the girls, Cheese would always have some nice cut coke, Baby!

Everyone on campus called Cheese by that name because he had about a million holes in his nose from sniffing cocaine and his nose looked like Swiss cheese. Between the bums and hangers-on, Cheese was the one who really got me hooked. Old Cheese could sniff an ounce of coke in one nostril! You see, I started sniffing cocaine at first just to have fun when I was going to have sex. Coke makes sex beautiful and funky and sometimes extremely rude! It makes your dick hard, you dig? But that shit got out of hand. Can you dig this, I had a fifty dollar a day habit, just to get my dick hard! I got paranoid about everything: my dick, people, money, eating the right foods. Man, I was all fucked up.

That's how I got to know my roommate Kareem Kareem. We became true buddies. Kareem was from the northwest part of Africa, Mauritania. It is a poor nation of one and a half million people, near the Sahara Desert. Kareem was the son of a government minister. He was rich, kind, polite and extremely smart. Anyway, Kareem and I became very close friends after his advising me on many occasions against the use of drugs.

He would tell me off in my room, at dances, or in the basement of the campus church where I would sometimes play ping pong. Everywhere I turned there was Kareem! And when we weren't talking about my drug habit, it was a

Africa and girls, or what country had the best girls, and who had the best asses. Being African, Kareem had a passion for big ass girls. I knew he would go on to become a great doctor, especially if he specialised in big asses.

Back to the point. I was using much less cocaine than before. I was gaining a new sense of pride about myself. Kareem being the son of a diplomat, and rich, knew many African statesmen and their families. No way did he know any broke bastards!

Kareem was invited to many parties and socials. He was a 'hawk for a piece of ass,' but he never liked going alone and would ask Cheese and I to accompany him almost always.

One day, as I was coming out of football practice, Kareem and Cheese called out to me 'Hey Robbie!' I looked around, but saw no one. Again, 'Hey Robbie!' I turned to see Kareem and Cheese running to me with a small white envelope in their hands, and with big smiles on their faces.

I said, 'What's up?' Cheese replied, 'Pussy galore'. Kareem spoke up quickly 'Be cool man, don't talk like that about the ladies.'

'Robbie?'

'Yeah?'

'Robbie would you like to come to a African United party?'

'When?'

'Saturday night, man, what are you a detective?'

I thought silently to myself for a moment, the game would be finished at 5 o'clock Saturday, so that would leave me time to party all night. 'Hey man, that's cool! Where is this funky party?' I asked.

'Prince Jah Sing Kahn's house in Los Angeles, Beverley Hills baby,' Kareem answered. Cheese, pushing a fistful of cocaine up his nose, shouted 'Yeah man, high class bitches, Rolls Royces, and champagne all night.' Kareem and I gave out a loud laugh as we watched cheese foam at the mouth with excitement.

I hadn't been to a real prince's house before and I was getting excited just thinking about it.

'Kareem, is this on the level man?' I said with a smile. 'Yes, mon,' he said with an African accent. 'Com mon, I will find you a pretty African girl who will tear your Rolls Boli off.' (Rolls Boli means balls in his native tongue.)

'Right on, baby, right on,' I said. We all laughed and gave the Black Handshake. About this time Kareem's chauffeur walked over and asked if he could put the top up on the Rolls Royce as it looked like rain was coming. 'That's OK Mosi, we're leaving now,' Kareem said. All the way back to the dormitory we were like school boys. I'll never forget how happy we were.

Talking about booze, the food, the girls, and how on the night of the party Cheese and I would have to call Kareem 'Lord Kareem', as he is a Lord in Mauritania. Mosi was laughing so hard, he pissed himself the poor bastard.

Kareem shouted at his chauffeur, 'Mosi, you African cunt, you had better wash that front seat with soap and water good tonight.' Cheese jumped in quickly, 'Yeah and wash your nasty ass too!'

At last the big night was here. It was Saturday night. Ring, ring – I jumped out of the shower to get the phone.

'Hey Robbie, get your ass ready quick! This is Kareem, Cheese and I will pick you up in twenty minutes, man. Cheese is getting fucked up, man. If you don't hurry I don't think Cheese will make it. OK Robbie?' I laughed, 'OK Kareem, I'll be ready when you come. Just honk your horn twice.'

You will never guess what happened. Kareem had invited Cheese to a film premiere at the local cinema. There was dinner and champagne being served, and Cheese drank two bottles of champagne without the meal. Cheese was beginning to feel real good about now. What with jamming a fist full of coke up his nose and feeling the waitress's tits as she served drinks behind the topless bar. It all proved too much for Kareem to take.

I suddenly heard the horn of Kareem's Rolls. I pulled back the curtains and saw Cheese running to a nearby bush to be sick and Kareem waving me quickly to come down to the car.

I grabbed my coat and hat and took one last look in the mirror at my beautiful self. I blew a kiss and said 'Go get 'em Robbie' and ran out the door. When I arrived downstairs, Kareem shouted 'Robbie! let's go man, before old asshole Cheese falls apart.'

I said 'Cheese, you OK man?'

'Yeah man, let's get to this party, man,' Cheese replied. As Kareem was driving us, I knew he was feeling very embarrassed about his chauffeur Mosi being drugged out of his head in the back seat with Cheese.

Cheese had slipped Mosi some cocaine outside in the parking lot, while Kareem was making his apologies to the waitress for Cheese's bad behavior.

I tried to cheer Kareem up by saying 'Kareem, man, I bet all the girls will go for you tonight.'

'Bullshit,' replied Cheese. Mosi began to laugh out loud and this made Kareem really angry as Cheese and Mosi laughed like Miss Piggy in the back seat. I stepped in by saying 'Come on fellows, calm down and let's be on our best behavior.

'Yeah, you guys be cool tonight. Mosi, no more drinks or anything or I will report you to my father,' Kareem replied. Just then a man in a red and gold uniform stepped out in front of our car with a sign saying Stop. 'Be cool everybody, we're here now. No bullshit, man, or we don't get into the party,' Kareem said.

'Excuse me sir. Shall I park your car sir?' said the car-park attendant. 'Well thank you,' Kareem said as we all got out of the car. Cheese spoke up. 'Hey man, are there many bitches here tonight?'

'Pardon?' the attendant answered. 'Sorry fellows, 'Cheese said laughing. I butted in. 'He said are there many ladies here tonight?'

'Yes sir. The place is full of gorgeous girls, sir,' the attendant replied with a smile.

As we walked away, Kareem spoke with seriousness. 'Please fellows, have a good time tonight, but be cool. Some of these people know my mom and dad, so be cool.' Cheese answered coolly, ' I know you're talking about me you bastard, but I will act like a perfect gentleman, tonight.'

As we walked up the driveway, all you could see was Rolls Royces lining the kerbs and foxy ladies walking through big double gold doors. As we approached the door of the house, an attendant asked for our invitation cards. Kareem answered quickly 'I am Lord Kareem Kareem and these are my guests.'

'Come right in, sir.'

'Lord Kareem Kareem of Mauritania and his guests,' the doorman said in a loud, husky voice.

Everyone looked as we strolled across the floor 'looking good' to the bar. This party was like something in the movies. There were six huge chandeliers in the main ballroom, three band-stands, with fifty musicians and dancers from Africa. There were wild exotic flower displays in every room from all parts of Africa. The food was extravagant and colorful with wines and cham-pagne from France. As the orchestra played, Lords and Ladies, Princes and Princesses danced. There were also some very shady characters here, doing some reckless eyeballing at the jewels.

They came in all kinds of lies and make up. Phony Lords and Princesses, expert pickpockets and we also have five or six trans-vestites here tonight. Cheese went into the men's room for a piss and ran out quickly, grabbing me by the arm, 'Hey Robbie, there is a damn fag in the toilet, dressed like a woman.'

'Don't bullshit me, ' I said. Cheese, shaking with embarrassment, replied 'No man, I thought it was a girl at first. She was looking good. I was going to talk to her after I had a piss, when she strolled over and pulled up her dress, pulled down her drawers and pulled out a bigger dick than I have.'

'No bullshit, man?' I began to laugh and tell Kareem as he walked over to me, what had happened to Cheese.

This was a hot party. You didn't have to worry about racism here, baby! Everybody, well, almost everybody, was as black as the ace of spades.

I had never seen so many beautiful black girls with such big asses in one place in all my life. I felt like a rat in a cheese factory I thought to myself. About this time, Prince Jah walked over and asked Kareem, Cheese and I if we were enjoying the party. I thanked Prince Jah and smiled, but he noticed Cheese said nothing to him.

'How about you, sir, are you having a nice time?' asked the Prince. Cheese replied, still feeling good, 'Does a bear shit in the woods?' The Prince laughed out loud with joy and said to Kareem, 'This nigger is crazy,' and walked away smiling.

Kareem said to me and Cheese, 'I'll be back later, meanwhile you guys walk around and mix with the guests, ok?'

'You got it, baby,' I said. As Kareem was walking away, Cheese said 'Hey Robbie. You want some cocaine to get a little loose, or some magic mushrooms?' I knew he had some just for this party and they were from Mexico, beautiful stuff it was and made you feel loose like a long necked goose.

Yes sir, that's just what I need to make me feel mellow and cool. I took four and about ten minutes later, I felt like walking on air and dancing on an egg, so light on my feet, and in my head at the same time.

As I was walking alone without old dogass Cheese, I heard this voice coming from a small room on my right, next to the shit house. I stopped and looked in. To my surprise, there stood this beautiful big tit girl. She had this magic smile, and her teeth glittered like ivory. She was about five feet two in height and had a body shaped like a Coca-Cola bottle.

That white dress she was wearing made her look like a black angel. It was clinging so tight to her body, you could see that she had that Special Something... and a lot of it. Oh, she was a juicy momma!

All of a sudden I felt a unique feeling rushing all over my body, which ended with a sudden swelling on its way to my knee. It was a bit psychic, really. I didn't know what it was, or why I felt this way, as I had seen and met thousands of girls before.

I decided to sit down quickly and check this young lady out. As I sat smiling and looking in a daze, she caught my eye, turned, and began to move in my direction, as she was singing with this jazz trio. At times she sounded just like Nancy Wilson, who was my favourite singer anyway.

Now dig this little bag of goodies. She walked over, sat down on my knee with her little round ass, and looked dead into my eyes. She broke into the song 'I Want To Be Loved By You'. I was thinking to myself, don't move baby, don't you ever get up from here. I could feel her small waist, her tits was all in my face, her soft ass was resting on my knee and the bulge in my pants was getting bigger. Jesus, Jesus, Jesus. I must be in love with this bitch, I thought to myself.

As the song finished, she got up off my knee and gave me a wink, saying 'You're cute, baby.'

'I know,' I joked. She laughed and walked away to the dressing room. Some drunk guy sitting at the next table and looking with envy said to me 'You lucky bastard. You Mexicans get all the girls.'

About this time Cheese walked in the door and shouted 'Hey Robbie. What's going on man?' Before I answered, I took a good look at Cheese and he looked like a hurricane had hit him after a truck had run over his face. I said 'Cheese, man, I have just met the most beautiful girl in the whole wide world.'

'Yeah I know. She's probably one of those fat sons of bitches I turned down, God dammit!' Cheese replied. I said 'Cool it you silly bastard, watch your mouth. I'm in love and going to marry that girl one way or another.'

'I'm sorry Robbie, about what I said. Here have another mushroom,' Cheese replied.

'OK man, only four more. I don't want to get fucked up and begin to look like you,' I rapped back to Cheese.

'Cheese, man, I'll be back later man, I'm going backstage to see if I can talk to that girl singer, OK?'

'Yeah. I'll be here, later baby.' Cheese replied.

As I went in the stage door, I could see this very distinguished looking old gentleman waiting outside this girl's door. This bastard was standing outside my girl's stage door, licking his big lips, with some cheap-ass roses. Now what kind of shit was this, I thought to myself. He knocked on the door. 'Shilee, hurry, hurry out my sweets. I want to show you off to the President of Syria and the rest of my friends,' he said, smacking together his liver lips. That bastard!! Just then out popped Shilee in a dress so tight you could see what she had had for dinner.

I jumped back before she could see me, but all I could see is she was dressed all in red and looking like Lady Madonna. All kinds of thoughts went round and round in my head as I seen my girl, Shilee, walk away arm in arm with that jerk-off-Johnny.

Maybe she likes rich men. Maybe he's her sugar daddy. Maybe she's going to marry that old man. Maybe I ought to kill myself right now. Oh God! Oh Mercy Jesus! Please let me have the love of my life, Shilee. This was my Southern Belle, my Southern Fried Chicken, my kind of woman that I could run away with and never be seen again. Oh, take me now, Lord!

Fight you bastard, fight! I said to myself, don't let some fancy pants diplomat take your girl away from you.

I quickly regained my composure with the feeling that she was already mine. I made a beeline for the cocktail bar, and there she was, sitting in the corner of the bar drawing a small crowd. I sat down. 'Hey, pretty lady. May I have this dance?' I asked. 'Sure if you promise not to ask again,' she smiled. 'You got it lady,' I said.

'Oh, please don't call me lady, my name is Shilee Ali Shilee.'

It was supposed to be one dance, but we stayed on the floor twenty-five minutes. My rap was long, hard and fast and my pants were getting tighter. I told her I loved her five hundred ways and how nice it would be living our lives together. I was even quoting Shakespeare – Shakespeare, who by his friends was called

Willie the Shake.

All the time I was talking to Shilee, I could see and feel my life would never be the same again. I would need no dope, booze, or anything that was artificial. I wanted to live, live, and live forever with my Shilee.

As I talked, she would move her body close to mine and give me that baby doll look, that kind of look that makes a man feel ten feet tall. She had a way of making a man feel super-macho like a cave man, but filled with love.

With her arms around my waist, smiling like she knew something I didn't, Shilee whispered to me 'Robbie, stop talking so damn much. I fell in love with you the very first I saw you. OK baby-cakes?'

My mouth fell open. I was stunned. I had my baby at last. If I never had nothing else in my life again, I had the love of Shilee. At that moment I could see out of the corner of my eye that diplomat fellow, looking with some concern. After all I had kept Shilee all to myself for half an hour and here I was a complete stranger.

As the music stopped, Shilee pulled my jacket and said 'Hey baby, I'm going to powder my nose. Wait for me at the bar, I won't be long. And hey! Don't talk to any other girls, you hear?' laughing as she walked away.

When I walked back to the bar I met up with Cheese again. 'Robbie, you old bastard, are you trying to avoid me?'

'Me avoid you, Cheese? Hell no man,' I said. 'How is it with that girl you was telling me about Robbie?' Cheese said smiling.

'Listen Cheese, man, not so loud! Everything is fantastic with Shilee and me. But that damn diplomat fellow keeps looking over here and might give me a bit of trouble later.'

Cheese whispered 'Which son of a bitch is that?' Cheese could hardly stand or see straight. I mean his eyes were so red, they looked like a mad dog's balls. Anyway, before I could say anything Cheese had ran over to this diplomat fellow's table and began to grab him by the collar, shouting to me 'Robbie, Hey Robbie! Is this the son of a bitch that won't leave you alone? Stand up and fight you silly bastard!' Cheese shouted in a fit of temper as he was pounding the diplomat over his fat head. I ran over to try to stop the fight. 'Let him go. Let him go. Cheese for God's sake let the poor bastard go!' I shouted as I was kicking the diplomat in his ass and stepping on his balls. Tables, glasses, plates, and chairs – everything that was not nailed down went flying in the air, and Cheese and I were on this diplomat like white on rice.

I tried to help Cheese, but there were too many people kicking his ass, like kicking asses was going out of style. They were on Cheese like stink on shit. I could hear Cheese shout after every six blows to his head, 'Fight fair, you sons of bitches, before I really get annoyed.'

I could hear people shouting 'Break it up, come on break it up, dammit.' this huge big nigger with a deep husky voice shouted 'God dammit I said break it up or I will crack some heads.' This nigger had muscles everywhere. His hands looked like a foot and I swear he had muscles on his fingernails. He was the type of big nigger that when he sat on the toilet, his dick would hang in the water.

Everybody ran away and all the white people that were near the fight watched in amazement. This big nigger was sweating and started shouting how he would tear off anyone's arms if another punch was passed, and how his foot would stretch somebody's asshole if the fighting didn't stop immediately.

Anyway, the fight was over and Shilee walked over to me and asked what had happened. I told her and to my surprise, she began to laugh out loud, with tears streaming down her face, laughing with joy. Apparently the diplomat fellow was a prince and the local bully of whom everyone was terror-stricken when in his company. His name was Prince Ben Ali Hassan.

He was a shrewd, shitty, murderous man who made his fortune by selling humans – the slave trade. He was the biggest slave trader in Mauritania, and also was to be the next ruler of Mauritania. This was the story Shilee told me after she stopped laughing.

She had seen everyone so frightened of this man, and along comes Cheese, who don't give a shit about anything, and fights like a wild bear with the prince and his bodyguards. I must confess, if I knew that the prince was that bad and had so many bodyguards, shit, I wouldn't have gone over there in the first place. I wouldn't give a shit who was getting their ass kicked, Cheese or my mother. Anyway, that was the first time I met Prince Ben Ali Hassan, and I wished it was my last.

About this time, Kareem Kareem walked into the room. 'Hey, Robbie, guess what? I heard there was a big fight in this room twenty minutes ago. I wonder who was in it?' Kareem said smiling.

'Ah, it was nothing,' I explained. 'Hey Kareem, I want you to meet my main lady from now on,' I said, trying to change the subject as the floor attendant was mopping up the blood, glass, and shit stains from the floor.

'Shilee, meet my roommate. Kareem this is Shilee, my future wife,' I said, introducing the two.

About this time I could see the prince and his bodyguards walking over our way. I was glad Cheese was in the toilet, washing the blood off his face, head, and legs. Why hell, he was washing everything after taking an old fashioned, country boy beating.

One nurse had never seen so many black people and black eyes in one place. She thought Cheese was in a fight with everybody and that Cheese was the only one without a tomahawk, he was so fucked up. Anyway, before the prince arrived, Shilee quickly slipped her telephone number into my coat pocket, told me to call her tomorrow, and don't for God's sake make any problems with the prince.

But you know me. I had to show a little bit of courage. You know what i mean. Some kind of shit like 'hold me, let me at him,' Errol Flynn kind of stuff.

So, just before the prince got near, and I knew Kareem would hold me tight, I shouted 'I'll kill the bastard if he comes over here. Where's my damn knife? I'll cut his balls off. Hold me, please don't let me get my hands on that son of a bitch.'

Kareem was shocked. 'Hey Robbie, what's going on man? You know these guys?' Before I could answer, that big nigger with the big hands rushed over. He looked like he wanted to kick some wise guy's ass real good. 'What the hell's going on here, huh?' he shouted loudly, shaking the floor, pacing around, and foaming at the mouth.

The prince, his bodyguards, and the big nigger with half the people in the room gathered around me. It was a very tense moment. Everyone wanted to see what was going to happen. Would I fight? Would I run? Would the big nigger rip my arms out of their sockets? Or would the prince and his bodyguards, plus the big nigger, commence to stomp another hole in my ass?

I had to act fast. There was nowhere to run. As I looked around, all I could see was a thousand big white eyes staring at me. Some of these niggers wanted to see me get a good ass kicking just to make the party worthwhile. As I was looking around, a quick flash went by my mind. Don't fall, Robbie. You see, if you fall fighting a bunch of niggers, here's what's gonna happen. Two will jump and kick your ass, while another nigger will be going through your pockets for your money, or if there's one more he will be shaving your ass with a razor.

All this happened so fast, my head was spinning. 'Are you gonna fight or shut up, sucker?' Somebody shouted. Shilee and Kareem started to beg 'Please don't fight Robbie, we hate the sight of blood.' I knew the joke had gone too far, but I had the perfect plan even though I knew I had let my mouth get my ass in trouble. I slowly removed my coat, calmly unbuttoned my shirt, and rolled up my sleeves as Shilee began to cry and called out for the attendant to bring back the mop. Cool as ice I said 'Kareem, hold my coat please.'

Just as the big nigger and the bodyguards began to move the people back to make room to kick my ass, you guessed it right, I fainted. That fucked everybody up. I could hear the shouts of 'That dirty bastard fainted, wake that nigger up and kick his ass.'

I even heard one old lady about eighty years old shout 'Piss on the son of a bitch, he'll wake up then.' After a few seconds the old lady said 'That nigger ain't fainted. I seen him move his lyin' eyes.' I wanted to laugh, but that would have meant these people disconnecting some parts of my body, mainly my head.

As I lay on the floor waiting for someone to revive me, I slowly opened one eye, slightly, I could see the prince grab Shilee and tell her he's taking her home. I noticed she was not worried about me. I guess Kareem had told her that I always faint when things get hot and nasty.

I am not ashamed to faint. No sir, you try it sometime. It will save your ass when you need it most, but don't get me wrong now, I'm no coward, but when I am outnumbered nine to one, I'm going to faint. No ass kicking for this boy, no sir!

Anyway, as I came around slowly and somebody revived me with a whisky on the rocks, and a James Brown song being played by the band in the background, Kareem smacked me on the back and said, 'Robbie, that was close, man.'

'All in a good day's work,' I replied calmly with nerves of steel and my fist balled up ready to kill at a moment's notice.

I was explaining to Kareem how the fight started and why, when all of a sudden I noticed Cheese was nowhere to be seen. 'Kareem, have you seen Cheese?'

'No man,' Kareem said.

'Let's go and look in one of the bedroom toilets. He must be in one of them being patched up,' I said to Kareem.

As we walked upstairs, people were kissing and hugging on the stairs, in the corners of the hallways, or dancing to the loud, blasting music from downstairs.

I opened room number three. There was a couple standing on the bed with no clothes on, naked as jaybirds, reciting Shakespeare and licking cream cheese from each other's body, working their way downward. They stopped, turned slowly, and stared at me with cream cheese dripping from their jaws. After five seconds, he said 'That's the nigger that fainted downstairs.' I shouted back 'It wasn't me, it was another handsome black man that looks like me, cream chops.' Laughing, I slammed the door and carried on to the next room.

As I opened the door, the sounds of soft moans and heavy breathing stopped; silence broken only by the blasting music from downstairs. 'Where's the lights,' I said.

'Don't cut on them damn lights you asshole,' A familiar voice shouted from out of the dark. Kareem shouted, 'Cheese, you old bastard, what the hell are you doing here?'

I quickly turned the lights on and shit, I never have seen such a fat woman. Cheese was on top of her and he looked like a monkey trying to fuck an elephant. Her lips were the size of Mohammed Ali's fist. Back home we call lips like that 'soup coolers'. This bitch could get a job as the Fat Lady of a circus anytime.

'Cheese, come on get up. We are going home now. I've got to get up early and call Shilee tomorrow. She's also bringing a friend for you,' I said lying through my teeth. Just then the fat bitch spoke. 'What's the other girl got that I don't have?' I said 'Nothing. You just got ten times more of it.'

'I'd like to whip your ass,' she said.

'You got about as much chance of that as waking up skinny in the morning,' I replied, and Kareem and Cheese fell over laughing. 'It's been a long day fellows, let's go home,' I said.

As we were leaving the party, and checking out our hats, I tipped the check girl five dollars. Walking toward the door, I heard her whisper to another girl, 'That's the cheap bastard that fainted in the main ballroom.' I turned and gave her a shit-eating type of smile and said 'It wasn't me. It was another handsome black man that looks like me, Miss fuck face,' and kept on walking out the door laughing.

As we walked to the car we saw that Cheese's clothing was full of blood. Kareem said to Cheese 'Have you been fighting tonight or something?'

'Yeah,' Cheese answered sharply, 'I was fighting two big bastards at the party tonight. I would have kicked their asses if I hadn't slipped in my own blood.'

With that we went back to the dormitory, laughing and having a night to remember for life.

The next date with Shilee was the start of many more to come. All that summer and the last half of my senior year, Shilee and I had hardly left each other's side. Sometimes we would go for long drives, or walks on the beaches, or just be lazy and stay on campus running in and out of each other's dormitory rooms. While this lovey-dovey was going on, I began to receive threatening letters against my life. In plain old English, somebody wanted to put the snuff on me.

At first I thought it was a joke, as they only came every two months. Then they began to come once a week, and I started to worry.

Each time a letter arrived it would say 'Leave Shilee alone or I will kill you, MIBUKO DELIA.' For readers' information, MIBUKO DELIA means 'Man with the face of an ass'. The lettering was from newspaper cuttings. I called the local police, but they said it must be the work of a crank trying to put me off my football games. I told Shilee about the letters and told her not to worry, but you know women. She would always say 'I bet it's that damn Prince Ben Ali Hassan's people who are sending the letters to scare you, Robbie.'

Yeah, and he's doing a damn good job too, I thought. I said to Shilee loudly and strongly, 'Don't worry baby, I'll kick his ass like last time,' and that would always make Shilee laugh. As time went on things progressed to the worst. I began to see and feel guys following me everywhere. Cheese was too stoned to notice and Kareem thought the whole thing was very much exaggerated.

The police thought I was girl crazy and a little off my rocker when I demanded police protection – not for me mind you, but for poor little Shilee. One night somebody lit a paper bag in front of our dormitory door, then shouted 'Fire, Fire!' and ran away.

I ran downstairs and stomped on the bag trying to put out the fire, only to find that the bag was full of horse shit. It splashed all over my shoes and pants. Shit flew everywhere. luckily I had my brown pants on.

Everyone said it was only kids having a joke. So I let it go and began to see the funny side of it. But old man trouble was not very far away. It was one afternoon as I was lying across my bed, when Shilee opened the door of my room with her pass key. She shouted 'Let's make love all day, you fool,' quickly undressing as she moved closer to my bed in the nude. I grabbed her sweet body when suddenly there was a ring at the door. Ring, ring, and again ring, ring. 'Shh Shilee,' I said, 'that's the doorbell downstairs.'

'Stay in bed and let your friend Bobby get the door,' Shilee whispered in my ear. Her body was so warm and nice, I could feel her leg moving slowly up and down my thigh.

I shouted out 'Bobby, get that damn door please.'

'OK Robbie, but you owe me one the next time,' Bobby shouted back. Kissing and hugging and grabbing all of Shilee's beautiful body that I could get into my two hands, I felt like a rat in a cheese factory.

It seemed like there was pussy and tits everywhere. I was trying to put my dick anywhere and everywhere, when Bobby shouted 'Hey Robbie, it was the mailman with a package for you. The wrapping looks fantastic, and it smells of some kind of exotic perfume.' Just then Shilee said 'What bitch has been sending you presents smelling like perfume, you two timing bastard?'

That was funny because there was a song being played on my radio in the background called 'That Bitch Is Back Again' by the Paducah Cats. Anyway, I was thinking to myself, who in the hell would send me a present smelling like perfume?

I answered calmly to Shilee 'Nobody baby, I swear to you on my mother's grandmother's life honey.'

'Shall I open it? You already got a girl, Robbie,' Bobby shouted back, laughing. About this time I could see Shilee was getting as mad as a junk yard guard dog.

'Tell him to open it, if you don't care who it's from,' Shilee whispered, looking very annoyed and pulling the sheets over her body. I thought to myself, I don't want to lose a good piece of ass over some shit package, tell him to open it and be done with it.

I shouted downstairs 'Bobby open that son of a bitch package, please and leave me alone, OK?' Bobby shouted with joy 'Far out. That's really cool of you Robbie.' I could hear the footsteps of the guys in the pool room downstairs running to see what was in the package, when all of a sudden we heard a terrible explosion.

There were screams of horror, 'Oh God, help me!' Another voice shouted out 'I'm dying, help me.' The blast was powerful, but only broke the windows, glasses and plates in my room. The after effect of the blast had knocked Shilee out of the bed and onto the floor, sliding over on my brown pants, luckily. (When you're scared shitless, best to have brown pants to match the color.)

While I regained my composure, I saw Shilee was only a little shaken up. As I held her close to me, I wiped the dust and glass from her face and quickly pushed my brown pants under the bed. I tried to put on a brave face as I said 'Shilee, honey, you stay here while I go downstairs and see what the hell happened, OK honey?' With that she nodded her head and I noticed there was a strange silence downstairs. As I helped Shilee back on the bed, I said 'I'll be back in a minute,' and slipped into a clean pair of brown pants in case of emergency.

I ran down the stairs to see what was going on, and tripped

over a leg of somebody and fell ass over elbow down the stairs. Glass was everywhere, the walls were a mess of human flesh and blood. Some of the furniture was still on fire, as well as parts of the room. There were only two complete bodies left, the others were in bits and pieces. A leg here, a hand there, it was just awful. The work of an inhuman bastard. Poor Bobby who was near the fireplace, all that was left of his body was an ear with an earring he had just bought in Beverley Hills. I leaned over and whispered to the ear, 'I'm terribly sorry, Bob.'

I had to crawl on the floor to find the door as the smoke was so thick with poisonous gas from the broken mains. It made it extremely difficult to inhale air into my lungs. It was like trying to breathe under the armpit of a wrestling gorilla.

Shilee called out to me, 'Robbie, Robbie baby, are you all right? Speak to me for God's sake.'

'Yes Shilee. Get back. There's poisonous gas down here, get to a window and break it for fresh air.' I could hear sirens coming on campus now, getting closer and closer as I was trying to find the door. I felt a huge thumb on my back; something very heavy fell on top of me like the foot of an elephant.

I thought, oh God it's got me. I tried to jump up at first, but whatever it was felt like a ton, so I rolled over on my side and was able to push what turned out to be a body off me, rather easily really. Crash, bang, as the door flew open from a hard kick from a fireman. 'Here,' I shouted, 'Down here, nigger,' as he was looking up at the ceiling and scratching his ass. As he dragged me out the door, I shouted in all honesty, 'My girl is upstairs, rescue my girl please. I don't want to live without my sweet Shilee.' Naturally I fainted momentarily.

As the fireman went to rescue Shilee and anyone else of importance in the dormitory, I picked myself up off the ground, dusting off my brown pants, and walked back to the door to look in. I could see little Billy Joe's body lying face down in a pool of blood in the same spot I pushed that heavy body off me. (Billy Joe was hired to clean the toilets and cook dinner for the students who were working their way through school.) There was a large bookshelf which covered the wall near the door. Little Billy Joe had been blown by the blast on top of it. You could still see a mass of blood dripping from the top shelf. I guess when he fell off, he fell upon me as I was crawling in the smoke on the floor.

As I was standing in the door, Shilee ran over to me shouting 'Robbie, without a doubt, that bomb was meant for you.' Sorrow and pain swept through me. An innocent person and dear friends had been killed by a bomb that was meant for me.

The police asked me all the usual and unusual questions, but never found any clues to the murdering bastards. It was in all the papers, on national TV, with headlines that read 'Attempted murder on star football player'; 'Six killed in bomb blast.'; 'Lucky he had his brown pants.'

It was hard to believe that some sons of bitches would go this far just to keep me from my Shilee.

My parents phoned every night to see if I was alright. Cheese and Kareem went everywhere I went to protect me. Shit, Kareem couldn't even squeeze a grape and Cheese was getting worse now. When he talked, he would get tongue-tied and his ass was really starting to drag the ground when he walked.

The police assigned me a twenty-four hour guard, but after one week I told them 'Thanks, but no thanks,' because with Cheese always around me, I didn't want him busted for cocaine by my own police guard. Here I am, scared as a bastard and worrying about old fucking Cheese.

The funeral was set for two weeks after the bombing, because some of the relatives had to be reached in Japan, Spain and Germany. By that time the glue factory smelled good. All the bodies were to be cremated at St James Funeral Parlor at one o'clock in the afternoon on a Sunday. We had to bribe the funeral attendants to even carry the caskets. Already the casket tops were starting to swell up, popping the nails that held them. As I didn't want to go in a hearse, Kareem suggested that Shilee, Cheese and I go in his Rolls-Royce. On the Saturday before the funeral, Shilee, Kareem and I stayed in the dormitory and had a candlelight dinner and some French wine, while Cheese and the chauffeur made last minute funeral arrangements downtown.

As the chauffeur was parking the car, Cheese was loading and unloading some flowers for the funeral. Two masked men jumped out of a speeding red Ford Thunderbird, pointing .38's with silencers. The boss yelled 'All right you dumb shits, hands up, if you move we'll blow your asses away.' The big one spoke next: 'How much money you got? If you don't have none, I'm gonna kill you, ya hear?'

To cut a long story short, the two masked men robbed Cheese and the chauffeur of $4,000; three thousand belonged to the chauffeur and Kareem to pay for the flowers and get the Rolls Royce serviced. The other thousand was Cheese's money, $500 in cash and about $500 for his watch which they took after a hell of a struggle.

After robbing Cheese and the chauffeur, they put laundry bags over their heads and bound and gagged them, leaving them locked in the trunk of the Rolls-

Royce.

Kareem, being a nervous sort of chap, summoned the police when there was no phone call by two o'clock in the morning from old dead ass Cheese and Mosi. Meanwhile, a patrolman making a routine check downtown, saw some Mexican teenagers go through a red light in a Rolls Royce that was being driven like a low rider and gave chase. When the officer finally stopped the kids, he found they were either only ten years old, or a pair of midgets, but it turned out they were a boy and girl who couldn't speak English.

When the officer opened the trunk to check for illegal Mexican aliens, out rolled Cheese and the chauffeur flashing big white eyes. 'Are you guys wetbacks?' the surprised officer asked, as Cheese had something stuffed in his mouth resembling a large white taco.

As you can imagine, we were all very worried back in the apartment, not hearing for so long from Cheese. Knock bang knock on the door, 'Open up in there.'

'Cheese is that you?' Shilee shouted with joy. 'Who else do you think it is, Donald Duck?' Cheese replied.

Cheese and Mosi kept us up to six o'clock in the morning telling us all about what had happened and how they would kick ass if they ever saw the muggers again.

Suddenly there was a long ring in my ears. It was my alarm clock set at nine in the morning. I rolled over and switched it off. I felt like death. Three hours ago I was up bullshitting with Cheese. The phone rang and I knew it was Shilee calling to get me out of bed. 'Are you up?' she asked.

'My dick or my body?' I said laughing.

'Why is it you are always talking about your dick? Look Robbie, pick me up in an hour, OK honey?'

'Yeah, see you later,' I said as I hung up the phone.

I got dressed and went downstairs to the dining room for some breakfast and bumped into Cheese and Kareem stuffing their faces with food.

'Here comes the King. Praise the King,' Kareem shouted. Everyone calls me the King because I have my own private room since I started getting the threatening letters. 'We have to pick up Shilee in an hour, you two. Are you ready to push off soon?' I said reaching for a box of orange juice. 'Calm down, Robbie, we have been up for an hour,' Kareem said. 'Yeah don't give me no shit man, this is Cheese you're talking to man. I'm never late, right?'

'Right Cheese,' I said, stuffing a boiled egg in my mouth and reaching over for a chicken leg left over from last night's dinner.

'The car is ready, sir,' Mosi said to Kareem as we sat talking at the breakfast table. 'Let's go fellows. It's about that time to leave,' I said.

'Mosi, go to Robbie's room and pick up his luggage and coat and we will be waiting in the car, OK?' Kareem instructed Mosi.

As we drove off to the funeral, we were not our normal happy selves. There was a long silence before Cheese suggested to Mosi to put on the radio. With the music in the background, we began to talk about what we were going to do after we graduated from college.

As we were on a hill waiting for a traffic light to turn green, Cheese shouted 'I got to piss and badly, dammit.'

'Save it, buddy or tie a knot in it,' I said.

'Save it shit,' Cheese insisted.

'OK, OK but we're late picking up Shilee already, man. Mosi, as we go down the hill on the other side of the street , stop and let dog-ass Cheese piss, please,' I said sounding pissed off with a frown on my face.

The light changed to green and Mosi pulled away slowly at first and we began to talk about Vietnam and how it would affect most American families. Just as Kareem was thanking God for not being an American who had to fight in Vietnam, and possibly leaving his ass in Shit Jungle, the car began to go downhill very fast. This hill went straight into a busy freeway at the bottom. This freeway had ten lanes. It was covered with cars like flies on grandma's apple pie. From the top of the hill to the bottom it went straight down. If something went wrong on this hill, it was curtains on your life, you know what I mean? Finito, kaput, ended baby. No more Saturday night balling and no more grandma's apple pie. As the car picked up speed we all looked ahead and saw two hundred yards of straight road with no turns, just down. Kareem shouted at the top of his voice 'Mosi put on the brakes, put on the fucking brakes, man.' Mosi stomped on the brakes very hard two or three times but nothing happened. Cheese shouted 'Come on man, stomp harder, much harder than that. Put some muscle behind it.' Mosi gritted his teeth, raised his foot higher and stomped a crushing blow on the brakes. I thought his foot was going through the floor, but still nothing happened to slow the car. If anything it went faster. 'Oh shit,' Cheese said, throwing both hands over his eyes. (Our pants were slowly changing from black to brown.) Kareem closed his eyes and began to pray out loud. 'Lord, don't let me die in America. Don't let me die so young, without seeing my family in Africa again.' This damn Rolls Royce was going downhill at about one hundred and ten miles an hour. Everything was just a blur as you looked out of the windows. It was awful as the four of us were sliding on the seats on our brown pants.

The chauffeur was so scared his eyes looked like they were going to pop out of his head. Me, I was shit scared. I bit off all the fingernails on my right hand with one bite. It was all happening so fast. Just then Mosi shouted 'I'm going to turn up on the sidewalk. I've got to.'

'No, no, the trees, the fucking trees,' I said with a lump the size of an egg coming up in my throat. But before Mosi could turn back, crash and thump as my head hit the floor.

I looked up but couldn't move as the front seat had me trapped after it had moved back on me. Fire and smoke was everywhere. Shilee popped into my mind like a flash. I was never going to see her again as I was going to be burned alive, I thought to myself. I could hear someone kicking and pulling on the doors trying to save us and saying 'Those are niggers trapped in this Rolls Royce. They must have stolen it.' Then I passed out, falling on Cheese, who looked like he was dead.

You know how you wish when something is going real bad in your dreams, like falling out of a crashing aeroplane or a big shark is about to bite you in half, you wake to find it was only a dream and how happy you are? Dig this. I did wake up. (You bastards out there thought my ass was dead, didn't you?) Like I was saying, I woke up in a bed in a hospital.

'Glad to have you back with us, Mr Jones.'

As my eyes adjusted to the light, I could see that it was a doctor speaking to me with a fat nurse standing near my medicine table coyly scratching her ass.

'Would you like some soup, Mr Jones?'

'Not unless you wash your hands first,' I replied, knowing that Blue Cross were paying the bill anyway. 'How long have I been out, Doctor?'

'Two weeks my boy. You were in a coma and you have a broken leg, the right one as a matter of fact,' replied the doctor. 'But don't worry, we'll have you up and about in two or three weeks.'

'Thanks, Doc,' I said feeling a bit weak. As the doctor was leaving he looked back and said 'Cheese and Kareem have been asking for you.'

'Oh thanks, Doc, that's the best news I've heard all day.' I said.

That night a police inspector came to see me with Shilee. At first we made a lot of small talk, mostly about the apple pie my grandmother used to make, and how some of his best friends were colored folks. Then the Inspector began to ask about the accident while gorging himself from the fruit bowl next to my bed. I told him about the Prince Ben Ali Hassan incident, he sat listening and from time to time he would write something down in his little black book.

As he finished writing, he looked up and said 'That Rolls Royce you niggers stole –'

'Stole shit.' I said.

'OK George –'

'My name is Robbie.'

'OK Robbie or Snobbie, this is what happened, boy, the Rolls was tampered with.'

'What do you mean officer?' I said, shocked.

'Well Bobbie,' he said, 'I had my Sergeant look over your car and he found that the brake cable had been cut.'

'My name is Robbie, officer.'

'Anyway Robbie, someone wanted to kill you or someone else on that car pretty badly. Also, we found some fingerprints on the car that belong to a gunman out of Chicago.'

'You mean a hit man?' I asked.

'That's it,' the Inspector said, 'His name is Robert Leroy Carson, better known as Sharp-eye Carson, but sometimes goes under the alias of James Carson or Carson Carson. Anyway, it's something Carson. He's thirty-six years old, black, and is a member of a terrorist organisation financed by some East African country. This Carson fellow now goes by the name of Midoo Ali Jamal. We picked him up and advised him of his rights then questioned him about breaking his parole, carrying a gun with a silencer, and about the ten thousand dollars cash we found in his suitcase when we picked him up at the Greyhound Bus Depot.

After interrogating this Carson fellow for about ten hours, he broke down and admitted cutting the brake cable. His partner has escaped back to Africa,' said the Inspector, looking very proud of himself.

'Boy, you have been working hard,' I said. 'But who paid money to the bastards?'

'Aha, that's a point. Well the money was paid by a bodyguard of Prince Ben Ali Hassan. But we have no evidence that the prince was involved personally,' he said as he stuffed a banana into his mouth and blew his nose into my dinner napkin.

'I bet that bastard has skipped the country by now,' I said.

'You're right, he's gone. He got a plane out of Los Angeles two hours after the explosion, I checked with the airport personally,' said the Inspector, smiling to reassure me I was in no more danger.

After that, I asked Shilee how were Kareem, Cheese and Mosi. Shilee spoke with sadness and grief. 'Robbie, Mosi is dead. He died instantly as the steering wheel went into his chest.'

'And what about Kareem and Cheese?' I asked, hoping for better news. 'Cheese is in a wheelchair, paralysed from the waist down, and Kareem has lost his right eye.' After saying that, Shilee burst into tears, resting her head in my arms.

Tears came to my eyes. I could not hold back the hurt and sorrow. As Shilee and I began to cry, the Inspector left the room quietly. Shilee stayed with me at the hospital the whole night, and even with her soft comfort it was one of the worst nights of my life.

As I lay in bed, I was thinking to myself how all this had happened to me and my friends after I had met Shilee, the girl I loved, and how horrible Prince Ben Ali Hassan had made our lives. I was so happy all the time with Cheese, Kareem, and my pals on the football team. I had everything going for me. Now this tragedy had to happen to me and my pals and spoil everything.

Well, after three weeks went by and I was up and about, of course I couldn't walk but I had an electric wheelchair to ride in. I would wheel down to Cheese's room and have a chat. Most of the time Kareem would be there also.

Kareem was taking the loss of an eye very badly, but Cheese was still his old self even though he was paralysed from the waist down. As always we would discuss the Vietnam war, and how more and more American boys were being sent to their deaths.

Cheese would always say 'It's none of my worry now, baby, it's nothing but beer, wine and women, TV, and cocaine for me. I'm on easy street, baby,' he would say laughing. But I felt the sadness he tried to hide with not being able to have a choice. Shit, Cheese loved a good fight, he'd kick his mother in the ass, I know that for a fact, I thought to myself. I would always joke back 'Yeah Cheese man, you lucky old dog, you're gonna have all the bitches running after you now, man.'

Cheese and I would do our best to try and cheer up Kareem, as he was always in some kind of depression about his eye. Kareem was worried about how people in Mauritania would take to him now.

You see people in his country are very superstitious about someone with one eye. They still believe in witchcraft. Most people there would never, but never, go to visit a doctor who had one eye. For they believe that an evil spirit has taken his eye away and that his other eye might be bad also. (Would you go to see any doctor with one eye?)

Anyway, between the two of us and his father, we managed to get Kareem back on the right track. His father would telephone everyday and Cheese and I would fill his head with self confidence about his future. After a while that old smile would come back with a glow.

Well, it was about two months before the end of the term. I will have made it at last, the first in my family to have gone to college and graduated with honors and national recognition as a football star. Cheese was moved to a local hospital back in his home town, so his family could visit him and give him the love and attention he needed so badly. We hugged and cried as we said goodbye to one another and I promised him I would always write no matter where I was in the world.

Kareem, well, he was a new man now. He was full of confidence and was going to go to a university in England for his master's degree. He was most excited, as his brother was living in London, working with the Mauritanian embassy there.

Shilee came to visit me everyday, but one day she looked very upset. 'What's wrong?' I asked. Then she explained that if she went back to Mauritania she would have to fulfil a marriage contract her father had made with a very wealthy older man whom she despised. 'What? What kind of shit is that?' I shouted angrily. She explained to me that in Africa, the fathers pre-arranged all marriages for their children. All the more if you happen to be a beautiful young lady, as the money paid to the father makes it very worthwhile for him.

I said calmly 'Do you know who you're going to marry?'

'Yes,' she said openly, 'but I don't know if I should tell you.'

With that I shouted 'Tell me, Goddammit.'

'It's Prince Ben Ali Hassan,' she confessed, 'I am to be his third wife.' And she hung her head in shame.

'Say no more, my love, get dressed now and pack your bags. We are going to Las Vegas to get married tonight.'

Shilee jumped with joy and with a big smile shouted 'I love you, you big, black candy stick.' She threw her arms around my neck and planted a big kiss on my lips, and on my ears, and my neck, and then my chest, and at that moment I quickly jumped back saying 'Don't give me no pussy, baby, because we don't have the time. We have a long drive to Las Vegas.'

We hit Las Vegas about ten o'clock that night and drove around the streets until Shilee saw a sign that she liked. 'That's the one. Stop baby, that's the place over there.' I stopped the car in front of a little pink and white motel. The sign read 'Open twenty-four hours a day. Vacancy. TV in every room. Exotic movies free. Every room has a waterbed.'

The marriage ceremony was over in ten minutes. The preacher who married us was known as Rev. James, the fastest in the west. 'Excuse me sir,' I said. 'May I have two roast chickens, two bottles of French champagne, and also a carton of Russian caviar, if you can find any please?'

'I can find anything in this town, sir, for the right bucks, Praise the Lord,' he said, holding out his hand. I pushed two one-hundred dollar bills into his hand and went to find our rooms.

We spent two weeks in this little motel. It was smashing. The Rev. James liked us very much and often he would come upstairs and listen to music with Shilee and myself. Sometimes when I went to fix the drinks for Shilee, the Reverend and myself, I would pretend to be looking away and catch the Rev. James watching and studying Shilee's big ass as she walked by or bent over to change the records.

He would sometimes say 'A woman like that could ruin a man, if he was lucky.' This old preacher after two or three drinks would begin to foam at the mouth every time he saw a big legged black girl. He was a white Southern red-neck, and you know what they say down there when they are away from their wives, 'The blacker the meat, the sweeter it is, Praise the Lord.'

As we were packing and getting ready to leave, I got to talking to a fellow who had lost at the dice table in one of the casinos. He told me that the Rev. James was the local pawn shop and the local ten-dollar-a-bag marijuana man. He was like your friendly neighbourhood toot man, and he got more people high than Jesus ever did. I thought something was a bit strange the first time I went to his church and it was packed out with standing room only, and as the Rev. James walked up to the pulpit, all the the people gave him a standing ovation.

I noticed a lot of people crying, well I thought they were crying at the time. But now I know that they were wiping their noses from all that cocaine sniffing.

Anyway, as Shilee and I were pulling away from the motel, the Rev. James walked over to the car and said a short prayer and wanted to know if I wanted to buy a dime bag of weed. He assured me it would make me loose like a long-necked goose. I said thanks, but no thanks,as I had to drive a long way and be straight.

When Shilee and I arrived back on campus, there was a dark gloom all around, bad vibes, man. Kareem waved and ran over to the car. 'Hi Shilee, or should I say Mrs Jones?' said Kareem.

'Hi Kareem. What's going on?' I butted in before Shilee could answer.

'Well,' Kareem said, 'Look around you.'

I did. There were hippies everywhere. Peace signs, the beads, and everybody saying 'Peace man, make love not war.' The music was blasting out loud and there were about six girls running around naked with ducks on their heads shouting 'Peace not War, Peace not War.'

'It's always been like this, Kareem, only now a few more signs of protest,' I said.

'Are you in the the Reserve Officers Training Corps?' Kareem asked smiling.

'Yes,' I shouted, 'Now tell me what's going on, dammit.'

After Kareem stopped laughing, he told me a lot of ROTC guys were being shipped over to Vietnam for the war effort. another one of Richard Nixon's great strategic moves, I thought to myself.

Shilee gave me that worried look, which made me think to myself, shit, it would just be my bad luck to be drafted. Anyway, I put on a cheerful face to not scare Shilee. Kareem reassured Shilee a little by saying that they only took cadets from the eastern states and had filled their allotment. 'Anyway, if they did need somebody else, they would have to be mighty desperate to want to take Robbie.'

Trying to convince myself, I said, 'Yeah. They wouldn't want me. I'm a married man now.' This really made Shilee happy and forget about the war. As time went on with one thing and another, Shilee and I moved to about six blocks from the campus in a two room apartment. It was small, but who the hell cares when you are in love. Shilee would clean and cook exotic foods, and introduced me to famous wines from France.

Most nights we would stay in our little love nest with soft music playing, and just talking husband and wife talk, you know what I mean. Things like how many kids we would like to have, where we were going to live, where we were going to study for our master's degrees, or if we were going into specialised medicine or not. Things were working out fine. Shilee was everything I had ever dreamed about. I was happy living in my own little world of wine and roses. The best way I can explain this happiness is 'I was like a hound in a dog food factory'.

After I moved off campus, I didn't see much of Kareem as he had a steady girl now and was thinking of marriage himself. But when the big day rolled around – graduation time – Kareem and his family were at the ceremony, my family were there, as was Shilee's family. With all the hugging, kissing, drinking, and lying, we became one big happy family. As Shilee was from a rich family with money running out of their ears, she decided to invite her whole new family to a local restaurant which specialized in Peking and Mandarin Chinese food.

As I gave my diploma to my mom, tears came to her eyes, my dad tried not to cry but his emotions of joy and happiness overcame him. I then looked around me and there were thousands of people in the main hall hugging and kissing and crying their eyes out.

So I guess it was all right if my old man and mom had a good cry. It was becoming very crowded now, so I shouted to Kareem and Shilee 'Let's get these cry babies out of here and go to the Chinese restaurant.'

As we all packed into the restaurant the waiter met us in the lounge. 'How many, please?' he said. 'Thirty,' I said. 'This way sir,' and the waiter showed us to our tables. We wined and dined into the early morning. Some of us danced to a trio of Chinese musicians playing cover versions of the top ten records of the national charts. One of the most requested songs was 'Does Your Chewing Gum Lose Its Flavor On The Bedpost At Night' and 'My Old Dog Still Likes Spinach'. They were terrible, but after five or six glasses of wine they began to sound better and better. Mother even got out on the floor and asked if the Chinese knew 'Danny Boy', to which the boys who had been sipping sake all night replied 'Does a bear shit in the woods?'

By now everybody was shouting,laughing, blowing horns, and just being a general pain in the ass. Kareem was leaving in the morning, the minute the college dean walked into his office and signed a letter of introduction to his new university. All he could talk about was tomorrow and how he'd got everything packed. Kareem and his girl sat with Shilee and me. We talked and laughed about the good old days and how we missed Cheese.

As the party broke up in the early morning, I said goodbye to Kareem outside the restaurant and Shilee began to cry as we parted. I told Shilee not to cry as we could always fly to England to see Kareem. As it turned out, that was the last time I saw Kareem for many years. It was something I thought would never be possible, not seeing Cheese and Kareem for that long a time.

With college over, there was not that much to do but laze around and go to the rock concerts. Shilee and I planned to study in Strasbourg, France for our master's degrees when September came round again. We would someday open a clinic together. We were young, in love, and full of spunk. Everything was so mellow.

Then, one day after Shilee and I came back from hiking above the San Fernando Valley, while I parked the car, Shilee walked up the driveway to check the mail. Carl, my neighbor was working on his car next door. He called to me 'Hey Robbie, did you enjoy your hiking trip?'

'Yeah, it was wonderful. The weather was much the same as today really,' I said. The sun was bright with not a cloud in the sky, the birds were singing, and the butterflies were flitting happily. For a minute I felt like Davy Crockett looking into his back garden.

Carl was a bastard. He was a nosy fucker and never. but never cut his damn grass. I never once saw his wife's legs or his feet all the time I lived next door to him. His grass always came up to his knees.

I knew he was waiting to say something and then it came.

'Hey Robbie, I don't mean to be nosy, but the police came by your house while you were gone. Well, not really the police but the Military Police, that's what I mean. I hope you're not mad that I said something.'

'No way Carl. Did they say what they wanted?' I said, looking nervous and worried.

'Well I'm not one to pry into people's affairs,' he said.

'Carl, tell me what they said.'

'Well,' Carl said, 'You didn't register for the draft and they have been writing letters telling you to, but have been receiving no replies.'

As I walked into the house, Shilee was sitting on the floor crying. 'What's wrong honey?' I said.

'It's the army,' she said. 'They want you to report in four days.'

'What? I'm not going. I'm a married man. I've got responsibilities.' I then fell on the floor, rolled on my back and began to kick my legs up and down like a spoiled kid.

Anyway, six days later I was at Ft Campbell, Kentucky, marching like a bastard, and my damn feet were killing me. We had a sergeant who looked like Joe Frazier.

'Jones!'

'Yes sir,' I shouted back.

'You march like you got a stick up your ass. You're not playing football now, you little sissy,' the sergeant shouted in my ear.

I'd like to beat the shit out of you. I'd like to kick you in the ass until my leg got tired, I said to myself.

'You look like you want to say something, Jones. Do you?' the sergeant asked, looking mean and foaming at the mouth.

'No sir, I was just admiring your shiny gun,' I said.

'Well, you can keep your bastard eyes looking straight ahead,' he said before walking off calling cadence: 'Hup 2,3,4, Hup 2,3,4, Hup 2,3,4…'

In the day time we marched and went to school or we went to school and marched. One hour for lunch, half hour for breakfast. The rest of the time was marching and school. It was what I always wanted to do, wear my feet down to the ankle bones.

Because of my college training to be a doctor, they made me a medic. You know like in the John Wayne movie when a guy gets shot up and John Wayne jumps up with a hand grenade clenched in his jaw and shouts 'Medic, medic!' and a little guy comes running with a red cross painted on his helmet. Well, I'm that poor bastard with the big red cross that makes a perfect target for the enemy rifles.

In my company there are one hundred and six of us. My company is 'D'. We are the best of the eight companies that are in medic training. The sergeant made us a fighting team. I found to my surprise that I liked the army. I guess I like the army because I'm a uniform freak, really. There's nothing like being number nine in a gang bang with a chick and looking up to see your buddy standing number two and he recognises you because of your uniform.

Every night I would write to Shilee and she would write to me every other day. She missed me very much, but was doing fine as my sister went to live with her to keep her company. I told Shilee to keep a good eye on my sister as she was always a little too butch, and was known to carry a big black dildo in her handbag. She said it was to fight off muggers and any other undesirables. Shilee wanted to move near me, but I advised her not to as I was shipping out soon. Sure enough the sergeant called us to attention. 'Men, the captain wants to talk to you!' the sergeant shouted in his usual gentle manner while rolling his big bloodshot eyes.

'At ease, men. Smoke 'em if you got 'em,' the captain said with that forced Richard Nixon smile. Shit, this is beginning to sound more and more like a John Wayne picture, I thought. There was a silence among the men as the captain started his spiel.

'Men, America needs good, strong, healthy men like you. Two days from now, you will be fully trained medics. America has spent a lot of money to give you the training for this war. Make America know that the money has been well spent. Do you realize how expensive bandages are? Do you realize how much it costs to send you half way across the world to a jungle paradise? You had better write or phone your loved ones, as most of you are going to Vietnam. The list will be posted tonight. I know you will do your best for America and keep our country a free land for all men, and I say this with all sincerity, and honestly this includes you black soldiers too. You men have the unique opportunity of stopping the Communist tide in the trenches before it reaches our shores. Any questions? No questions, then carry on as normal,' said the captain. 'Attention!' the sergeant called as the captain departed.

As the captain disappeared into the orderly room, the sergeant shouted 'At ease, men! The list of all personnel shipping out to Vietnam will be posted on the right side of the Company bulletin board, the others being processed for assignment in the states will be posted on the left. I suggest all of you polish your equipment for captain's inspection tomorrow morning at 0800 hours. Carry on men, and kill a gook for God and for your country.'

Everybody was shocked. Nobody thought we would be going to Vietnam this soon. Of course we all thought that the other guys were going.

Then some wise ass started talking about how the Vietcong cut your head off when they capture you and if not, they are likely to cut off your manhood with a dull knife. Finally, somebody in the back yelled 'Shut up you asshole, before I break your head.' Then in walked the sergeant, nailed up the two lists, faced us with his usual possum-eatin' shit grin and left without a word.

All the men dashed to the bulletin board hoping to see that their best friends were going to battle instead of them. Around the bulletin board there were all kinds of reactions. Some of the men were crying, some were so mad they began stomping the ground in frustration, some of the blacks started taking about their Vietnamese Brothers, and two or three of the less masculine started for the hospital to claim latent homosexuality. The guys with names posted on the left were laughing, yelling, and making plans to get very drunk that night. Outside of the Post Exchange it was packed with guys trying to phone their loved ones and asking each other who had some dope for sale.

I sat on my bed too scared to go out and look. Dammit man, you're an American; this uniform means something after all, you are a professional soldier, I said, trying to convince myself to have the courage to go look at the list. With this pep talk, I stood up and calmly buttoned my uniform. I walked up to the board with my chest out, feeling proud to be an American soldier. I ran my finger down the list thinking to myself, fuck it man, you got to go; you got to go. I can take it like a man, thousands of other guys do, why can't I.

As I got down to the J's, my hand began to sweat and shake. And then suddenly there it was, my name, my serial number, in big capital letters. A lump the size of a watermelon cane into my throat. My eyes shot out of their sockets. Piss began to run down my leg like Niagara Falls. I would have shit right then, but I had been just before the sergeant came in, so instead I fainted.

Did you know that you can hear people talking after you have fainted? Well. you most definitely can. I swear to you on my grandmother's mother's life. I heard one of those good old Southern boys say to another guy, 'It's nothing very serious, niggers faint all the time. Why, back home my daddy – '

'Cool it, Winston, that fellow just fainted and shitted on himself from the shock of going to Vietnam. So don't bring racism into this, you big asshole,' said one of the guys nearby.

As Jackson, the guy who sleeps in the bunk next to me, revived me (and I felt so ashamed, Lord I felt so ashamed) I got up calmly and walked into the shower room with my head held high just like John Wayne, smelling just as shitty as the average bear in the spring. Everyone let me have the showers to myself by running out. 'Phew, boy, you smell shitty,' the sergeant said as he passed to go upstairs to his office.

Well, after the shower, I went to call Shilee on the phone to tell her that I was shipping out in two days for Vietnam. As we talked, I could feel the sadness in her voice and something else I could detect. At first I thought she's found another guy and then all kinds of things went through my mind.

'Shilee,' I said, 'all this time I've been talking to you, I haven't heard you once say you're going to fly down to see me,'

'Robbie, honey, I guess I'll have to tell you. I can't come to see you because I slipped in the bath tub and broke a bone in my hip. You should see me now with this cast on my hip,' she said, crying over the phone.

'Oh honey, I'm sorry,' I said and I began to tell her what to do and what not to do. This went on for nearly two hours, talking man and wife talk. The main topic of the conversation was 'Don't give no pussy up, and if you have to, charge for it and put the money in the savings account.' (I ain't proud, shit.) Just then, a jeep pulled up with two Military Police in it. 'Hey soldier, let me see your ID, and what the hell are you doing out of the barracks so late?' said the cross-eyed one.

I said 'Shilee, I got to go now. I'll call you when I reach my destination. I love you,' and hung up the phone quickly so I could answer shithead's question, trying to look into both his eyes at once (it wasn't easy). 'Sir, I was only calling my girl as I am shipping out to Vietnam in two days, sir,' I said to him as I handed him my ID cards. Handing them back to me he said 'OK you're alright. You can go now,' as he motioned me back to my barracks. With that shit over and done with, I fell into my bunk and dropped into a deep sleep, dreaming of kicking the sergeant in the ass until I wore out a set of kneecaps.

The big day was finally here. Thousands of men lined the parade ground. American flags were everywhere, and then came the army band playing high spirited marching music by John Philip Carson. '1 2 3 4, sound off 1 2 3 4,' the sergeant shouted as the men passed the reviewing stand looking as sharp as a country preacher. 'Company halt! Right face! At ease!' the Master Sergeant shouted, proud as a mother hen.

Then the captain took the stand to announce that the Base Commander wanted to say a few words of encouragement. A little fat, balding man with a uniform two sizes too big for him, stepped up to the microphone. 'Men, I am General McKissic, your Base Commander, and I am so proud of you and America is so proud of you. So I say, do your duty for America and go into battle with your heads up high. You are the bulwarks against the Communist Tide, and remember the words of John Leslie Wayne: 'The only good gook is a dead gook.' That's all, men. God Bless America,' shouted the piggy General as he backed away from the microphone and sat down, breaking the wooden chair under his excess weight.

Standing in this hot fucking sun and hearing this John Leslie Wayne shit, I whispered to the sergeant 'Is this all there is?'

'What do want, a watermelon?' he laughed back like the good old boy he is.

# 2

Twenty-four hours later, and here I was in sunny Vietnam. I was stationed about ten miles from Saigon, which was a very large overcrowded city, with a lot of cockroaches and rats. Hell, I've seen a cockroach with a switch blade take a rat's cheese. But other than that anything you wanted you could get in this city, which was why I liked it.

For the first four days, the sergeant said to the new recruits which were nine men, that we could have leave in Saigon as our records had not yet arrived from the States. I went to town on my own, something I should not have done. On my very first night in town, this Vietnamese guy walked up to me and said in very broken English, 'You want to fuckee fuckee my virgin sister yes?'

scratching his balls and looking at me with his lying eyes. I looked down at this bastard smiling with one tooth in his mouth and thought to myself, I hope his sister looks better than him. Anyway, as I wanted to help this fellow out and maybe his family could use the bucks, and maybe he really did have a virgin sister, and me being a good soft hearted American boy away from home, and missing grandma's apple pie, I reluctantly said yes. (Pushing my dick away from my throat.) 'Where is this virgin sister and how much?' I asked,wanting to be of help to the family.

'My sister home. You come now,' he said.

'And how much for the ass?' I asked.

'Twenty dollars Yankee, but she Young and pretty,' he said pointing the way. We walked through many small alley ways, turning right then a left and a right and a couple more lefts until I said 'Hey man, how much further? Shit man, I could wear out a set of knee caps doing this much walking.'

'We here now Yankee, we here now. You give me money now, yes?' he said.

'No, I see pussy first, yes?' I said.

'That's not possible. You give me money now. I show me sister money now. Me sister dress to look good to Yankee and I call you upstairs. But moma-san stay in next room so you no hurt me sister, yes? OK Yankee?' After walking all this way, and my dick was playing baseball with my balls to my pants, I said 'OK'. I gave him the money and he disappeared up the stairs and through a door.

I waited, and waited, and waited. I waited about an hour before someone said anything to me or passed by. 'Hey Yankee,' I looked up and an old woman was shouting to me. 'What?' I said.

'You big fool. You be what they say in America, a asshole. Man always brings Yankees behind this house. He take money, come up stairs and go out front door. This is rice and tea house. You stand where we bring rice.' Then she began to laugh and sing 'No fuckee, no fuckee fuckee. Silly Yankee, no fuckee fuckee.'

I felt like a fool. 'I'll kill that bastard. That little one tooth, short leg, fat foot, son of a bitch,' I shouted in a puff of anger. Anyway I'm gonna check that shit out as this old lady might be in on it. I walked upstairs and looked around. The old lady was right. There were four rooms, three were packed with tea and rice, and one was an office. It wasn't the money that made me mad, it was being ripped off so easily that bugged me as I walked down the front stairs into a main shopping center.

Feeling pretty bad, I went for a Chinese meal in the market place. On the way to the restaurant, I would stop and look in the many windows of the different stores. You know what I mean, like a clock shop or specialty food store, anything of interest really. Dig this. I found this lovely Peking Chinese restaurant, it was packed with people. You know the types, the local people, GI's, sailors and many tourists from all over Malaysia. Anyway, I sat down and ordered a dinner for three which included everything. I couldn't go wrong, baby, this meal was only thirty dollars and that was with all the drinks. I was waiting with chopsticks like a native and was feeling good now baby. The waiter put thirty-two dishes in front of me and tasting all these exotic dishes really got the best of me. Everytime I would chew down, the juices of the food would splash against the walls of my jaws. My fingers were all greasy from picking up the barbecue ribs that I had dipped in brandy sauce. Of course, I was washing this all down with a good red wine from France, it was Bordeaux from 1959 to be truthful. As the waiter brought over the bill as I requested, he said, 'Would there be anything else sir?'

'No thank you, but you can bring the chef out here so that I can thank him personally,' I said looking for my wallet in my back pants pocket. He spoke a few words to another waiter who soon emerged from the kitchen with the chef. Both had big smiles on their faces hoping for a big tip. 'The chef is pleased you have honored him for his cooking sir,' said the waiter smiling from ear to ear. The chef butted in by saying 'My brother who waited on your table is a most good waiter too, yes?'

'Hell, yes,' I said still looking for my wallet in my coat pocket, then my inside pocket, then I thought maybe it's in my pants front pocket, yeah that's where it is, sure I thought to myself. 'Hey fellows, would you accept a drink on me while I'm looking for my wallet?' I asked.

'Sorry, we no drink on duty, but will accept most gracious tip, sir,' smiling like a bastard he replied.

'Yeah, you're a damn good waiter,' I said. 'Some of my best friends back home are Vietnamese waiters,' I joked, looking a second time in all the pockets I had. Oh shit. Oh big balls. Someone has pickpocketed my wallet while I was in the market place, I thought silently. As I looked up at the faces of the chef and waiter, the smiles turned to anger, and I mean quick.

'Joe, you have no money, no?' (they call all GI's Joe over here,

well most GI's anyway.) Suddenly everyone's head turned
around and all eyes were on me. There were majors and captains
with their families and they were looking to make sure I didn't
embarrass them and my uniform. I looked up and smiled with a
shit-eating grin and asked 'Hey fellows, can't we work something out like washing dishes or maybe I could wait tables for
y'all, or maybe I could cook up a mess of chitlins?' I asked sinking
lower in my chair.

All of a sudden that broken dog English vanished. 'Look, you
silly son of a bitch, pay us our goddamn money now or we'll
break your fucking head, and stop talking that "can I wash your
dishes" shit. Is that kosher, motherfucker?' the chef said, showing me a large butcher's knife tucked under his apron which was
stained with somebody else's blood who didn't pay the bill.

I thought to myself, it was never like this in a John Leslie
Wayne movie. I began to move my hand slowly under the table
grabbing the table cloth. The hot dishes were still on top of the
table as I hadn't eaten all of the food. I asked the waiter 'Can I
have a word in your ear?' I told him that I had a proposition that
would make him more money that he could imagine. His eyes lit
up again and the smile returned to his gook face.

As that fucker bent down for me to speak in his ear, I took my
right hand and put it on his yellow bone head and shoved it
down into a dish of hot soy bean sauce and chicken. Upon hearing his screams of pain and seeing the chicken leg go into his
nose, I pulled the table cloth off the table, throwing it at the chef.
All hell broke loose as I ran over to where there was a bunch of
sailors eating and drinking heavily.

'Hey fellows, they say that all GI's are shits and sailors are no-
brain shits and that all you guys at this table are cheapskates. I
heard the chef tell the waiter that when you walk your asses
squeak, you're so tight with money. I got so mad I smacked one
of them in the mouth and then ran over here,' I said quickly as a
crowd of Vietnamese heavies looking mean started across the
floor with their stained aprons and dirty yellow teeth. (Some of
my Vietnamese friends are very nice and keep their place.)

'Oh yeah, show me these fucking gooks who said that,' said
one of the biggest and meanest sailors I have ever seen. With that
remark about ten husky, burly, and mean sailors and about
sixteen gooks went at it like stink on shit.

People were running out of the place led by the officers who
did not wish to be embarrassed. as one major ran by me, I could

hear him say to another officer, 'I knew there would be trouble when that nigger ordered Peking duck. Niggers eat pork.' By now everything was being smashed, plates, chairs, glasses and tables were bouncing off people's heads, and mostly gook heads.

'Take that, yank,' Wham up side my head. 'Take this, you fucker,' the waiter said after punching me in my damn eye making it swell like a watermelon. Now I was really mad. I reached in my back pocket and out came old Betsy. (Betsy is my knife. A nigger always has a knife handy when someone wants to fuck with him.) I jumped on that gook's ass like stink on glue. I put so many marks on his ass with Betsy, he thought I was Zorro.

'The police. The police are coming,' someone shouted from beneath a table. Suddenly someone grabbed my arm and shouted 'This way, soldier. I know a safe way out of here. I had no time to argue, so I followed him out the emergency exit. We ran out on to the street and into a taxi. 'Hey driver, take us to 159 Kiloon Street and make it fast, OK,' said this odd-ball stranger. As the taxi pulled away with the tires screaming I asked 'Hey man, who are you and where are you taking me?' (You never know, this guy could be a fag, right?) He said, 'I will explain everything as soon as we get there. Please relax, you are in good hands.'

We pulled up on a river front, I got out and the stranger paid the taxi fare and led me onto a boat, a Vietnamese junk. On the outside it looked like a brick shithouse, but when we went below deck, it looked more like the Hilton. Man, everything was so classy. For a minute I thought some gook was living better than me. Zip. An electric door opened and a big man with a full beard walked over and said 'Hello soldier. I'm Major Mays, Commander of Seventh Army Intelligence for Saigon. Please be seated.' As the stranger and I sat down, the major asked if we wanted a drink after our ordeal. Zip. The door opened and a Vietnamese girl entered and began to pour a whiskey on the rocks for me. I noticed that I was the only one drinking. 'Don't be alarmed by us not drinking, but we're on duty just now,' said the major.

'My name is Charlie,' said the stranger who had helped me to escape from the gook horde. 'I am a captain in Army Intelligence, but don't call me captain, just Charlie or Charlie the Fox. As you probably guessed, I am from New York City and I'm hell when I'm well. So call me Charlie, please Mr City Slicker.' he said to me laughing. With that, this beautiful Vietnamese girl said 'My name is Jackie, and I am a captain in the Vietnamese Central

Intelligence, but only call me Jackie as we use only first names here.' Jackie did have a body better than the average bear.

'Well,' I said, 'I'm private Robbie Jones, a medic who's just been stationed here in Saigon. And by the way, major,' I said with a shit-eating grin, 'I really did mean to pay the bill in the restaurant if–'

'My dear boy, I know you meant to pay the bill, with you being a good American and all,' he said smiling and giving back a shit-eating grin.

'Well, now that we understand each other and have got that out of the way, I think I'll be going now,' I said knocking back my drink quickly so I could get the hell out of there.

'Don't be in a hurry. We like the way you handled yourself in the restaurant. You could be of some help to us, old buddy,' said the major, motioning for Jackie to pour me another drink.

'In what way?' I asked, while I sneaked a look at Jackie's big ass.

'We know that you have trained at Stanford University to be a doctor. So how would you like the army to give you a special course to make you a doctor in three years instead of the normal four?' asked the major.

'Yeah, I would like that very much,' I answered, 'But wait a minute. What would I have to do to deserve this special treatment?' I said suspiciously.

'Join Army Intelligence is all you have to do. Would you like working under cover?' replied the major as he motioned Jackie to pour another large whiskey on the rocks for me. 'Yeah that's cool,' I said, almost falling out of the chair to get a closer look at Jackie's ass.

'Oh by the way, as you are a college graduate, from this moment forth, your new rank is Second Lieutenant,' the major said, shaking my hand. Charlie picked up the phone as the major was pinning on my new lieutenant bars, and told some guy named Joe to come in to the office immediately. Zip. The electric doors opened and in walked a Master Sergeant. 'This is our pal Joe Farrell, and he's on our team,' the major said as he motioned me to shake Joe's hand.

'Joe, I'm Robbie – Lieutenant, that is,' I said shaking Joe's hand. (I didn't want no shit from Joe now that I was an officer.)

That's how I met my new friends, Charlie, Jackie, Joe Farrell, and Major Mays. As time went on we became like brothers and sisters, but right now they had a plan for me which I knew nothing about. I was sure of one thing, though. They wanted more from me than just being a doctor.

The training they put me through lasted three years. I had a special teacher in Dr Albert Von Ryker. He was a world famous surgeon, and nearly as famous as a pharmacist. Working with Dr Von Ryker was very hard indeed as he was so demanding, but I made it with flying colors. Up to now, I had done no undercover intelligence work whatsoever. It was all studying in the daytime and on the job training at night. All I saw were classrooms and lots of underground hospital rooms filled with other students and surgeons with whom I was not allowed to talk.

Most of the time I was alone with Dr Von Ryker learning the finer surgical arts. These three years training under one of the world's finest plastic surgeons had given me the best possible knowledge of this art and built myself confidence for the mission ahead. There was very little time to socialise, but every Sunday I would meet with Major Mays, Charlie, Jackie and Joe Farrell. They would take me out on the town in Saigon for dinner or a movie, and after we would do a little night clubbing near the red light district.

One night as I was relaxing in my room, a little bored as my training was over, the phone rang. It was Major Mays. We talked awhile and then he wanted me to get dressed and come over as he had a surprise for me. He told me I wouldn't be able to resist it. With that kind of news, I grabbed my coat and ran out the door, letting it slam and jumped into my jeep and drove off to the headquarters junk. Parking my jeep on the pier, I noticed there was an unusual silence all around me. No people, no cars, nothing but the headquarters junk bobbing quietly in the river.

As I went on board, and still heard no sound, I was beginning to get worried. So I tip-toed down the steps silently to the below deck and as soon as my right foot touched the floor – Zip – the major's door flew open and out popped Charlie, Jackie, Joe and Major Mays singing all around me 'For he's a jolly good fellow'. They gave me such a fright, I almost shit myself. 'What's going on?' I said, laughing.

'Promotion time, Robbie,' Charlie said clapping his hands.

'Well kiss my old boots,' I shouted with joy.

'Yes my dear man, you have earned every bit of it and more. Dr Van Ryker says you are one of the best students he's ever had the pleasure of working with,' the major said as he pinned two captain's bars on the collar of my shirt.

'All right, Joe. Don't give me no shit. I'm a captain now,' I said jokingly.

'You don't give me no shit and there won't be any shit,' Joe answered while shaking my hand in congratulation.

Things were going fine, everything was so mellow. What with my favorite food and champagne to wash it all down, I felt like a big-dicked boy in the YWCA.

'Robbie, we have another surprise for you. Would you like it now?' Jackie asked, smiling and looking all sweet and innocent, wearing a satin dress so tight you could see the seams on her panties.

'Oh boy, would I,' I shouted, (thinking some big Amazon-looking bitch was gonna jump out of a cake and say 'Fuck me quick, Robbie.')

'You are going on your first combat mission with us in two weeks time, behind the enemy lines.'

'Congratulations,' said the major, knowing my ass would fall out of the chair. Well, shit, what could I say? Fuck all. Nothing. A big lump came into my throat like a Georgia watermelon and I was just gonna shit and then faint when the major said quickly, 'Hey, you nasty bastard, don't shit in here. Go outside if you got to.' Everybody was laughing until tears ran down their faces.

Starting the next day, and up to the day we were to go on the mission, all we did was plan and rehearse at a secret site.

The mission was to capture a top general in the Vietcong army and replace him with a phony one who was our man. I was to do surgery on our man, who was a South Vietnamese officer, and make him look exactly like the general from the north.

Jackie's job was to visit a whorehouse in the jungle and pretend to be a prostitute. Once there, she was to get General Ho Fok alone in the bedroom. Upon getting the general in the room, Charlie and the major would come from behind a secret panel and would break in the general's ass with their boots, giving him a severe case of piles.

Joe would help protect our phony general and get him into the house safely, and help get Major Mays, Charlie, and Jackie out of the house with the real general into a waiting jeep which I would be driving.

I didn't have much surgery to do really, as most of it had been done by Dr Von Ryker. I just put the finishing touches on his mug. But it took two weeks more than we planned as the swelling in the face stayed a bit too long. Still it was a most difficult job as I had to take many inches off our man's nose. This old boy had a nose like Pinnochio, I don't know where the hell they found him, but he was an extremely nice chap.

We had a helicopter to drop Jackie and some supplies in the jungle, and also arranged for a loyal North Vietnamese guide to take Jackie to the house in the jungle and introduce her to the Madame's long-lost sister. The Madame of course would be working for US Intelligence for a low price as she was a foreigner.

The rest of us, Joe, Charlie and the major and the phony general plus two Vietnamese guides and myself went by gunboat on the river. We had helicopter cover until sixteen miles into North Vietnam.

Now we were on our own, with no radio as the major wanted total radio silence so as not to give our position away. We slept in the day and moved through the jungle at night. I had to stay in the lower deck with the others during the daytime, if we really had to travel and make up time, which was only occasionally. The phony general and the two guides stayed on deck dressed as North Vietnamese farmers. As the Vietcong jets flew over, the guys on deck would look up, smile, and give a wave. Once, I was caught on deck as a jet swooped over and he returned to have a closer look. I guess a nigger did look a little out of place in his neighborhood.

After five days and five nights on this damn boat, I was glad to land on shore. At last we were at our destination, the right spot and we were all alive. Everyone got off the boat but the two guides. They were to come back in two days and pick all of us up at the same spot.

Charlie whispered to everyone 'Heads up and be alert. This is the big one you guys.' It was hot, stuffy, and felt like a gorilla was breathing down our necks as we walked through this hell-hole of a jungle. There were snakes and monkeys of all kinds mingling in the jungle. (I knew we wouldn't starve to death with all these monkey elbows and snake steaks around, they make damn good vittles.) Thousands of birds and monkeys were jumping from tree to tree. It was so damn loud, with the birds singing and monkeys shouting at each other. Sometimes the monkeys would come down out of the trees and start to fuck with your hat or the pack on your back. I like monkeys just as much as the next man, but I had to kick a few monkeys' asses to make them leave me alone. After walking about ten miles, the major said 'Halt men. Let's take a break here until we meet our contact,' and he wiped the sweat from this forehead.

Just as we sat down, it began to rain. I have never seen it rain so hard. It was like a thousand elephants pissing at one time. 'Somebody's coming,' Joe called out.

'Be cool everybody, keep your heads down and let me do all the talking,' said the major.

The major and Charlie did all the talking to our new guides as we loaded everything into two jeeps and began our journey to this house in the jungle by road. We arrived about ten o'clock at night. They had four guards walking around the perimeter of the house. They must have thought nobody was going to attack this far behind their lines, and normally they would be right, but they hadn't reckoned with crazy Americans like us. There were nine staff cars outside the house, all looked to be very high ranking. Over near the right of the house was a camp fire where all the drivers sat and talked, while drinking a little rice wine. We settled down in the jungle waiting for a signal, which Jackie was to give. Click, clunk, and more clunks sounded out around our campfire. 'Hey you guys, not so loud as you load your weapons,' whispered Charlie as he stuck a stick of chewing gum in his mouth, or I could have been mistaken. It could have been a cocaine leaf, knowing old Charlie.

On and off, on and off, we could see Jackie giving us the signal we had all been waiting for. 'Charlie, Joe and Pak-Kun you come with me (Pak-Kun was the replacement general). Robbie, you stay with the guides and the jeeps,' said the major.

'Please major, let me come with you,' I said as I forgot about the danger and only thought about all that ass in the house. The major looked at me with surprise and then smiled and said, 'OK, Joe, you stay behind. Robbie, you come with us,' and then gave the motion to move out. On and off, on and off, Jackie was standing outside the house near the basement hatch doors flicking a light as a signal. As we moved across the field trying to avoid the drivers sitting around the campfire, Jackie ran back into the house and disappeared. As one of the guards passed, the major and Pak-Kun ran across the dirt road and down through the hatch doors into the basement first. Then as another guard passed, Charlie and I ran over to the basement doors. 'Shh,' said Charlie as I let one of the hatch doors slam.

We could hear Vietnamese music being played upstairs and lots of dancing and loud laughing. We moved through the dark in the basement into a candle lit room. 'Psst,' and again 'Psst, over here,' said a whispered voice. It was a small Vietnamese girl dressed in silk. She was hot shit man, I would have bought some of this bitch's pussy if I hadn't been working.

Anyway, she knew a secret passage that would take us to Jackie's room where the real general would be. As we passed through the passage, we could hear giggles, laughing, and the other assorted sounds of the officers and some of the prostitutes enjoying their love-making as the walls of the passage were very thin. This was the first time ever that I was going in to battle to kill with a hard on, I thought, with a big smile on my face and a bulge in my pants.

'Shhh, we are here,' said the girl. There was peep hole in the wall so we could watch everything going on. The general was sitting on the bed with Jackie, hugging and kissing while trying to unzip Jackie's dress from the back.

Jackie jumped up off the bed and began to run and tease the general with one of her long stockings. Strangely, both were speaking English through all this, as both had studied in the US. (Jackie's story was that she had been a student at UCLA when the war broke out, and he had been a military attache in the US.)

The general asked 'What do I get if I catch you, my little flower?'

'What do you want, my sweet general?' Jackie said blowing a kiss at him.

'I would like you to tie me up in bondage and beat me, and piss on me before we have beautiful sex together,' he said, and reaching into his top jacket pocket, he pulled out a gold hair clip. 'And I'll also give you this – is it a deal?' he said, grabbing his balls frantically. As he said that, all of us behind the wall were nodding our heads with excitement as we wanted to kick him in the ass at the same time. Jackie paused, smiled sweetly, and agreed. She turned on some loud party type music on the radio, and sprayed the room with an exotic perfume, and closed the curtains. 'I'll lock the door, my angel,' said the general removing his gun and holster from his waist. 'Ready, go,' he said, chasing Jackie and foaming at the mouth with his crazy desires It was funny watching these two silly bastards laughing like eight year olds playing tag. Of course the general was able to catch Jackie, and as she slowed down to let it all happen the general began to undress. Soon he was as naked as a jaybird. Jackie began to tie up the general's hands and ankles with the rope going around his neck and between his legs and balls. The general then pretended to cry and shout out 'Beat the shit out of me. I'm a bad boy, Lord knows I'm a bad boy. Beat the living shit out of me.' He would foam at the mouth every time Jackie would grind her high heels into his foot and kick him fiercely in the balls. 'Suffer, you son of a bitch,' she said as she grabbed hold of his dick and wrenched it as hard as she could. The general went crazy with delight. 'Talk dirty, whore, I love it when you talk dirty to me.'

'Is everybody ready? Dammit, is everybody ready?' the major whispered twice as we were so involved watching the scene and getting with it ourselves. 'Yes sir,' everyone replied. As I was nearest the secret exit, I was the first to enter. 'Let's go now,' the major commanded. Bam. We kicked in the secret panel. In I jumped with a Browning machine gun, doing my John Leslie Wayne bit, when this little fat, ugly bastard general tied up on the floor looked up at me with shock and shouted 'It's a nigger. I don't believe it. Kiss my ass.' *Whomp*. Upside his fat head went Major May's pistol butt.

Everything went great. It was like clockwork. Pak-kun looked fine in his new uniform. We had delivered Pak-kun safely, and now our mission was over. All but taking the real general and ourselves back to our lines, which we thought would be a very routine operation.

Jackie was so happy to see us, and as we all hugged and kissed, there were two knocks at the door, and a loud clunk as one of the rifles fell to the floor. 'Are you all right, General?' said a voice.

Jackie quickly motioned us all back into the secret room, as she and Pak-kun pushed the real general's body, tied up and gagged under the bed. 'General, are you all right? This is Major Le Wi,' said a voice outside the door. Pak-kun said very sternly, 'I left a message not to be disturbed under any conditions. I am most annoyed with you, major,' acting out his part like a pro.

'But sir, you said to let you know at once when the gold shipment had arrived, sir,' the major said.

'You stupid shit of an animal,' shouted Pak-kun, you come here and disturb my night of love with this pretty Love Flower over some shit gold shipment. You are a stupid – gold? Oh yeah, the gold shipment,' Pak-kun pretended to remember, 'Come on in, major. You must not think badly of your general. You just knocked at the wrong time as my mind was full of love and the smell of exotic perfume. I mean look at this young flower, major. How could you resist her?' said Pak-kun pointing to Jackie.

The major looked at Jackie as she raised her dress to show just a little bit of hairy pussy, and slowly let the dress down again. The major's face lit up as he smiled at Jackie with a pussy-eating grin. 'Do you like her, Major?' Pak-kun said, teasing the major, whose glasses were now starting to steam up. 'Oh my General, you're much too kind to me. She is most nice and delicate. I would give my right ball to fuck her,' the major said with saliva flowing down his chin.

'Well, before you give away your right ball, where is this lovely gold you were talking about?' Pak-kun said, slapping the major on the shoulder in friendly fashion.

'It is outside in the truck sir. Where should I put it?' said the major, turning his head and winking at Jackie, who was gently rubbing her right thigh.

'Tell the men to unload it and bring it into this room. You can stay and watch over it with this young flower until morning. Then we shall move it to the main camp bank. Oh and major, I want you to supervise the unloading personally, and that is an order,' said Pak-kun warmly with an apple pie-eating grin.

'Oh my General, bless you, you are so kind to me.' said the major, backing toward the door and stealing one last glance at Jackie who was now slowly rubbing her pussy with her slim, elegant, hand. The major withdrew and closed the door softly.

As he left the room, the secret door opened and Major Mays, Charlie and myself rushed over to Pak-kun and congratulated him on a great performance. As I listened at the door, Major Mays gave instructions to the group. 'Pak-kun, when Major Lee Wi comes back with all the gold unloaded and stays with Jackie, you leave the room and go to the bar and talk with some of the other girls and get drunk. This will keep you in the clear. We'll take care of everything else this end.'

'And what about m y share of the gold, you sneaky bastards?' said Pak-kun rubbing his hands together with excitement.'

'I will put your share in a Swiss bank account and give your mother the number. Is that OK?' said Major Mays.

'I was only joking, you guys know I can trust you,' Pak-kun said with a smile.

'I hope to see you guys after the war is over,' Pak-kun said, hugging all of us and feeling sorry to see us go.

'Someone's coming up the stairs,' I whispered.

'Quick, get back behind the wall and best of luck,' said Charlie.

'Yeah, I'll see you after the war, Pak-kun,' I said as I ducked behind the wall quickly. Just as the secret door closed, in walked one of the guards carrying a box the size of an egg carton. 'Is that all there is?' asked Pak-kun disappointedly. 'No sir. There are twenty more coming up,' the guard said happily. In our hiding place, we looked at each other and smiled with visions of riches.

The gold was unloaded quickly and stacked neatly in the corner of the room, as Major Lee Wi was so hot for Jackie and rushed his men to finish the job. 'That's all of it, Major,' said the last guard while watching Jackie put on lipstick in front of the mirror.

'Very well. Do not disturb me under any condition until eight o'clock in the morning. And that is an order,' said Major Lee Wi. As the guard left, the major walked over and locked the door, and out walked Pak-kun from the toilet, wiping his hands on a towel. 'Oh, my General, I did not know you were still here,' said Major Lee Wi.

'That's OK, major. Just take it easy with my little flower and I will hold you personally responsible for the gold. Oh by the way, sign this paper saying as much,' Pak-kun ordered the major.

'Well, I am leaving now,' he said as he picked up the paper the major had signed. 'Jackie, take real good care of the major while I am gone. See to his every want. And try to find new ways to bring up his love fulfilment,' said Pak-kun, blowing a soft kiss to Jackie as he closed the door. The major wasted no time in chasing Jackie round the room. His pants were below his knees and his ass was in the breeze as he was chasing Jackie over and across the bed. Jackie let him catch her, and suggested he wash first in the toilet and then come back in the room, so she could look her most desirable to him.

As Major Lee Wi was singing a lullaby and washing his ass in the tub, Charlie and I were unloading the gold from the room. Major Mays was waiting near the toilet door with a bamboo club, ready to hit Lee Wi as he came out the door. Finally, 'I'm coming out. Are you ready my sunflower?' asked Major Lee Wi from the toilet, sounding like an oriental teenager in heat.

'Yes my little soldier boy,' replied Jackie in a soft sexy voice while motioning to Major Mays to get ready to clobber the bastard.

Out jumped that poor son of a bitch smiling like a country preacher, when Major Mays slammed him over the head with that bamboo club. Wham. His legs went to jelly and his eyes rolled up into his head as he hit the floor.

Quickly we began to unload the gold through the secret passage, over the dirt road and into the jungle. As it was neatly packed and small, it made it easy to carry. It took us only about twenty minutes and we were on our way.

'Hey, Robbie, don't forget the real general under the bed,' said Jackie.

'I won't. Charlie, give me a hand with this fat bastard,' I said as I pulled on the rope around the general's waist. With Charlie pushing and kicking the general in the ass, we made it through the secret passage and into the jungle quickly. Joe was waiting and guarding the jeeps as we appeared. Major Mays was the last to arrive after having left behind three grenades to cause a little diversion. 'Move it! Move it on the double, as the charges will go off in seconds,' he hissed. At that moment, all the staff cars gathered at the brothel went up in flames. There was no pursuit for now.

As we moved through the night, I think we all thought about the gold, and what each of us would do with so much money, if we ever made it back to our lines. After traveling all night, when the sun began to shine throughout the jungle the major ordered 'Halt. We will camp here, and remember, no fires as the damn Vietcong can smell a fire a mile off.'

'You won't make it back yanks, my men are all around you. They will soon discover your phony general you know, we may look stupid but we are not. Why don't you give up. I will save your lives,' said the real general, now dressed as a peasant farmer.

'Shut up, old man,' said the major, 'You are not the general anymore, you're just a peasant farmer now. The real general is back at that whorehouse or fucking your wife by now. So get some sleep.'

It was a bitch trying to sleep with all the ants and insects biting and crawling all over you. The sounds of birds and monkeys screaming didn't help either. We had to put cotton in our ears to get some sleep as the two guides kept watch. As the night fell upon the jungle again, we began to move out slowly. Suddenly, BOOM, BOOM, BOOM, BOOM, all around us. One of our guides had stepped on a land mine, setting off three more nearby.

'Kiss my ass,' said Charlie in a fit of temper, 'We only drove into a minefield, dammit.'

'Get the field packs with the gold and everybody walk in a

straight line behind me. Move it quick,' said the major.

'Yeah, them fucking gooks must have heard that explosion,' remarked Charlie. Moving slowly at first, then picking up speed, after twenty yards we ran quick time. Jackie fell, stumbling over a tree trunk.'Robbie,' she called out. 'Come help me.' I turned and ran back to help her. ZIP, ZIP, ZIP, a burst of bullets went by my head into a nearby tree. 'Stay down Jackie, I'll get that gook,' I said, feeling brave, like Rockwell Hudson in the movies.

WHAMMO, the whole top of the tree went up in flames as Charlie threw a hand grenade up into it. The dead gook hit the ground like a sack of Indiana potatoes. Joe ran back to see if Jackie was all right as he was deeply in love with her.

'They must have heard that also, so let's move ass,' shouted Charlie, chewing his cocaine leaf. Finally after running and walking about five miles, we came upon our boat with our guides on board. Man, that was a sight for sore eyes. We had made it back to our lovely boat. 'Hurry my friends, hurry, they have gun boats that patrol this part of the river frequently,' said one of the new guides, motioning us aboard.

At night on the river everything was fine, but sometimes we had to travel in daylight. On this particular day as we were fixing a broken engine, one of our guides saw a Vietcong PT boat, fully armed and moving at full speed in our direction.

'Everybody down below quickly,' said the major. 'Jackie, you stay up on top with the guides. Let the Vietcong come aboard if they want to. Don't fire your guns or do anything until I give the signal.'

The captain of the PT boat spoke over the loudspeaker: 'Pull over. This is a routine search. May we come aboard?'

Joe, Charlie and I each had some homemade bombs of six sticks of dynamite taped together. The major gave the nod for us to get ready and told the guides up on deck to tell the captain of the PT boat to come aboard. In one of the small portholes on the side of the boat, the major mounted a bazooka. This one was a special 956X portable rocket gun. It could knock anything out of the water at close range. 'When I fire the rocket, Joe and Charlie, you guys jump up on deck quickly and throw your dynamite into the smokestacks of the PT boat,' ordered the major.

'Are you sure they have smokestacks on a PT boat, sir?' asked Joe.

'Who gives a shit. It's only a book we're in. Just throw the fucking dynamite,' said Charlie, unwrapping another leaf.

'Robbie, you stay down here and watch the general,' ordered the major. 'If he moves anything other than his bowels, kill him.'

As the PT boat drew closer, WHAMMO – the major fired the 956X bazooka into the smokestacks. About four huge explosions ripped open the whole boat. Those poor bastards never knew what hit them it was so fast. Burning wood and smoke was everywhere. 'Hey everybody. Help put out the fires on our boat,' shouted Joe. I went up on deck to lend a hand with the fires, but while doing this, I had forgotten the general below deck, like everyone else had. As we were cleaning up the mess and bragging about our success, the general had worked his ropes loose, and now there he stood holding a gun on all of us.

'Hands up you dirty rats and drop your guns. I've got you bastards now,' he snarled with a shit-eating grin o his face. Foolishly, the two guides tried to jump overboard and he shot them. Jackie, being a quick thinker, kicked over a petrol can, making it roll toward the general. It hit him from behind, taking away his legs. As the general went ass over elbow, I jumped over and stabbed him with my jungle knife. I was taking no chances, so I jabbed the knife into him two or three times. It was all over in a matter of seconds. I was on his ass like funk on a skunk. The poor bastard never had a chance dealing with a professional killer like me.

'Good job, Robbie. Damn good show, old boy,' said the major, proud of his student who only a few months ago couldn't even squeeze a grape. 'Well men, we are now behind our own lines. We made it and we can live to tell about it and be very rich men besides,' said the major, holding up a small box of gold. Joe went over to give Jackie a kiss and had a quick feel of her ass, as Charlie and I dumped the dead general's body overboard.

As night fell upon the river, and all was very quiet but for the crickets in the jungle or the occasional gunfire of a distant battle, we went below deck to enjoy our dinner and wine. For dessert we sat and shared out the gold, The major, Charlie, Joe, Jackie, one guide, and myself all received five thousand dollars worth of gold, not counting Pak-kun's share. Incredible as it may seem, we did remit to him his just share, which was probably the only really honest action we ever took.

Some weeks later, on the morning I was to fly back to the States for discharge, Charlie, Joe, Jackie, and Major Mays came over to my barracks and said goodbye. The major had arranged away for me to collect cash for gold from my bank in America. All

I had to do was walk into my bank and sign for the money. The major had paid a diplomatic courier to smuggle the gold into the US and into the hands of the buyer. Money for this small deed came out of 'expenses' the major had put aside.

As you can see, the major was one hell of an organiser, huh? We didn't call him Papa Money for nothing. I exchanged numbers with everyone, and we all promised to write to each other now and after the war was over, but you know how that shit goes, each lie was more sincere than the last. Charlie even had to chew another leaf to keep from crying. As the plane took off, I felt the sadness of leaving my dear friends behind., and at the same time happy that I was going home to my wife Shilee and all that beautiful money. The medical plane was full of GI's, some well and some not so well. Most had a leg gone, or an eye missing. It suddenly seemed as if the plane was full of Long John Silver impersonators. But seriously, some were suffering from shell shock and other personality disorders. Some of the men were very pleasant, but thought they were someone else. Most of the journey I was sitting next to Robin Hood who introduced me to his buddy, Jesse James. But we all had one thing in common: we were all going home to our loved ones.

# 3

As the plane landed and began to park, I looked out my window and there was the same band playing the same music that I had heard when I was leaving for Vietnam. It only took me ten hours to check in and out of headquarters and to receive my discharge papers. I walked off base and flagged down a taxi. 'Take me to the airport in Louisville quick,and if you get me there in one hour there's an extra ten dollars in it for you,' I said to the driver. Cruising down the highway at high speed, the driver started a friendly conversation with me. 'I'm not really a cab driver, you know,' he said.

'What are you, a brain surgeon?' I asked.

'Of course not. Don't be stupid. I'm Frank James, Jesse's brother.'

Trying not to smile, I asked 'Were you in Vietnam?'

'Yes,' he answered, 'The 101st Airbourne Division. Man, was it rough fighting those yellow-skins.' As we arrived at the airport I rushed through the doors and checked in my luggage. Just then an announcement on the p.a. system said 'Flight 109 to Los Angeles is now boarding.' As one of the ticket girls looked a nice sort , I paid her five dollars to call my wife and tell her what flight I was on and to meet me at the airport. Sure enough, as the plane arrived and I walked through the passenger door in uniform with all my medals and captain's bars shining, there stood my beloved Shilee. She was one of the first in line. 'Shilee,' I shouted, 'I'm here. Don't you recognize me?' I said jokingly.

'Robbie, Robbie you old bastard Robbie my baby,' Shilee called out with tears streaming from her eyes. That first touch was magic. I promised myself there and then that I would never leave Shilee again. We hugged and kissed as we moved through the crowd trying to find the exit. I shouted to the red cap to get my luggage, 'Hey boy, pick up that luggage, please.'

'Boy?' said the black red cap, 'I got a dick hanging down to my knees and you call me boy?'

'You're just a big dicked boy, now pick up the damn bags and earn this ten dollars.' I said. A smile came over his face and he said 'Yas suh, Mr Uptown Boss Man,' swallowing his pride over that greenback ten-dollar bill.

For the first month, Shilee and I just stayed in bed making love. I got to tell you. Shilee had some of the best pussy on this side of the Mississippi. Sometimes I would get so excited, I wouldn't know whether to beat it or eat it. All we did was to get up to take in the food that was delivered at the front door or go to the toilet to refresh ourselves. One day as we were laying in bed, Shilee asked what our plans were now that I was back and she had just finished studying for her master's degree.

'Well, Mrs Jones, now that you are a doctor also, I think we will go into private practice together. We can open a nice place in Beverly Hills on Wilshire Boulevard, if you like my dear. But first we are going to travel a bit,' I said, feeling like a rich man. Hearing that, Shilee screamed with joy. 'Hot dog. Kiss my old boots. That's what I was hoping you would say.' Four times that night, Shilee showed me how grateful she was. Grateful, grateful, grateful, grateful, boy was she grateful. Lord knows she was grateful.

From that moment on, Shilee and I became big time jet setters. We went on shopping sprees every day, buying new clothes and jewelry for our new adventure. I went out and bought a new Rolls Royce for Shilee, a Silver Cloud to be exact, just to show her how much I loved her, and hoping she would be grateful again and again. As she was waiting for me to come home from shopping for some new shoes, I pulled up in front of her apartment window and honked the horn. Shilee looked out of the window and ran downstairs and over to me. 'This is for you,' I said. Shilee was to stunned to talk. She just held me tight and stood in silence, weeping with joy. 'Don't cry, honey,' I said, 'show me how grateful you are.' She grabbed my hand and we ran into the house and up to the bedroom. Boy was she grateful that night, and we had our dinner in bed (fur-burgers).

After everything was packed the next morning, we drove up to San Francisco and rented the penthouse on the 34th floor of the Hyatt Regency Hotel. The luxurious suite came with three shifts of butlers for round the clock cocktail and food service. Breakfast in bed was served by a butler who brought up trays of coffee, orange juice, sausages and eggs, and french rolls. Another butler would draw the baths, keep the fruit baskets filled and the champagne chilled, and run little errands for Madame. This was the life and it only cost a measly six hundred dollars a day, quite a bargain don't you think? We stayed there two months before moving to another playground. As I had always wanted to see New York City, I asked Shilee if she would like to go there.

'Is pig pussy pork? Stupid,' she said. That cheeky little smile came upon her face and cat's whiskers, we were on the plane to New York.

We checked in to the Berkshire Place Hotel in Manhattan, and took a suite on the twenty-first floor. It had a wrap-around terrace with a breathtaking view of the city and a Chinese red kitchen. Oh, I almost forgot. Each night we had a candlelit dinner prepared by a master chef from a different country each night, and a helicopter tour of the city for only a trifling $1450 a day.

After staying for another two months in New York, we moved on to Hawaii to get away from the chill. (Shilee is less grateful when it's chilly.) I booked a suite at the Kahala Hilton. It was a beautiful room. It and a grand piano in it, and from a balcony you could see the fishermen far below. Shilee and I would lay on the beach all day becoming more black than the average bear, then go back to our suite and have sex, sleep, get up, wash, and then descend to a magnificent dining hall to partake of some local and imported delicacies. The food was bitching and the wine wasn't bad either. This went on for six months or more. No, I lied. It was eight months to be exact. It was pure living. Shilee would always say in gratitude 'Ooh baby, don't you just hate it? Living so damn good.' I must admit I was getting a little out of condition, a little soft around the edges.

Shilee wanted to see Paris before we set up our private practice and settled back down in Los Angeles, so I agreed. Anything to make madame grateful every day. Cat's whiskers. Off to Paris for a one-month stay, we thought. But we stayed on for one year. We walked in the city looking at students, painters, old buildings, and the lovely Seine river. It was so much fun to sit in the small cafes and speak to the local people, tasting the wines and cheeses from all over France. If I had the time, I could tell you every kind of wine made in France.

One night Shilee and I sat in a small cafe, holding hands, listening to an accordion player who played a song that seemed familiar: 'I'm Broke And I'm Busted.' About this time I happened to mention to Shilee that we were down to our last seventy dollars plus aeroplane tickets back to Los Angeles. 'What do you want me to do, sell some pussy?' she asked with a pout on her lips. Then she smiled and said, 'So what? We had a good time together, didn't we? I'll just tell daddy to give us some money from my inheritance. Daddy knows best in these matters.' I slid back into the chair feeling so much better and relieved as I was beginning to have trouble sleeping at night. (Also, that lump like a watermelon was starting to come back into my throat like it used to.) Two weeks later we flew back to Los Angeles with about ten bucks between us, and dressed like dog catchers as someone had stolen our luggage as we left Paris.

Shilee's dad had put aside for each of his children some inheritance money that was to be paid after each had been married for three years without a divorce. When the money arrived and we saw the size of the cheque, we nearly fell on the floor laughing with joy. How much do you think it was for? Take a guess – without looking on the next line. Dig this. One million dollars to be paid upon signing the back of the cheque. With all this money, Shilee and I was in hell when we was well, man.

Having had more than a year of playing in the luxury capitals of the world, the time had arrived to plan for the future. We were ready to begin serious plans to set our long-range dream, our own surgical clinic. With some hard bargaining and looking all over the city of Los Angeles, we found a building at last to set up our clinic. After working day and night and saving every penny we got our hands on, we bought a house in Beverly Hills for a staggering one million and a half dollars, from a fading rock singer whose name was Sharp-Eye McKissick. We still had our old Rolls-Royce, but decided to buy another one as our accountant advised us to, as a tax write-off.

Things could not have been better. We were working hard on the clinic, which gave us a lot of satisfaction, and the clinic in turn had paid us handsomely. Lord knows we were living the real Beverly Hills Life, but as they say downtown, we were living high on the hog's ass. One rainy and stormy night Shilee came home with a girlfriend who was in a bad way. her boyfriend had just left her, and left her pregnant. She wanted Shilee and I to perform an abortion on her as a special favor. What she did not tell us was that she had tried two days before with another lady, not licensed, who did abortions on the backstreets of downtown. We felt a great deal of sympathy for the girl as she was not streetwise, the poor bitch really didn't know whether to beat it or eat it. After a couple of hours of her pleading and a little good head for me when Shilee went upstairs, we relented and admitted her to our clinic under an assumed name, Betsy Mae McDonald, as she was still nibbling on a cold, limp hamburger.

Anyway, as the nurse wheeled her into my surgery I asked her once again if she was sure and did she feel OK. On both accounts, she said yes. But as Shilee and I were about to start this delicate operation, the girl began to bleed very badly. Before I could stop the bleeding, and weakened with the previous infection from dirty instruments in her first abortion attempt, she died on the operating table in no more than ten minutes.

Well, after the shock of all this shit, Shilee and I looked at each other and sank to the floor and held hands, knowing our professions as doctors were over then and there. Having this girl die in the midst of an illegal abortion, our names would be mud in the medical profession now. We couldn't even get jobs giving band-aids to wetbacks coming through the barbed wire fence from Mexico. We couldn't even give injections in a whorehouse.

Now that I look back, I see how innocent we were. Hell, we could have hidden the body or something. But not stupid old me. Like an ass, I called the police and the ambulance, and soon after this the shit hit the fan. The next morning's headlines screamed 'Black Couple Kills White Girl'; 'Was Black Couple Qualified to Practice Medicine?'; 'Sex Triangle Suspected – Traces of Fresh

Sperm Found in Victim's Mouth'.)

Anyway, the case went to court, and with all the legal jogging, the trial lasted six months. We were found guilty, lost our license to practice medicine in the United States, and were very fortunate to stay out of jail. Just to top it all off, the girl's family also sued us for millions, and we lost the case again. We lost our Rolls-Royces, the house, and the clinic. All over some pussy someone else had enjoyed, I thought to myself later.

Shilee and I owed money everywhere and to everybody. We had to travel hard and fast to stay out of the way of the many debt collectors. Our lazy nigger butler, Charlie, stole the silver we were going to pawn, and the Mexican gardener chased us in his pick-up truck all over Los Angeles for a measly $3.50 and a can of Rival dog food we had cooked for hamburger. In fact things were so bad when the garbage man came to the house, we asked him to leave us three cans of his best garbage.

We found a room in downtown LA in a cheap hotel called the Roselake Paradise. It cost us three dollars a night and was full of drunks, dope addicts and male prostitutes. The room was dirty, stinking and full of huge rats, and the hotel cats were so frightened they walked in two's for protection. It was the best we could do at this moment in time. Shilee got a job working at McDonald's in Hollywood and I got a job singing in a pizza place in the San Fernando Valley, just out of LA.

One dark, rainy night I was singing on stage doing my Sammy Davis Jr bit when somebody shouted 'Get the bum off, that bum can't sing, he's singing out of his ass,' And I stormed off the stage feeling very hurt, knowing I wasn't that good anyway, but that son of a bitch shouldn't have said it out loud as no one then would put money in the glass rabbit that was sitting on the stage for tips.

As I was changing out of my gypsy costume, Shilee walked into the dressing room, sat down on my violin, crushing it, and said calmly, 'Can you imagine, I got fired from that shitty hamburger joint. The manager said I was eating up all the profits.' And she handed me a cold burger for my supper.

'Let's go,' I said grabbing her arm and running out the backstage exit. There was a taxi free and waiting there like it was meant for me. As Shilee and I sat in the taxi talking, the driver took a wrong turn while driving like a mad man. 'Hey buddy, you're going the wrong way,' I shouted. I could see that bastard looking into his mirror and smiling like a Cheshire cat.

Just then we heard the doors all automatically snap locked, and a glass panel shot up, separating the driver from us, and our compartment began to fill with gaseous white smoke. Shilee and I felt like we were going to choke to death. And then that awful sinking feeling as we lost consciousness and the world began to spin, like being on a country ferris wheel.

When we finally came to, we found ourselves lying on a bed in a luxury hotel room. Looking around the room, I could see a note written on the mirror in lipstick saying 'Welcome, Robbie and Shilee. Ring this bell when you are awake.' There was a small bellpush below the mirror.

'Honey, what kind of shit is this?' Shilee whispered to me.

'I don't know baby, but I'm going to find out quick,' I said, as I shoved Shilee behind me and pushed the bell. Soft Vietnamese music came through the speakers and then a voice spoke. 'Welcome Robbie and Shilee. You are among friends. I am Major Mays.'

'Hi, I'm Charlie the Fox.'

'Hi, I'm Jackie.'

'Hello Robbie, I'm Joe, remember? Walk through the doors in front of you so we can meet your sweet wife, and of course you, you old bastard.'

'Be careful Robbie, it could be a trick,' said Shilee squeezing my hand tightly.

'It's OK baby, I know all those bastards,' I shouted with joy as we hurried through the doors. Sure enough, there they were. It was like being in heaven with a bunch of master thieves. Charlie, Joe, Jackie, and the major all ran over and hugged Shilee and me. Tears, tears, I could not hold back the tears of joy at seeing my old mates again. I felt even happier at seeing Shilee fall in love with my old, dear friends too. After all the hugging and kissing, we sat around a huge table and had a meal fit for a king. I was sure sick of eating cold, greasy hamburgers and Rival dog food. Everyone looked fine, healthy and as if they were rolling in money.

'Major,' I said, 'there is just one question I want to ask. Why did you have to meet up with us this way? You know what I mean, kidnapping and shit like that.'

'Sorry about that, Robbie, but it was the only way I could get you and Shilee here without being traced or followed,' said the major.

'What is the one thing we all have in common right now, Robbie?' Charlie asked me.

'Oh that's easy. We were all in Vietnam together, we all like grandma's apple pie, and we are all the best of friends,' I said.

'Yeah, that's true, but the main thing is that we are all broke, no money, and that's not kosher, baby, to be broke,' said Charlie, turning his pockets inside out. We all looked at each other and nodded our heads in agreement, and started to laugh, as we had all thought each of the others was doing so well. After everybody finished laughing at Charlie standing on top of his chair with his pants pockets turned out, the major spoke up.

'Robbie, would you and Shilee like to be a part of our future plans, whatever they may be?'

Shilee looked at me and nodded.

'Yes, major, you can count on us, whatever it may be,' I said, kissing Shilee on the cheek.

# 4

This was the beginning of many jobs to come. Our first job was to track down and bring to justice a Nazi war criminal by the name of Karl Hans Hurbert. He was responsible for killing fifty-five Hungarians in a church basement in Budapest. All were Jews, of which seven were of the Zagora family. Mr Sam Maggra, now of Maggra Electronics of Australia, was a small boy in Budapest at the time of the massacre. He had managed to escape out of the toilet window as Major General Karl Hurbert ordered his troops to round up the unfortunate victims of the mass murder.

So Mr Maggra paid Major Mays one million dollars to bring Karl Hans Hurbert to justice and back to Israel to stand trial as a war criminal, using any method we were forced to use. After spending a lot of money on informants, and traveling thousands of miles chasing false leads in Europe and South America, we found him in Halifax, Nova Scotia, working as an undertaker. He had not changed his ways in all these years. He made an enormous profit dumping fresh bodies into the ground and selling the same caskets over and over again. After searching for six long, hard months, we finally hit pay dirt. We caught him in church one afternoon as he went to one of his confession sessions with his priest, whom we had paid handsomely to disappear while I took his place in the confession box. This Karl Hans Hurbert fellow confessed to me about his desire for an eleven year old girl in the next block, and asked was it a mortal or venal sin to have taught her to masturbate him in the church basement where he taught Sunday school. And this was only the beginning. But when he began to confess his necrophiliac practices as well, I interrupted the sordid tale by pulling back the curtain and giving him one of my special injections. After seeing my face and before passing out, he asked, gasping for breath, 'Why me, nigger?' and I just gave him my best shoe shine boy grin and left him to wonder.

This injection gives the appearance of being dead. The name of the chemical we used was Gesthemane 19X, and it is so powerful doctors can't tell if a person is alive or dead as no pulse or heartbeat is detectable. Given this injection, you are dead to all concerned, except the CIA or Dr Albert Von Ryker, its inventor and my teacher, and of course myself. We are the only people who know about this special injection. Anyway, back to the plot. To all appearances he was dead, so we drove his body back to his own funeral parlor, dressed him in the priest's clothes, and shipped his body back to Israel in one of his own used, used, caskets, which by now didn't smell too fine.

When he arrived, they revived him with the second part of our secret formula, called Viock's S-96g. Then they put his caught ass on trial. Meanwhile, the major, Charlie, Joe, Jackie, Shilee and me split the money during lunch on the terrace of the Grand Casino in Monte Carlo. Not bad for six months work, huh?

Then there was another time when fighting had broken out in Africa. Uganda was the place, and General Amin was the problem, a big problem. General Idi Aloysius Frank Amin was the ruler of Uganda and ran the country with an iron hand., or it could have been a foot as he kicked so many asses. Everyone in this country was frightened of this huge, cruel black man. Not the UN, the US, The Red Cross, The Blue Cross, no person or organisation could talk to this man or help his country to be rid of him, that is until we came along.

A group of businessmen from South Africa, England and America, who together had huge investments in Uganda, paid us ten million dollars to do our special little job on him. This was our special little job: with the assistance of corrupt government and business people, we were to bring financial chaos to Uganda and later do any personal damage to General Amin possible. I went to Kampala, Uganda and met with some top diplomats and high ranking officers of the Ugandan armed forces. After making many friends in the civil service also, and having them provide me with all the proper permits and official papers for a price, I set up my own private surgery and began medical practice.

At first it was only the local poor people visiting my clinic.Then one major, then two, three... and soon my whole clientele were diplomats and generals. This had taken me six months to set up, remember, and I still had not met general Frank Amin. To his closest friends, he was called Ol' Blue Eyes.

Meanwhile, as the country was nearly bankrupt, Uganda had to pay for all its imported goods with cash, so the black market thrived on the shortage of goods. Meanwhile the major, Charlie, Joe, Jackie and Shilee spent their time flying to Kampala and Entebbe, the two largest cities in Uganda, with goods that were in short supply. They would then sell thousands of dollars worth of stuff such as whisky, vodka, gin, champagne, sugar, ladies' stockings, mushrooms, motor cars and many more things that I can't remember or don't want to lie to you anymore about.

Anyway, they made the Ugandans pay for all these supplies with cash, whether dollars or English pounds. Sometimes they would accept German marks from the rich Nazis still in hiding there. Just before the major,Charlie and company would depart for each trip, they would drive to the outlying towns and villages to circulate thousands of counterfeit Ugandan pound notes with the help of the interested businessmen, and after a year of passing these phony bills, the country's economy was almost ready to collapse.

Now back to my part in the scheme. One night I got a call asking me to come to the presidential palace, for some good down-home soul food. Monkey elbows and zebra chitlins, cooked by his personal chef Big Mama Loula Mae, who apprenticed with a chief of a cannibal tribe. This became the first of many meetings with General Idi Aloysius Frank Amin. The general liked me very much because I always talked bad about America and the Jews. I knew he hated Jews in South Africa and Israel. He always said that because they were such good organizers, Jews made money exploiting lazy Arabs, blacks, or uneducated people throughout Africa.

This was an in for me. So I pretended that I hated Jews also.

(Can you imagine a nigger hating a Jew? I mean we both get treated like shit most of the time, right?) I wanted to laugh at this big, fat fucker, but I kept cool. I didn't want to kick his ass on a full stomach. Anyway, that's how I became his private doctor, and he also made me a captain in his army. What was really going on was this. I was giving him general injections of male hormones to improve his masculinity for public appearances, and mixed in with the hormone injections were special injections. The really special injection was syphilis class G. This type of syphilis is different from the normal high-school type you find in the west. this kind is the worst known venereal disease ever. It eats your body. It's a cannibalistic disease. After a short time, you wish that your dick would fall off, then it attacks your spine, chest and then the brain. While all this is going on, your balls swell up to the size of two cantaloupes. Other than that, I don't think that I was too hard on his ass, right?

As the months went by, General Amin was getting weaker and weaker. Also most of his decisions were wrong or crazy or just plain stupid. The old boy was becoming nutty as a fruitcake. His commanders knew this so they began to take bribes or steal fortunes and then escape to neighbouring countries. By now, the general was spending most of his time riding on a wooden hobby horse in the palace living room, listening to Chopin. I also performed plastic surgery on a secret service man from Tangiers. He was an out of work actor, and was transformed to look like Major General Mosi Ali Mahakma. This general was Amin's right-hand man, though he had been left-handed since puberty. General Amin trusted everything that General Mahakma said or did, as Mahakma was the commander of the 5th army group on the north side of Uganda. We exchanged him for our man, the out of work and cheap actor who bore a strong resemblance to General Mahakma, fat in the head and skinny in the legs. Our phony general's mission was to invade Tanzania and start a war on that front with the troops under his command. He was to make sure that all was lost in defeat, men, tanks, jets, and to destroy all communications between the capital and the northern part of Uganda.

With General Amin's mind going and his body becoming weaker, he became impossible to deal with. He was constantly suspicious of an army coup and ordered most of his high-ranking officers murdered, replacing them with ex-taxi drivers, butchers, and cinema attendants who had convinced him of their loyalty. All politicians that were opposed to his rule were killed or imprisoned. At the same time, the secret gravesites around Kampala blossomed with thousands of fresh graves from the purges. Amin also had his second wife killed for infidelity with a young musician. In his private refrigerator, he kept the kidneys of his slain enemy which were later fried with garlic. (In his tribe, it was believed that if you ate this part of your enemy, his spirit could not come back to haunt you for your deed.)

All of Idi Amin's opponents were killed. Thousands were killed every month and buried in the huge gravesites outside of Kampala, never to be seen again by their families and loved ones.

Uganda was now officially bankrupt and as you can see, this did not happen overnight. It took all of us, and the many who died, to bring down this mad, vicious dictator, general, doctor, the protector of Uganda, marshal of the army, Idi Aloysius Frank Amin.

After three years of our work in Uganda, the country was in bad shape and going downhill fast. General Amin was by now mentally incompetent and the formation of a new government was imminent. Major Mays received a message on our radio from our employers in Europe saying that it was time to pull out of Uganda and that our money would be paid in full in neighboring Kenya.

I was still in Kampala waiting for my half-blind guide to get me out of the country while the major and gang were waiting for me in Kenya. One day as I was saying goodbye to my last patient for the day, two of Amin's personal bodyguards knocked at the door and said that the general wanted to see me at once. I knew then that it was my time to die. The general had chosen to do away with me like the others before. I pulled out a bottle of whisky and offered the guards a drink while I went to my room to get dressed. 'Hey you with the big fucking head,' shouted one of the guards.

'Who me?' I said with a smile so as not to piss off the guy.

'There's nobody else here with a big fucking head but you. don't try to run away or I'll have to shoot your ass, OK, and that would be a waste of a good bullet, sucker.' I gave him a smile and nodded that I understood perfectly. As I closed the door I tied a hand grenade to the door handle so that when these two assholes outside opened it, everything would go up in smoke and plaster the walls with black greasy meat. Before I jumped out the window in my room (wearing my brown pants) I shouted 'Hey you silly black African bastards, kiss my big black ass.'

Just then the door opened, the hand grenade fell to the floor, and a lump the size of a watermelon came to the throats of the two black bastards when WHAMMO – shit flew everywhere as the explosion ripped their asses wide open. After I regained my composure, and feeling very pleased with myself, I jumped into the jeep that the soldiers came in and calmly drove to a town called Jinja while eating the delicious white meat of turkey sandwiches that were left by the soldiers. While stopping in the town and putting more gas in the jeep, someone tapped me on the shoulder. As I turned there was Shilee. My heart jumped with joy.

After kissing and hugging and running into the woods for a quick piece of ass, we drove across the border into Kenya to a town called Mombasa. After checking in at a hotel called The White Duchess, Shilee and I went straight to bed. Boy, was she grateful. Lord knows, I was grateful. I didn't know whether to beat it or eat it, it had been that long since I had seen Shilee on white sheets.

The second morning, Charlie, Joe and Jackie came to our room and divided up the money from the Ugandan mission. Our share of the money came to two and a half million dollars paid in English pound notes. Everyone was talking about retiring and the good life on some peaceful tropical island in the Pacific, when I asked 'Where is the major?'

'Oh he's gone to set up one last quick deal,' said Joe, rubbing his hands with excitement.

'What kind of quick deal?' I asked while stuffing my millions in a pillowcase.

'You tell him, Charlie, you know more about it than anybody,' Joe said.

'Well, everybody wants to retire now, so the major thought we should go out with a bang. The country of Mauritania needs guns to fight the rebels, right? Well, the major flew to Maputo, Mozambique to buy guns shipped from Cape Town, South Africa. He'll bring them back and sell them to Mauritania before they can buy everything from the Russians. It's as simple as that,' said Charlie, smiling.

'How much do you think we can make selling guns?' I asked.

'Oh, I would say about a million and a half, split six ways again, OK?' Charlie rapped back smiling.

'Yeah, you know me, whatever the major says goes,' I said, pulling Shilee down on my knee.

'Oh honey,' she said, 'that's wonderful. We can go and stay with my family once the deal is completed.' Shilee was so happy as she had not seen her family in eight long years. Until the major came back, all we did was play cards and swim in the hotel pool, and at night count our money thinking about the good times ahead.

Three days later, ring, ring, the phone rang just in the middle of Shilee being grateful again. It was the major. He was back and wanted Shilee and I to go and get dressed as everyone else was up, packed, and ready to go. Driving to the airport, we were so excited at the thought of a little extra pocket money to be made. We jumped out of the taxi and ran to the waiting plane. As the plane lifted up in the air, so much wind came rushing through the many cracks and holes in the plane, that I went up to the cockpit and asked the major, 'Where did you get this damn plane?'

'Aah, some old boy from London, England that I met in a bar in Nairobi sold it to me. I know it's a pile of shit but it is all I could get on such short notice,' said the major, laughing as he pointed at one of the plane's engines which had stopped at that moment of time, scaring the hell out of me. As I went back to my seat, everyone was looking out the windows at the dead engine. 'One engine has stopped,' shouted Shilee above the roar of the other three engines.

'I know baby, just relax. We will be landing in fifteen minutes,' I said, trying to sound like Humphrey Bogart.

As the plane landed on an old inactive airfield and rolled to a halt, two trucks came out of the woods and drove up alongside the plane and began to unload the guns. 'Hold it you bastards. Let them guns be until I see some money,' I shouted. As they backed away slowly the major told Shilee and me to collect the money, as we spoke the language of Mauritania, which is an Arabic-African mixed language. A short, fat, balding man motioned for us to follow him. Helping Shilee into the car, I checked to see that I still had my gun strapped to my leg. I then looked to see if the major and Charlie were following us in the car behind. Joe and Jackie decided to stay and watch the plane and guns until we returned, as these Mauritanians would steal the white off rice.

This car journey seemed to last for hours before we stopped next to some beach with tents put up all over it. As far as you could see there was nothing but tents. The driver motioned us into the largest, with guards all around it. After negotiating with the generals for over an hour, then a meal, we came up with a deal. Maybe not the deal we wanted, but a deal. The major wanted a million and a half dollars and the Council of Generals wanted to pay a million or kick our asses and take the guns. 'What kind of shit is this?' said the major angrily.

'It's inflation, my boy, it's killing all of us. You must understand this,' the general responded without being impressed. The price stayed at one million.

After the deal was clinched and the money was being paid out, in walked a man I thought I had seen before. As he moved out of the dark and into the light of the campfire, I could see it was Prince Ben Ali Hassan, as all the princes and generals gave him the Arab handshake with great deference and respect.

'Who is this bastard?' the major whispered. But before I could answer, Prince Ali Hassan said 'Aah! Ho, ho, ho, look what we have here! Why it's Mr Robbie Jones and his little pissy wife from America. I am going to give you and your gun-running friends one week to leave my country or I will kill you. Do you understand, you filthy dogs?' shouted the prince.

'Well you hold on a damn minute,' said Charlie. 'One of the engines in my plane is broken down. It will take at least three weeks to get the parts and fix it.'

'For you, my friend, I will give you three weeks from today to fix your plane and take these two dogs and anybody else with you, but leave my beloved country quickly,' Prince Ben Ali Hassan shouted as he stormed out of the tent with his bodyguards.

'What the hell's fire was that all about?' asked the major.

'Let's go now and I will explain on the way back to the plane,' I said as I motioned to Shilee to hurry as all these Arabs had their eyes popping out looking at her low cut dress. 'What are you looking at?' I asked one Arab who was staring at me.

'I don't know, the label has fallen off you,' he answered back sarcastically.

As I explained to the major and Charlie on the way back our little troubles with Prince Ben Ali Hassan and how it all started with his love for Shilee, the major told me not to worry as it would only take two weeks to fix the engines. So we might as well calm down and have a holiday before flying back to America. The major, Joe, Jackie and Charlie went to stay in one of the local hotels, while Shilee and I went to stay with Shilee's family while the plane was being repaired. One day as Shilee and

I were sitting by the pool in the back garden, Shilee began to cry.
' What's wrong?' I asked as I stopped writing my letter to my
mom and dad.

'It's that damn Prince Ben Ali Hassan. I hate him. He's already
killed many of your friends in college with bombs and messing
with peoples brakes on their cars. Why, this man is horrible and
insane. I wish we could leave now.'

Holding her close to me I whispered 'Please baby, stop
crying. Now calm down. Just think about America, and all that
money you've got to spend on new dresses. You see, that's better,
huh?' And a smile spread over her lovely face. Staying with
Shilee's family was swell. The major, Charlie Joe and Jackie
would come up to the house sometimes for a meal or a drink or
sometimes just to chew the fat. Late one evening as Shilee's
family and our gang were having dinner together, we heard a
special radio announcement being broadcast interrupting the
music by Possum Mouth Capone.

'Long live the new revolution. Our President and Chief of the
Armed Forces, Protector of our grape fields will speak to you
now. Take it away, Mr President,' said the announcer. About this
time Joe had just come up from the wine cellar and shouted, 'Hey
everybody. Look what I've found.'

'Shh,' I whispered. 'Let's hear the new President's speech.'

'This is your President speaking to you. I am President Prince
Ben Ali Hassan. There will be Martial law in Mauritania until all
imperialistic traitors have been eliminated. There will also be a
ten o'clock curfew in all cities starting tomorrow night. Long live
the revolution. Allah is my guide and protector. I can not and will
not betray my people. May peace be with you.'

As the music began to play again, some of Shilee's family
began to cry. Shilee and I just sat and looked at each other in
silence, as Joe began to pour the wine for the others. At this
moment Shilee's father spoke to all of us. 'My friends, do not
worry yourselves over us. For we in Mauritania are used to this
as every few years there is a new revolution. You had better take
care of yourselves. I ask only one thing of you, please take my
daughter with you to America.'

'Drink up everyone, we go tonight. the plane is fixed and we
cannot afford to get caught up in a revolution that is not paying
us any money,' said the major. As we all kissed and hugged and
said our goodbyes to Shilee's family, we felt a sadness in our
hearts as we were leaving and they were staying here with a mad

president like Prince Ben Ali Hassan. As we waited in the car Shilee ran and kissed her family once more like she knew it would be a long time before she was going to see them again.

As we drove through the streets, all you could see were soldiers of the new revolution, people being dragged away in waiting vans, and kids throwing rocks and bottles at the soldiers. As we approached the airport, the major stopped the car some hundred yards from the entrance. 'Hey Robbie, go have a look and see if anyone is guarding our plane,' he said. Joe got out of the car also and helped me get over the fence by letting me stand on his back. As I was crawling in the dark, I could see only one guard near our plane. He walked around the plane singing softly to himself. When his back faced me, I threw my knife into it. Thump. The knife hit dead center. He took one more step and collapsed to the ground. At that moment I ran back to the car and shouted 'Let's go, I got him.'

The major pushed down the accelerator and we went through the checkpoint at eighty miles an hour. Bullets were flying everywhere. 'Stop. Stop you sons of bitches,' shouted the sergeant of the guards as we went speeding by. The car stopped in front of our plane and the major gave us our orders. 'Joe, you and Robbie hold them off until I get the engine started. Jackie, Shilee, you two jump in the plane and help Charlie prepare the dynamite in case we might need some.'

Putt, putt, putt, putt, the damned thing wouldn't start right away and again the major tried to start the engines. Putt, putt, putt, putt, putt putt. Nothing. The engines were cold and wouldn't catch. Meanwhile, there were two trucks of Revolutionary soldiers coming our way at full speed. Machine gun fire splattered everywhere. 'Kill. Kill the Yankee pigs!' shouted the soldiers. Putt, putt, putt, putt, putt – pop! rip! zig! First one engine then the other caught and the props were spinning like mad when Charlie shouted 'Get your asses in here.' As Joe and I dashed to the aeroplane door, Shilee and Jackie let their machine guns rip into the upcoming trucks. As we jumped into the plane Charlie slammed the door behind us and shouted 'everybody get down.' As the plane wheeled and started down the runway past two of the trucks, a dozen or so bullets ripped into the side of the plane. When we took off, I asked the major if we could empty our spare dynamite on the airport we just left.

'My dear boy, I was hoping you would say that.'

On our first pass we dropped a pillow case full of dynamite

smack dab in the center of the control tower. The tower disintegrated in flame. The second pass we dropped a second pillow case on one of the trucks that shot at us. Only a puff of smoke and a huge hole in the runway was left. We dropped four more pillow cases before we were through and the whole airport was alight as we lifted into the clouds. After all the laughing and shouting at what a good job we had done on them good old boys, Jackie asked if anyone wanted a Mauritania beer. It was called Tab Bola, it was supposed to reach places other beers couldn't reach. Finishing the case of beer everybody hit the sack in the rear of the plane, except Charlie who went into the cockpit to keep the major company. After sleeping about three hours, I woke up as it was difficult to snooze with the noise of the engines and the wind rushing in the cracks and bullet holes. I let the rest of the gang sleep while I got up and went to the cockpit to see what the major and Charlie were up to. 'Where are we?' I asked. 'We're just over Kiffa and about one hour before we reach Saint-Louis, Senegal which is our destination,' replied the major.

'That sounds fine to me, but what happens when we get to Saint-Louis, Senegal?' I asked, rubbing my hands with joy.

'When we get to Senegal the first thing is we'll be out of Mauritania, which means no police or dictators will be chasing us. The second thing is we travel from Saint-Louis to Dakar by bus, from Dakar to Accra, Ghana, by boat, and fly from Accra to London, and London to New York, and from New York the world is yours with two and a half million dollars. Now get the fuck out of my cockpit and get some sleep,' the major said, laughing at me.

As I lay down on my bunk, I went to sleep with a smile on my face. I still remember the dream I had on the plane. I dreamed I had washed up on an island of Amazon women and they wanted to make me suffer as I was the only man on the island. The wicked queen who was built like a brick shit-house ordered all the women under twenty-one years old to rip off all my clothes and lay all that good hairy stuff on me. They really wanted me to suffer.

Just as one of them sweet, naked, tan, pretty young things touched my penis with her greedy hands and looked at my body with her man-eating eyes, WHAMMO. A damn crate full of oranges the size of coconuts smashed upside my head. Blood went everywhere, and Shilee and Jackie began to scream and panic as the plane began to sputter and went into a spin, falling fast.

'Everybody prepare yourselves for a crash landing. Two of the engines are on fire and we've lost power,' said Charlie, dashing back to the cockpit. What had happened was, the major was having a little nap in his seat and let Charlie pilot the plane for a while, when suddenly it became very cloudy with a rainstorm. So Charlie decided to come down a couple of hundred feet, but hit a mountain top, knocking off parts of the two engines on the right wing.

It was a sorry sight to see my friends and my wife shouting and screaming from fright, begging God to let them live one day more. Hell, I knew I was going to die, so I just tried to calm down Shilee and be thankful that if it was my time to go, I would go out at least holding my darling Shilee as I went.

Bam, boom, smash. All hell broke loose. Then all of a sudden there was no pain, worry, or sound. It was like walking and running in a dark tunnel for a lifetime with no end in sight. The next thing I knew when I did open my eyes, there was the biggest damn crab sitting on the sand near my face and staring me dead in the eyes. I tried to jump up from the fright, but the pain in my legs and chest was so bad I just rolled over on my back trying to get away before that damn monster locked his pincer onto a delicate part of my body. I wasn't scared, mind you, I just didn't want one of those piercing claws to cut into my rectum. 'Oh my poor head. Oh what pain, pain, pain,' Charlie said as he began to come around. 'Robbie are you OK?' he asked as he reached over to me holding one side of his head, to keep it from falling off.

'I don't know, Charlie man, I can't feel my legs and there's a terrible pain in my chest. Other than that I feel great,' I said, trying to make a joke of it.

'My head feels like someone hit me with a hammer and a runaway truck loaded with bricks has run over my face, but don't worry. Robbie, I want you to stay here while I go and try to find the rest of the gang. I'll be back as soon as I can. Will you be OK until I get back?' Charlie asked, getting to his feet and brushing sand from his clothes.

'Go on, I'll be fine right here,' I whispered as I could hardly talk with this burning pain in my chest and having the feeling that my ass was somewhere up on my back.

As the waves from the sea came upon the beach and the breeze hit my face, my mind began to wander back to my past life. To show you how bad my luck was, dig this. You know how they say your life flashes before you as you're going to die? Well,

it's true. I saw where I grew up in New York, I saw myself on the
tennis team at college, I saw myself receiving the key to the city in
Atlanta, Georgia. Then I suddenly realized: Shit, this wasn't my
life at all. (That quote was first used in 1779 by Arthur Macklefish
Hackenbush, who was the first lawyer to be scalped by the
Indians in the New World.)

As my mind and thoughts came back to the sea, the crab was
still there wondering if he should fuck with me or not, and I
looked across the beach and could see two people coming closer
and closer in my direction. As they came near, I could see one of
the outlines to be that of a woman. At first I thought it was my
love Shilee, but as the two figures came close I could see that it
was my friend Charlie with Jackie.

'Where is everybody? Where is my Shilee?' I began to shout
and beat my fist into the sand in anger. Charlie grabbed my
hands and Jackie began to cry as she spoke to me.

'Robbie, we have some very sad news for you. Shilee, Joe and
the major are all dead. We are the only ones to survive the crash.'

I fell back into the sand and lay there in silence, totally numb
with shock. This time for real.

'You stay here and watch Robbie, Jackie, and see that he don't
do anything silly while I'm gone to get some wood for a fire, OK?'
I heard Charlie say as he walked away.

'I'm going to get some sleep now, Robbie, as I'm sore and very
hungry. Now you won't do anything stupid, will you?' Jackie
whispered to me, holding my hand.

'I'm sorry I lost my cool awhile back, but I'm OK now. You go
ahead and get some sleep,' I said, biting my tongue not to cry, as
I felt so much sadness in my heart.

As night began to fall and with the incoming tide, it became
cooler and then downright cold. Charlie came back with an
armful of wood and shouted 'Hey look what I found.'

'A chicken,' I shouted thinking of my empty stomach.

'No. I found some matches to light a fire.'

When Charlie dropped the wood on the ground he also had
two black bags hanging over his shoulders. 'What's in the bags?'
Jackie asked with curiosity.

'I was hoping someone would ask me that question,' Charlie
remarked, looking over my way to see if I was interested. I
turned and looked. Charlie opened one of the bags and dumped
some cans onto the sand. It was about ten cans of chicken noodle
soup which had been the major's. The major would always carry

this little black bag filled with tins of soup everywhere he went, Africa, Vietnam, Nova Scotia, that black bag was always there. 'I found the major's bag of soups washed up on the beach behind some rocks. This will keep us going for two days until I can get some help,' Charlie said.

'And what's in the other bag, pal?' I asked, hoping it was medical supplies.

'Well it's not much but it will do for now,' Charlie said as he opened the second bag and showed us the money inside it. It was the boat passage money that was to take us from Dakar, Senegal to Accra, Ghana. 'There is about twenty-five thousand US dollars in here. This will buy the right kind of help and get us back to America safely,' Charlie whispered just in case somebody might overhear.

It was very dark on the beach. The only thing you could see was our campfire, and the three of us sitting eating soup. 'Robbie, I'll go and try to find a doctor for you first thing in the morning,' Charlie promised as he began to show me on the map where we had crashed and the location of the nearest village.

'Thank you, Charlie, I really…' Before I could finish Jackie whispered 'Shh. There's someone out there in the dark moving around.' At that moment Charlie grabbed a burning piece of wood in his hand and ordered Jackie and me to stay together while he would go out and take a closer look. 'Watch yourself, they might have guns,' I cautioned.

# 5

As Charlie disappeared into the dark, all we could see was the burning torch. Suddenly a shot rang out, then two more. At that moment the torch fell to the ground.

'Charlie, Charlie. Answer me, for God's sake, answer me,' I called out into the dark. There was no answer from Charlie. There was only silence except for the crashing surf on the rocks. As Jackie moved closer to me and asked my advice about what we should do other than faint, the whole beach lit up bright as a football stadium at night. There were about sixty Arab nomads fully armed and shining hand-held lights, plus the headlights from six trucks all beaming into our faces.

Jackie began to cry and I could not move because of the pain in my chest and legs. I shouted in anger 'You silly, fucking, murdering, bastard Arabs. I hope your mothers rot in hell.' As I kept up a continuous barrage of abuse, they surrounded Jackie and I with their camels and horses and began to move closer. They stopped about five feet from us, and a voice spoke in English.

'I am Prince Rashid Ben Acbar the leader of the Bu-Anan tribe. You are now my slaves. You girl, I can get two thousand British pounds for you on the open market. And you, nigger with the big head, I will make you work in my fields and guard my many wives.'

At that moment I shouted out 'Look you silly asshole, I am an American citizen, and so is my friend.' Smack across my face and upside my head went a smashing blow. Some fucking Arab hit me with a hand that looked like a foot.

'Ha, ha, ha!' laughed the Prince, blowing his nose into his silk burnoose. 'I like a man with guts. I will make you the head guardsman in my harem. But first you must have your balls cut off. Take them away.'

As I was loaded into one of the trucks, I looked to my left in the glare of the headlights, and could see Charlie's body lying in a pool of blood. Jackie was taken to the open slave market to be sold to the highest bidder, so that was the last time I was to see my dear friend. I was taken away to the Prince's palace. As I arrived behind the gates and then at the slave quarters, I was taken to the medical room where I was put to bed by two big fat mommas. There were bars on all the windows and the doors were kept locked at all times.

I stayed in the medical room for about six months, confined to my bed with two broken legs, broken wrist and four broken ribs on my right side. Other than that I felt just fine. The doctor was a decent sort of fellow and attended me very well considering the lack of modern medical equipment and drugs. Sometimes when on his rounds he would stop and talk to me for five or ten minutes as he was amazed that I knew so much about modern medicine and practice. One day the doctor told me that Prince Rashid Ben Acbar wanted him to perform the necessary operation of cutting my balls off so I could work in the harem.

I pleaded with the doctor to help me, everyday and all day for three days. I begged like a son of a bitch for the doctor to delay the Prince's orders for a while at least. Finally the doctor broke down and said yes, he would help me, as I fell to my knees and begged

'No, no, not my balls, man.' The doctor came up with a plan.

He would leave open my room door. I was to go downstairs to his operating room, where a hand grenade was hidden behind the fish tank, and I was to take the grenade and blow up all of his equipment. At that point the doctor would be unable to perform the operation for lack of equipment and the necessary drugs to do a proper job. After the explosion, I was to move as quickly as possible back to my room and pretend I knew nothing at all. You see, if I escaped, the Prince would kill the doctor and sell his family into slavery because the doctor was the only one with the keys to all the medical rooms.

As you can guess, I went through with the plan. It was one afternoon. As the doctor was leaving the room, he stopped, turned, and said 'Tonight's the big night. don't fuck it up because if you do, it will be my neck too. Remember, behind the fish tank.' As darkness fell upon the palace grounds, and the door had been left open as planned, I jumped out of bed and went downstairs. As I was going out the door to the main courtyard, I heard laughing and music coming from one of the rooms. I was curious to go see who it was, but thought I'd better not if I wanted to save my poor balls.

As I went into the courtyard, I had to duck behind a wagon full of hay as two guards walked by into the tire shop. I then jumped up and ran under the rain roof and into the doctor's office and operating room. It was very dark in the office, but with just enough light coming through the windows from the moon. Dig this shit. The doctor told me to look behind the fish tank for the hand grenade, right? Well this son of a bitch had eight fish tanks in the room, so here I am in this damn room looking like crazy in the dark for that grenade, when I noticed that I had left the front door open. As I have not found the hand grenade, and as I am standing in the middle of the room looking stupid at the open front door with about twenty cats running through the door and jumping into the fish tanks, I wanted to cry. I just took pot luck and looked behind the tank that was under the picture of his dear, dead mother that was hanging on the wall. Gee fucking whiz. Sure enough there was that sweet little hand grenade with a note on it saying 'Please don't fuck up. If you do keep on running.' I picked up the grenade and ran to the door, as the cats were screaming, jumping in and out of the fish tanks and shitting all over the floor.

As I slid across the floor on the cat shit, I saw two guards coming down the stairs from the recreation room to change guard at the front gate. Just then, *kersplash*. Over went those giant fish tanks about the size of a refrigerator, smashing to the floor with a bunch of cats hanging on to it.

I looked out of the window and I could see the guards running in my direction. This all happened so fast. I jumped behind the office door and clutched my sweet grenade, waiting for the bastards to enter. As the guards ran into the office and tried to chase all the cats away, I pulled the pin on the grenade, threw it in the direction of the guards, and got the hell out of there most quickly. Just as I hit the ground, an explosion ripped through the office. Arab arms, legs, blood, and pussies sprayed the courtyard like a Jackson Pollock painting.

I quickly jumped up off the floor and ran upstairs to my room, straight into my bed like a naughty kid who had just stolen a cheese and onion sandwich from the refrigerator. Just as I pulled the sheets over my head, I heard someone at the door putting a key in it and turning the lock. I could hear shouts of 'Fire' and 'More water' from outside my window as the soldiers yelled to one another. Then suddenly I heard the key in my door again, and in walked Prince Rashid and the doctor, making sure I was in my room.

'You son of a bitch,' said the Prince, 'I know you had something to do with this bombing, but I can't prove it. If I had caught your ass down there, I would have kicked another hole in it. I was in America too, you know, and you niggers are a sneaky lot if I say so myself. It looks like you will have reprieve on your operation until we get some new equipment. But I promise you this: I will have your balls to feed to the dogs,' said the Prince as he stormed out of the room. (Balls to the dogs? That sounds like Shakespeare, doesn't it?) With the Prince gone there was only the doctor and me in the room. 'You're very good at your work, Mr Jones,' he said with a smile.

'Thanks Doc, I owe you one,' I said shaking the doctor's hand.

'I can't help you any more. You are now on your own as you will be transferred to the main slave quarters in two days time,' whispered the doctor, then said 'Oh I almost forgot, watch yourself in the main slave quarters as the Prince has spies everywhere.'

'Thanks for the advice,' I said softly as I was thinking out my next move.

Sure enough, the Prince and his four outhouse guards came to my room and personally escorted me to my new cell in the slave quarters. As the cell door closed, the Prince made a wise crack to me. 'Yank, your ass has had it now,' he said motioning in the direction of my new cell mates.

The cell smelled like cow shit and it looked as if nobody had cleaned it for a year. I wouldn't let my dog sleep on that floor it was so nasty. As I walked across the cell, all eyes were on me, and I mean big bad eyes. There were ten Africans and six Arabs in this one cell with me, and each had his own little place to sit and sleep on the floor. The slaves were given a bowl, a blanket, and a newspaper each day to use when they had to go to the toilet. The toilet was a hole in the wall, and that's not easy to shit into, and mostly they missed the hole. But the newspaper made good reading. I guess I was lucky to be in this cell as I didn't have to worry about no punky fags. Everyone in this cell worked in the Main House with the Prince's wives, which meant they had been castrated and their dicks couldn't get up in any circumstances, and I mean any. This was why I was put into this room. I was to be next as soon as the new equipment arrived. Some times the guards would come around and tease us by throwing books of naked women to the slaves. I heard a young slave say to an old one, 'Put down that book. You're too old to cut the mustard.' The old one answered 'Yeah, but I can still lick the jar.'

The first week everybody stayed away from me, but nodded or smiled as we passed in the courtyard. Our day would start at five in the morning and end at nine o'clock at night, with twenty minutes break for eating. Oh, I almost forgot. We got a nice bowl of rice, red cabbage and those big white beans at the end of our day. The farts of sixteen men in one cell sounded like a band playing the marching music of John Phillip Carson.

The work was very hard and the hours long and I was losing a lot of weight as the guards took an instant dislike to me. For two months I worked with the other guys in my cell and no one spoke to me. Until one day a wagon full of rocks was coming down a steep hill and its brakes failed. The driver jumped out, letting the wagon and horses crash over the mountainside. As the wagon crashed on the side of the mountain and rocks flew everywhere, 'Look out for the rocks, rock slide, run,' someone shouted, and everybody ran for safety. Some of the men working below were too slow and weak to get out of the path of the rocks and were crushed to death.

As the rocks rolled over some poor bastards' bodies, there

were screams of agony from the dying. When the dust cleared away, a guard shouted 'Burn the dead and shoot the badly wounded.' While the men were piling the dead in neat stacks, shots rang out all around us. Suddenly I saw a slave from my cell with a huge rock resting on one of his legs, shouting at the guards not to kill him.

I quickly ran over and begged the sergeant of the guards to spare his life and let me try to save him. 'If you fail, Yank, the punishment will be death for wasting our time on a shit slave. You understand, you dog?' shouted the sergeant, smiling and hoping that I would fail.

'All you men come on. Give me a hand with this big rock,' I yelled while trying to calm the wounded man. Most of the men were already dog-beat tired but came and gave a hand to move the huge rock. As it rolled off the badly crushed leg, I knelt down and began to wrap the leg in my head cloth which I wore to keep the burning sun off my head. 'You men grab his arms and his legs carefully and put him in the back of the water wagon,' I yelled.

'Who are you giving orders too?' shouted the sergeant as he drew back his whip to hit me.

'The Prince paid a lot of money for this slave, now you wouldn't want it to get back to him that you shot one of his slaves that could have been useful for many more years, would you?' I asked.

'OK you smart shit, but like I said, you'd better not slip up. That's all I'm going to say,' remarked the sergeant, tapping the handle of his whip. When the water wagon started back to the camp with the wounded slave and me, I could hear someone shout out an order in a husky voice: 'Alright. Don't stand around like a spare prick. Get your asses back to work. You bastards have been having it too easy lately. Good thing the Lord let the rocks fall on you, or you wouldn't have had that rest.'

Riding in the back of the wagon was hot as hell. The sun was burning down on us, my mouth was dry, and I was fed up with this slavery shit. I was just about to jump from the wagon in chains when this poor bastard with the bad leg opened his eyes and touched my hand motioning me not to go.

We pulled into the camp and all the slaves ran over to stare into the back of the wagon at me and the wounded slave. 'Don't just gaze with your mouths wide open, you stupid shits. Help the nasty dog to the hospital room, and be quick about it,' shouted the captain of the house guards. 'Hey you, skinny ass. What do you think you're doing,' he shouted as he saw my trying to stop the bleeding of the wound.

'I am a specialised surgeon,' I answered calmly. The captain laughed and said 'You a surgeon? Surgeon my ass.'

'Your ass my need some surgery, but right now I must try to save this man's leg in the hospital operating room,' I said walking away and hoping the bastard wouldn't shoot me in the back.

As the Captain quickly ran after me shouting filthy abuse and trying to hurt my feelings, the Prince yelled from an upstairs balcony adjoining his rooms, 'Leave him be. Let him try to save the slave's life. If he fails, shoot him in both knee caps for being a smart ass, the black bastard.'

As I had to be clean to perform the operation, they let me wash and change into clean whites. When I looked into the mirror, I didn't recognise myself. I was so thin and my eyes were sunk back into my head. I looked like I was dressed in whites to go to a concentration camp ball. I entered the operating room where two nurses and my pal the doctor were there to assist me. The operation went like clock work. The old skills came back to me as if I had been operating on a regular basis. I couldn't save the leg as it was too badly damaged, so I amputated the slave's right leg just below the knee. At least after this was all over, he could go into show business as a Long John Silver impersonator.

When I changed back to my old shit clothing and went back to my cell everybody ran to me and began to hug me and shake my hand in friendship. I learned that night that they had had to be careful of me in case I was one of the Prince's spies. I also learned that they were planning an escape. Now this really turned me on as I was up to my teeth with this slavery shit and couldn't stand any more. The very next night I sat in on the escape committee meeting and was invited to give some of my views, as I had told them of my work in Vietnam. Each night every one of us made something for the escape or brought something into our cells that would be useful in our escape plans. As the floor was covered with hay, it was easy to hide things in our cells. The guards would come and feed us and hurry away so that they wouldn't have to smell the stinking shit on the floors and walls.

Life is funny, isn't it? I used to say what a shit-hole this place is and wished some of my cell mates would use the toilet-hole instead of shitting on the cell floor in a mad kind of way. Now we wanted everybody to shit on the floor or the walls, depending upon how badly you had to go, just to make it smell terrible and stop the guards searching for weapons.

The slaves that worked in the hospital rooms took wood from the bed slats to make ladders to go over the walls. The slaves who worked in the kitchen stole knives, spoons and forks to sharpen into razor-like little daggers. One day as was coming back to camp from working in the wheat fields, I leaned over as I was walking and grabbed some wild berries while the guards were not looking. I then quickly stuffed a handful of berries into my mouth, as I knew they would make me ill and give me a bad case of the shits. I would then be sent to hospital and could see my friend the doctor. You see, I wanted to see the doctor and ask him at least one favor before I escaped, and this was the only way I could speak to him, as only two types of patients saw the doctor in this camp, the dead and the almost dead – it's cheaper.

I continued to walk in line with the other slaves back to the camp. I fell out, staggered over to a rock, and passed out. 'Doctor, give this nigger Yank something now, we need his ass working in the fields tomorrow,' yelled the sergeant as the doctor came out the toilet scratching his ass. Upon hearing the yelling of the sergeant, I came around with a terrible pain in my stomach from eating the wild berries.

'Doc, hurry up and give me something for this pain,' I shouted as the sergeant and guards left the hospital where they had carried me. 'What have you been eating, green watermelons?' the doctor said laughing , thinking I was from Georgia where all niggers eat watermelons by the truckload. 'Them fucking wild berries by the wheat field,' I said in pain. The doctor began to laugh and said, 'You'll be all right with these pills I gave you, but you sure are going to have a bad case of the shits as those berries are nature's most powerful laxative. The local natives give them to their camels when they want to fertilize their gardens. I was wondering of you would mind shitting in my flower box on the balcony. I would be most grateful.'

'Doc,' I whispered, 'Forget my bowels, please do me one more favor and I will never ask anything of you ever again,' I begged in all seriousness. The doctor looked around to see if anyone was listening to our conversation and said ,turning back to me, 'What do you want now, Robbie? You know how dangerous it is to talk about escaping if that's what you're thinking about.'

'Yeah I know doc, but the slaves and I need your help badly. That's why I am asking you to please get us two hand grenades for our escape.

'OK, but this is the very last time I will help you. I will wrap a bandage around your waist and tape two hand grenades inside it,' whispered the doc. I gave him a big hug out of excitement. When the doctor finished wrapping the bandage around my waist I quickly pulled my shirt down over my pants to hide everything.

'Goodbye, doc,' I whispered. 'This may be the last time I will see you as we have plans to escape tomorrow night,'

'Goodbye my friend, may your God be with you in these hard times,' whispered the doctor as we hugged and shook hands. Just then a knock on the door and in walked the captain of the guards. 'Is this dog ready to go back to work, doctor?' asked the captain as he stood tapping his whip in the palm of his hand.

'Yes, he's all yours. I just bandaged his ribs as he had bruised them rather badly falling on the rocks when he passed out. But other than that, the dog is ready for a good day's work in the fields,' said the doctor, motioning for the next patient to come into his office. The next patient looked like he had a bad case of leprosy or elephantiasis. Whatever it was, he had the deep uglies.

As I arrived back in my cell, an old man I had helped earlier in the day motioned me to his side with his walking stick. 'My Yankee friend, we will have to escape tonight, so be prepared for action,' he whispered to me while keeping an eye on the cell door at the same time.

'But why tonight and not tomorrow night as we planned?' I asked curiously.

'Because three slaves were captured today carrying knives and homemade clubs. I am sure they will talk after being tortured by the captain tonight,' whispered one of the other slaves standing near us as he raised his shirt and showed the scars on his chest, arms, and back. The old man nodded and said, 'The captain has a new way of torturing the slaves now. He has two guards wrap fine piano wire around the penis, then they pull until either you tell them what they want to know or your penis is amputated at the base and they let you bleed to death.'

'OK tonight it is,' I said, smiling but feeling something very bad was about to take place tonight.

When it became dark and all the cell lights went out, the guards began to play cards and listen to the radio in their office. The slaves began to crawl on the floor and search for their home-made weapons hidden in the hay laced with shit. As the other slaves had not trusted me at first, they now wanted to show me a surprise. The surprise was fantastic to me, a sight for sore eyes. It was a tunnel dug out of the wall in the cell that led under the walls that surrounded the main slave quarters and out into a small market place where the farmers and peasants sold their goods. 'That's nice,' I said, rubbing my hands with joy. 'Fucking bloody marvellous. But what about the other slaves. How will they escape?'

'Don't worry, Robbie my friend, all is taken care of. First two of our men will go out this tunnel and come back over the walls into the camp. Then they will do away with the guards in the office, and come and open all the other cells so that everyone can go out the tunnel. Simple, huh?' said the old man, patting me on the shoulder.

'But everybody can't escape through this small tunnel, and even if they could, it would take hours for everyone to pass through,' I said .

'Calm down, calm down, Yank. We're not stupid. Most of the slaves are only peasants and want to remain here, while the young and strong want to leave and live in the city or escape to Algeria,' remarked one of the bigger slaves, breathing into my face and smelling like he had just eaten ass for dinner. I could see there was no use in explaining more as they were already set in their minds to go tonight, so I let it be, not wanting the big nigger to breathe on me again.

The guards were playing cards, listening to the radio, and laughing up a storm as we in our cells were waiting for the right time to begin the escape. As we lay on the hay in our cells and showed each other the different weapons we had made for this very moment, screams of the tortured slaves rang out over the courtyard. I got up and walked over to the old man and suggested that now would be the right time to give the signal, as the screams from the tortured slaves were making our men a bit jumpy and fidgety. The old man agreed with me and gave the signal. As we pulled on the rope, eight stones came out of the wall and in went two of the strongest slaves to deal with all the climbing, crawling, and the guards' asses.

When the two slaves went down the tunnel, the old man said it would take a half hour before they got back into the camp to help us. So we just all sat and waited and listened to the screams of pain and horror coming out of the torture chamber. Once in a while we would hear the captain laugh, the crack of his whip, and 'Attaboy. Get the son of a bitch. Fill his ass with more water,' and then more screams. I was getting nervous. About an hour had gone by and still nothing had happened. Suddenly there were screams of mercy from the guards in the front office: 'Please don't kill me. Some of my best friends are slaves.'

From the screams of the guards, you could tell the two slaves were kicking asses with a vengeance. (Like we say back home, kicking asses first and taking names later.) Then the two slaves ran back to our cells and began to open the cell doors with the guards' keys, shouting:

'Burn this fucker down.'

'Kill the Prince.'

'Kill all the women and fuck all the men.'

And these were the mild tempered slaves. Just as I had said all along, all the silly bastards were all trying to escape through the small tunnel at the same time. Like the song says, 'If it don't fit don't force it.'

I ran quickly over to the tunnel entrance, jumped up on a stool and pleaded with the slaves not to try to escape all at once through the tunnel as it might collapse on top of them. 'Move away, Yank. Fuck off you old bastard. You just want to jump in line first yourself.' All I got was abuse and obscenities for trying to save them.

About ten minutes later, sure enough the tunnel collapsed, killing some thirty men. Five slaves managed to escape death by crawling back through the fallen rocks and dust into the cell block. Now things got really out of hand, everything was so disorganized with everybody talking at one time. 'Let's storm the main gate.'

'Let's go out and kill,' a group from another cell began to shout and chant over and over. 'Hey look. The guards are lining up outside itching for a fight.'

'Let's give them one, men. Let's give them an ass kicking that will make their noses bleed,' shouted some crazy bastard as all the slaves dashed for the main doors shaking knives and clubs in the air. I knew at that moment if I stayed in my cell I would be killed and if I went outside I might be killed. What a choice, huh? As I unwrapped the bandage from around my waist to get at the hand grenades, I could hear screams of death and gunfire all around me. I dashed out into the courtyard where there was fierce hand-to-hand fighting going on between the guards and the slaves. Some of the guards were on the walls firing out of date, single shot rifles into the melee below them. As I knelt down beside an overturned table, I could see the main house was now on fire along with the buildings and slave quarters around the courtyard. Most of the slaves were being killed near the main gate trying to get past two machine guns firing two hundred rounds per minute directly into them. When I saw this slaughter, I felt the need to help. With me doing my John Leslie Wayne bit, I jumped up and tried to pull the pin out of the hand grenade with my teeth and almost broke my damn jaw. Anyway, I ran in the direction of the main gate shouting 'Attack the gate. Storm the gate, men,' as I threw one grenade, wiping out the machine gun nest. I looked down and saw a German Luger pistol in a dead sergeant's hand. I knelt down to pick it up and ZIP, something nicked me near my right ear. Everything suddenly went hazy and blurry.

'Throw the other hand grenade, Yank, they are killing us.'

'Throw the hand grenade, what the hell's got into you?' a slave shouted near me. I couldn't see very well as everything had a blur to it, so I got up onto my feet and looked in the direction I thought was the main gate. I could only see something bright red, which I remembered was the stop sign that was nailed to the gate. Digging down deep inside myself, mustering all the power I could raise, mustering all the strength at my command, I hurled the grenade at the gate.

A huge explosion ripped open the main gate and all the slaves stood up and shouted 'The Prince is back with more men. The bastard won't let us be free.' With that a cannonball landed near me, knocking me to the ground.

'Yank, you alright?' asked a slave, stopping to help me. Before I could answer, he whispered to me 'We have lost. We will be hanged when it's all over. The captain will drown us each, one by one, like rats. The Prince has a fresh four hundred men out there ready to storm in here and kill us.' I thought to myself at that moment, this is it. I'm gonna die in a strange land and a slave like many of my ancestors before me.

'Just help me to my feet and find a place for me to rest,' I said to this helpful slave, as I felt him going through my jacket pockets. Suddenly cannon shots began to fall all around the courtyard, tearing out huge chunks of earth and killing most of the slaves as they ran wildly screaming, crying and shouting like scared chickens going to market.

As this slave helped me to my feet, we began to move slowly across the courtyard looking for some cover. A cannon ball landed in front of us knocking me ten feet in the air and into a water well. I hit the cold water with a bang. My head cleared and I got myself together quickly and tried to climb up the walls of the well, as the thought came into my head that I was going to drown. I was half way up the well and could hear the very slave who had helped me to my feet and half way across the courtyard plead for his life as the soldiers shot him three times. 'Did you kill all the dirty rats you saw?' the Prince asked the captain. 'We killed everything with two legs,' laughed the captain.

'Hey captain, what shall we do with these two wounded slaves?' asked a soldier, who was brown-nosing the captain. 'Take out their eyes with a hot poker,' yelled the Prince, taking a swig of whisky to celebrate his victory. While this was going on, I was still trying to keep my balance by pushing two feet against the walls of the well. 'If you men catch another slave, bring him to me immediately. I want that dog to suffer by putting a hot poker up his asshole,' shouted the Prince as his men cheered him like crazy and gave him a standing ovation. Upon hearing this, and trying not to make a sound in the well – just keeping my grip was putting a terrible strain on my poor weak body – I managed to hold on, hoping that the Prince and his men would leave soon.

'Your most gracious prince, our valiant leader and protector, master of lands to the sea, filled with heavenly kindness, will you drink the water from the sacred well and bless our soldiers for this victory today, if it pleases your highness?' said the captain to the Prince, who by now had mounted his white stallion.

'Arise, my captain, and bring me a bowl of water from the sacred well,' said the Prince as his fighting men cheered again and waited for his blessing. All this time I've been in this filthy well trying to keep my balance and this kind of shit comes up, I thought to myself. Anyway, I quickly let go of the walls and fell again into the cold water below, making a loud splash as a soldier approached.

'Your Highness, come quick. There's a slave in the well,' shouted the soldier, looking down at me with his bloodshot eyes.

'Kill him. Kill him,' I could hear the Prince shout at the top of his voice. Bullets started flying around me as I dove to the bottom of the well. In my haste to get away from the bullets, I hit my head on a rock and felt a strong current swirl around my head as I passed out. I don't know what happened, but when I did come around, I found myself in an underground cave that was dark and full of bats as big as footballs. No, I tell a lie, watermelons. I pulled myself out of the water and sat on a nearby rock. I was exhausted and felt like wild bulls had stampeded all over my body, but I knew God wanted me to live for another adventure.

# 6

I also found out why the current was so strong near the well. The water comes down from the mountains, meeting with two other rivers and creating a very strong undercurrent. Between you and me, I didn't give a shit as long as I was alive.

I picked myself up off the ground and began to walk and walk until I discovered I had been walking in circles. After going nowhere for six hours, I decided to sit down and have a little sleep before moving on further. As I awoke, I found my body covered with big black razor toothed, red eyed rats. These ferocious little beasts were all over me, biting huge mouthfuls of my flesh and leaving gaping holes in my poor, weakened body. Have you ever seen a Swiss cheese nigger? I'd never been so scared in my life as I began to beat the rats off me and run down into another tunnel entrance. I was truly hauling ass, and said those famous words, 'Feet don't fail me now.' Now I really had a problem. I knew that if I went to sleep I would be eaten alive by the killer rats, and if I didn't find food soon I would starve to death, but the good news was that I had water and plenty of it.

In this big cave were a hundred little tunnels leading into or out of one another, which was confusing to say the least, old boy. I walked and walked for five days and managed to keep from falling asleep the whole time. My body became very weak as I had now gone for seven days without any food. Five days in the tunnel and for two days before the escape. My every thought was about food, mainly hamburgers, and this kept me going. Just around every corner I looked for the golden arches where billions had been served.

As I dragged my poor body along the floors of the cave, becoming weaker and weaker, I decided to give up. My body was now like a skeleton, my ribs were sticking out of my skin, and my stomach was paining me like hell for food. The only good part of this, was that there was no mirror, as I used to love looking at my muscular body. As I lay on the ground trying to keep my eyes open, I became aware of the rats moving closer and closer to me in the dark. I guess I was on their menu as black steak.

I was hoping that I would be too tough and bony for them or hoping that the sons of bitches would choke to death on one of my bones. The rats began to run in circles and scream, and I began to pray to God and ask him for forgiveness for the killings, the stealing, and the lying to so many sorry bastards in my life. I also told God that if he got me out of this mess, I would devote my life to healing the sick, helping thee poor, and go to church every Sunday. Halfway through my prayers I could feel the rats biting into my legs and toes then darting away quickly with my blood dripping from their ferocious jaws. I just kept on saying my prayers to God as I was too weak to move or fight back. The rats were moving from my legs to my chest now, clawing and biting and attacking each other for the best parts of the meat. It seemed like thousands of them judging by the pain everywhere. The excruciating pain from the thousands of sharp, razor-like teeth was quickly becoming too much to endure. With all my might I dug deep down into myself once more and let out a scream for help. Over and over I shouted 'Help me, I'm dying!' Just as I was about to close my eyes and end the struggle in horrible death, I saw a light coming toward me and heard a loud explosion before I passed into unconsciousness.

When I came around I saw two women standing over me loaded down with bullets in bandoliers over the uniform of an unknown army.

'Here, have some water and don't try to talk as you are very weak,' said a soft luscious voice. Was I still in some kind of dream? Had I died? Would misery be over at last? Were these two angels really soldiers of the Lord? After I drank a few sips of water, the two ladies put me on a donkey loaded down with small boxes of some sort and led me away to another tunnel. Feeling badly dazed, riding on the back of the donkey as the women walked, I could see lights at the end of the small tunnel. As I rode out into the open, I could see a camp of some sort.

'This is our home. We will take you to our house and care for you, Bones,' said the lady with the bigger tits.

The two women led the donkey and me into the camp and stopped in front of a market stall to pick up some food. A group of men gathered around me looking curiously. 'Where did you girls pick up this scarecrow?' asked a big guy with a pot belly. Everyone began to laugh when one of the women quickly answered back 'Don't laugh. Can't you see how badly hurt this man is? Sometimes you're so stupid,' and she shook her head in disbelief at their crass behavior. Just then a captain walked over and asked the two women where they had found me, and if I had been in an accident. I could not hear their reply, but could see the women pointing and explaining all that had happened. After talking to the women, the captain walked over to me and looked at my body with chain marks on my legs and neck and knew at once that I was an escaped slave, and not a spy as he had first suspected. After looking me over and seeing the rat bites and the chain marks, he motioned to the two women that all was OK and that we could leave.

As we moved through the camp, all eyes were upon me and the women with wonder and curiosity. 'Marra, can I help you with your friend? He looks like he has been in a nasty accident,' asked an old woman grinning with a one-tooth smile as the donkey stopped in front of a nearby hut.

'No thanks. Irma and I will be able to get him into the hut,' said one of the women. From the time I hit that hut things began to look good. The two women who saved me were soldiers of the White Army fighting the revolutionary Red Army headed by Prince Ben Ali Hassan and equipped by the Russians. The names of the two women were Marra Anna Idriss and Irma 'Tits' Balanco. They both had studied in America before the revolution and both had been married but their husbands had been killed in the revolution like those of so many of the other women in the camp. That is why many of the women had become soldiers. Anyway, there was a shortage of men around and as time went on, I taught the girls Irma and Marra not to be greedy over my poor little body as I had enough love for both ladies, even if I did have to suffer a little bit.

The girls had to wash, shave, and feed me. They had to do everything for me. I couldn't stand, walk, or even go to the toilet by myself for nine long months. For all this time, Marra and Irma nursed me back to the best of health with tender loving care. I'll always be grateful to them for saving my life.

When I was able to move around on my own, things really moved to the better. I was constantly walking around humming 'How Sweet It Is To Be Loved By You'. Marra, Irma and I were always together. We'd walk on the many beaches at night, or go riding in the mountains together. I became an authority on the animal and plant life of the mountains. Life was one big bowl of cherries. Why, these ladies were real firecrackers when it came to loving, and they showed me how grateful they were too. Grateful, grateful, grateful, Lord knows they were grateful. Oh, please! Sometimes in turns and sometimes together. Marra, why she was the one with the big tits, forty-two inches to be exact. she could do things with her tits and tongue to a man that would make his toes curl up and cause him to scream obscenities. Marra had a tongue like an ant eater and was dangerous when she moved it all over your body slowly and delicately. Fellows, don't you just love it? And when I talk about Irma, she was hotter than a Mexican tamale. When she moved her hips so fast, you became hypnotised, and the faster you fucked the more your dick became tenderized and satisfied, and eventually homogenized.

I tell you this with no lie. Marra and Irma made up for the nine months we couldn't get it on in one month. These girls made me suffer, 'every day in every way' was their motto. Why hell, it got so bad at times that when the girls came back from patrolling the mountains looking for Red Army soldiers, they wouldn't fix me any food until I made love to them savagely. I even had to whisper dirty rude suggestions in their ears. Now you know that ain't right for a good Christian boy like me. Boy, they made me suffer, Lord knows they made me suffer, but I was grateful for the chance.

I was as happy as a nineteen year old big dicked boy turned loose in the YWCA until one day a knock sounded at the door. 'Marra, Irma, open up. This is Sergeant Meknes. The War Council wants to speak to old lover boy,' said the sergeant.

'Just a minute. Let me get dressed,' shouted Marra looking frantically for her silk panties which I had put on earlier. What the hell did the War Council want with me, I thought as I rolled off Irma and handed the panties to Marra. 'Come in Sergeant. Don't stand in the street like a common beggar,' Marra said, smiling to an old comrade.

'The War Council wishes to speak with the American in half an hour. That's an order,' shouted the sergeant, making sure I heard him as he could see Irma and I playing under the bed covers. As the sergeant left the hut in a puff, Marra jumped back in the bed and began to feel my balls as I was feeling Irma's tits.

Just then another knock at the door and some shouts. 'Stop joking. I gave that fucking Yank an order from the War Council.

Now jump to it,' yelled the sergeant as some of his men tried to look in the windows. At that moment, Marra, Irma and I looked at each other and began to laugh as we jumped out of bed to dress.

'I'm coming, sergeant, just give me time to dress,' I shouted to the sergeant as I smacked away Irma's greedy hands from my no longer private parts. When I came out of the hut with the girls, all the men looked at me with envy and began to foam at the mouth when Irma kissed me and said she would be along later. As we rode through the camp I couldn't help but wonder what was going to be my fate, when the sergeant shouted 'Halt. Dismount and stand to attention.'

'Yank, you and the girl come with me,' ordered the captain of the guards. Marra and I walked quickly into a big cave. It was full of tables with men and a few women seated at them. The room seemed like a smaller version of the main speaking hall of the United Nations building.'Sit here and be very quiet,' ordered a captain, taking his job too damn seriously. There were two other guys waiting to go before the Council sitting next to me. 'What are you here for?' I whispered to the one on my right. He just looked at me and began to cry out loud, which distracted the hearing of another man that was taking place. Everyone turned and gave the guy sitting next to me dirty looks. I began to slide down in my chair when a guard walked over and said 'You're next.'

'Who, me?' I said, pointing to myself.

'No Yank, the asshole next to you. You'll get what's coming to you in plenty of time,' he said with a shit-eating grin. The guards dragged the other guy screaming and crying before the Council. I began to worry about my neck then. Suddenly cries of 'Kill the dog, stone the bastard to death,' rang around the room.

'Silence. Silence, I say,' shouted the chairman, as the room slowly went quiet. 'I see here, Mohammed Rabat, you have fought in many battles with our army, is that right?' asked the chairman, pouring himself another glass of wine.

'Yes, my General,' answered Mohammed.

'Then you know what we stand for, right? We stand for liberty, justice and freedom for all our people in this land, right?' asked the general of this poor man named Mohammed.

'Yes, but I was going to pay all the money back, my General. Please have pity on me.'

'I will show some kind of mercy upon you as you've been a

good man and soldier before this little transgression,' said the general in a kindly forgiving voice. At that moment a big smile came on the face of Mohammed. He was filled with joy and relief when the general called the room to order to pronounce sentence.

'Mohammed Ali Booboo Rabat will you stand please?' asked the general with a fatherly smile. Mohammed jumped to his feet with a smile on his face, remembering that the general had said he would show mercy upon him. He was sure he would be free and be given a new start in life as he shook the defence lawyer's hand in gratitude. 'Mohammed, we the War Council of the White Revolutionary Army find you guilty of all charges which are: stealing from a shipment of gold coins, adultery with your brother's wife, animal fornication with army camels, purveying pornographic literature in the mosque basement toilet, and selling narcotics to our brave innocent soldiers who are no longer with us after the last bag you sold them.

We will, however, show you mercy as I have promised. You will be taken to the market center near the rose bushes where a headsman will chop off both your hands with a dull rusty axe and burn out one of your lying eyes with a hot poker,' said the general as he motioned one of the guards to quickly get a mop from the hall cleaning room as Mohammed first vomited and then pissed on his nasty self without restraint.

As I wasn't there when the original accusations were made, I asked the guard what Mohammed had done to deserve such a harsh sentence. He replied that Mohammed was an accountant for a bank that the White Army used and he had been stealing gold from the vaults, plus there were a few other social infractions not connected with his job at the bank.

Meanwhile as the guards were mopping up the piss off the floor, left behind by good old Mohammed, another guard from the back of the room walked over to me and whispered 'You're next, Yank'.

Walking up to the front of the Council, I almost slipped and fell as there was still some piss on the floor. Laughter and shouts of 'Stupid bastard' rang around the room. I looked around the Council slowly. I could see some of these silly fuckers wanted me to fall on my ass in Mohammed's piss. They all had shit-eating grins on their faces as if to say 'We've got something for your ass, Yank.'

'Are you an American?' a member of the panel asked me.

'Yes I am, and proud of it,' I answered.

'Do you like living in our camp?' asked one of the women on the panel.

'I like it very much, man. But I'll have to be going back to America very soon. If you people can help me, I would be most grateful,' I said, giving a warm shit-eating grin. Cries of laughter filled the room at that moment. Just then from behind the curtains stepped another general wearing sunglasses. Immediately, two guards rushed over with a chair so that he could sit down with the rest of the Council.

'What is your name?' asked the general with the sunglasses.

'My name is Robbie Jones, sir. I'm just a poor lost American boy trying to get back home to see my poor little loving mother, who I adore,' I said, holding my head down in sorrow. The general began to laugh so hard and loud, he had to leave the room to regain his composure. When he left the room the first general took command of the hearing again. 'Well, Mr Robbie Jones who is lost from his mother. We have a very serious problem as to what to do with you,' said the general as he looked through some papers before him.

'There have been some very serious allegations made against you. Number one, all you do is eat our food, drink our wine and make love to our women. This makes you an expensive man to keep as you bring in nothing to help the people in our camp. Number two, in the one year you have been here, you have not once offered to help fight for the revolution. Number three, now that you have your health back, you want to leave and go to America without making some generous contribution to our war effort,' said the general, looking rather mean. 'In your absence, we have reached a fair verdict. Guilty,' shouted the general.

'Guilty, guilty, guilty,' was the chant of the Council. I looked to the back and could see Marra and Irma hugging each other and crying their poor hearts out for me.

'Hold on. wait just a damn minute, fellows. Let me have a few words,' I shouted at the top of my voice. Just as I said that, the top general came back into the room and sat down still wearing the sunglasses. 'Mr President, generals, and the brave people of the White Revolutionary Army,' I shouted forcefully, 'Listen to me. Why hell, I know I was a little wrong in waiting so long to join you in your fight against the Red Army, but I have been trying to figure out how I could best serve you in a skilled capacity.'

An old man shouted, 'Have you found a way to help us yet?'

'I'm glad you asked that question,' I said, smiling with a shit-eating grin. 'Why hell, it was only yesterday that I suggested to Irma and Marra that I'm gonna go and join the White Army and help fight the revolution.'

Just as I said that, again the general with the sunglasses ran out of the room laughing and holding his stomach. 'What can you do, Yank?' asked a captain on the Council.

'I am a trained surgeon. I can care for the sick and wounded. All I ask is that you make me a major in your army and I will organise for you the best medical corps you have ever seen. And I will throw in my special knowledge too, just out of friendship,' I said, smiling all over so as not to piss anybody off. Everyone on the panel put their heads together and discussed the matter for a whole two minutes, thoroughly. Then the general turned to me. 'Guilty. No deal, Yank,' he bellowed.

'You must be punished, but we will give you a choice and you must pick one or be hanged until you are dead,' said the general.

'What are the choices?' I said jokingly, 'Fighting a wild bear with my bare hands?'

'Funny you should say that,' said the general, 'You were very close in your guess. First you must walk across an open pit on a board about six inches wide three times without falling off.'

'And what is the second choice?' I asked.

'Being sold immediately into slavery for three thousand dollars to help our war effort,' remarked the general as he stuffed a grape into his mouth.

'My dear general, I can see you and the Council are a loving bunch of people and are being more than fair with me on this little innocent misunderstanding,' I said as I went to shake hands with the War Council members individually.

'Will you please tell the people and the Council your final choice?' said an old lady on the Council as I kissed her soft wrinkled hand which looked like a foot. After shaking a major's hand and kissing another old lady's pistol, I turned and made my choice.

'People of the White Army, to the generals that lead you, Allah that loves you and protects you, I have made my most difficult choice. I will walk over the pit three times and…' before I could finish speaking, the whole room cheered and gave me a standing ovation. You can imagine how good I felt when I saw everybody cheer and chant 'Yankee!' over and over. As the people cheered, I raised my arms into the air for everybody to stop cheering so I could speak to them again. As the cheering stopped and all eyes and ears were looking and waiting for me to speak, I stood on top of a table and shouted to the people. 'I don't think walking across the pit three times is enough. I'll show you how an American will do it. I'm gonna walk across six times.' The people jumped and cheered again with joy. With all the cheering and passing the wine around, Irma and Marra ran to me and began to hug and kiss me with such passion and lustful desires. With so many people dancing and drinking, the whole room became one big party. Suddenly into the room marched six trumpeters. They played a melody that was so sweet, tears came to my eyes. When the trumpeters finished playing and were about to leave the room, Irma looked up into my face. She wiped away the tears and Marra whispered softly and lovingly into my ear, 'Are you crying because you may have to kill the bear?'

'What bear?' I asked, giving Irma a kiss on the cheek.

'Why, the bear that is going to be in the pit as you walk across it,' said Marra looking very serious.

'Bear? What fucking bear? That low down, dirty, chicken livered, fat bacon ass, son of a bitch general never told me about no damn bear,' I shouted as I rolled on the floor kicking my legs into the air and beating my fist repeatedly into a package of vanilla marshmallows that some kid had left on the floor.

'Get up, Yank, and fight the damn bear like a man,' yelled the cleaning lady as she was cleaning under some chairs. 'Up yours, lady,' I yelled back. Just then two guards called out to me all formal like. 'Mr Jones, the bear is waiting. Let's not keep him waiting for long, please. He gets real ornery when he has to wait on his meals.'

As I walked into the huge tent covering the pit, there was standing room only with ticket touts doing a roaring trade outside. The pit was twenty feet wide and ten feet deep, and it had the biggest damn bear you ever saw walking from side to side waiting for a meal. 'Are you ready?' asked a sergeant to another man who was about to walk the pit with a knife in his hand. 'I'm ready,' said the man as he stepped on to the board for his first attempt. The whole tent suddenly went quiet, everybody wanted to see this big moment. The man ran across the first time easily as the bear was too slow grabbing his legs. Everybody cheered as the man crossed safely. Now it was time for the second attempt. As the man moved across the board slowly, the crowd became silent again. He was almost across when the bear stood up on his back legs and breathed into his face. Of course this made the man frightened and very tense and he lost his footing and fell into the open pit. The bear jumped on him with all four claws, he scratched and bit and stampeded the poor man's balls. That man was put to death because he made love to an officer's wife and mother while the officer was away fighting the revolution. An older grandmother had revealed this secret to his commanding officer.

'Bring on the Yank now,' shouted one of the guards. Up to now, I thought I would make it to the States safely, but this really had to be the end. There was no way I could kick that bear's ass. Marra and Irma ran over and kissed me good luck and tried to give me some confidence by saying things like 'Get him, muscles.' They really thought I could kick that bear's ass, foolishly. One of the guards gave me a club shaped like a baseball bat, as I requested. 'Are you ready?' he asked, smiling from ear to ear like a nigger eating a Georgia watermelon. 'Yes, I'm ready,' I said as I ran across the pit in five seconds and smacking that damn bear up the side of his damn head with my club as he raised up on his hind legs. I ran across the pit so fast, I kept on running into the crowd and then crawled on my knees under tables, over people's feet and escaped out the back of the tent. As I crawled on my knees out the back of the tent, I saw two horses tied up to a post. Making a run for the horses, a guard saw me and shouted 'Halt. Don't run or I'll shoot. I know who you are.' I ran away into another tent and crawled out the back right into the arms of about twenty people who were looking for me to fight that damn bear again. 'We got him. We got the scared bastard,' the mob chanted over and over.

As the crowd manhandled me back into the main tent there were shouts for my head as they almost pulled my arms out of their sockets. Suddenly a shot was fired into the air. Everyone at that moment turned to see who fired the shot, when a voice yelled 'Let him go free'. It was the general with the sunglasses who had been laughing at me all night. 'But my General, the bear is waiting to fight him. He's only had the first course,' remarked a major.

'Do as I say, damn you man. Bring this man to my tent before I rip out your arms, you silly little man,' the general ordered. Upon walking into the general's tent, he motioned the guards to leave so that we could be alone. 'I knew a jive-ass, two timing, cocaine sniffing bastard in America about eight years ago,' said the general as he offered me a drink of whisky from his private cabinet. I tried to avoid talking about the American and just thanked the general for my drink.

'Most black Americans take dope and carry knives to mug old ladies. In fact, I think all black Americans are stupid, don't you?' asked the general, moving his hand to his gun slowly.

'Well general, I think there are some good and some bad Americans and the same thing applies to black Americans,' I suggested, taking the liberty of pouring myself another drink of the general's best whisky. At that moment the general went into a rage. Ripping out his pistol from his shoulder holster and pointing it between my eyes, he shouted 'Get on your knees and beg me not to low your damn foolish head off.'

I looked up at the general and smiled. I then got up from my chair and calmly poured myself a triple shot of whisky and yelled 'Bring on that fucking bear now, general'. At that moment the general fell about laughing. Tears of joy were running from his good eye. 'Robbie, you will never change. I haven't seen you in about eight years, or is it nine? Don't you recognize me? I'm your old college pal, Kareem Kareem,' yelled the general as he removed his sunglasses and began showing me his bad eye, that he had lost in the car crash with me and Cheese.

'Kareem, is that you? You old rascal, you,' I said as I gave him a big hug. This was one of the most precious moments of my life, meeting my dear friend Kareem Kareem after all these years. Kareem and I sat in the tent and talked all night and most of the next morning. He explained to me how his mother, father, and two brothers were executed by hanging and how the Red Army took over all of his family estates just like in Russia. And also how he worked his way up through the ranks as he was only a propaganda minister at the start. And I told him all that I had been up to also. I guess we were in the tent for so long his staff officers were getting a little bit worried by now as someone knocked at the front. 'Who is it?' yelled Kareem.

'Major Casbazo, sir. There are two women here who claim to be a friend of the Yank and won't leave unless they can speak to you, general. Shall I tell them to piss off, sir?'

'Don't be such a stuffed shirt, major. Send them in on the double,' ordered Kareem, giving me a wink and motioning me to pour us another drink. I turned around and it was Irma and Marra with swollen eyes from so much crying. 'My general, please save the man we both love. We beg you, please show a little mercy,' Irma pleaded as she and Marra fell to their knees.

'Get up you silly old bitches. How can I kill my best friend? I have only just found him after eight years,' said Kareem as he threw his glass of whisky over the heads of Irma and Marra, laughing out loud.

At that moment, Irma and Marra looked up at me with a joyous smile on their little sweet faces. They both jumped to their feet, ran over to me, and gave me the biggest, most succulent kiss I ever experienced. 'Do you two really know each other?' Marra asked throwing her arms around my neck.

'Is fat meat greasy?' I said. 'Of course, we know each other very well. We studied at Stanford University in America together and became dear friends,' I replied as Kareem nodded his head in agreement. Just then Major Casbazo and another young lady I did not know walked in from the back of the tent. 'Robbie, Irma, and Marra, I want you to meet my sweet baby now. Tira, meet Robbie and his friends,' said the general as he smacked Tira on her ass playfully.

'So you're gonna let the Yank live, huh,' snapped Tira like a deadly scorpion.

'Watch your damn mouth girl, now you apologise to my friends,' ordered Kareem as he winked at me and the girls. Tira gave me and the girls a shitty look for a second and then turned and walked out of the tent. 'Pay her no mind, Robbie, these old black girls from Mauritania will drive you crazy if you let them. Let's have another drink before we all turn in for bed,' suggested Kareem, trying to make me feel welcome and to forget about the bad vibrations left in the room by Tira. 'Major, take a note of this. My friend Robbie Jones from this moment in time will have the rank of major, and will be commander of all hospital personnel in the White Revolutionary Army. Read that back to me and post it for all the battalion commanders to see in the camp tomorrow morning,' ordered Kareem.

As the major began to read back what the general had ordered, he would glance up at me and give me a look like I was pure dog shit. I could see that making me a major hurt that son of a bitch's pride, because when he was reading back the notes he could hardly speak. Boy, was this son of a bitch mad. I told him 'Take that dick out of your mouth so you can talk better.' I mean even the girls noticed a lump in the bastard's throat as he was talking. 'I hope that son of a bitch chokes,' Marra leaned down and whispered to me. When he had finished, Kareem dismissed the major promptly. As the major turned to leave the room, I could see steam coming out of his ears, he was so mad at my good news. 'I don't think he likes me very much Kareem,' I said as I kissed Irma on the cheek.

'Major Casbazo don't like nobody, not even his mother. He's a bit of a stuffed shirt, really, but he's a damn good fighter and the men respect him,' Kareem said, pouring another drink.

'Thanks for making me a major and putting me in command of the hospital group. Now I don't want to seem ungrateful or a bit pissy, but man I got to get back to America, Kareem.'

'But we need you to help fight the revolution. My men and I also know you and your friends from Vietnam helped supply guns and rockets to Prince Ben Ali Hassan's army, right? Now if I told my men you wanted to go home just now, without fighting for our victory for two years, let's say, they would take you outside and kill you in a most awful way. My dear friend Robbie, now don't you want to stay and help our revolution?' said Kareem playfully but meaning every word at the same time.

'Hell, I was only joking with you, man. I was gonna stay about two years anyway. Hell I might have stayed four, things are so nice here,' I said, biting the inside of me jaw so as not to cry in front of the girls. I just hate to see a man cry in front of a girl.

'Well I think we all better turn in now,' I whispered as the girls had fallen asleep.

'No way man am I gonna let you and the girls ride all the way back across camp at this hour! I'm gong to bed and I want you and the girls to stay here and be my guests,' whispered Kareem as he waved and left the room.

As time went on, thoughts of escape went right out of my mind. Hell, I was too busy setting up a workable hospital command all along our western front and operating on the wounded and sick to worry about escaping. Some nights I would work so late, I would just fall asleep in my office or on a vacant operating table. This was a hard fought war and a war that I thought would go on for many years to come. Just my luck, wouldn't you know it? I noticed the little power struggles and corrupt officers and politicians in both armies. Take my good friend Kareem for instance, most of his office holders and army staff officers can be bribed and are corrupt and vicious. There are too many chiefs and not enough Indians. Everything is power and money here, which makes the men corrupt and vicious to one another. For five American dollars, you can pay to have anyone killed. A man can lose his life here by snapping his fingers too loud, that's how bad things are. In the main cities, the black market thrives. That's where we get most of our medical supplies and anything else of value from. As I was working so hard most of the time, I didn't see much of my old friend General Kareem, who was away on different missions or planning battle strategy for the front line troops.

One afternoon I was having a long-deserved break near a small lake with the girls, Irma and Marra that is, I don't want people to think I am a playboy as I am strictly a two-girl man. Major Casbazo rode up on his smiling horse and gave me a message that my friend General Kareem wanted to see me on the double. 'Do you know what it's all about?' I asked. The major just looked at me without answering, kicked his horse slightly and rode off.

'You had better watch him closely, my love,' whispered Marra.

'I think he thinks I want his damn job or something,' I said laughing as I motioned the girls to mount the horses.

When Irma, Marra and I arrived at General Kareem's headquarters, a sergeant ordered the girls to stay on their mounts or go for a bite to eat as the general only wanted to see me. I walked in to the meeting room and Kareem motioned me to sit near him on his right. 'Men, you all know my friend Major Jones, don't you? He'll be coming along on this mission,' the general suggested as the men nodded in agreement. 'I want everyone to look in front of you and you should find maps. I want you to familiarize yourselves with them very carefully,' said the general as he pulled down a larger map hanging over the blackboard.

'The French Air Force are going to make an air drop of heavy artillery and the newest rocket launchers about five miles from the town of Nema. Look at your maps and see spot twenty-three. That's where we will intercept the drop. Don't worry about the other marks on the maps as the tank commanders will handle them. Any questions?' asked the general.

'Who will be in command of the camp while you and General Fez are away?' asked one of the staff officers.

'Well, as General Fez will be with the tank command, and I will be at the French air drop securing the weapons, I guess Major Casbazo will be in command until I return. Now is that all, as I must be going now,' said General Kareem. No one had any more questions so a baby faced captain shouted 'Attention,' and everybody jumped to attention as Kareem and I left the room. Hey, this is some big time shit, I thought to myself.

'Robbie, I will meet you in about half an hour. Be ready on time as I want you to set a good example for the other men,' Kareem said, giving me a wink. I hurried back to my lodgings and told the girls to pack my clothes and equipment that I might require for such a journey, as I had never been to that part of the country before.

After getting a quick piece of ass from the girls, I dashed back to the general's quarters ten minutes late. 'You ain't shit, boy, you dip-shit you. You thought we were going to leave without you. No such luck, old boy,' shouted Kareem at me, motioning the men to move out at the same time. Riding through the desert for about five hours, I noticed some of the men begin to split up and go in another direction. 'Hey Kareem, where are they riding off to?' I asked as I was feeling a bit nervous.

'Call me general in front of the men, damn you Robbie. Now to answer your question, my dear man, we are splitting up so as not to draw too much attention to ourselves as we move through the villages,' whispered Kareem as he pointed to a blown up jeep in the sand with his army markings on the side. As we rode into the town of Nema, the people ran out to greet us with flowers and wine. Some of the women kissed and laughed with the soldiers and wanted some kind of souvenir for their kids or family. Some of these old girls really looked good. I wanted to leave a personal souvenir, but just didn't have the time. It was all innocent fun as the people of the town and the soldiers mixed happily.

'Robbie, we'll pick up some supplies later on the way back. Right now, I am going to a good cafe to eat. You want to come?' asked Kareem.

'Yeah I'll hang out with you, Kareem,' I said.

'*General*, you asshole. How many times have I got to say it before you understand it in your big rock head? Call me general in front of the men,' yelled Kareem as he threw his hat at me.

'Stop all this bullshit and let's get something to eat, Mr General,' I yelled at the top of my voice, frightening the horses and a couple of Arab fags who were walking down the street hand in hand. The general and I sat at a table eating and talking about old times in a small French-style cafe, when a beautiful black girl with pearly white teeth walked into the cafe and ordered a tea mixed with a little whisky from the bar. Kareem's eyes almost fell out of his head looking at the girl.

'Now, now, Kareem, you don't need any more problems. Tira, remember? You'd better pass this one up, old boy,' I whispered.

'Pass my ass, do you see what I see? Shit man, this is once in a lifetime,' remarked Kareem as he called over a waiter.

I knew I was in trouble, Kareem was in trouble, and that girl was going to be in the shit when Tira found out about it. As the waiter came over, Kareem slipped some money in his hand and told him to ask that fine young lady to come and join our table. Sure enough she got off that bar stool and walked over real slow, moving her lovely big sweet ass like a tidal wave. I was personally getting sea sick watching all that hip and ass movement going on. Kareem whispered, 'Don't you look too close with your big eyes, you son of a bitch. It's all mine.' Kareem was like a kid with a new toy rapping to this lovely young lady. He talked and talked and talked. After two hours of non-stop talking, the girl said yes, she'd come back to our main camp with us. This was going to be trouble. Tira would never stand for this shit, I thought to myself, knowing Kareem had forgotten all about Tira and the ass kicking that was waiting for him. When I could get a word in, which wasn't often, I found out the girl was from Chinguetti, a city up north. She had been a university student before it was burned down and the city taken over by the Red Army. Her parents were killed six months ago and she was trying to find her brother who lived in this town up until three weeks ago. 'Where is your brother now?' asked Kareem.

'He ran off to join the White Revolutionary Army,' said the girl.

'We will find your brother for you, my dear. I am the commander of the whole White Revolutionary Army,' boasted Kareem. With her big baby doll eyes, she looked into Kareem's eyes and whispered real sexy-like, 'Thank you, my big handsome general.'

Talking shit like that almost made Kareem fall out of his chair. 'Oh, I almost forgot,' he said, 'Tillie, I want you to meet my most trusted friend in the whole wide world, Major Robbie Jones.'

'I'm very glad to meet you, Tillie,' I said as a big smile came upon my face. I was happy for Kareem. I had never seen him so happy before.

As we were about to pay the bill, a car came around the corner at full speed heading in our direction.

'Get down!' I shouted as the car went by at high speed, shooting about forty rounds into the bar. Instantly, the car was out of sight turning another corner, and I called out to Tillie and Kareem 'You can get up now, they're gone'. As I picked myself up off the floor, I drew my pistol and went over to the main bar. Up jumped a bartender with a big wooden club, big enough to kill an elephant, screaming and shouting at me. I quickly let three rounds of cold hard steel blast into his chest.

'What did you do that for?' shouted Tillie as she dusted the dirt off her low slung dress, stuffing her tits back into the bodice. 'Yeah, he was a nice guy, why did you do that?' asked Kareem.

'Well, that nice guy almost helped his friends to kill you. That son of a bitch gave the signal and dropped down behind the bar with the other barman. Look for yourselves. Where are the other barmen? Case closed,' I said as I dusted myself off and asked Tillie if she needed any help with her bodice. 'I thought you said this was a friendly place,' I remarked jokingly.

'Well it is, most of the time, but those crazy fools tried to kill us. I'll make them pay when I come back this way,' said Kareem, ordering his men to mount up. As we were moving to the drop zone, a funny feeling came over me. I couldn't put my finger on it, but I knew something bad was about to happen.

When we got near the drop zone and made camp, General Kareem called all the men together and gave them some last-minute instructions. After the briefing, Kareem asked me if I wanted a drink in his tent to calm my nerves. We sat listening to the military radio when a message came through from head-quarters. 'Sir, the French will make the drop in ten minutes,' said the radio operator in a voice like Tiny Tim's.

'Sergeant, tell the men to move out to the drop zone. We have ten minutes to get there,' ordered Kareem as we both jumped to our feet. All the men gave a cheer and dashed off to the drop zone. As we waited for the plane, I went for a piss in the nearby woods. I thought I heard something move near me, when one of the men shouted, 'The French are here, Major Jones.' I quickly ran out of the woods, trying not to piss on my leg, and forgot about the movement in the woods.

The men lit the fires on the ground to outline the drop zone clearly, and it was a beautiful sight to see all the fires burning brightly and the men standing and cheering. Very quickly the lights came on in the bomb hatch of the aeroplane and out came some packages floating to the ground attached to parachutes. As the big white parachutes descended like giant butterflies in a strong wind, the men cheered as they ran to collect the supply of guns and especially the F12 rocket cannons. 'Load the weapons quickly, men, and let's go home,' ordered Kareem as now he was walking ten feet tall and feeling proud as a country preacher who had just laid the deacon's wife. 'You see Robbie, I told you everything was going to be alright. I'm gonna make those suckers in the Red Army beg for mercy, now that I have my new F12 rockets,' shouted Kareem with pride and joy as he shook my hand, almost breaking it.

At that moment, all hell broke loose. No, I tell a lie. The whole world caved in. Gun shots, machine-gun fire, rocket launchers, tank fire, heavy artillery fire. It was a bitch. Somebody was kicking our asses real good. 'Ambush. Ambush, man. get on your mounts and retreat,' the officers shouted to the men. 'Blow your damn horn, man,' I shouted at the bugle boy. As he sounded retreat, a shot hit him in the throat and only a gurgling sound came out of the trumpet. When he fell, I dashed over and picked up the bugle and began to blow the best I could. For a minute I thought I was Louis Armstrong. After trying a couple of toots, I gave up and began to shout 'retreat' to the men again. Bodies were everywhere, either dead or badly wounded. Somebody knew exactly where we would be, at what time, and why. Out of about sixty men, only seven were still trying to fight back at the attackers.

A shell-shocked soldier walked up to me and tried to explain how he would have killed one of the enemy had he not slipped in his own blood and fallen. 'Let's get out of here, Kareem. Most of your men are dead and gone,' I yelled over the gunfire still raining around us unmercifully. Quickly, Kareem and I and the few remaining soldiers hauled ass out of the drop zone and then slowed the mounts to give them a little rest after reaching a safe distance from the ambush. 'I'm gonna make those bastards pay for that, they are gonna pay with their asses, damn it,' Kareem kept repeating over and over. When we rode back into the town of Nema, nobody ran to us. Everyone had closed their doors and windows and would only peek from behind the curtains as we went through the streets.

Let's keep on going through the town,' I said to Kareem as I still had that bad feeling in my stomach, and my stomach is never wrong.

'I'm not going to let some small-time bandits run me put of town. Furthermore, you silly frightened bastards, I'm gonna get my girl, Tillie, and then have a drink in this damn place before I leave. You hear me? I want all you dog-people of this one-horse town to know that I am still military commander of this area,' shouted Kareem at the top of his voice and looking around for any who dared object in any shape or fashion. As we went to the place where Tillie was staying, some of the people were looking out from the corners of their windows with fright. Slowly we rode down the side streets and house after house slammed their doors closed and pulled their curtains in hiding. When we stopped our horses in front of Tillie's house, Kareem ordered a private to dismount and knock at the door. Before the soldier could knock, the door flew open by itself. 'Sir, I think you had better have a look,' said the private, shaking nervously.

'Come with me, Robbie,' Kareem said as we both dismounted and walked into the house. When we walked into the main bedroom, the room was in a mess. It was like a hurricane had hit it. Kareem became suspicious and began to call out Tillie's name hysterically. He was like a mad man, running and looking in every room and screaming for Tillie. In his fury, Kareem wanted to go out in the street and take a hostage and force him to tell where Tillie was. 'Calm down, Kareem. We'll find Tillie if we have to rip this town apart piece by piece,' I said, trying to reassure him that everything would be fine.

'General, I think we have found her, sir,' said a private with a croak in his voice.

'You what? I'll be down right away,' yelled Kareem, jumping down two stairs at a time to get to his sweet, beloved Tillie. When I got downstairs and walked into the backyard, I saw Kareem on his knees with his head in his hands, crying uncontrollably.

It was Tillie, hanging at the end of a rope tied to a tree, dead. Someone had cut off all her hair, covered her beautiful body with hot tar and feathers, put a rope around her neck and hanged her from this tree.

'Those dirty filthy bastards. Robbie, they killed my baby. How could they do that to a sweet innocent girl? How could anybody take a sweet girl's life?' Over and over Kareem repeated to himself, 'How could they kill my baby?' Finally he said 'Leave me alone for a bit, Robbie. I'll be OK. I just want to be alone with Tillie for a while,' and he cut down Tillie's body.

I came back to pick up Kareem after sitting in a cafe for about two hours and drinking twenty cups of coffee. 'General Kareem, I think we'd better be moving, sir, before the Red Army comes back this way,' I suggested. 'We can't leave Tillie like this. I'm not leaving until we bury her body properly,' said Kareem as he motioned to some soldiers to place Tillie's body on a wagon that was across the street.

After loading Tillie's body and moving off slowly to a small hill on the outside of town, a shot rang out, knocking the general to the ground as his horse ran off back down the street bucking and kicking in a wild panic. 'Get down, men, somebody is firing from the church tower,' I yelled out loud. 'Kareem are you hit bad?'

'No. Don't worry about me. Get that bastard in the church tower,' ordered Kareem. I noticed that each time a shot was fired from the church tower, something would shine very bright in the sun. It could have been the marksman's glasses catching the sunlight. I decided that the next time something sparkled in the sunlight from the church tower, I would fire directly at it. I quickly ran across the street and jumped behind a water barrel that was meant for watering horses and camels, when two shots from the tower just missed me and went into the water. Now that I was closer to the tower and could get a better shot, I waited for that sparkle once more. Sparkle again you bastard, just one more time and you're dead, I thought to myself as my finger closed in on the trigger.

As I stared, something moved, then a sparkle. I let off three shots directly at the sparkle in the tower. My shots ripped into the tower and I heard a scream of death as the soldier fell from the tower to the street below like a sack of sand, his head bursting with blood like a ripe Georgia watermelon. Just then a sergeant ran over shouting 'Got 'em major. You got the bastard good,' as he reached into the gaping wound and extracted one of the bullets as a souvenir.

'Thanks, sergeant, take another man with you and check out the whole church while I go and see about the general,' I ordered as I ran back across the street to find my dear friend Kareem. 'Damn good shot, Robbie. Damn bloody good shot, my dear boy,' shouted Kareem as I knelt down to check his wound, 'How bad is it?'

'You'll live, you old bastard, to fight another day. The bullet went straight through your arm. As soon as I finish to bandage your arm, you will be able to ride OK, so don't be a cry baby,' I answered, wondering why all of a sudden so many people wanted to kill us in our own territory.

After saying a small prayer over the grave of Tillie, we

mounted and started for home base. I paused for another look down in to the village where crowds of people were shouting and singing the anthem of the Red Army in celebration. To the peasants, survival depends upon supporting the winner, not necessarily the side of right.

Riding off at a fast gallop, we crossed over some hills and rode on until we came to a rocky stream. We dismounted and walked our horses. Walking slowly on the stream I whispered to Kareem, 'You know we were set up, don't you? You have a spy on your officer staff. We rode smack dab into the middle of an ambush and got an ass-kicking.'

'I'll admit we rode into the ambush, but my dear man, to say that one of my own staff officers is a spy and was responsible for the killings is just not on,' said Kareem, putting it down as just another case of bad luck.

'Maybe I worry too much, but just the same, somebody in our camp is working against us and doing a damn good job. But I'll do my best to find his ass before he gets us all killed. Let's hope to God it's only one bad apple in the barrel,' I said to Kareem as I rode off to check the point. With me riding point and the rest of the men following slowly behind licking their wounds, I stopped a moment, and through my binoculars I saw a cloud of dust moving fast in my direction. As the dust cloud got nearer, I could see riding out of it about a dozen men wearing the colors of the White Army. As the men rode up to me in a slow gallop, a master sergeant yelled out 'Major, what are you doing out here alone and this far away from camp?'

'I am riding point for General Kareem's party, as the general has been shot,' I answered calmly.

'The general! Why we heard our beloved general had been killed in an ambush by bandits,' said the sergeant.

'See for yourself. He's coming up now,' I said, pointing behind me.

'What's going on here? What's all the fuss?' asked General Kareem, holding his aching arm.

'Sir, it's so good to see you alive and well. The news around the main camp is that you are dead, sir,' said the master sergeant, shaking with fright.

'Dead! Who said I was dead?' yelled Kareem.

'Major Casbazo, sir,' answered the sergeant.

'Oh he did, did he? Well, he'll see how dead I am when we get back to camp,' said Kareem, motioning me to take command.

'Move out men, back to the camp and on the double,' I ordered, getting a hard on with the power of command. After riding two long hard ass-breaking days, we finally reached camp headquarters. 'Look sharp when you men ride through the gates,' ordered the sergeant.

At first when we rode through the main gate no one noticed that the general was alive. 'You see that? These silly bastards don't care if I am alive or dead. After all I've done for them, not one looked up and recognized me,' said Kareem, shaking his head in disbelief.

'Take the general to the hospital first and then back to his quarters,' I said to the sergeant as I went on to make my report to the Acting Commander. Walking by General Kareem's quarters and making my way upstairs to his main office, I could see out of the corner of my eye the secretary reaching for the phone to warn Major Casbazo that I was coming. Sneaky bitch, I thought to myself.

'Why major, it so good you no hurt. I hear you and my dear friend the general was killed. I will have soldiers punished for such lies,' said the major, sitting in the general's chair, smoking the general's best Cuban cigars, and with the general's old lady Tira standing on his right all cozy-like.

'Major Jones, you must excuse Major Casbazo's English as he did not learn English in our schools like so many of our people,' remarked Tira all sweet but deadly. 'How is my husband-to-be, the general? I do hope he is not wounded badly,' she said, with a shit-eating grin splitting her face.

'He was wounded, but nothing very serious. Why he was telling me on the way back how good he felt and how he'll be back behind his desk tomorrow. Won't it be nice having the general back in command?' I said with a smile on my face to match hers. Just then the smiles went from the faces of Tira and the major and they looked at each other in shocked surprise. 'I guess I'd better go and see about my dear husband-to-be then, huh? The poor dear may need me at his side at a time like this,' said Tira as she walked to the door.

'I hear the general's chair never once went cold while we were gone,' I said sarcastically, looking directly at the major.

'What do you mean, Yank?' snapped the major looking angry.

'Meant nothing bad, Major Casbazo, only that you had been very busy and were doing a fine job as Acting Commander.

That's what I meant. If I offended you, I am sorry,' I said. The major looked at me with death in his eyes and a smile on his lips as he walked over to the door where Tira was waiting. 'Yank, if only I could beat the...' Quickly Tira butted in, warning the major not to say anything further, and opened the door for them to leave together.

Coming down the stairs, I whispered to the general's secretary, 'You're gonna get yours too, bitch.'

'But Major Jones, what are you talking about?' she answered back with her shit-eating grin as I walked out the main doors and into the courtyard. Anyway, two weeks have now passed without any major problems. Irma and Marra are giving me all the loving and home cooking any man could ask for. It's rough fellows, believe me it's rough. One day as the girls and I were walking in some caves that we thought were deserted, we came upon hundreds of large snails as the cave was dark and damp.

'Let's take some home for tonight's dinner. They would be great with the new wine we brought back from town,' suggested Irma, rubbing my leg.

'Yeah, I haven't had no snails in about, I don't know how long,' I said, laughing. The girls and I were very excited thinking about how delicious they were going to taste tonight cooked in fresh garlic. Suddenly I whispered 'Ssh.'

'What's wrong, Robbie?' asked Marra.

'I thought I heard voices on the other side of this tunnel,' I said.

'I don't hear nothing,' answered Irma, rubbing my middle leg.

'Maybe it was my imagination,' I said, 'I'm so jumpy these days.'

On reaching the end of a small tunnel, Marra suggested we go into another small passage to pick some more snails as it led back to the main camp and was a short cut. 'Robbie, you lead the way. You are a big strong man and our leader,' joked Marra, kissing me in the ear. Bending over and picking up so many snails was beginning to give me a pain in my back so I suggested that we sit and rest awhile. 'Let's sit near that hole in the wall up ahead,' suggested Marra.

'Yeah, we can get some fresh air by sitting near it,' I said as we moved to the hole and sat down to rest our poor paining backs.

'Men put on your masks. The meeting will now take place,' said a voice from the other side of the hole.

This time I knew I wasn't just imagining voices. 'Hey girls,' I whispered. But before I could finish speaking, Marra butted in and whispered 'We know. We heard someone speaking too.'

I rolled over on my side and looked through a small hole in the wall of the tunnel and saw some kind of meeting taking place. 'Let me see too,' asked Irma. 'Is it something kinky?'

'Sssh. There's a meeting of some kind happening in there, so don't make any loud sounds,' I whispered to the girls as they pushed me out of the way so they could see.

'Men of the Ouzoud Brotherhood, your leader will now take the stand and will speak to you.' With the chairman saying that, a man dressed with a red hood over his head and face stepped up on the speaker's platform and began, 'Men, the White Revolutionary Army is a joke. we cannot continue to follow a man like General Kareem Kareem. We need a military man, not some washed out, one-eyed doctor who trained in America and England. He doesn't care for poor bastards like you. I say here and now, kill him. Kill him now, or let him lead you to your deaths. Are you with me, men?' About a hundred men, all with white hoods, stood and cheered frantically. Irma and Marra looked at me and suggested we leave quietly and inform General Kareem of what we had seen.

Getting to our feet very slowly, we suddenly heard a woman's voice begin to speak to the hooded men. After listening to that voice for about two minutes, I asked the girls if they recognized it, as I thought I had heard that voice before somewhere. 'That sounds like that bitch Tira speaking, but it could be somebody else also,' whispered Irma. I know Tira is a bitch, but she couldn't be so stupid as to get involved with this bunch of maniacs, I thought to myself. 'Let's get out of here while we can,' I suggested. As we moved through the dark tunnel, Irma bumped into a steel oil can, knocking it over and making a loud noise.

At that moment the woman with the hood over her face shouted, 'Somebody is out there in one of our tunnels. Get them and bring them to me, dead or alive.' The darkness was slowing us down as we could not see without our light. 'They're over here,' shouted a hooded attacker. 'Don't let them escape, kill them first,' yelled a guard in front of us who couldn't see us hiding in a dark corner.

'Don't make a sound girls, keep your heads, and I think we'll make it by playing cat and mouse with these chumps,' I suggested as we crawled on the cold wet floor of the cave.

'Keep looking men, look everywhere, they must not escape,' someone yelled two tunnels down.

'Let's make a run for it while they're over there looking,' I said as I pulled the girls along.

Just as we got to the end of a small tunnel, two shots ripped into a rock above my head and bounced off, almost hitting one of the girls. 'Get down, Irma and Marra,' I shouted as I let rip four quick shots from my pistol, killing the two attackers who were coming after us.

'I've found them. We have them trapped like rats now,' shouted one attacker as about twelve of his mates surrounded us and blocked off the main cave entrance.

'What are we going to do now?' asked Marra nervously.

'I don't know, but don't lose hope,' I whispered as I continued to load my pistol and watch the guarded tunnel exits.

'Hey, you people, you come out and we no hurt you. All we want is to talk to you, honest,' a voice shouted to us from the dark.

'Don't answer to them or trust them. They can't let us live because we know too much now,' I explained to the girls. Again a voice shouted out from the dark, 'We will give you ten minutes to surrender. If you don't come out, my men will hurt you, no? We no bad men, but we may have to kill you if you no come out.'

'That leader guy must be from the north of Mauritania as he talks such bad English,' I whispered to the girls.

'Yes, because our people in the south have talked English for many years now,' said Irma as she agreed with me.

'That guy could be any one of a thousand of our men, one third of all our men are from the north,' suggested Marra.

'Look, something is moving to our right in the dark,' Irma whispered to me as she drew her pistol and prepared to fire.

'Let 'em get a little closer, then I'll give the signal to burn their asses, and remember, don't shoot until you can see the whites of their eyes,' I said. I could see someone moving really close to our position and then stop like a frightened rat.

'OK – give it to 'em girls.' As I gave the signal to fire the girls and I let our bullets rip into the bodies of our attackers and heard them call out for mercy or scream in pain as old man death was about to pay a visit.

'You people fight mean, You force me to kill you now,' yelled a voice from the dark as the guns stopped blazing.

'Check your ammo in case they try to rush us all at once,' I whispered to the girls. The girls were re-loading their pistols, when a woman's voice called out from the dark.

'We know who you are.You'd better come out now or we'll

burn you out like rats. I'll give you ten seconds to surrender. Take your choice.'

Oh shit, I thought to myself. 'Think girls, and think good about how we can escape from being burned to a crisp,' I said in a low voice. (The low voice was my macho bit, as when I am scared my voice goes up – five tones.)

'Robbie, I got an idea. No, it's probably no good. We better drop it,' said Irma. Just then the voice in the dark began to count out loud: 'I'm counting down now, whether you live or die is your choice. Ten nine, eight, seven, six, five, I'm halfway. Are you coming out?' she called out.

'Robbie, there's a stream back down this tunnel, but it's got too many strong currents in it. You always hear about people drowning in these underground streams,' Irma said, pointing out the danger to me.

'Three,' a voice called out.

'Well, it's a case of being burned alive or being drowned in these underground streams,' I told the girls.

'What about taking three of the oil cans that are empty and using them to stay afloat?' asked Marra, trying to make me look bad with a brilliant idea.

'One, zero,' the voice called out while Marra waited for her answer.

'I was going to say before I was so rudely interrupted by you, Miss Big Tits, that we should try to escape by using some empty oil cans to stay afloat in that damn stream you have just been telling me about,' I said, showing the girls that I was still boss.

'We are coming out. Please don't shoot or burn us out,' I shouted as I motioned the girls to push two oil cans through the tunnel and down to the stream.

'What's that noise we hear? what are you doing with the oil cans?' shouted the masked lady in the dark, sounding like a detective.

'It's difficult to see in the dark. We just knocked over a couple of oil cans and they're rolling on the floor, but we are coming out,' I shouted back, trying not to laugh.

'Now we really know who you are. Yank. Do you really think you can fool us, you silly man? We got your ass now, boy. Light the fires and burn them out like rats. Burn in hell, Yankee,' shouted the mystery woman as she also ordered her men to shoot and kill. Suddenly the place was all in flames and bullets were flying everywhere.

Running through the tunnel with the fires licking at my ass and thinking 'Feet don't fail me now', I called out to the girls as they were waiting for me near the stream, 'Throw in the oil cans quick, I'll share one with somebody.'

'OK, jump in and share one with me,' Irma called out. Diving into the cold water and just missing the many sharp rocks, I could feel my balls go blue. It was cold enough to freeze a polar bear's testicles, let alone mine.

'Hold on very tight and try not to hit the sides of the tunnel, because the rocks will rip your skin wide open like a meat cleaver,' I shouted as we moved down the stream at a terrifying speed.

'There they are in the stream below. I'd know that nigger's big head anywhere. Shoot quickly Don't let that Yankee dog and his whores escape from us,' shouted the mystery woman, shaking her fist in the air as we moved into another tunnel. The oil cans now began to move, gathering speed by the second. I could see the girls becoming more and more frightened as the force of the currents would make the cans smash against the walls of the tunnel. Also the cans would dip, dive, and stay submerged for long periods of time.

'Hang on in there girls,' I shouted as the water splashed once again into my mouth.

'I can't hold on. I'm losing my grip. Oh, my can's gone, help me Robbie, help!' Marra screamed as the currents swept her along and pulled her body down at the same time. Oh my God, I've got to think quickly to save Marra, I thought to myself. Lucky for Marra that she had been in front of us when she lost her grip. 'Hold out your arms as I pass,' I yelled. As we went by, Marra held out her right arm and grabbed hold of my left arm. 'Hold on tight, wrap your arms around my neck and I'll get you back safely,' I yelled over the loud noise of the water splashing against the tunnel walls. Moving at terrifying speeds through these underground waterways was a bitch. I mean pure hell, like heading at sixty miles an hour downstream into a stone wall and knowing you won't make it without some kind of miracle at each turn.

'Robbie look, rocks and then a huge waterfall up ahead,' Irma yelled. At that moment I said two quick Hail Mary's and I think I pissed in my pants.

'If we gotta go, we gotta go. Let go of the cans and just pray,' I shouted, crossing my fingers. The girls let go and began to scream in terror. 'Watch that rock, Marra,' I called out, but it was too late. I saw Marra go under the water after smashing into a huge rock, but I didn't see her resurface. Searching frantically for Irma, I looked up and there was the huge waterfall coming up in two seconds. I gave out a loud yell as I went over the falls with tons of water smashing my body like a toy matchstick in the ocean. I never knew what hit me and I don't think the girls or anyone else could explain surviving that living nightmare.

'Good afternoon, Robbie.'

I thought I was in heaven and an angel was talking to me.

'Come on, Robbie, I know you are only pretending you're asleep.' A soft sweet voice was speaking to me. I opened my eyes very slowly and lo and behold, there was a beautiful big, huge fat lady looking down at me. I quickly regained my composure and asked the nurse how long I'd been in hospital.

# 7

'Slow down Robbie, all your questions will be answered as soon as your doctor comes to see you. OK?' answered the nurse.

'I'm sorry nurse, but are the girls all right?' I asked as I was getting ready to get up and dress.

'Hold on major, you can't get up until your doctor says its OK. And to answer your question, what girls? I ain't seen no girls. You must have got hit on the head. All I know is some men brought you here in a coma, from which you were not expected to recover until a few days ago when you started to respond to the treatment. Your dear friend General Kareem Kareem has been coming to visit you every day for a month. Why he's the one who has been talking you out of your coma and you surely should thank him for saving your life,' the nurse explained.

After the nurse left my room, I laid back on the bed thinking that something was very wrong. Even if they found me alive, they should have found the girls' dead bodies somewhere in the water. Then a doctor and nurse walked into the room.

'Hello, major. It's good to have you back with the living,' remarked the doctor jokingly.

'Thanks doc,' I said, and asked him about the girls and their whereabouts.

'I'm sorry major, but there were no women with you when they brought you to the emergency ward. The men who brought you in said they had found you face down and unconscious on a small river bank. Nothing was said about any women being with you. I'm sorry major,' said the doctor.

'Can you tell me the name of the village where I was found?' I asked.

'Sure major, it was a village called Ain-Diab. I hope I have been of some help,' remarked the doctor as he left my room, patting the young, pretty but fat nurse on her ass. I got up and walked back and forth across the room thinking of what I must do. I had the feeling that Irma and Marra were not dead. I picked up the phone and was told that the general was on his way up to the room. I quickly jumped back into the bed and a few seconds later came the knock at the door. 'Come in, general,' I called out.

'Hey Robbie, how is everything now that you're back with us?' the general asked.

'I thought that I had gotten away from low class trash like you, Kareem,' I said, shaking his hand.

'Robbie, I am very sorry about the death of your friends Irma and Marra,' said the general, taking off his hat in courtesy.

'That's one thing I want to talk to you about, Kareem,' I whispered as I turned to make sure no one was listening. I told Kareem to pull up a chair as I had some very important information to give that was vital for his survival. I then began to tell Kareem my story and how his life was being threatened. I went on to explain how this secret organization that the girls and I had stumbled upon was going to intimidate some of his officers in the future. All the time I was telling Kareem my story I could see him looking at me as if I were crazy.

'Robbie, Robbie, Robbie, my dear friend,' Kareem said, 'slow down a bit. This all sounds so fantastic. Gunmen? Secret clans out to kill me? And some of my trusted officers turning against me? This is a most fantastic story, old boy,' the general said, laughing and shaking his head in disbelief. No matter what I said or how I explained it , General Kareem was not going to believe me. 'I'll look in on you tomorrow, OK?' the general said.

'Kareem,' I called out before he left the room. 'Maybe you're right. I need a good long rest. How about you talking to the doctor and getting a month's sick leave so I can go fishing, huh? What do you say, Kareem?' I asked. I could see this made Kareem feel much better, as he quickly pushed a button calling for the doctor before I could change my mind. When the doctor arrived, Kareem asked him what were the chances of me getting a month's sick leave. 'Well,' said the doctor, 'I think that would be an excellent idea as Major Jones has had a terrible time settling down here in the hospital.

'Alright, with that out of the way, Robbie, I'll send you my private chauffeur to pick you up and drive you anywhere you desire,' said the general, giving me a wink.

'That's great, now carry your nasty ass out of here and let me sleep, as I am a very sick man,' I said, laughing at my dear friend.

After eating a good supper and feeling my stomach almost about to burst, I decided to read a bit to let my food digest. My eyes were beginning to get very heavy after reading for two hours, so I checked to be sure my pistol was near my bed, rolled over and switched off the lights. I had almost dropped off into a deep sleep when I heard somebody walking on the roof of the hospital and stopping over my room. I reached down and got my pistol out of the shoulder holster that was hanging on my bedpost and waited for something to happen. I didn't have to wait long before somebody slowly opened up the sun hatch in the ceiling of my room.

It was so dark, I could not make out who or how many were up on the roof planning to do me in royally. As the hatch opened about six inches wide, I heard one of the intruders say 'Drop it over his damn head,' and then snicker to his pal.

'Ssshh', said one as the sun hatch opened a few inches more. I could see a hairy, dirty hand which looked like a foot, reaching in and slowly lowering something in a basket down on my head. It's now or never, I thought to myself, as I let off three shots at the attacker, who was leaning through the hatch at this time.

'Tatoe, my brother. He shot you. That black bastard shot you,' one attacker shouted out in anger as his brother was shot all to hell. He panicked and opened the sun hatch wide and began firing like a wild man. No, I tell a lie, a stupid man. 'You Yankee bastard. May your bitch of a mother die in hell. May your mother grow balls,' he called out as he filled my room with flying bullets. It was a good thing I had jumped under the bed. While I was waiting to get a good clear shot at the guy on the roof, I noticed something moving on the floor in front of me. 'Holy shit, It's a fucking snake,' I shouted out loud as the shock was too much for me to be quiet about.

'Yeah, and he's gonna bite your big black ass too,' shouted my attacker on the roof as he let rip more gunfire into my bed.

Just then my doctor and a male nurse rushed into the room. but before I could shout 'Get back' machine-gun fire ripped into their bodies, and they fell to the floor in a pool of blood. Lucky for me, the male nurse fell upon the snake as he was dying and trapped it under his stomach.

With all the gunfire, somebody in the hallway pulled the emergency fire bell and called the hospital guards to my room,driving away my attacker. 'I'll settle with you the next time, Yank,' shouted the mystery attacker through the hatch as he disappeared into the night.

'My God, what's going on here, sir?' asked the doctor who was on duty that night.

'I'm Major Jones, Hospital and Medical Commander of all White Revolutionary forces in the southwest,' I said, explaining to the captain why the two attackers tried to put an end to my life.

'Captain, have all my belongings moved to another room, will you please. Oh, and have that beastly snake removed from this room before someone hurts himself,' I suggested. The next morning the general and his chauffeur arrived at the hospital front desk where everyone was talking about how I had survived the attack upon my life. The phone rang while I was packing my bags. It was the general waiting in the lounge for me to come downstairs. As I arrived in the lounge we shook hands. 'Good morning, general, lovely day for it huh?'

'Lovely day for what?' asked the general of me.

'I meant a nice day for fishing, old boy,' I said jokingly in an English accent.

'Now see here Robbie, what's all this attempt on your life stuff I have been hearing lately?'

'I don't have the slightest clue, general,' I said with as much innocence as possible.

'Now see here Robbie, old chap, you know damn well what I am talking about,' yelled the general, throwing his cap to the ground in anger.

'When I tried to tell you the first time, you thought I was crazy. Now all I want to really do is go fishing and not think about your problems, old chap,' I said, acting like a smart-ass.

'I'm very sorry for acting the way I did, Robbie. What are you really going to do? I personally know that you hate fishing,' said the general, smiling now.

'Give me two of your most trusted men and I will go back to the village where I was found in a coma and start looking for my girls,' I said, motioning that we should leave right away.

'I'll give you Master Sergeant Sahara and Sergeant Jamai with four of my best Arabian stallions. Anything else that you need, just take it and sign for it on my authority, and I mean anything,' said the general as he dropped me off in front of Sergeant Sahara's office.

'I'll be with you in a second, sir,' said a sergeant as I walked into an office with throwing knifes decorating the walls. 'I am Sergeant Sahara, sir. I was just putting another of my favorite knives on the wall as a trophy.'

'I'm Major Robbie Jones.The general said that you can be trusted and has assigned you and Sergeant Jamai under my command for an important mission,' I explained as I walked around his office admiring the many knives on the walls that sparkled like jewels.

'I'm at your service,sir. Glad to be of some help. Sergeant Jamai and I have known the general for a long time and have fought many battles together. We look forward to serving with you as we would the general. Shall I call Sergeant Jamai on the phone, sir?' asked the sergeant politely.

'Yeah. Tell him to get over here on the double, please,' I ordered.

Sergeant Jamai ran in to the office ten minutes after the phone call, huffing and puffing like a wild boar. I explained to them my sad story and the dangers involved on this mission, and each assured me they were eager for adventure. As the two sergeants knew the country better than I, they suggested we change out of our uniforms and into the clothing of the nomads. Also they suggested we ride camels instead of horses. This proved to be a bitch, trying to stay on the back of a camel when he's running at full speed. Shit, sometimes I was up on its neck, and then I would slip back to the hump, hanging onto anything I could as it swayed and lurched at full gallop.

After three days of teaching me how to ride a camel, treating the huge blisters on my ass, and warning me never to kiss a camel as they have the worst breath of anyone or thing, we set off to find the girls, not knowing whether they were alive or dead. It took us four days of hard riding to reach the village of Ain-Diab. By talking with some villagers, we could see that most were Red Army supporters, not like some of the Georgia red-necks I've known.

'We are going to need a lot of money to spend to make these people talk, my friend,' suggested Sergeant Jamai, scratching the bald patch on his head from a ferocious camel bite.

'I thought of that,' I said as I handed each of them a small bag of American dollars. 'There are ten one hundred dollar bills there, that's a thousand American dollars,' I explained. 'We will go in to the village and spend, spend, and spend until we find someone who talks our kind of talk. I want you to mix with the locals, buy the men drinks, make friends, visit the whore houses, and spend like money is going out of style. But keep your eyes open and hear everything that's going down,' I ordered the sergeants, and they nodded in agreement and grinned from ear to ear.

Three weeks went by and nothing happened. Not even one clue. Even the camels were bored. Then one day as I was sitting on a cafe having coffee with the two bored sergeants, a note was found hidden in a tomato salad that we ordered after our main meal:

'For five hundred dollars, I will give you the information that you seek about the women. Come alone. Will meet you at number A-16, Medina Street, at nine o'clock tonight. Don't bring the camels.'

'You're not going alone, are you major?' asked Sergeant Sahara with concern.

'Yeah, I'd better. I've got to find the girls at any cost,' I said as Sergeant Jamai stuffed the note and some pieces of tomato into his mouth and began to chew with vigor.

'Please let me go in for you, major, as I know these people and I can pay them as well as you can, right?' begged Sergeant Jamai as he continued to stuff tomatoes and pieces of Sergeant Sahara's fried camel balls into his mouth.

'They sure put a lot of garlic in that salad,' I said as the sergeant merely nodded. 'OK,' I agreed, 'But don't take any chances. The first sign of trouble, you fall to the floor and fire off a shot for help. That's an order,' I said, patting Sergeant Jamai on the back. 'When we get to this address, Sergeant Sahara, you take the back and I will take the front, is that clear?'

'Yes, sir,' Sergeant Sahara answered as I called over the waiter to pay the bill.

'Go out the back door. You are being watched,' the waiter whispered to me as he picked up the small change from the table with a look of dissatisfaction.

'Let's get the hell out of here by going out the back door.

Quick. One at a time,' I whispered to the sergeants as I pretended to tie my shoelace.

When I was going out the back door of the cafe and in to the small alleyways, it reminded me of my old school days. I used to steal apples and pears off the trees of some of my white neighbours, hearing the shouts of 'Stop stealing my apples, nigger, take the watermelon instead, you bastard.' I would keep running down the alleys laughing like a son of a bitch. Today I wasn't laughing at all. Somebody out there wants to kill my ass.

'This is the street. Shall we go in now, sir?' asked Sergeant Jamai, still carrying one camel ball in a paper napkin.

'Hold on a bit. We still have ten more minutes before it's time to go in,' I said as I noticed how dark the streets were. Each street had one light for one block, and then some of the lights were missing or broken by kids throwing rocks. This was a cold miserable night with fog about to move in. A thought crossed my mind as I saw a poor starving cat across the street, dragging his ass along in the dirt. That's the way the girls found me the first time we met, I thought.

'Sir, it's time to go,' said Sergeant Jamai.

'Now remember, don't take any chances. Just fall on the floor and call out for help or fire a shot in the air, you understand?' I said.

'You worry too much, major. Just wish me luck,' said Sergeant Jamai as we shook hands and off he went down the street. It was very difficult to see a long way as the fog was coming in off the river, but I could see Sergeant Jamai walk up to a door, knock, and then go in. The moment he went through the door, a huge explosion ripped out the front of the house.

There was no use in running to help. The sergeant never felt a thing. The building never even caught fire as there was nothing left. One minute there was a house and the next nothing but dirt and dust. Sergeant Sahara ran back with tears in his eyes. I knew how he felt, Sergeant Jamai had been his best friend for more then ten years.

'Those dirty bastards. They don't even have the guts to fight fair anymore,' the sergeant said as he wiped the tears from his eyes.

'Come on. Let's leave here quick,' I suggested.

Two weeks have now gone by since the explosion that killed Sergeant Jamai, and still no clues or big breaks to help us. Then one night as Sergeant Sahara and I were coming home after sitting in a cafe most of the night, we saw three man jump on a man and begin to kick the shit out of him unmercifully.

'Hey you, what the hell's going on here?' I shouted as I ran over to help the old man taking an old fashioned country beating. After I threw a couple of left hooks, a body punch, and two right crosses to the heads, the three men picked each other off the ground and disappeared into the darkness shouting 'That big nigger hit me. Where in the hell did he come from?'

'You all right, Sahara?' I asked.

'Yeah, just a small cut on my arm. How about you, old man, are you OK?'

The old man explained to us that even though he had been stabbed many times with a knife, he wanted to go home as his wife was waiting for him with his supper.

We helped the old man to his feet and began walking slowly to his place. After arriving at his door and explaining the stabbing to his wife, she invited us in for tea while she put him to bed immediately. When she came back into the room, she said 'Thank you very much for giving me some advice about how to bandage his wounds and for saving his life.' She spoke to Sergeant Sahara as she did not speak English.

As we sat having tea and just chewing the fat, the old lady took a liking to us. But suddenly she pointed a finger at me and said 'You Yankee, bad man.'

'Find out what she means, Sahara,' I ordered. Sahara then explained to me that some men came into the village with food and money and told them not to talk to any American about anything or risk being put to death.

'Ask her where are these men now,' I ordered Sergeant Sahara quickly as I didn't want the old lady to stop talking just when things were getting good. She said

'The men are gone, but one of the leaders runs Volubills cafe and lives upstairs in an elegant apartment, it even has an indoor toilet.'

We thanked the old lady for the tea and left her home without eating the baked camel's balls dipped in shredded coconut that she had offered.

'This may be our first big break, I said to Sahara as I rubbed my hands with joy. 'Shall we fall into the restaurant tonight or tomorrow night?' I asked, knowing Sahara was in a fighting mood.

'Fuck it. Let's get his ass now. Let's kick his ass tonight like ass kicking is going out of style, baby,' said Sergeant Sahara as he did an imitation of me talking.

'OK smart-ass, you take the front and I'll take the back,' I whispered to Sergeant Sahara as we passed the side of the restaurant, you know, the one with the toilet upstairs.

'Right, see you upstairs,' Sahara called out as he ran across the street to take a quick piss behind a rose bush. I went around the back and jumped over a fence and landed in a chicken pen. Those damn chickens let out an almighty scream, pecking, biting, and began to jump all over the place when suddenly a light went on upstairs. Some guy came to the window with a shotgun and leaned out. 'All right. Whoever's down there, you'd better come out with your hands up or I will be forced to let this shotgun loose on you and I'd hate to do that,' he said talking slow and cool.

'All right, I'm coming out. Don't shoot. I'm just a poor lost American boy who has strayed from the tourist attractions and has lost his traveler's cheques somewhere here in the dark.'

'Well, well, well, if it ain't the Yank with the nine lives. Come out and walk slowly up the back stairs in the light where I can see you,' he said, holding that shotgun on me. As I came out of the chicken hut and started up the stairs, I heard him say, 'Hey Yank, I used to study in America before the revolution. I thought I'd never get a chance to meet you. Everybody talks about you and your nine lives,' he said laughing.

When I reached the top of the stairs, I saw him drop his shotgun down to the ground, the smile turn to a frown, and then walk very slowly in my direction, with Sergeant Sahara holding a gun at his back.

'My, my, my, you do speak real good English. Now I hope that we don't have to beat the living shit out of you just to make you talk, fatso,' I said as I slammed my fist into my other hand trying to give him a hint of what I meant. 'Where are the girls? We don't have all night to play games with you, so please tell us quickly,' I asked sportingly.

'I'll never talk. You can beat me, shoot me, fuck me in the ear, anything, but I still won't talk,' shouted the greasy pig of a man. This man was a typical fat, greedy Arab, who sweated like a greasy pig when he was scared.

'What's your name?' I asked after getting nowhere for the last twenty minutes of questions. He was a stubborn bastard.

'I don't mind telling you that as you two will be dead by morning,' answered the sweating pig, making me angrier by the minute. 'My name is Beni Mellal, Captain Beni Mellal Khan, at your service,' he said, smiling from ear to ear. 'Now that's a real pretty name,' I said as I looked over at the grand piano tucked away in the corner. 'I'll tell you what. Let's make a bet. Are you a betting man?' I asked.

'Yes, I would like to take your money before you die,' Beni replied greedily.

'I bet you can tell me where my two girlfriends are. If I make you tell me where they are, you'll give me all the money in your night safe and I will let you go free. If I don't make you talk and tell me everything I want to know, I will give you the five thousand American dollars I have here in my pocket. Is it a deal?' I asked. 'Let me see the money on the table first, Yank,' he answered, foaming at the mouth with greed. I then threw down on the kitchen table five thousand new American dollars. Old Beni's eyes got real big staring at all that money. Beni was a very wise man, for he knew I wouldn't kill him because I would never find the girls if I did. He also knew that he could take a punch at me, but that we couldn't beat him to death. But he didn't know that I had a master plan that I had learned in Vietnam.

'OK now you open the safe, Beni, and we've got a deal,' I said. Sergeant Sahara walked over to the safe with Beni and let him open it. When the door flew open, it was packed with money.

'Look now, Yank, because you'll never spend any of it before you die,' said Beni as he laughed out loud.

'Come over here, Captain Beni. Sergeant Sahara, I want you to tie his hands behind his back,' I ordered the sergeant, giving him a wink.

'What are you going to do to me?' asked Beni.

'You'll see later,' I answered.

I could see the fat bastard was beginning to worry and sweat as I kept on looking at him and laughing.

'Sergeant Sahara, go over to the piano and cut out some piano wire and bring it to me, please,' I said, still keeping my eyes on old fatso. When the sergeant brought me the piano wire, I ordered old fat Beni to get up and walk out on the kitchen balcony into the moonlight.

'Now look, Yank. No rough stuff, or I won't tell you where the girls are,' Beni was sure to remind me.

'Pull down his pants, Sergeant Sahara,' I said as I grabbed the piano wire from the sergeant's hand.

'You need me alive. You need me, Yank. You'd better not kill me if you ever want to see the girls alive again,' Beni shouted out loud as he began to tremble with fright. I drew back my hand and gave Beni a smack so hard across the face that it made him see stars in the moonlight. 'Now if you don't be silent, I'll give you one harder, you fat, ornery, little man,' I yelled into his face as I pulled hard on his nose. 'Now pull down his underwear, Sergeant Sahara, and let's see his fat stomach and little shrivelled cock,' I said, laughing. The sergeant pulled down fat Beni's underpants to his knees and started to laugh as old Beni tried to hide all that greasy fat and small cock by crossing his legs. 'Goddamn,' said the sergeant in a true American fashion, 'Don't you ever wash your drawers, fatso?'

'You two must be some kind of sex perverts,' Beni shouted to me in anger.

'Funny you should mention that, Beni,' I said, swinging the piano wire near his small cock. 'Sergeant, tie one end of this wire to the balcony banister and the other end around Captain Beni's cock and balls, please,' I ordered.

'Sir, it will be a pleasure,' answered Sergeant Sahara, as he began to tie up the wires to the parts that I had ordered.

'Now this has gone too far, Yank. I'll have your head for this. I'll...' At that moment I let go a smack upside the fat head of Beni that almost knocked him over.

'I told you to be quiet. If you want to talk, whisper my dear man, whisper,' I said in a low Dracula-like voice. 'Now I'm gonna ask you just one more time and I mean just one more time, where the girls are. Now I hope you understand, because if you don't, I'm gonna push you off this balcony down into the chicken shit, with your cock and balls tied to the banister. Now this won't kill you, cause I like you, but you can kiss your love making days goodbye, old boy,' I said as I stood eye to eye in old fat Beni's face. 'Just think, no more pussy ever. Why you won't even be able to be a fag. You'll have nothing to stick with,' I said, laughing out loud.

'Now look, Yank, have mercy on me. If I tell you I'll be killed. They will hunt me down like a dog. Please don't make me tell everything, please,' old fat greasy Beni begged and sweated.

'As nice as I am, I still must know where the girls are. They are my dear friends,' I said. 'I have wasted too much time already, where are the girls, sucker?'

'If he doesn't answer in five seconds, push him off the balcony, sergeant,' I ordered. Beni looked at me in fright and waited for the count.

'1, 2… you had better talk now before it's too late, Beni,' I remarked. '3, 4…'

'Please I beg of you, don't do this. I'm a family man,' Beni shouted as he crossed his legs tighter, making his balls start to turn blue.

'5. Time's up. Push him off the balcony, sergeant,' I ordered with a serious expression on my face. The sergeant grabbed old Beni by the arm and was about to push his ass over the side, when suddenly old fat Beni broke down and cried like a baby and told all.

'Now you see, that wasn't so bad after all, was it? You should have told me all this at first and saved yourself all this unnecessary roughness and brutality to your cock and balls, old boy. You know I hate myself when I do these things,' I said jokingly to old fat Beni.

Beni had told us that the leader of the Ouzoud Brotherhood had sold the girls into slavery to a Moorish sultan, about two hundred miles from here. 'What's this sultan's name?' I asked as the sergeant was untieing the ropes on Beni's arms and legs.

'His name is Sultan Moulay Ben Saad,' old Beni said in a hushed voice.

'Does this sultan have many men?' I asked.

'He has more than enough to deal with you, Yank. He has hundreds of men all around his palace and guard dogs to bite you in the ass,' Beni said, laughing nervously.

'What are we going to do with him?' asked the sergeant.

'We'll let him go free like I promised,' I answered, trying to be a gentleman. Not really trusting old fat Beni, I decided to keep an eye on him until we left his house. After we down for some coffee and talked a bit more with Beni, I gave Sahara the nod to go. 'I'm going now, it was so nice taking your money and seeing you do a naughty strip show for the sergeant and I, but we must go now,' I said. 'I'm asking you nicely, Captain Beni, not to run to the door and call out for help for at least ten minutes. I don't want to kill you, but I will if I'm forced, sucker. Now is that a deal?'

'You have my word as an officer and a gentleman. Don't worry, my word is my bond, Major Jones,' answered Beni, trying to give the impression of being an honest lad. The Sergeant went first and I backed out the door second, still holding my pistol on old fat greasy Beni with his swollen blue balls dangling in the breeze.

As we got to the foot of the stairs and were about to leave

quietly, minding our own business, not wanting any trouble from no one, stepping carefully through the hen shit, sure enough Captain Beni Blue Balls ran to the door and gave the alarm, breaking his officer's agreement.

'He's here! Don't let the Yank escape! Help, help, search all the grounds around! Help, help!' That son of a bitch was yelling at the top of his voice like a country whore who just got paid with a nine dollar bill, when I let three shots rip into his chest. As the bullets hit, he staggered, spun around, then crashed through the balcony to the ground below, burying his face in hen shit.

Now the place was crawling with fat Beni's men. 'Have you seen anything of the American running through here?' asked the leader looking for me.

'Yes. He went running that way with blood all over his shirt,' said Sergeant Sahara quickly, pointing the direction to the bandits. The six men ran off into the darkness looking for the phantom American, while we made our way to the camels and rode off looking for the girls.

After riding several days and most of the nights, we arrived in a city called Akjoujt. It had taken us nearly one week of hard riding to get here this fast. The city was crowded and the people lived and worked like ants. It seemed like everybody was in the slave trade. Men, women, children, and camels were all that the people wanted to buy or sell in most places at the markets.

In a way these people were lucky that they were missing the war. The market was full of Red Army units on leave or helping the local police force to maintain law and order for the decent folks. This was a very dangerous city as most of the people were war refugees from other parts of the country. Most had no money, food, or place to sleep at night. It was a bitch trying to stay alive in this city of violence and lust. Some of these people would have cut your throat as much as look at you.

'Let's find a place to water and feed the camels,' I suggested to Sergeant Sahara. After walking about an hour, we found a place. A camel-smith. 'You two can stay in the top of the barn as long as you don't touch my three beautiful daughters. (I know all the jokes say the three daughters are supposed to be beautiful, but these three bitches were so ugly, they had to sneak up on a glass of water top get a drink.) The camel-smith was a very nice man and we thanked him for his hospitality and he farted as he bent over to pick up our heavy luggage.

'Wow, that was a whopper,' said the sergeant to the old man.

When the night came, the camel-smith asked the sergeant and I if we would like to have a meal with his family. 'Thank you very much,' I said politely. 'I haven't had a good old-fashioned home-cooked meal in a long time.' The old man couldn't speak English, but I knew he was very happy when we accepted his invitation to dine with him.

That night we went down to the old man's house and were let in by two big black slaves who motioned us to sit and be comfortable. The table had been set, and in walked the three ugly sisters and their fat ugly brother. As they sat, the father and mother walked in and sat next to me. After everybody said a short prayer, the food was served by the slaves. The food smelled and tasted delicious, but there was just one thing I didn't like. I was just pissed off. One of the slaves, whenever he served me something, had a bad habit of putting his thumb in my dish. That nigger had a thumb like a foot. 'Get your fucking thumb out of my food before I kick your ass,' I said quietly as I rolled my eye at him trying to show my displeasure.

I guess he knew he was getting on my nerves and pissing me off badly, because everytime he would bring me something, no matter what it was, he would jam his thumb down deeper in what I was having. But you know me, right? I had something for his ass. As I was talking to the father, I could see this smartass slave with the big head and big rolling eyeballs coming my way with his hands full of dishes, walking just past me with a special dish of food the wife had made for me and Sergeant Sahara. Still taking to the father about the high price of camel-balls, I stuck my foot out slightly and tripped that smartass slave waiter as he walked by. He gave out a loud Tarzan-like scream and went ass over elbow down onto the floor, smashing plates and sliding head first into the food. The father jumped up and screamed at the top of his voice in anger. 'I'm gonna...' then he stuttered out of anger, 'I'm gonna kill him, I'm gonna murder that son of a bitch, I'm gonna personally kick his ass until I wear out a set of knee caps,' and the slave was dragged out of the door with the brother and sisters and the mother stomping his ass unmercifully.

'You speak very good English for a man who only a few hours ago didn't speak any,' I said calmly as I was buttering my bread.

'I speak only a little. I learned a little from the American priest who used to hire my camels, before the war,' answered the old man, knowing that I had caught his hands in the cookie jar.

'Do your children speak English?' I asked.

'Yes, they studied in New York before the Revolution. The Red Army does not like it when our people speak in English, but French and Arabic is all right,' the old man answered, winking at me. 'Your picture is posted all over the city. We know who you are. You can stay tonight, but you must leave early in the morning. I am most sorry, my friend, but I have a family to think about,' said the camel-smith sadly. After our last cup of coffee, we said goodbye to the old man and his family. Sergeant Sahara and I got up very early in the morning before the markets were open and made our way across the city before the streets filled with traffic and people. After traveling about fifteen miles, we came upon the sultan's palace. It was surrounded by guards. Only guests and workmen were allowed inside and we were neither. Just our luck, huh?

Watching the palace for one week, day and night, we noticed that the women came out and worked in the fields every afternoon. This was our chance to rescue Irma and Marra. While I stayed and watched for the girls, Sergeant Sahara went back to town and bought some dynamite and a couple of Browning machine guns, just in case things got funky. This was the best guarded palace I had ever came across. There were two jeep patrols that patrolled the outside grounds, plus many wall guards, and a dog-patrol unit walking inside the palace grounds. The only way was to attack the guards outside the palace gates at some place where they wouldn't be expecting an attack, I thought to myself. When Sahara got back, I had it all figured out.

'Now here's the plan,' I said as I went on to explain to the eagerly listening sergeant. 'The guards will bring the girls back from the fields, coming through the main gate about noon, right? Well, about noon there's only a few guards on the wall, two at most. Also every afternoon the pilot of that helicopter starts up and warms up the engine.'

'What helicopter? I ain't seen no damn helicopter anywhere,' Sergeant Sahara said, laughing and looking at me as if I were mad.

'That's because you haven't been here at noon when they open the underground hangar doors and up comes a fully armed helicopter,' I said, knowing Sahara didn't believe me for a second.

'I'll show you later, but first let me finish explaining to you the rest of the plan, Goddammit. What kind of shit is this anyway? A shitty little sergeant arguing with a major,' I said jokingly. 'Now look, we need one more man for our plan to work. Do you know anybody?' I asked, hoping that the sergeant could have obliged.

'We go back to town tonight. We'll get somebody. Don't worry about that. Explain the rest of the plan,' Sahara said.

'OK, we need a jeep with a heavy machine gun for a start,' I said excitedly.

'No problem. Go on, this is getting good,' Sahara said.

'We've got to get some officer's uniforms. Also, when I give the signal, you and this new man charge in a jeep, attacking the guards of the girls. Meanwhile, I'll attack the pilot of the helicopter and hold him hostage until you and the girls arrive,' I said, explaining how simple it all was.

'And how are we going to get out of this place when all the shooting starts? You just tell me that, smarty pants,' said Sahara, thinking that I had not taken that into consideration.

'The helicopter, dummy,' I answered. After a few minutes of silence, I did admit the plan was a bit risky and highly dangerous. 'We might not make it,' I suggested.

'Yeah, I know, but what the hell, they can only kill us once,' the sergeant said with a short laugh.

We went back into town that night and paid one thousand dollars for two of the most proficient killers in the city. They were right handy with knives and handguns. As I was explaining my plan to one of the two paid killers, the other whispered in Sergeant Sahara's ear.

'What's wrong?' I asked.

'Nothing's wrong,' the sergeant assured me, 'Do you still want the uniforms and the jeep?'

'You know I do,' I answered.

'Well for another thousand dollars, they will get you the uniforms and the jeep. And because you are a friend, they will get two of their best killing partners to fire rocket launchers at the guards on the walls.'

Now that's hot stuff, I thought to myself as I paid out another thousand dollars for a job to be well done. On finishing my coffee, I shouted out 'Waiter, another bottle of whiskey for my friends.' Everybody at the bar suddenly turned and looked at me. Two or three of the men drinking at the bar, quickly departed out the front and back doors simultaneously. When I realized what I had done, Sergeant Sahara suggested we leave right away. Sahara quickly explained to our paid assassins where we were to meet tomorrow morning and the time. We all quickly knocked back our drinks and departed in the dark, as the police would be coming to the bar looking for me. (Remember, I was a celebrity, as my picture was posted all over town.) When the morning rolled around, our two paid assassins and their two pals met at the designated spot and on time.

I went over the whole plan once more, just to be sure there would be no slip-ups, because if there were, it would be curtains. Everyone then went to their positions and waited patiently for my signal. Something was moving a long way off in the sunlight, but I could not make it out for heads or tails. 'Hey Sahara, pass me my new Foster Grant binoculars,' I called to the sergeant as he was making last-minute checks on the jeep machine guns. That movement was the girls coming back to camp. 'The girls will be here in about half an hour,' I remarked to the men. Just then at exactly twelve o'clock, the underground hangar doors for the helicopter opened, and up popped a beautiful blue and black helicopter on a hydraulic platform.

'Well, there's your helicopter, Sergeant Sahara,' I said as the pilot turned the key and started the engines running.

'Look at the guns on it. I bet she flies like a baby,' Sahara said as he looked on smiling.

'What do you think of this idea?' I asked Sahara. 'Don't attack the guards of the girls at first, but ride up and tell them the sultan wants to see Marra and Irma quickly and that it's very important. With you being in an officer's uniform, they won't think anything is wrong. But if they do, let them have it.'

'Sounds great except for one thing,' said Sahara.

'What's that?' I asked.

'You go,' he answered, and he was serious.

'OK, you take the helicopter pilot and I'll go and take care of the girls,' I said as I ran and jumped in the jeep ready for a good fight. 'Attack in ten minutes if you hear gunfire. If you don't hear any firing, be cool until the wall guards start to open fire,' I ordered. Dressed as officers, one of the assassins and I drove off to meet the guards who were walking with the girls, and getting a lustful eyeful. When we stopped the jeep, the assassin quickly began talking in the local tongue and laughing with the guards who were leading the column of dark-eyed and lightly clad big-busted women. All the guards gathered around the jeep as one guard brought up the girls in chains. Irma and Marra still looked as succulent as ever with their big tits easily seen under the light shirts soaked with sweat. I wanted to scream when I saw their hips swaying from side to side like a rowboat on the sea. The girls looked up at me, but did not recognize me with the strange officer's uniform and Foster Grants over my eyes.

They got into the back of the jeep with one big huge guard handcuffed to them. I was beginning to pull away without any problems, then all hell suddenly broke loose. That damn stupid son of a bitch assassin who was riding with us reached over and slit the guard's throat in a matter of seconds. He then jumped into the back, and began firing the machine gun into the crowd of guards we had just left behind seconds earlier, for no reason.

'Die, you filthy dogs. May your mother eat camel shit, and lots of it,' he shouted as he pulled the trigger of the machine gun like a mad, frantic mercenary killer, and enjoyed every minute of it as he burst into uncontrolled laughter.

'You crazy bastard, why did you do that? You had no call to do that, fuckhead,' I yelled over the roar of bullet fire whilst traveling at sixty miles an hour.

'Robbie, is that you? That's our darling Robbie,' shouted Irma to Marra.

'Yes it's me. Who else would be crazy enough to go through this to rescue you,' I answered as the girls, who had now found the key, were unlocking the handcuffs and freeing themselves from the dead guard.

Now the hell really broke loose. The guards on the wall began to fire cannons at our jeep and the assassins we had left behind began to fire at the wall with the rocket launchers. 'Hold on tight everybody, I've got to zig and zag to keep us alive,' I yelled into the speeding wind. I could suddenly see the helicopter on my right, when I yelled to the girls in the back, 'Take the guard's gun and start firing. We're going to try to make it to the chopper over there near the palace walls, can you see it?' I asked, feeling a bit nervous by now.

'Yes, we're ready when you are. You just drive, we'll take care of everything back here,' replied one of the girls as that silly bastard firing the machine gun in the back was still laughing and enjoying himself so much, he didn't even hear me. Making for the chopper, zigging and zagging like a scared rabbit, I could see Sergeant Sahara waving his rifle as he stood in the doorway of the chopper. 'We're almost there girls, hold on just a little bit more and then it's home sweet home.' Just then a cannon shell hit near us on the right side and made the jeep overturn, throwing us free of it and on the ground. 'Is everybody all right?' I called out.

'No. That crazy bastard with you is dead,' shouted Marra as she helped Irma to her feet.

'Forget bout him, run, and keep your heads down, over to the helicopter as quick as possible.'

Bullets landed all around us. I've never been so damn scared in all my life. While helping the two girls run faster, I heard someone shout out behind me, 'Run Yank, we're coming too. Don't think you're going to leave our asses here.' It was the other three assassins waving and laughing as they too zigged and zagged through all the cannon fire on their way to the helicopter. Those crazy fools. They'll be blown all to hell, playing Mister Hero, I thought to myself.

'Give me your hand and I'll help you in the door,' Sergeant Sahara called out to the girls as we got near the chopper.

'I'm hit. Go on without me,' Marra called out in agony.

'Don't be a fool, you're coming back with us. We've come this far, and we're not leaving without you,' I said as I picked up Marra's limp body and put her on my back. 'You run on ahead,' I called out to Irma. Seeing Irma go safely into the chopper with Sergeant Sahara, I began to run with more speed and determination. I knew I had to get Marra back to safety after all the nice things she had done for me in the past. 'We're gonna make it, Marra, just five more feet and we're there,' I shouted with joy.

'Here, let me help you with Marra,' Sahara said, reaching out with both hands to help us aboard.

'Take it easy with her, she's been shot,' I said. Irma began to comfort her as we laid her between two seats in the back. 'Marra, my dear friend Marra, I pray to God you'll be alright,' Irma called out sadly, and crying hysterically.

'Alright you bastard,' I said to the pilot, 'You'd better get us out of here safely when the other men come aboard and quick.' With me just saying that, a cannon shell made a direct hit on the speeding assassins' jeep.

'Those poor stupid bastards, what a waste of life,' the sergeant remarked as I gave the order to take off to the pilot, who was shaking nervously. When we got out of the range of the machine-gun fire, I went to the back of the helicopter to check on my dear friend Marra. 'It's too late. She's dead, the poor girl,' Irma said, trying to hold back the tears. I felt I had lost a big part of me, with the death of Marra. It was hard to imagine life without her. It was she and Irma who had kept me going all this time. Irma and I just sat down and cried in the back of the chopper, while Sergeant Sahara kept an eye on the pilot, making sure that he tried no funny stuff. On the way back to camp, I promised Irma that we would always stick together and that I would always look after her in times of crisis. She knew what I meant, as she was the one who had saved my ass more times than I had hot dinners.

As we returned back across our lines, I ordered the pilot to get in contact with our main headquarters so that I could speak to my friend, General Kareem. 'Hello, General Kareem, this is Major Jones. What has been going on since I have been gone?'

'Oh boy, Robbie is that you? Where in the hell are you? I almost gave you up for dead, old boy,' Kareem said, happy to hear from me.

'Man, you should see this helicopter I'm bringing you back for a present,' I said. Just then the pilot gave me a dirty look.

'You had better keep your hot biscuit eyes over there on them controls, unless you want me to butter them for you, sucker,' I said, laughing.

'Who's that with the biscuit eyes you're talking about?' asked Kareem.

'Just a private pilot of Sultan Moulay Saad,' I answered, chuckling into the microphone.

When we sat the chopper down, Kareem was there to meet us with a five-piece raggedy band of shoeless musicians who sounded like dog doo-doo. 'Boy, she sure is a beauty. What a super machine,' Kareem said as he shook my hand like a jack-hammer, almost dislocating my right shoulder. 'Where is the other girl?' he asked, not knowing of the tragedy that had befallen poor little Marra.

'I'll explain later, right? Now let's just take Irma to the hospital and give her a check-up and have some of your musician friends take Marra's body to the mortuary,' I suggested.

'Very well, I'll see you tonight then,' answered the general.

# 8

That night as we sat and had dinner with General Kareem, Tira walked in with Major Casbazo following like a lost puppy. 'Hello major, it's good to see you and your lost friend back among us,' Tira remarked in a sarcastic way.

'It is good to see you back with friends, no?' spoke the major in his broken English.

'Yes, it's nice to be back, watching over my dear friend, the general, and seeing that he comes to no harm from the sneaky people around him,' I said as I gave Tira a wink.

'It's such a pity that your other young lady met with an untimely death, isn't it?' Tira said as she leaned over my shoulder to take an olive from my salad plate popping it into her piranha mouth. Irma jumped up at that moment and started to go for Tira, but I quickly pulled her back down into her seat. Irma was steaming. She would have kicked another hole in Tira's ass if I had let her.

'Maybe you stay close home with girl, now, and let real soldiers fight, no?' said the brown-nosing major as he walked out the door with Tira.

'Yes I will, and keep an eye on other things also,' I shouted as they closed the door.

'What gives, Kareem, I thought she was your girl, but I always see her with Major Casbazo. Whose girl is she anyway?' I asked, looking a bit puzzled.

'Now calm down, old boy,' said Kareem smiling. 'She's my girl, but she is also on my staff holding the rank of Captain and advisor. She and Major Casbazo are from the same village and tribe,' he explained to me as he carried on talking. 'When Tira and Major Casbazo came to me, they brought four thousand men with them. These men respect them and in turn respect me because I am their leader. And your last point about them being together, well I know Tira. She would never marry a lowly ranked man like Major Casbazo. She's much too ambitious for that sort of horseplay, old boy. That's why she treats him like a dog,' Kareem answered calmly as he poured himself another glass of his favorite wine.

'Well, there is still something funny going on. I don't care what anybody says, I smell a rat,' I said.

'You smell your upper lip,' Kareem said laughing and almost falling out of his carved wooden chair. Seeing Kareem laugh, made Irma and I also begin to chuckle. Trying to change the subject, as Tira was a sore point for the general, I asked

'Anything out of the ordinary happen lately while I have been gone?'

'No. Nothing really. Now I tell I lie, yes there was, now that you bring it to my attention, old boy. About three weeks ago, the main warehouse where we keep our new M-16 automatic rifles was broken into,' said the general as he went on to explain rather badly because of the booze he had been drinking most of the night.

'You will never believe this, old chap, but I had made plans to attack an arms train on the other side of the town Kiffa. We were to attack as the train was taking on water and guess what happened?' the general asked Irma and I shaking his head in disbelief.

'Nothing surprises me with that bitch Tira around,' Irma remarked.

'What happened?' I asked, knowing it was going to be a real dandy of a story.

'Well,' said the general after taking a long puff on his Havana cigar, 'As my men and I approached the train, all was quiet, then suddenly, out of nowhere, the doors on the side of the boxcars opened up and there were our new M-16 rifles staring us in the face. Each train had about forty men and they opened up on us with our own guns. They knew we were coming and cut us down like dogs. Out of two hundred men, who were highly trained, I came back to camp with just twenty-five. Now what do you think of that?' Kareem asked, still shaking his head in disbelief.

'I already told you what was going down,' I answered.

'Yeah I know. But I just can't believe that someone on my staff is a traitor to the Revolution,' said the general.

'It's getting late, general, Irma and I are going home to get some sleep. We'll see you in about three days after Marra's funeral,' I said as we made our way out the door.

After the funeral Irma and I went up into the mountains to get away for a while, as the house reminded us of Marra too much. One day as we were making love in some high grass, we saw Tira and Major Casbazo ride by with a covered wagon heading in the direction of a road which led to a river. 'Why are they going that way? It's nothing but a dead end,' remarked Irma as she pulled up her pants.

'Well,' I said, 'Let's follow them and see for ourselves,' as I was rushing and trying not to catch my balls in my pants zipper. We jumped up and ran through the woods trying to keep back far enough to just see which direction they went or turned. Riding to the end of the road, Major Casbazo ordered the driver of the wagon to cross the shallow river and go through the giant waterfall that lay ahead.

'Kiss my ass,' I said, 'Did you see that?'

'I see it but I don't believe it,' whispered Irma. 'This must be where the secret brotherhood headquarters is,' I said stunned.

'Yeah, let's go back before something bad happens, Robbie please,' begged Irma.

'You wait here. If I'm not back in twenty minutes, you go for help. You got that?'

'Yes, but please be careful and don't get into any trouble,' Irma answered feeling a bit nervous.

I then ran into the giant waterfall leaving Irma to watch for me. After passing through the waterfall and walking down a large dry tunnel, I saw a light at the end. Near the light, a guard was smoking a cigarette and sitting on a rock, while some other men were loading boxes onto a wagon. As soon as he got up to put his cigarette out in a special container, so as not to cause a fire in the tunnel, I quickly jumped in behind the other men and helped load the heavy boxes onto the wagon.

'These damn guns are heavy, man, I wonder why they don't get slaves to do this shit, don't you?' one of the men asked me as he struggled to load a box. I didn't say anything, I just nodded my head and agreed, not wanting to give away my American accent. A loud horn sounded which meant the men could take a break to eat or have a drink. This gave me a chance to look around and play detective like my old friend and idol, Dick Tracey.

As the men all gathered together in a corner joking with each other, I went on my own to another part of the tunnel and began to look into the many rooms filled with boxes of all sizes. Any kind of gun or rocket you wanted, this place had it. This place had more weapons than Carter had little liver pills. There were so many boxes of hardware that I couldn't begin to look at all of them in the short period of time that I had.

As I was looking in a room that specialized in electronics and was about to leave, I heard footsteps coming so I jumped back into the room and hid behind a huge box. The door opened, and in walked Major Casbazo and Tira as proud as peacocks. 'What's this room for?' Tira asked her guide who walked in behind them.

'This room is for storing electronic bugging devices and other top secret electronic equipment,' he answered.

'Is this the same kind of stuff you use to bug General Kareem's operations room with?' Tira asked with a smile.

'The very same, so you know they must be good,' replied the guide.

'Show me some other rooms before we have our meeting,' ordered Tira as they departed out the door.

I quickly stuffed some electronic devices into my pocket to show the general, and left in a hurry to rejoin the other men still having a tea break and talking shit. 'Back to work, men, the break's over I want to see every man with a swinging dick and an elbow working up a sweat and earning your pay. You lads have been goofing off lately,' shouted a guard who carried the rank of sergeant major in the Red Army. The boxes I was loading got the best of my curiosity, so I dropped one as I took it off the pile. 'You dog shit of a man. You bird brain,' the guard yelled at me as I stood and looked at ten new Russian 774 repeating Mountain Guns. They were beautiful, you couldn't miss with this gun unless you were blind, and that would still be almost impossible.

'I'm sorry, sergeant. Please forgive me,' I said, as I kicked one into the dark shadow. All the men ran over to help pick up the rifles and began to reload the box as I sneaked off into the dark with the one rifle that I had kicked behind me earlier. Running so fast in the dark, I tripped on a small bump on the ground and fell ass over elbow.

'Anybody there? Is there some bastard out there?' shouted a guard shining a searchlight down the tunnel just to make sure. They must have seen me because the alarm went off fast as a whippersnapper. (You know how fast a whippersnapper is, don't you?)

'Intruder in the tunnel, intruder in the tunnel,' a voice shouted over the loudspeaker.

I turned and fired my new Russian 774 mountain rifle and knocked out the searchlight and ten guards who were running down the tunnel at the same time, in about four seconds flat. OOWEE, the Lord knows I was fast, and looking good. I then ran out of the tunnel and under the waterfall into the woods to the spot where Irma was supposed to be waiting for me to return. As I came to the tree, I felt very strange, something psychic really.

Walking up closer to the tree, I saw Irma sitting on the ground with her back resting up against a big oak tree. She didn't move a muscle. Moving in closer with a lot of caution, I noticed blood all down the front of the pretty blue dress I had bought for her weeks earlier. Some son of a bitch had put his foul knife to the lovely throat of my dear friend Irma, killing her instantly. This was a very sad moment in my life. If I had seen anybody at that moment, and I mean anybody, I would have shot him dead as a bastard. I was so mad I couldn't cry. I couldn't even scream in anger. I just sat and held Irma in my arms, and remembered all the happy times we had lived together.

When nightfall came upon the woods, I was still sitting with Irma in my arms. Some soldiers came out of the tunnel looking for me, but didn't see me as I backed into the bushes still carrying her. After they left, I put Irma's body on her favorite horse and rode back to camp feeling the terrible emptiness throughout my poor little body. I rode up to the general's private quarters and asked the officer in charge to take care of Irma's body while I spoke to the general about a matter of urgent importance.

'Robbie my dear boy, you look like you have been to hell and back. What's going on, old man?' asked Kareem as he poured me a long tall drink of Scotch.

'They killed my babe. Some rat infested bastard murdered Irma. Now they're both gone,' I shouted at the top of my voice in angry grief.

'Who's gone? Make sense man,' said Kareem. 'Irma and Marra, who else. While you are pussyfooting around here, people are being killed all around you,' I shouted.

'Calm down, Robbie, that's just not true, old man. Why, just the other day I brought in a new law and...' Before Kareem could finish speaking I butted in,

'Law my ass, old boy. Kareem, it's all for nothing if you can't see what's going on under your nose, man.'

'Your sweet little Tira and Major Casbazo are planning to overthrow your little White Army now, man,' I insisted.

'What do you mean. Bring me some proof, then I will believe you,' Kareem said 'And not before.' With that comment, I brought out my little bag of goodies and began to show Kareem what I had found in the tunnel under the waterfall.

'These bugging devices can be found all over your rooms, and this is one of the best new rifles on the market that money can buy,' I said as I showed Kareem the 774 Russian Mountain Gun.

'Man, this is really something. I wish my army had some of these babies,' Kareem said, smacking the rifle with the palm of his hand.

'Well, I'm glad you like them old boy. Tira and her lover, the major, have got an aeroplane hangar full of them just waiting to be used on your ass,' I replied sarcastically.

'OK I've got your point. I've made some mistakes about the whole mess. Now what do I do? You tell me since you are the only one I can really trust,' Kareem acknowledged.

'Well, now that we are on the same wavelength again, I suggest we pay Tira and the major a little visit to the tunnel and blow everything sky high, and then we'll come back and deal with them and the other rats that are loyal to those two shit-heads,' I said enthusiastically.

'Yeah, that sounds good.You draw up the plans while I go and get Sergeant Sahara. Sahara will pick my most loyal men to come on this mission with us. We'll show the bastards who they're messing with,' said Kareem as he ran to the other side of the room and began to dial a number on the phone. While Kareem was on the phone, I had it all figured out, how we could bust their little asses. We'd wait until nightfall, and about two o'clock in the morning, go in the tunnel while they were asleep, set charges in every room and blow it up while the bastards slept in their beds. Kareem came back over to the table and said the sergeant was coming over right away.

'We had better wait until Sergeant Sahara comes, so I will only have to go through the plan once,' I suggested to Kareem.

'Yeah, let's have a quick little drink while we're waiting,' Kareem said as he poured one for each of us. Meanwhile I walked around the room looking for bugging devices.

'What are you doing?' Kareem asked like a dummy. 'Ssssh,' I whispered, and motioned at him at the same time to keep on talk-ing about anything he could possibly think of. Sure enough, there was one behind a picture of an old American Sherman tank, and one under Kareem's writing desk. I ripped each one out in turn as I came across it, and showed them to Kareem. About this time, Sergeant Sahara knocked on the door and asked if was all right to enter.

'Come on in sergeant,' Kareem called out. The sergeant came in and gave me a warm greeting and smile.

'How has life been with you?' I asked Sergeant Sahara, as I was hoping things were going really well for him with his new promotion and all.

'Allah has been good to me. I have more money now with my new promotion, and my wife and kids are happy too,' Sergeant Sahara said as he accepted a drink from General Kareem.

'Let's move over here to the big table and I'll explain the plan to you and the general,' I suggested. An hour later, after going over the plan in the most minute detail, and trying to seal off all possible avenues of failure, Sergeant Sahara was the first to speak.

'Yes it's a good plan. I can organize our best men overnight and arrange to get all the supplies you need for tomorrow night with no problems,' he assured us.

'Good, we'll move out tomorrow night and crush the dogs once and for all,' Kareem said, smacking his hands together in excitement.

'Oh, do not tell the men what, how, when or where we are going under any circumstances. I think it's better to tell them of our mission after we are half way to the target,' I said.

'I think that's fine,' answered Sergeant Sahara, rolling his big eyes around his head. 'I had better be going now if I am going to get things moving for tomorrow night. Will you two please excuse me as I know you have a lot to discuss together.' Saying this the sergeant saluted.

'Oh sure, my dear boy,' the general said, and waved him toward the door.

As the sergeant opened the door to leave, in walked Tira in a most revealing nightgown. To me, she was a cobra with a hairy snatch. 'I heard about your other friends' unfortunate death from the officer of the day. I am truly sorry for you. Seems like you draw trouble to yourself everywhere you go,' she said, in her usual sarcastic way.

'Yeah, I guess you're right, old girl,' I said, not wanting to let slip anything that this bitch could use to get the upper hand in our coming mission.

'Honey, I think you'd better come to bed so that I can give you your daily loving,' she said laughing, pulling Kareem up from his chair by the crotch of his baggy pants. Kareem looked at me and shook his head in disbelief at how bold Tira could be.

'Yeah, you'd better make tonight a good one, you never know when she might stop giving you that hairy stuff,' I said, trying to be a bit sarcastic myself and pushing down the bulge in my pants as I looked at Tira's body through the see-through nightgown.

If looks could kill, my ass would have been dead right then by the look Tira gave me as she pulled Kareem to the door without saying another word.

'See you tomorrow, old boy,' Kareem shouted from the hall, pushing his dick away from his chin.

The next morning, Kareem called me at eight am. 'What the hell. Why are you calling me this damn early,' I shouted into the phone.

'I found a note in my office this morning saying my time is up,' Kareem said with a shaky voice. 'Calm down. All will be put to rest once and for all tonight. So go back to sleep. Tomorrow at this same time, you'll be laughing about it all, OK?,' I said, trying to calm Kareem down.

'You think so? Yeah I guess you're right as always,' Kareem said, feeling much better now.

'Get some sleep, you'll need it for tonight, old boy. Goodbye and later to you buddy,' I said, as I hung up the phone and went back to sleep.

After taking a quick shit, shower and shave, and fixing myself a fried camel ball sandwich, I quickly drove over to the meeting place on the other side of town near the old cemetery called Shoe Hill. 'Are all the men here, sergeant?' I asked.

'Yes sir, and fully armed the way you like, if I may say so myself,' answered Sergeant Sahara looking sharp as a tack and ready to nail.

'Have you seen the general?' I asked.

'Yes sir, that's him coming out of that church next to the cemetery,' answered Sergeant Sahara.

'General, we are ready to move out. Shall I give the command?' I asked.

'Look Major Jones, you are in command. Don't give me any shit. Do what you have to. Just let me be there when you catch the sons of bitches off guard. Now let's get moving, dammit,' General Kareem shouted a little nervously.

'Move them out slowly and quietly, sergeant,' was my order.

We reached the waterfall at about midnight and made a fireless camp for a few hours in the woods. Up until two o'clock in the morning there was loads of traffic of men and wagons going in and out under the waterfall, as we sat and watched from a safe distance in the woods.

'I haven't seen Tira or the major,' Kareem said to me quietly.

'You will see them soon enough, my dear boy. Soon enough,' I said to the general, motioning him to keep his big head down behind the bushes. I then called Sergeant Sahara on the radio just to make a last minute check on the position of the men.

'How's everything on your side?' I asked.

'The men are in place and ready to fight,' Sahara answered.

'How many men do we have all together?' the general asked me.

'Only two hundred sir, so as not to draw too much attention to our mission,' I answered.

'Ah that's good. Just enough to surprise them,' Kareem said.

'General Kareem, I want you to take command now, and guard the outside of the tunnel while I take half the men to set the charges inside the tunnel. Too many men moving through that tunnel at one time will lessen the chances for our little surprise. Now you don't want that to happen, do you?' I asked, laughing softly.

'Anything you say, just do a good job on those sons of bitches, will you please,' Kareem whispered. I called Sahara on the radio and ordered him to move half the men to the tunnel.

'Tell the men to move with caution and be very alert. Oh, and sergeant, see that the men make a good fight of it.'

'Good fight shit, we're gonna murder the bastards,' answered Sergeant Sahara with total confidence.

'Good luck, old boy,' the general called out to me as I ran off to join my other men moving through the waterfall into the secret tunnel. 'Everybody down on your bellies. I want every man to crawl softly and quietly through this part of the tunnel as it is very important to surprise the guards. pass this order down the line, Sergeant,' I ordered. As we slithered through the tunnel, I gradually worked my way to the head of the column. Leading my men to the opening where the guards were, I stopped and signaled that the guards were just ahead and passed the word for total silence.

'What shall we do now?' asked the sergeant when he saw the two guards walking back and forth across the entrance and one more standing near the searchlight.

'Bring up the six archers with their bows and arrows,' I ordered.

'Now I know why you asked me to find six good archers. Good thinking, major,' Sergeant Sahara said with a soft pat on the back.

'They're all here, sir,' Sergeant Sahara said, looking excited to see the results.

'Ready men?' I asked.

'Ready when you are, sir,' answered the lead archer wiping hot dog mustard from the string of his bow.

'Fix arrows and shoot when I drop my hand,' I directed.

'Which hand, sir?' asked a stupid soldier with a patch over one eye.

'Sergeant Sahara are you sure these are your best men?' I asked. Sahara shook his head with some disbelief. As I dropped my hand, the arrows went off with such power and speed, hitting their targets with ease. All three guards fell to the ground like sacks of potatoes.

'All right. Half you men go down to the right and lay some charges. Meet me back here in twenty minutes and not a minute longer,' I ordered. 'The rest of you keep with me and Sergeant Sahara. There are the rooms we really want,' I pointed out to Sahara.

'Yeah, but what about that radio operator in that room in front of the main rooms?' he asked.

'Get one of the men to take him out with a silencer on his weapon so as not to wake the other sleeping beauties. It's easy old boy, you sure are a little worrier aren't you?' I teased. Sergeant Sahara sent over an experienced private first class to do the job neatly and properly. After blasting the radio operator in the chest two times and once in the ass as he spun to the floor, the private gave the signal that all was clear and the job was done.

'Split up into groups of three and plant the dynamite where the marks are on your maps. We'll meet back here in twenty minutes and not a second later,' I ordered, as I almost slipped on a half eaten hot dog bun that was overloaded with mustard, relish, and garlic. The private with the eye patch said,

'Sir, I can't read the map you gave me. There's mustard all over it.' Before I could answer, Sahara sent him to the ground with a terrible kick in the balls.

'Twice is too much, sir,' Sahara said as he lifted the private to his feet.

The men divided into threes and went their ways laying charges everywhere I had marked on the maps, without disturbing the Red Army soldiers asleep in their quarters. After twenty minutes of nervous impatience I asked 'Is everybody here?'

'No sir, Private Juenka and three other men are still putting charges on the electric generator,' one of the men replied, saluting and digging in his ass at the same time.

'Run and tell 'em to hurry. we've got a timetable to keep to,' I ordered a runner.

'Major, we had better move quick. In ten minutes another set of guards will come on duty,' Sergeant Sahara suggested. Just then a thought went through my mind. How did Sergeant Sahara know that the guards changed in ten minutes? It was a silly thought, and I am always jumping to conclusions, so I put it out of my mind. After all, this was the man who had saved my ass many times. If I couldn't trust Sahara, who could I trust?

'Everybody's back and ready to move out, sir,' Sahara whispered to me as he motioned for the men to start running out of the tunnel.

'Yeah, tell them all to get the hell out of here,' I said, as I began to run with the rest of the men. Everybody was out of the tunnel now and had retaken their original positions in the woods.

'Tell everybody to put their heads down now as she's gonna blow in five seconds from now,' I said on the radio to Sergeant Sahara. About the time he said 'Yes sir' to something I was asking, WHAMMO. The blast ripped out the whole side of the hill, sending the stream flooding the tunnels and the surrounding areas outside.

'Whoever was in that tunnel, never knew what hit 'em.' I said. My guys knew their dynamite, I thought to myself happily. After everything settled down, and with the many bodies of the Red Army soldiers floating in the stream, the men stood, gave a loud cheer, and began to dance a little jig in joy. Little did they know that the fight was going to get hotter now. I mean, Tira and the major weren't going to like us blowing up millions of dollars of Russian and American weapons, were they?

'Let's get back to camp and arrest the whole damn bunch of disloyal sons of bitches,' ordered General Kareem, feeling proud as a guy with a twelve inch hard-on.

'OK, I'll tell the men to mount up and move back to camp promptly, sir,' I answered.

'General, I know a quick way back to camp. We can get back before any of the traitor dogs escape our clutches. Want me to show you, sir?' asked Sergeant Sahara with such enthusiasm.

'Yeah, and hurry up before they escape me,' ordered General Kareem as he bent down to wipe some mustard from his boot with my handkerchief. Off we went on this short cut across small rivers and over many bumpy hills on our horses and the two jeeps loaded down with our equipment and some left-over hot dogs. All the men were talking about how we had fucked up the cave and about how much dynamite they used or should have used.

As we were riding along peacefully back to camp to arrest Tira and Major Casbazo, the general struck up a conversation with me. 'Robbie, I owe all this to you,' the general said, being grateful.

'Now hold on, general, things are long way from being over. I just pointed out to you that Tira and Major Casbazo were planning to do your ass in royally,' I said laughing.

'Yeah I know, but I am gonna be a better leader from now on. I'm gonna put a chicken in everybody's pot. I'm gonna start listening more to my lower ranked men,' said the general, like the true politician he is. 'Oh yeah, this is what I want to say to you before I forget. When we get back to camp, you are to be promoted to the rank of Colonel. How do you like that?' asked the general.

Just as General Kareem said that, all hell broke loose. About six giant search lights came down upon us with rockets, cannon fire, heavy artillery, and machine gun fire mixed in for good measure. This was killer stew. The rockets and cannons were just ripping us apart. Whatever was left, the machine guns took good care of.

'Ambush. Retreat,' someone called out in the dark. Somebody knew just what they were doing when they decided to ambush us at this spot. With nowhere to run, we just had to stand and fight. The men were dying like flies when someone began to speak on a loudspeaker. (Over here they like to talk to your ass while they're kicking it. They seem to think Allah appreciates it that way.)

'General Kareem, tell your few men who are left to throw down their weapons and surrender to the new Casbazo Revolutionary Army. We will give you five minutes to make up your mind.'

'That son of a bitch. After all I've done for him,' Kareem said in anger, foaming at the mouth. 'What can we do now, Robbie?' he asked nervously.

'Wipe that foam from around your mouth,' I said laughing.

'This is no time to be joking, you fool. Earn your promotion, dammit man,' Kareem said, looking very disturbed.

'Sergeant Sahara, how many men do we have alive?'

'About twenty, sir,' he replied.

'Come over here. I want to speak to you,' I ordered. When Sahara arrived, I explained my plan. The general agreed to it as nobody else had anything better to offer. The only thing we could do was to shoot out the giant searchlights, and try to escape into the dark.

'Is everybody ready?' I asked.

'When you are, sir,' Sahara whispered.

'OK, wait until I give the signal, and then we take out the lights. Any questions?' I asked.

'Major, I don't know if this can be of some use, but I know a house not too far from here that has a radio. We can call some of our most loyal troops to the rescue, if we can make it out of here in one piece,' suggested Sahara with a gleam in his eye.

'Yeah. That's just what we need, to get out of here in one piece,' said the general, agreeing with Sergeant Sahara eagerly. 'OK, we'll go if we get out of this alive,' I said.

'General, your five minutes are up,' a voice said on the loudspeaker. Suddenly Tira shouted into the speaker,

'Kareem darling. Don't be a fool like you normally are. Give up, you asshole,'

'Did you hear what that bitch said? If I ever, I mean ever, get out of this, I will personally kick that bitch's ass until my kneecaps fall off from kicking it so hard,' the general said, trying to assure me of his kinky intentions.

Those damn big lights were still glaring down upon us as if we were the main attraction in a tree ring circus, when I gave the signal. 'Now, take out the lights; shoot out the lights and follow me, men,' I screamed out loud, and almost choked on my Bazooka bubble gum. Machine gun fire burst into the big searchlights and suddenly the whole valley was in darkness as if someone had blown a fuse.

'Don't let the rats escape us, kill 'em, shoot every last one of them in the ass,' I could hear Tira shouting into the loudspeaker like a raging mad woman. (I wonder if I am a little freak, because every time I hear a woman mouth obscene talk into a loudspeaker I get a hard-on that just won't quit.)

Although Tira and her men couldn't see us running and crawling in the dark like rats, they sure made it tough by hitting us with everything they had. It looked like the fourth of July in this valley, with bullets, rockets, and cannon fire raining down and across the hole-in-hell that we were trapped in. As I ran in the dark, I could hear some of my men call out for help, as they were dying and mortally wounded. I was thinking what a nightmare this is as I stepped onto dead men's chests, or tripped over arms and legs of bodies sprawled in this dark valley of death as I was trying to get away from the rocket fire.

'Sergeant Sahara, Sergeant Sahara, where in the fuck are you?' I called out in anger.

'Here, sir, just a bit over to your right,' Sahara called out, forgetting to make his eyes glow in the dark.

'Dammit man, get us out of here,' I ordered.

'Follow me, but tell the men to keep low and be very quiet,' Sahara whispered.

'This way men, keep low and follow the sergeant. That bastard has cat eyes in the dark,' I told the men with a struggle, as I had gotten my dog-tag tangled in my Bazooka bubble gum in the excitement of trying to stay alive.

Keeping low and quiet, we managed to escape along the side of one of the hills that once had us trapped. Tira and her bunch of cut-throats were still firing into the valley and shouting rude remarks that would make a country deacon blush. Looking back into the valley reminded me of some fireworks displays I used to see at some of the pro football games back home during half-times, only this time there were no cheerleaders dancing and showing their crotch pieces to the onlookers.

'How many men made it?' I asked, feeling a bit brave by now.

'Four, sir, counting myself,' answered Sahara also sounding a bit more brave than usual.

'You all right general?' I asked.

'Yeah, but I am shot up pretty badly,' the general answered in pain. 'How about you soldier, are you fit?'

'Yes sir, I'm all right. They can't kill me,' the soldier answered finishing the last of a hot dog soaked in mustard.

'Sergeant Sahara, I want you to lead the way to that house you were telling me about earlier,' I ordered.

'Right sir,' he answered. We started for the house with the soldier and I helping to a carry the wounded general.

After walking about three miles and looking back to see if we were being followed by Miss Dirty Mouth and her men, we could still see the fires in the valley raging on. 'How much further?' asked the general, as he was losing a lot of blood.

'Not much more, sir,' answered Sergeant Sahara. 'Just over

the hill up ahead and we'll be there.' After walking over the hill Sahara had pointed out, the general wanted a drink of water.

'I can't go any further without a drink. I'm sorry but I've got to rest and have a drink,' the general shouted out.

'That's all right. We can stop a few minutes for our favorite general,' I said jokingly.

'While you and this soldier wait with the general, I'll go and check out that house and check on the radio at the same time. Is that OK?' asked Sahara rather enthusiastically.

'Yeah, let me rest a bit. You give us the signal if everything is OK, and then we'll come to the house,' answered the general, trying to take advantage of the rest period. We all lay on the side of the hill and watched the sergeant as he approached the house. He zigged and zagged all the way to the front door in fear of another ambush. Trying the door knob slowly, he burst in holding his machine gun ready for action. He wasn't about to take anymore shit from anybody. After being in the house about five minutes, he came to the door and waved us all to come on in.

'There's the signal, general, shall we move out now?' the young soldier asked, finishing off another hot dog and swearing that this was definitely the last one.

'Help me to my feet, Robbie. Now we can go and call my most loyal troops to come and then we'll see to those stupid bastards back there in the valley,' the general said with new excitement. As we walked up to the house, Sergeant Sahara turned and went back inside.

'You think he's found the radio?' asked the young soldier, as he pulled a huge kosher pickle from under his steel helmet and began to munch ferociously.

'I hope so,' I replied snatching the pickle from his hand.

'Yeah, he's found it. That's why he went back in the house so quickly. He's probably calling headquarters right now. Good old Sergeant Sahara has been with me a long time. He always knows the right moves to make in a tight spot,' the general said with pride, as if the sergeant were his own brother.

As we got to within five feet of the door, the general called out 'Sergeant Sahara, are you calling my men on the radio? Tell 'em to bring the heavy stuff, and send about six jets armed with rockets,' the general looked at me, gave me a wink, and began to laugh.

'I'm calling them now, sir, just come in and rest yourself,' Sergeant Sahara shouted back. When we walked into the house the general asked if there were any way to make some coffee.

'I've gone without my coffee for so long, I just got to have some,' the general said laughing.

'I'll make you some, general,' said the young soldier trying to be useful for a change.

'How are you doing on that radio?' I asked.

'I've lost headquarters, but I got the general's orders off before I lost the signal,' Sergeant Sahara assured me.

'Did they say how long it will be before they get here?' the general asked looking unusually nervous.

'One hour, sir. That's the fastest they can move as some of the men have deserted in the night. Plus it's early in the morning now and some of the men have gone to town to meet the Moslem prophet Mohammed Idriss Mohammed Hammerhead,' answered Sergeant Sahara. After drinking about four cups of coffee each and finishing off k-rations, a half hour had passed.

'Where the hell are those guys,' asked the general again for the sixth time.

'Calm down. It's only been a half hour,' I said.

'Would anyone care to share my last hot dog?' the young soldier asked trying to change the subject. Just as he said that, three helicopters flew past and fired some rounds into the house.

'I'll be damned, those silly bastards are shooting at us. Don't they know I called them to save me?' shouted the general in anger, waving his arm wildly and knocking the hot dog out of the soldiers' mouth, smearing mustard all over the general's shirt. I looked out the window as they made another pass and saw that the helicopters had the general's private marking on their sides.

'Yes, they sure got your markings, general, but I don't know whether they came to rescue you or bury you,' I said, with that strange feeling in the pit of my stomach, kind of psychic really.

'That's right. I called them to help me escort you to my new leaders. Don't anybody move, or I'll shoot you all like dogs,' Sergeant Sahara ordered.

'You. I don't believe this shit. For God's sake not you, Sahara. Why, I've treated you like a brother. I just hope you get yours real good when the time comes,' shouted the general, in a towering rage and foaming at the mouth.

'I know what. Ya definitely gonna get yours, old boy,' Sergeant Sahara said very sarcastically, smiling from ear like a Cheshire cat.

'Why? The general has always treated you very fairly at all times. He even gave you his old golf bag last year. Just tell me one good reason why you would turn traitor just when things are going well for you,' I said, appealing for honesty and love of a brother general.

'Money. Rank. And most of all, this country should be run by Moslems and not some pro-Yankee, high ass, fat lipped, knock-kneed, one-eyed, high living Christian bigot, That's something you wouldn't understand, you Uncle Tom Yankee,' answered Sergeant Sahara angrily, with his eyes almost popping out of his head. I turned to the general and said

'I guess that's a pretty good reason.'

At that moment the young soldier made an attempt to get his pistol lying on a chair near him, but slipped on the half eaten hot dog on the floor that the general had knocked out of his hand earlier, letting out a loud scream of 'Oh shit,' as he fell on the floor. Quick as lightning, Sergeant Sahara let his machine gun rip into the poor young soldier's body. The soldier never had a chance as the sergeant was an old fox from way back and knew all the tricks in the book.

'I guess you feel proud of yourself now. He was only a kid,' I pleaded.

'Fuck him. He was a Christian pig,' Sahara said, laughing like a man possessed of evil.

'I want you to step outside with your hands in the air and don't try any funny stuff or you'll get this machine gun in your asses,' Sergeant Sahara said laughing, knowing that he had the drop on us. 'Look out the windows before you go out. I think you might know some of my dear friends,' Sahara joked, rolling his bloodshot eyes. It was Tira and Major Casbazo who was dressed in a general's uniform stepping out of a helicopter. 'Let's go boys, and no tricks,' Sahara said motioning us to walk in front of him.

'Well, well, well, look what we have here. Old dog nuts himself and his shit Yankee dog,' Tira said laughing almost uncontrollably.

'It is most regrettable. Your military days are over at this point,' Major Casbazo said in a low gravely voice.

'General Casbazo has a light cold. He's been waiting for hours for Major Sahara to bring you two to our little ambush, so you must excuse him if he doesn't talk too much,' Tira said laughing so hard that drops of something began to run down her leg.

'Is this what you turned traitor for, a promotion to major?' I asked Sergeant Sahara.

'It's just one of the nice things that happen with a Moslem

government,' Sahara answered back with a shit-eating grin.

'You two make a sorry pair. I never would have believed you would go with a no-talent shit like Major Casbazo,' General Kareem said to Tira, shaking his head in disbelief. With saying that to Tira, Major Casbazo walked up calmly to General Kareem, faked a right cross to Kareem's head and kicked him in the balls. The general moaned, groaned , and fell to the ground holding his crushed nuts with both hands.

'Don't talk dirty to my wife again, big balls,' shouted Casbazo as he danced a little jig on top of Kareem's cap on the ground.

'What's going to happen to us now?' I asked with some apprehension.

'We'll hang the general and sell you into slavery, or we may give you to the Red Army leader Ben Ali Hassan, your old enemy from way back. They have my brother in prison, so I think I'll make a trade for you, Yank.' Tira answered in her normal shitty way.

'Do my friend a favor, please let him live,' I begged to Tira and Major Casbazo, who was still standing and admiring his new general's uniform

'Do the Yank a favor, honey,' as she gestured to the major to oblige. Major Casbazo walked over to me slowly and then quickly kicked me in the balls several times as if his knee had a spring in it.

'I told you, don't talk dirty in front of my wife, big balls Yank.' As I fell to the ground moaning in pain, all the soldiers started to laugh and chant out loud 'Big Balls Yank, Big Balls Yank,' over and over.

'Let's kill 'em now, let's hang 'em both now and get it over and done with,' Sergeant Sahara insisted, forgetting about all the old times we had previously shared as fighting men.

'I'm the leader here, Major Sahara,' Tira said. 'I'm gonna exchange them for my brother. The Red Army will deal with both of them like dogs anyway. Load them in the helicopter safely as they are very valuable now,' ordered Tira to the two big guards who were picking us up of the ground. Taking Kareem and I over to the helicopter, one of the guards could not find the key to the cabin door.

'You stay here and guard the Yank and general closely while I try to find the damn keys before somebody finds out that I have misplaced them,' the shorter of the two guards said to the other.

'Yeah, you hurry back quickly before I shoot these two big

balled bastards just for the fun of it,' answered the bigger guard whose hands looked like feet.

'I've got a hand grenade tucked away in my jacket,' Kareem whispered to me.

'What are you going to do with it now? You know that when we get back to camp, they're going to make a thorough search of us,' I said to Kareem, feeling nervous at what he might do in his rage at being captured.

'I don't know what I'm gonna do, but I do know one thing. I'm not going to let those bastards hang me, no way baby am I going out that way,' said Kareem rolling his big eyes and meaning every word of it as he began to squirm in his brown pants. About this time, Major Casbazo and Tira walked over and began to shout at the guard.

'I thought I told you to put these two dogs in the helicopter ten minutes ago,' Tira said to the shaking soldier.

'You did sir, I mean ma'am, but my friend has misplaced the keys to the chopper and he's gone to find them,' answered the guard holding his big bloodshot eyes fixed on the ground in embarrassment.

'When he comes back, you take the general with his fat self and we'll take the Yank in our helicopter back to camp. Now you can do that without fucking up, can't you?' asked Tira.

'Yes ma'am, yes ma'am, yes ma'am. I'll take care of everything personally,' answered the guard.

'Don't worry Yank, you'll see the general back at the camp,' Tira said laughing, and then turned and spat in Kareem's face.

'I hope you rot in hell, you sleazy bitch,' the general shouted at Tira.

'It takes one to know one,' Tira answered back, motioning me to follow her and Major Casbazo.

'I'm back, sir, sorry for being late, sir,' said the guard as he showed Tira and Major Casbazo the keys he had misplaced.

'Very well, take the general with you in your helicopter and we'll meet you back at the camp. Now get on with it man, don't just stand there looking at me like a God,' ordered Tira.

'I'm on my way now, sir,' the guard said as he ran away like a frightened kid.

'Power, Yank. That's what I like about being in charge of an army, a country, and my men,' Tira said laughing, as she gave Major Casbazo's ass a hard pinch. 'Get in and watch your step, Yank,' the pilot ordered. The co-pilot, who was a midget, closed the doors and then went to start the engines. 'I just love flying. Boy do I love flying. Allah knows I love flying. Don't you like flying too, Yank?' asked Major Casbazo as the helicopter raised into the air rather shakily as the midget could hardly see over the instrument panel, and headed back to the main camp. I didn't answer Casbazo's silly question.

Looking out the window, I could see the other three helicopters all moving in a line with ours when Tira asked me something over the engine noise. 'I hear you are a good surgeon. Tell me, how did a dip-shit like you pass the exams in medical school?'

'Well, I'll tell you since you're so goddamned nosy. She had a face like an ass, and she would pay me to piss on her face in exchange for passing my exams,' I said, with a big laugh. Tira then jumped to her feet and drew back her hand to slap me when all of a sudden we heard a huge explosion, interrupting our intimate conversation. One of the helicopters went down in flames. Everybody rushed to look out the windows to see the fiery helicopter go down crashing into the mountains below. A message came over the radio. 'That was General Kareem's helicopter, I repeat, that was General Kareem's helicopter that exploded in mid-air. What are your orders now?' The radio transmitted.

'Tell all the pilots there are to be no change in plans. Get back to base as quickly as possible,' Tira ordered our pilot.

'That fucking coward of a man, that silly son of a bitch, he tried to mess up my plans for exchanging my brother for you two dogs. It doesn't make a damn bit of difference anyway. I still have your black ass to exchange,' Tira said pulling my nose rather hard down to my chin.

'I'm lucky really, President Ben Ali Hassan hates you more than we do, Yank. You are more important to us than old General Kareem was. I hear you took President Ben Ali Hassan's girl away from him while you were at university in America.' I didn't say a word. I just stared at her with all the disgust she deserved.

'Shame on you to take his bride-to-be away,' Tira said, trying to gain more information to use against me. I continued to sit and say nothing. I pretended I didn't know President Ben Ali Hassan. Tira was guessing and was not sure until she touched that sore point – my Shilee. 'Do you know a pissy girl called Shilee?' Tira asked.

'Sorry, I don't know anyone by that name, especially if she's pissy as you say she is,' I answered with a smile trying not to give anything away.

'But if you don't know her, then everything is alright, ain't it, old chap,' Tira said while carrying on with her filthy talk. 'That girl named Shilee was a whore, she gave pussy out of both legs of her drawers at the same time. Why, she's seen more cocks in four years than you've seen in your lifetime and you piss every day,' she said, laughing in my face with her breath smelling like two mules grazing in a garlic field.

'Why you pussy-faced bitch,' I shouted out in anger, as my cotton-picking hands closed around her neck and I began to tighten my grip as a strange sexual feeling came over me that I had never experienced before. (Sticky drawers again, dammit.) Whamm. Some son of a bitch hit me from behind and all of the lights went out. He knocked the shit out of me.

I came around with the fuzzy feeling that I was drowning. Someone had thrown a bucket of water on me. I looked around and found myself in a cell with four other inmates. 'The sergeant of the guard threw that water on you, but you had better not make a fuss if you know what's good for you,' an inmate advised me. Just then a sergeant walked back into our cell.

'Glad to have a distinguished guest like you staying in my jail, Yank,' the sergeant said. 'I'm sorry we woke you up like we did, Mr Yankee shithead,' he said as he walked away in a fit of laughter.

'That was Sergeant Socco, a mean bastard who eats nails for breakfast,' an inmate whispered to me, as he was chained to the wall upside down.

'Are we at the main camp?' I asked.

'Yeah, but not for long. I heard they're going to move us soon to the main prison camp behind the Red Army's lines.' an inmate who was lying in the corner with a toilet seat tied around his neck said.

'Did you hear about some kind of exchange?' I asked, as he seemed to be well informed on most matters.

'Yes, you have been exchanged for the commander's brother and you see that big sergeant? He works at the main prison of the Red Army,' he answered.

'I see that my luck is going as normal,' I mumbled to myself.

'You say something, Yank?' the inmate with the chained toilet seat asked.

'No, I was just talking to myself,' I answered. 'Hey, what's your name anyway,' I asked.

'My name is Farouk Rana. I used to be a Captain in the Red

Army, but I got into some really bad things,' he answered.

'What bad things? Shit, I don't want to be sleeping next to a Jack the Ripper,' I asked.

'No, no, no, Lord knows no. Not that bad. I only killed my wife for cheating on me, only a small matter, really. Why all the fuss sending me to jail? I ask you, is it necessary?' Farouk asked most sincerely.

'Why don't the other two in the corner say something?' I asked again.

'They don't speak English. Only French. When you cross the heartland of the Red Army section , you will find nine out of ten people speak only French,' Farouk said smiling and picking a piece of paper out of the corner of his mouth.

'But everybody still speaks the normal Arabic mixed with an African dialect, don't they?' I asked.

'Yes. You're lucky, huh?' Farouk answered with that big smile once again. (This was one of the happiest and friendliest fellows with a toilet seat around his neck that I had ever met in my life.)

'Everybody on your feet back there. The general is coming,' Sergeant Socco shouted like an old fashioned US Marine sergeant. It was Tira and the self-appointed General Casbazo.

'We came to say goodbye, Yank. We really like you, really, but you have no place among us. Anyway, you will be with your old friend Ben Ali Hassan in about two hours. Isn't that wonderful, you little shit of a man,' Tira taunted, while putting another layer of bright lipstick on her dick-sucking lips.

'So you made the exchange,' I said, getting excited as I pictured lipstick on my dick.

'It was so easy when I told him it was you we had captured. He wanted you so badly, he even let three of my brother's best friends who worked in the diplomatic corps go free also. So you see darling, you will be well taken care of,' Tira said, smiling all over herself.

'Well, that's it, isn't it? May the sun shine all up your ass,' I said, as General Casbazo and Tira quickly departed from my cell for some refreshments.

'And yours too, darling,' Tira shouted over her shoulder with a laugh.

'You had better not talk like that when you're talking to a Red Army officer, or you'll have more lumps on your head than a bowl of cold Mexican oatmeal,' Farouk advised me, with a worried expression on his face that was framed with the rotting toilet seat and rusty chain, like a picture by Salvador Dali.

'It's OK. The bastards needed me for the exchange of her brother,' I assured Farouk, trying to loosen the chain to make him more comfortable.

After eating our lunch, which was a big bowl of potato soup, the sergeant came to pick up our bowls.

'Did you like your soup?' Sergeant Socco asked, smiling. The soup was like watery white vomit and I was ready to say stick it up your ass fellow, when Farouk kicked me on my leg just in time.

'Yes, sergeant. That soup was really good. Best I ever had and I am so full,' I answered with a big smile.

'Good. Then you won't eat tonight since you're so damn full,' the sergeant said laughing, throwing another big bowl of that soup all over my head, giving me an instant rash on the back of my ears and neck. As the sergeant walked away, laughing, the other prisoners rushed to pick up the potatoes that fell off my head to the floor.

'These potatoes taste so much better after they have been smashed upside somebody's head,' Farouk said laughing, stuffing a potato in his gaping jaws.

'Why did you kick me?' I asked.

'Because if you had said anything else, and I mean anything else, the sergeant would have pissed in your soup and made you drink it in front of him,' he replied, motioning me to sit and relax.

After getting one hour of sleep, again the sergeant came back to our cells. 'Get up, you lazy dogs. Yank, have I disturbed your beauty sleep again?' he asked sarcastically.

'No. I know you gotta do your job,' I answered.

'I like you, Yank. You got class,' he said laughing, as he continued to put the ball and chains around my ankles tightly.

'Yes, I think that should hold you safely until I get you back to your new home. Isn't it nice, Yank? Let's go everybody. We're going bye-byes to our new home,' the sergeant joked with his shitty jailhouse humor. (He was the worst comedian in the whole world. He couldn't swing if you hung him.)

After putting us on the plane, the journey took about three hours to the new prison camp. Before landing, the sergeant shouted out instructions. 'Listen up, everybody, I want you to be on your best behavior. When we get down there and meet the commandant. I want everybody to say "sir" when you are speaking to an officer or anyone else in uniform. Is that understood? I don't want any shit. So don't give me any, and there won't be none. If I get some shit, your ass will be grass and I'm gonna be the lawn mower. Now is that understood once and for all?' the sergeant asked, looking as mean as he possibly could.

'Yes sir,' Farouk and I called out, while the two other prisoners just looked and nodded yes as the sergeant shook his fist in their faces.

# 9

After the plane had landed and the doors opened, the afternoon heat hit you in the face like an oven. Our feet burned through our shoes as we stood to attention waiting to be checked in. Flies swarmed all over our bodies, and sometimes into our mouths and ears if we didn't keep slapping at them. It was pure hell. Our clothes were wet in seconds and it was like living in a steam bath all day and every day. The flies were almost as big as my thumb. They would charge at us and bite the shit out of us. And if you had an open wound, that was a fly delicacy. The salt from your sweat was a real seasoning for them.

'OK men. Walk in a straight line through the gate ahead and don't let me hear any of you talking,' ordered the sergeant. After checking the men in with a guard on duty, we marched through the main gates and up to the commandant's office door where the sergeant gave the order to halt.

'You men wait here while I see the commandant and I want to hear no talking.' That silly bastard left us standing in a spot in full sun. We had no hats on and after a while, the sun felt like a sledge-hammer smacking you in the center of your head.

To make things worse, we were standing at attention next to two garbage cans with about a million flies swarming all over and around us. If you didn't try to swat them away with you hands, they would cover you by the thousands in a matter of seconds. With the pain from the bites, I started to swat at the flies with my hands, trying to keep them off of me and out of my mouth like the other prisoners. With that, Sergeant Socco looked out of the window and yelled, 'I don't want to see anybody move or hit our flies. These flies live here and we like them. Before you leave here, you bastards will learn to love them too. Just think of them as meat in your soup. So, I don't want anybody hurting our flies any more or I will come out there and break some arms in nine places,' and he slammed the window of the air conditioned office. About this time, the guy on my right passed out. He fell face first into the sand on the ground. Farouk whispered to me, 'Leave him alone if you want to stay alive.' By now, flies were covering my whole face. It was like wearing a mask. Fuck it, I said to myself. I am gonna swat these damn flies if I want to. Fuck the sergeant. the pain was pure hell from all the bites, so I took my hand and swatted at the flies quickly hoping that the sergeant wouldn't see me hurting our dinner meat.

'I saw that, Yank. I told you not to hurt my flies, you big-head bastard,' he said, as he walked out the commandant's office door over to me. He took out his pistol and WHAMMO upside my head, scaring away the flies. The blow was so hard it made me see stars before I went unconscious.

When I came around later, a doctor was standing over me and looking down at my head. 'That was a nasty blow you got on your head. How did it happen?' he asked.

'That damned sergeant hit me. That's how the blow got there, shit,' I answered, feeling mad as a junk yard guard dog.

'Oh that explains it. He doesn't really mean everything he does. It usually means that he likes you,' he said giving a chuckle.

'Where is this place?' I asked.

'You are in a place called El Hank, better known as the Tropic of Cancer. Everybody dies here as there is no way to escape. But the place is not really bad, I enjoy living here,' said the doctor, as he continued to tell me of some of the lovely features of our new home. 'This prison has thirty-foot walls all around it and each wall is electrically charged. There are five walls each half a mile long. This is more than just a prison, it has many other things happening also,' said the doctor.

'What other things?' I asked.

'Like the arms factory, but you'll soon find out for yourself as you will be working here for many years to come,' he said smiling.

'Has anyone ever escaped from here?' I asked.

'Escaped from what? Death? When you come here, my boy, you are already dead. the work, the bad food, the beatings, or the disease will kill you inside of here for a start. Now listen to this,' he went on to explain, 'The desert is their watchdog. We are in the middle of a desert, one hundred miles from nowhere. There is nothing out there but three or four diseased oases and burning hot desert sun. That desert is so hot that if you don't have water every two hours, you will die like a dog. So, you are already dead my friend. Therefore you have no need to think about escaping,' he said, looking at me sadly.

'Thanks doc for warning me. By the way, I am a surgeon. I wonder if you could have a word with the commandant for me to help you with some of your work.'

'Where did you study?' he asked.

'Stanford University in America,' I replied.

'We'll see, but first you must stay out of trouble for six months before you can have such a good position as a doctor's assistant,' he explained.

Well I tried, I thought to myself. 'Don't forget about me anyway,' I said. Just then a guard opened the door and asked the doc if I was ready to leave.

'Yep. He's as ready as he'll ever be,' answered the doctor. The guard escorted me downstairs twisting my right arm behind my back, over to the commandant's office.

'Bring the Yank in,' shouted Sergeant Socco. I walked into the office and stood in front of the commandant's desk. I waited for the bastard to look up at me and say something, but he just kept his head down and pretended to be busy looking at some papers.

'Take off that hat in front of the commandant, Yank, before I take off your fat head,' yelled the sergeant.

'I can tell right away, that I'm not really gonna like you, Yank,' the commandant said with his head still looking down at some papers.

'I just want to serve my time without giving you guys any trouble. I must have made some small mistake to be here, but I am gonna try to be a model prisoner and become more spiritual. I know that I am fortunate to be with such nice people and that you are only doing your jobs in the best way possible,' I said in my best humble voice and watermelon-eating grin.

'You see. That's what I mean. Saying things like that to piss me off. I've lived in America for nine years. I know a jive-ass, no good loud mouthed nigger when I see one,' shouted the commandant as he got up from his desk and walked over to me, foaming at the mouth. If he calls me a nigger again, I'll kick his ass really good, I thought to myself.

'You probably think all Arabs are stupid, don't you?' asked the commandant, looking me dead in the eyes with his beaming bloodshot eyes. He then moved right up to my face, his breath smelling like a gorilla's armpit and asked me another question. 'You probably think that because I am an Arab, that I am stupid too, don't you boy?'

'No sir. I'm not that kind of guy. Lord knows I don't think that. Why some of my best friends back home are Arabs,' I said smiling, while I let him push my nose downwards to my lips with his right thumb.

'Would you like a cigar?' he asked, as he motioned the sergeant to give him a silver and black box of Chinese origin from his desk.

'I don't smoke, but I will just this one time as we are becoming friends,' I said, with a big smile on my face.

'You know sergeant, this Yank might be different from the other Yanks we know. He just might not give us any trouble at all. He seems like a wonderful guy,' the commandant said in a friendly voice.

'Please have one of my fine Cuban cigars dipped in brandy,' the commandant insisted. As I put my hand in the box, Wacko, my fucking fingers went numb. That dirty son of a bitch slammed the box shut upon my poor little fingers. The pain was like an elephant stomping on my hand. Closing the box tighter and tighter on my fingers, I fell to my knees and screamed in pain as the commandant also came down on his knees looked me in the eye and laughed at my suffering sat up in my face with his breath smelling of do-do.

I fell out on the floor and pretended that I had passed out, and let a small stream of spit run down the side of my mouth. The commandant and sergeant began to laugh louder than ever at my misery. 'Don't pretend that you passed out, sucker, if you don't get up on your feet in three seconds, I'll order the sergeant to kick you in the balls until they go blue and swell as big as your fucking head,' the commandant shouted in my ear. Not wanting to have crushed balls, I quickly jumped to my feet and hid my sore fingers in my pants pocket.

'Would you like some chicken?' asked the commandant sarcastically.

'No sir. Thank you very much, though. I'm so full I can't move,' I said, as the sergeant and the commandant fell over themselves with laughter.

'Now while you're here, are you gonna be a good boy and don't give us any shit?' asked the sergeant, giving me a wink.

'Yes,' I answered.

'Yes what?' shouted the commandant.

'Yes sir,' I shouted back.

'You will be assigned to kitchen duties and if you work well, we might think about assigning you to a higher position. But this will depend upon the sergeant's recommendation,' said the commandant, motioning the sergeant to take me away. As I was about to go out the door, the commandant shouted,

'Hey Yank, I almost forgot to tell you that Prince Ben Ali Hassan will be coming to see you in a few days. That should be exciting for you, huh?' he said, laughing again and lighting another cigar that was big enough to choke the average bear.

The sergeant took me to the supply room to pick up a blanket, a cup, one spoon, and then showed me my living quarters. After locking me in the cell, he smiled and said, 'Things get a lot worse around here if you don't keep your nose clean, and you've got a big nose to keep clean, Yank.' When the sergeant walked away, I heard a sound coming from behind me.

'Psst. Over here my friend,' someone whispered. I looked over in a dark corner of the cell. It was my friend Farouk, without the toilet seat around his neck. I hardly recognised the poor chap. 'I saved a nice dry corner for you,' he said trying to be friendly.

'Gee thanks pal,' I said, as I looked around and saw one big giant shit-hole of a place. Each cell housed ten men and had been made to hold six. Dirty straw lined the floors and housed ticks, roaches, and a whole lot of other bugs I was soon to become friendly with. This cell every day and all day, stayed funky, smelly, hot, and finally shitty. Every prisoner smelled like a gorilla and a country outdoor shithouse mixed together. The walls of the whole prison sweated and made you think you were in a Turkish bath or sauna room.

One day a guard brought our food in a mop bucket and served everybody our favorite dish: potato soup. Everybody rushed to get theirs and sat to eat with excitement. Sitting down peacefully, and about to taste my first mouthful of this exotic soup, I felt a cockroach crawling on my leg near where I was resting the bowl. I reached down calmly with my hand and flicked it off my leg knocking it to the center of the cell floor. About four prisoners saw this meaty cockroach hit the floor and made a frantic jump at it, smashing the poor little thing to the ground. 'Farouk, what's wrong with them?' I asked.

'My friend, you will learn never to throw good meat away

like that in the future I hope. Meat that big and juicy is hard to come by in a place like this. Allah be praised,' he answered taking another mouthful of potato soup and eyeing my bowl at the same time. The four prisoners who had leapt at the meaty cockroach were now looking at me in anger because I didn't give my meat away, and instead made them fight over it. This half assed place was the pits, the real asshole of the world, I shit you not.

After eating, everybody settled down to sleep. Between the mosquitoes, bug bites, and the fags making love in the corner, I couldn't tell you which was worse as I was trying to get some sleep for the next hard working morning that lay ahead. The next morning, Sergeant Socco came to our cell to wake us nice and early. 'Alright get up, you lazy dogs. It's time to go to work and I don't want no shit from anybody as I'm in a bad mood this morning. I didn't get no ass last night,' he shouted, slapping his whip at the same time. All the prisoners quickly jumped up from their beds and stood in line, all but one poor bastard who was too weak to move.

'Get up. Come on you dog. Don't make me stomp you in the ass before my breakfast,' shouted the sergeant, ramming the old mans head into the concrete wall. I started to move to help the old man when Farouk quickly tripped me, making me fall to the floor.

'Why are you down on the ground, Yank? You weren't thinking about giving me shit, were you?' the sergeant asked, pulling out his pistol. 'Were you gonna help this old dog? Well go ahead. Be my guest. Then I can put this bullet dead in your ass as well, sucker.' I got to my feet and kept my mouth shut.

'If you're not up and in this line in three seconds old man, I'm gonna end your suffering for good,' Sergeant Socco said, pulling back the hammer on his pistol. This was not an old man really, he was only twenty-eight, but this kind of life had aged him very quickly. Since he was too weak to move, the sergeant put two bullets in his head, killing him instantly.

'You Yank, and you there. Yeah, you with the big fucking head, prisoner 509, take this old beat up body out and bury it,' ordered the sergeant as he kissed his gun calling it Moobie, and returned it to its holster that hung down to his kneecap. Taking the old man's body out the main gates, and burying it about three hundred yards away from the prison, I noticed some camels near a small house by the south wall, drinking water from a wooden box. 'That looks good, huh?' I said to Farouk.

'Forget it. Don't even think about it. Don't even mention it again, please. That's where they keep the camels and wild dogs used to hunt down all escaped prisoners, if they get this far,' he answered nervously.

'But the doctor said that no prisoner has escaped this place,' I whispered to Farouk as I continued to dig the grave, not wanting the guard to hear me speak.

'Don't trust that doctor. He's married to the commandant's little fat sister,' Farouk said, laughing out loud, forgetting the guard.

'You laugh out loud again, and I'll beat the living shit out of you. I speak English you know. Don't laugh at me, you lousy bastards,' the guard shouted in anger.

'Don't freak the guard out by laughing out loud again, you silly cunt,' I whispered to Farouk. 'What's on the outside of the other four walls of the prison?' I asked softly.

'There's a whorehouse for the guards and the commandant's own personal house,' he answered, pretending to blow his nose into his shirttail.

'How do you know all this, Mr Wise Ass?' I said jokingly.

'I used to work here for three years, shit, that's why my wife took a lover back in my village. I used to leave her alone for six months at a time. Then the bitch got pregnant and tried to tell me it was because I wrote such sweet letters,' Farouk answered, shaking his head in disbelief.

'You lying little bastard. If that's so, why is it that Sergeant Socco doesn't recognise you?' I asked, knowing that he would have a good excuse.

'Because Sergeant Socco has only been here for two years, and I was here four years ago,' Farouk whispered to me as he kept digging.

'No more talking. Finish that grave in a hurry,' the guard shouted as he moved a bit closer to make sure there would be no more talking. I don't know why the guard wanted to get back to camp so fast, but that son of a bitch made Farouk and I run all the way with our shovels on our backs. When we got there, we were sweating as if we had stolen the preacher's bull. 'Did they bury that old dog right?' the sergeant asked the guard.

'Yes sir, sergeant,' the guard answered as the lunch bell rang in the background.

'Report to me after you eat lunch,' Sergeant Socco ordered.

'Yes sir,' Farouk answered. As Farouk and I moved down the

chow line, I couldn't help but notice a big black prisoner looking
at me and smiling like a silly bastard. Anyway, I put him out of
my mind and continued down the line with my bowl and cup.

Moving down to the last guy serving, after I picked up some
dishwater coffee in my cup, he stopped me and said, 'Oooweee. I
bet you like a big one,' as he slapped a huge pile of mashed potatoes in a bowl and squeezed my hand. I paid him no mind and
moved on to an empty table.

'His name is Magic Pussy and he told me to tell you that he
likes you very much and wants to be your friend, or whatever
you want him to be,' Farouk said laughing, looking at the big
portion of mashed potatoes piled on my plate.

'It's a shame a big muscled guy like that is a fag. Can you
imagine a guy kissing you with a fucking moustache and a dick
that is bigger than yours? That's fucking disgusting,' I said in
anger, as I dropped down on all those potatoes.

'Each man to his own. Anyway he's a very nice guy and a
friend of mine,' Farouk said, stuffing his mouth full of beans that
were hidden at the bottom of his mashed potatoes.

'Son of a bitch. Where did you get those beans? Nobody gave
me no beans. What makes you so special with your ugly face,' I
whispered to Farouk as the bean juice trickled down his jaws.

'I told you, Magic Pussy is my friend. Now don't you want to
meet my friend and stop being so damned skinny and weak?'
asked Farouk, smiling from ear to ear.

While I was eating and talking to Farouk about life in this hell-
hole, another three prisoners sat down at our table and began to
stare at me and my potatoes. When I paid no attention to them,
the big black one with hands like a gorilla, stuck his fork in my
potatoes and began to eat slowly, humming to himself.

Don't do that. Don't touch my fucking potatoes. You don't
know me that well, sucker. Don't you know that's bad manners?
Don't get me mad, dammit, I was thinking to myself. (I didn't
want to be unfriendly at first and have to kick some unfortunate
guy's ass who didn't know that I was a mean bastard.) Sure
enough, that son of a bitch did it again taking a bigger share this
time, really pissing me off.

'He's one of the big bosses around here. Don't mess with him
if you don't want an ass kicking and you want to live in peace,'
Farouk whispered in my ear as this big gorilla continued to fuck
with my mashed potatoes, which were rapidly disappearing
from my plate.

'I'm the big boss of this section, see? And I take half of anything and everything around here, including a piece of your ass, if I want to,' he said laughing, taking another spoonful of my potatoes. 'You surprised I speak English, huh? I tell you slowly in English, so you make no mistake, yes?' he said, wiping his mouth on his shirt that was stained with diesel oil. 'My name is Louie. I think that's too much potatoes for a little nigger like you to eat. So I think me and my boys will help you eat 'em,' he said as he and the two others reached over for the bowl.

I quickly threw the potatoes in the face of one guy while sticking my fork into Louie's right eye and twisting it as hard as I could. I tried to do some serious damage to that mother fucker's eye. The other guy quickly sat back down and shouted for the guards to come to their rescue. Louie fell back off the table and down to the floor like a heavy bag of shit screaming for bloody mercy. While I was smashing the guy with my potatoes in his face, against an iron bar attached to the table, the prison siren sounded summoning the guards to the cafeteria. The guards ran over and began to beat everyone around the table over their heads with their big nightsticks that were loaded with lead at the ends. After calming everything down quickly, one of the guards walked over to me and spoke. 'Now you really have done it, Yank. You really have fucked up now. I wouldn't like to be in your shoes, boy. The Lord Almighty Jesus Christ can't save you from a ferocious ass-kicking now. Do you know what you've done? You might as well beg one of the guards to kill you now,' he said, shaking his head in pity for the almighty ass-kicking I was about to receive. I looked around me and all the other prisoners nodded their heads in agreement with the guard.

'OK what have I done that's so bad? Who's the son of a bitch that's going to give me this almighty ass-kicking? Tell me, baby, what have I done?' I asked as everyone was so frightened. I couldn't figure it out as I had just kicked the biggest and baddest nigger's ass in the jail. So who would be left to fuck with me?

'You ask what you have done?' said the guard. 'I'll tell you what you've just done. You only just kicked Baby Louie's ass real bad, and now his brother, Big Louie, is gonna come looking to kill you when he gets back from working in the fields. That's all you done, Yank.' All the prisoners around the table nodded in agreement as Baby Louie was still shouting blue murder about his lost eye which was still stuck on the fork on the table.

'Alright. alright, break it up. Move back and let me through,'

Sergeant Socco said as he made his way to the front of the crowd jabbing his nightstick at the ribs and heads that stood in his way. 'Who started this fight? Speak up. I don't want no shit. Who started this damn fight? Show me the bastard, just show him to me,' demanded the sergeant as he pounded the top of the table with the lead filled stick.

'He did. That big headed nigger over there,' said a friend of Baby Louie, pointing a bony finger, dirty with mashed potatoes, right in my face.

'Aha, I knew you were trouble Yank, you're one of those niggers that don't believe fat meat is greasy. I'm gonna fix your ass so good you won't have any energy left to fight anybody, sucker. Take him to the cooler,' ordered Socco to one of the guards who was by now using a choke hold to keep me from moving anything more than an eyelid. 'Cooler' back home meant the jail, but over here in this hell-hole it means something else. The cooler is a tin box placed in a spot where the sun always shines at its hottest. They put you in this box stark naked, so that when it gets really hot and you bump into the sides your hide fries like mom's morning bacon.

This box is shaped like a telephone booth and you must stand all day as the guard will only permit you to sit at night when it is freezing cold in the desert. By the second day, my back, legs, chest and ass, I mean everywhere, were giving me terrible pain from stiffness and muscle cramps. My hide was burned in dozens of places from touching the sides of the box as I tried to move a little bit. My weight when I went in the box was 175 pounds of lean muscle, but when I came out a week later, I weighed 121 pounds. I looked like I was auditioning for a role in Auschwitz. I thought I was gonna die when they opened the door of the box to let me out with all that sun shining in my face and on my poor little body. When the burning sun hit my wounds, the pain was so bad I had only one choice left, so I decided to faint. When I finally came around, I was in the hospital bed bandaged all over like a mummy in a tomb.

'Mr Jones, how do you feel today?' asked a fat, greasy nurse with breath that smelled like do-do. I looked out through the slits of bandage and saw this big fat motherfucker smiling at me and trying to see if my eyes were opening.

'I feel a little better now than when I first came in here,' I answered, trying to be polite.

As the nurse was changing my sheets and pillows and doing

all that reaching over and around me, I noticed that the bitch was stinking badly, and when she talked in my face up close, her breath smelled like a gorilla's crotch on a hot Sunday afternoon. Nasty, fat bitch this was, or as the English say, 'A bloody nasty piece of work.' Just then the doctor walked in.

'Ah, I see you have joined us again,' he said as he put a lemon drop in his mouth. (I prayed he would give one to Gorilla Breath.)

'Yeah, I was just talking to your pretty little nurse here,' I said, lying like the bastard I am.

'So, you've net nurse Maha? Yes, she is a little beauty isn't she?' the doctor replied with a smile, knowing that she had a bad case of the deep uglies. As the nurse heard us talking about her, she began to blush all over her greasy face, and gave me a wink. I quickly turned my head and asked the doctor how bad my burns were and how soon I could leave. 'Now you don't want to leave us yet, Mr Jones. We're just beginning to like you,' the nurse said, pushing up my pillow and smiling at me without her two front teeth. Oh Lord, this bitch was ugly. She was the size of two Joe Fraziers and was the only woman I ever saw who became more ugly when she smiled.

'I see you have a admirer in Nurse Maha,' said the doctor.

'Yeah, she's sweet, isn't she? She certainly is a little cutie,' I said, trying not to hurt the poor woman's feelings. When the nurse left, the doctor grabbed a can of air freshener and sprayed the room, then leaned over to whisper, 'I know she looks like an old bucket now, but after six months here, she'll look more and more like Liz Taylor to you. And she knows it.' And he laughed so much he almost swallowed his lemon drop.

As he was leaving the room, I called out 'Hey, Doc. You never did tell me how long I have to be here.'

'You better not worry too much about leaving at this moment,' he answered.

'Why is that?' I asked.

'Because Big Louie has been asking about you and wants to come visit you,' he said laughing as he closed the door. I had almost forgotten about Big Louie looking for me. Anyway, this wasn't such a bad deal, being in the hospital. The food was much better in here and I was beginning to get back my strength again in my legs and arms. After nurse Maha took a special interest in me, my recovery speeded up. She would slip meat from the officers' mess up to my room and sometimes get me some chewing gum. Oh, and on Fridays of every week she would give me a hand relief special, using the dressing from my salad. Nasty bitch, really.

Nurse Maha really knew how to work her hands with a little bit of salad oil. Shit, it got so good at times, I thought I was having some real ass for awhile. In all honesty I must admit that she did begin to look more and more like Liz Taylor. (I shouldn't be telling you bastards this, should I?) After a few weeks I would do my exercises in the hospital yard in the fresh air, come back and have a good meal and a couple of cigarettes, provided by lovely nurse Maha. This was every day. Exercise in the morning, morning meal than back to bed. Lunch and a little more exercise, then back to bed for a nap. Dinner at night with a couple more cigarettes and back to bed for the night. This lovely life went on for three months until one day the door opened and in walked Sergeant Socco.

'My, my, my, I hardly recognized you with all them muscles,' joked the sergeant. 'I don't think you'll want to fight no more, huh?' he said, smacking me lightly on the face. 'You know you took out Baby Louie's eye, don't you? Well, you won't have time to worry about him and Big Louie now anyway. You have a very important visitor waiting to see you in the commandant's office,' he said, smiling and being overly friendly.

'Maybe you could ask my visitor to come up here to my room, as I am very sick,' I asked, testing the sergeant.

POW, across my face went his hand. 'Don't play with me Yank, I'll shoot you just as well as look at you, sucker. Don't you know the prisoners here call me Killer Socco? Well you'd better watch your ass from now on,' he shouted as he motioned me to hurry and dress. I walked into the courtyard and was told to stand at attention in the blazing sun until I was called into the Commandant's office. Sure enough, the damn flies started to buzz around my head and become a pain in the ass. Suddenly from around a corner, the biggest and meanest nigger I ever saw in my life walked past and whispered, 'I'm big Louie. I'm gonna crush your bone head and rip out your arms from their sockets when I get you alone, fucker.'

'Get the hell away from him, Louie, we want him first, and then you can have him after we're finished,' the sergeant shouted from the window as Louie started to raise his fist to clobber me. Boy, was I glad the sergeant opened his big fucking mouth this time.

That big black prisoner called Big Louie was about seven feet tall and weighed nearly three hundred and seventy-five pounds. That nigger was so big, when he sat on the toilet his dick would hang in the water, which was the only time he had a bath. And talk about muscles, he had muscles everywhere, even in his fingernails. But I wasn't scared. I'll kick that son of a bitch's ass good and proper, I said to myself as Big Louie strolled away, knocking over three garbage cans in anger.

'Hey, Yank, bring your ass in this office,' shouted the sergeant.

As I was about to walk into the Commandant's office, I could see Baby Louie with a patch over his right eye waving his fist at me from the back of the mess hall. I walked in the office and guess who was waiting. Yeah you're right. It was Ben Ali Hassan. He had come all this way just to see little old me. As I looked at him sitting in the commandant's chair, I could see the meanness, the hate, and the pain of losing a wonderful girl like Shilee to someone like me, written all over his face.

(You remember when I first met Shilee at a dance in Los Angeles and there was a fight? Well, this was the guy I was fighting. He was then and still is one of the biggest slave owners in Mauritania. And now he's President of Mauritania and Commander in Chief of all Red Army forces, answering to no one.)

Seeing that he was still mad at me and had not forgotten, I had to think quickly to cool things down a little between us. 'Why hello there, my, you're looking well Mr President. Sergeant Socco, did you know that the President and I were dear friends when he first came to America years ago?' I asked the sergeant, while keeping an eye on the President at the same time.

'You filthy dog,' said the President, 'how dare you mention my title in the same breath as yourself? I've gone through life all these years hoping that one day I would meet you again, and tears of joy now fill my eyes with this dream come true,' he said, choked with emotion. Taking out a handkerchief and wiping away the tears of joy, he asked the sergeant and commandant to bring me up to his desk so that he wouldn't have to reach too far to get at me. He could hardly control himself and began to shake with excitement at the thought of beating my head. As the sergeant and commandant pulled my neck across his mahogany desk, WHAMMO, that mother fucker hit me so hard I saw stars, planets and moons swimming by.

'I guess you were right to hit me like you did, after all, I did take your girl away from you years ago, sir,' I said with an aching jaw, trying to be friendly with the President. You know what I mean, let bygones be bygones. When he heard me say that, he let out a scream of anger and shouted 'You pig! May your mother suck dicks! I'm gonna kill you, you son of a bitch.' After calling me all the nasty names he could think of, he suddenly picked up a heavy cigarette lighter mounted in stone and threw it upside my head, causing me a great deal of pain. Blood went everywhere as I passed out. (I'm only human, you know.) Someone threw a bucket of water in my face to bring me around. 'Get up on your feet quick before I shoot you like a dog,' shouted the President, now foaming at the mouth and exhausted from beating the shit out of me. As I got to my feet I thought to myself very seriously, how I could have kicked all three of these bastards' asses good and proper if I hadn't slipped in my own blood before I passed out.

'Killing you would be too easy. I want you to suffer, Mr Robbie Jones, just as I have all these years,' shouted the President, spitting in my face as he yelled 'You will never know how I and my whole family suffered with shame when the people of my village found out Shilee was going to marry a nigger like you in America and not me after all the wedding plans had been made. Where is Shilee now? She's probably a prostitute somewhere in America, I bet,' he yelled at me as he reached up and tried to wipe my nose off the right side of my face.

'No, she's not. Shilee was killed in a plane crash right here in this country at the start of the revolution,' I answered calmly as I straightened my nose.

'You stupid rat-faced cunt, you deserve to be shit on,' the President shouted, and began to punch me, one blow after another in my stomach until I vomited potato soup all over his shiny new shoes and uniform pants. 'Get me a wet rag to wipe my shoes and get this filthy pig out of my sight now,' he shouted at the top of his voice as I tried to apologize for being a spoil-sport.

'Take him back to his cell,' ordered the commandant to Sergeant Socco. I was so glad to get back to my cell for some peace and quiet for a while. As I walked into the cell everybody moved away from me except for my dear friend Farouk. 'Psst, over here,' he called out from a dark corner.

'Why is everybody looking at me and moving away?' I asked.

'They don't want the word to get around that they are friends of yours and have Big Louie go after them also,' answered Farouk, smiling.

'Well fuck them guys,' I said, giving them all the finger.

'You are so brave. I have never seen a man so brave,' Farouk said, looking at me as if I were some kind of superman.

'Why do you think I am so brave?' I asked as I pinched out a tick from under my left armpit.

'The way you kicked Baby Louie's ass, and how you are just waiting to catch Big Louie alone in the dark to kick his ass even more unmercifully,' he said seriously and believing it to be so. Not wanting to damage Farouk's powerful image of me, I just rolled over and went to sleep, hoping I'd never run into Big Louie in the dark by my damn self.

The next morning early, the sergeant came to my cell. 'Get up, Yank. The President wants to see you again,' Socco said, smiling from ear to ear. On the way to the commandant's office we passed through the laundry section where Big Louie was working with all his boys around him. 'Hey Louie, there's the Yank that took your brother's eye out,' a small guy next to him yelled from a cloud of steam made by the pressing machine. As the sergeant made me walk right by Big Louie's work bench, Big Louie tipped over his wash bucket, which was dirty and stinking awful, all over my shoes and pants, getting me soaked to the bone.

'Oh I'm so very sorry for getting your pants all wet. Sergeant, please forgive me for getting his little pants all wet. Too bad he looks like he just pissed all over himself just when he's going to see the commandant; isn't it just awful, men?' Big Louie said with a grin on his face, while the sergeant and the rest of the men stood looking and laughing at me. I looked down at my pants and shoes and they really were a mess, all wet and stinking from the dirty wash water.

'Here, let me help you get out of them wet pants,' said Big Louie as he yanked my pants down to my knees with such force that he broke all the buttons on my fly and my belt buckle. On seeing my pants pulled down to my knees and my ass in the breeze, the whole wash section ran over to have a look and began to laugh hysterically.

While Big Louie was rocking back and forth on his heels, laughing at me with his big mouth open, I quickly jammed a big bar of soap into the bastard's mouth. That son of a bitch almost choked to death. He fell to his knees, begging somebody to reach into his mouth and pull out that huge hunk jammed between his teeth that was giving him hell. Big Louie didn't know whether to shit or wipe as his eyes started to bulge and his color went from a nasty black to a pale green as he gasped for air.

Suddenly everyone realized what was going on and stopped laughing while the sergeant and two other guys tried to help poor Big Louie. I was the only one laughing as I pulled up my pants and threatened to piss in Big Louie's ear as he was still begging for mercy. (I'm a mean son of a bitch when I get mad and someone picks on my poor little body.) After the doctor arrived on the scene, almost slipping on the dirty water which covered the floor, the sergeant called out to me that it was time to meet the President as we were already late for our appointment.

'I see you took your own damn time getting here,' the commandant shouted to the sergeant.

'He made me late by pretending that he was sick and I had to wait for him, sir,' the sergeant said, pointing at me.

You lying bastard, I said to the sergeant in my thoughts. Aloud, I said 'Yeah, I am sick and I am tired of people beating me like a dog. If you want to kill me, just fucking kill me and be done with it. I ain't gonna take this shit much longer.'

'Smack him upside his head quick, sergeant, before that boy lets his mouth get his ass in trouble,' ordered the commandant. After picking myself up off the floor, from a low blow to my balls as I tried to protect my head, the President spoke. 'Killing you is too good for you. You want me to kill you, don't you? Well I'm not gonna let you off so easy. You're gonna stay here until you're old and gray. I will make you wish you were never born, you son of a bitch, you! I'm going now, but I'll come back from time to time just to see how bad you're really doing,' he said smiling and holding his nose because of the stinky pants and shoes that I was wearing.

'Take him back to his cell and tomorrow start him working in the kitchen,' ordered the commandant to the sergeant, who was covering his nose from the stink with his shirt-tail. 'Yes sir. Anything else?' the sergeant asked as he motioned me to leave the room quickly. The commandant gave a negative headshake and continued talking to the President, who was reaching for the air freshener. 'Yank,' said the sergeant, 'You are very lucky that he didn't kill you. I'm really glad he wants you alive. I'd miss having your ass to kick.' And he smiled all over his unshaven shit face. As we left the office and entered the courtyard, the

President shouted from the window, 'Hey sergeant. I don't care what happens to him as long as you don't kill him. I want to see him suffer each time I come to visit him. I want him to beg me to kill him. That's an order, sergeant,' the President yelled, still filled with anger.

When I got back to my cell, I thought I saw a new man in it. Hey, Farouk, that guy is new isn't he?' I asked.

'Yeah, he's one of Baby Louie's men. You'd better sleep with one eye open tonight,' he said, cautioning me with a slight smile.

'Maybe I should call the guards and tell on that bastard, before he carves on my ass, or me his,' I whispered to Farouk, who answered, 'If you do that, all the other prisoners will want to fight you, because you told on a fellow inmate. Don't worry, I'll help you keep an eye on him at night.' When the night came around after the guards served us our potato soup with no potatoes to be seen, the lights went out and everybody turned in for exhausted sleep. 'Goodnight,' Farouk whispered to me.

'I thought you were gonna help me watch big Louie's man,' I said rather nervously.

'Yeah, I'm gonna help. I'm just pretending I'm asleep. And anyway he's not Big Louie's man, he's Baby Louie's man. I've never seen you so scared. Calm down and get some sleep. I'll keep watch just like I said.'

Farouk chuckled to himself. I could hear some voices talking quietly in the corner, and someone jerking off in another, and a midget trying to talk another prisoner, who was as fat as Kate Smith, into giving up some hairy ass. Normally I wouldn't be listening to this kind of shit and filth, I would be asleep dreaming of some exotic place and getting laid by an Amazon bitch. But tonight I've got to be awake and alert, all because of this new inmate who might try to cut my throat while I sleep. The night is very hot with the mosquitoes biting like a bastard, and bugs are crawling all over our poor bodies. Lying there in the hay, with the sweat running down my face and fighting off the bugs, I heard this unusual kind of conversation, definitely not 'Fit To Print' in the *New York Times.*

It was two fags talking intimately together in the night as the full moon shone on their entwined bodies. One fag said to the other, 'I think I'm pregnant.' The second fag raised up and said, 'By who, sweetie? Who is the father?' The first fag said 'I don't know, I don't have eyes in the back of my head.' I wanted to laugh out loud, but my attacker would know I'm not asleep, right? Anyway, I was just about to fall asleep from the exhaustion of the day's work, when I felt a hand on my ass. At first I thought it was one of the fags from the other side of the cell, then I thought to myself, the attacker is making his move.

I turned over quickly with my fist balled up tightly and was ready to put an unmerciful beating on some sucker's head, when Farouk ducked and shouted, 'Hold it, Robbie, I didn't have the heart to tell you sooner, but I'll tell you now so you can get some sleep. Everybody knows you thought that new prisoner was gonna try to kill you, so everybody wanted to have a joke no you.'

'What do you mean, joke?'

'That new guy is a fag. He paid one of the guards to stay the night with his new lover. Tomorrow he will go back to his own cell,' Farouk said, laughing and moving back to his spot, where the midget was waiting to give him a hand job.

'Are you bullshitting me, you asshole?' I whispered to Farouk without getting any answer. The only sound now was the slurping of the midget's lips at work.

# 10

The next morning everybody was looking and smiling about the little joke they had played on me. At least these bastards have got a sense of humor, I thought to myself. The sergeant unlocked the cell and burst through the door. He looked as if he hadn't yet been to bed after a night of hard drinking. He yelled at the men, 'Everybody up! Get your nasty asses off the floor right now. It's time to work and I want every swinging dick man outside on the double and standing at attention in five seconds from now,' as the cell quickly emptied.

As we marched across the courtyard to the back of the mess hall, Old Big Mouth pulled me aside. 'Come with me, Yank. You're working in the kitchen until I say otherwise,' he said, winking at a cook standing in the doorway eating some fried monkey's elbow with barbecue sauce. When I walked into the kitchen, the prison cooks were getting the food prepared for the lunch session to come. 'Here's the new man you asked for,' shouted the sergeant, pushing me in front of the main cook whose apron was covered with yesterday's gravy.

'Yeah,' said the cook, 'He'll do fine. Hey Magic Pussy, put this new man to work at once.' He picked his nose as he shouted these last words.

When Magic Pussy turned and saw that it was me with my handsome self, he dropped the salad bowl he had been holding and it fell to the floor and broke all to hell. 'You must excuse a poor girl like me, honey, I'm so crazy about you I'll drop anything, including my drawers for you, you little sweetie,' he said, trying to feel my cock as I jumped away from him.

'Now look, I don't play that shit, buster, I like pussy and nothing but pussy, you understand?' I shouted in anger.

'Why, that's what I'm trying to give you, fool. My sweet pussy,' said Magic, laughing and then showing me where I was to work. Magic Pussy was from Morocco and spoke five languages. He was tall, very well built, and good looking, but he was a fag. Outside of that he was OK. After a while we became the best of friends, for all he really needed was a true and caring friend, which he found in both Farouk and I. Of course he would play around and tease us for a joke, but he would never try and talk us into sex. Magic had a heart of gold. If you needed something and he could help, it was yours. Every prisoner, and I mean every prisoner, always had a good word for Magic Pussy. That bastard could out-charm a snake.

'You had better watch yourself. I heard that Baby Louie and Big Louie are going to try to get you this time tomorrow,' Magic Pussy whispered to me as I was peeling some potatoes for tonight's soup.

'You're working in the paper press section all next week,' the main cook butted in to explain.

'How do you know that for sure?' I asked.

'Because Sergeant Socco is hot on me and he told me last night when we were together making love,' he confided as Magic Pussy nodded in agreement.

'So you think they've got something planned for me, huh?' I asked again.

'Well, you figure it out They've already planned a party to celebrate your passing and I'm baking the cake. How's that for reliable information?' said Main Cook with a laugh.

'Don't fuck around, man, this is serious,' I shouted nervously at them.

'I am serious as cancer, fool,' said Main Cook. 'Look over there in my oven and see for yourself.' And he motioned me to have a look. I slowly walked over to the oven and opened the doors and saw a cake with writing on it. It read 'We Broke The Yank's Ass Good. Congratulations To Baby Louie.' I slammed the oven doors shut and thanked Main Cook and Magic for warning me about the planned attack tomorrow. Well, if they're gonna try to kill me I might as well go down fighting, I thought to myself as I checked my brown pants just in case.

When lunchtime came around and the prisoners passed through the food line, I kept an eye out for the two Louies and their boys. I was standing behind the counter serving food when a guy from Canada passed by with a sneer on his face 'Hey muthafucka, put some more goddamn food on my plate. What do you think this is, the Salvation Army?' he shouted at another prisoner next to me serving food. 'You fuckin' Arabs are all fuckin' alike,' he moaned as he moved to where I was serving cabbage. 'I hope you don't give me no shit, nigger boy, and just serve the fuckin' cabbage without no song and dance,' he spat, not realizing that I wasn't a local African.

He was a white Canadian with long blond hair reaching to his tits and he looked like a Jesus freak left over from a Grateful Dead concert. 'Hey, I said, 'what the fuck's wrong with your silly ass, cunt? You want this motherfucking spoon over your rock head, white boy?' And I brandished a huge steel spoon which was dripping hot cabbage grease from the delicious sauce. He looked at me in amazement and then started to smile.

'Hey man, I'm sorry about that. I thought you was one of these stupid African bastards that live here,' he said, and asked for another portion of cabbage, without the sauce. 'My name is Johnny Fuckerfaster and I'm from Quebec, Canada, and –' Before he could finish speaking a mess sergeant called out, 'Move along, bitch, don't try to sell no pussy in my food line.'

'I'll see you tomorrow or sometime in the exercise yard,' he said as he went on down the line, turning and blowing a kiss at me.

'Trying to fuck my girlfriend Johnny Fuckerfaster, are you? I'm not good enough for you, huh?' whispered Magic Pussy in my ear, laughing as he poured some more cabbage into the greasy, lumpy sauce in front of me. Before I could reply he kicked me on the shin and nodded to his right. I quickly looked over and saw the two Louies coming through the food line looking mean as a son of a bitch. Big Louie standing at seven feet tall and his shit of a brother Baby Louie standing at only six feet nine inches tall.

As they moved through the food line like twin elephants, all the other inmates moved out of their way and stood back without a murmur until they passed.

They made all of the prisoners serving behind the food counter very nervous, so naturally they filled the two Louies' and their boy's plates sky-high with food. As they moved through the line Baby Louie kept his good eye on me to see if I would panic. But I kept my cool. Shit, there was nowhere to run anyway. If push comes to shove I can always throw the hot cabbage on their ugly heads. When the two Louies came to me to be served, they stopped and gazed into my eyes as I looked up at them. I calmly served them without saying a word, but my big steel spoon rattled on the edge of the pan as Big Louie spoke with a deep, frightening, gravel voice. 'That portion you just gave me ain't big enough to wipe my ass on,' he said, as a scared hush came over the hall.

'Well I hope you don't try to wipe your ass in here,' I said, laughing weakly.

'Yeah,' shouted Baby Louie, 'My brother is a big growing boy, he needs more food than that.' And he stared at me with his good, bloodshot eye.

I said, 'Yeah, I can tell he's a big boy by his big mouth,' as I slammed my spoon into a pot of hot cabbage, making it splash all up in Baby Louie's face and bad eye. As Baby Louie wiped the cabbage from his eye, Big Louie leaned over the counter and whispered in my face, friendly-like, 'You're not a bad nigger boy, and it's gonna be a shame killing your ass, but Yank, when you come to work in my section, you'll be one dead-ass black piece of shit.' And he cracked his knuckles, making the sound of an exploding hand grenade.

'Thanks fat head, now get your shit people through the line please, as we have other people to feed,' I shouted back in his face, knowing he couldn't hit me in the cafeteria with all the guards looking. After serving the meal, I went to sit with Magic Pussy and Main Cook. 'Hey Magic, who's that Canadian guy named Johnny?' I asked.

'Oh you want to fuck him, yes?' he said laughing.

'No, if I was gonna fuck with anybody it would be you with your sweet ass,' I said jokingly.

'And what about me?' asked Main Cook, who everybody called Sweet Mama. (From this moment on I called him Sweet Mama as he was such a Tutti Frutti.)

Oh, I'll let you suck my dick if you beg me,' I said, laughing and almost falling out of my chair into a tub of apple sauce. (It is hard to imagine these big bruisers each standing over six feet tall, who looked as if they would kill you at a glance, wearing make-up and carrying on like such tutti frutti's. A real mind blowing experience.)

'Johnny is a darling. A real sweetheart of a girl,' Magic went on to explain. 'She gets along great with most of us girls, but she can be a real bitch when it comes to business.'

'What kind of business is he into, sweetie?' I asked as my curiosity got the best of me.

'Everybody else calls her Mr Fix-it, but all of us girls call her Miss Fix-it,' Magic said laughing. 'No, seriously, he can get you anything you want for the right price, and I mean anything, honey buns.'

'Anything?' I asked. 'Anything within reason,' Magic answered as he straightened up his padded bra.

'Yeah, and that bitch will make you pay the full price too, and check this honey, she gives no free pussy away either,' Sweet Mama said, almost crying with laughter.

'Look, I'm gonna finish doing my work on my side of the kitchen and take a walk in the exercise yard. Is that OK Sweet Mama?' I asked, getting up out of my chair.

'Yeah, but don't be long and don't do anything that will get me in trouble with Sergeant Socco,' Sweet Mama answered. As I was walking away, I heard Sweet Mama tell Magic about Sergeant Socco. 'Honey child, when Socco gets angry, he becomes too sexy for me to handle.'

'Well you better hope he loses his temper tonight and goes fuckin' crazy,' Magic said, falling all over Sweet Mama as they laughed together.

When I walked into the exercise yard hoping to meet Johnny Fuckerfaster, I heard a shout of 'Hey Cook, over here.' I looked around and saw Johnny with all his little boyfriends around him. 'Come on over man, I ain't gonna bite you,' he shouted.

'That ain't what I heard,' I said, laughing.

'All you American girls are the same, smart ass bitches. Come over here and meet my main squeeze that brings me to my knees. Robbie, meet Chellah. He's my heart and soul man,' Johnny shouted out loud so that the other girls around us could hear that Chellah belonged to him.

'Sit on down so that we can talk, man. Move over girls, and let a real man sit, with his big dick self,' Johnny said to me, motioning the other guys around us to move back and make room for me to sit. 'Now you tell old Fuckerfaster what you want, what's your desire. And don't tell me you don't want something, because I know you're lying by the way your lip quivers, bitch,' Johnny said as he rubbed his boyfriend's cock through his pants.

'Have you ever thought about escaping from here?' I asked seriously.

'I'll answer you that question and then let's change the subject and talk about asses, OK?' said Johnny. 'To answer your question, yes I have thought about it, but not lately. When I first came here, four years ago, that was all I thought about. But after three unsuccessful attempts to make it, with all the beatings and the pain that I suffered, I finally wised up one day and thought fuck it man. Now I am happy with my strong, handsome Chellah and I don't want to leave here. Now does that answer your question in full?' Johnny asked, still hanging over Chellah and grabbing for another handful of balls and cock.

'OK, I can dig where you're coming from, and I don't want to start no shit, but man there's a lot of other fishes in the sea out there,' I said, trying not to put my foot in it.

'I get your meaning, but you didn't get mine, old cock. I love Chellah more than I love myself or life itself,' he answered, trying to make his point in all seriousness.

'Say no more, mate, I think I understand you loud and clear,' I remarked as Johnny gave Chellah a big, wet, juicy kiss on the jaw.

'Don't get me wrong, Robbie, I will still help you in any way I can. Just ask and it's yours. I won't charge you for anything, because I like American girls like you. You're such a wild bitch when you don't have your way, aren't you ducky?' And he laughed and motioned for Chellah to take my hand in friendship. This was a very strange situation for me. I mean, all through the Vietnam campaign, the States, and West Africa, I'd never met one self-confessed, completely open fag in my life. Now I find myself surrounded by fags of all shapes, sizes and colors. But I will tell you this, in all honesty, I have never found more honest and true friendships anywhere than my compatriots here in prison.

'We got to get back to work now. We'll catch you tomorrow or whenever you can make it back here again. You know where to find us,' Johnny said as he and Chellah got up to leave, holding each other's asses with a tight grip.

'Later. I got to get back myself, girls,' I waved and started back to my work in the kitchen. When I got back to the kitchen, and was tying on my rubber work apron, Magic came up behind me and spoke. 'Did you see him? Did he want to suck your dick?' he asked, hoping for a juicy story of sex and filth to tell the other girls.

'Don't be filthy, cunt, where is Sweet Mama?' I asked, slapping Magic Pussy hard on the ass.

'She's in there with Sergeant Socco,' Magic said, pointing to the dark storage room. 'Come around to the side and I'll show you something funny, if you promise not to get a hard on, you dirty old man,' he whispered to me.

I went around to the side of the store room with Magic and looked through a knothole in the wall. In the dark room, I saw one hairy ass going up and one hairy ass going down over near some sacks stacked in the corner. I don't know if they were making love or not, with all that groaning and moaning, but if they weren't, then I guess they were going to shit on the potato sacks.

Magic and I went back into the kitchen and continued our work so as not to cause any unnecessary problems. After serving the night meal and cleaning the kitchen, Sweet Mama came over to warn me once again about the planned attack tomorrow on my life. 'Thanks once again, Sweet Mama, you're a real pal. A pain in the ass sometimes, but a real pal,' I said as I went to join the other prisoners in line waiting to be taken back to our cells.

The next morning while eating in the cafeteria, I noticed that something was different but I couldn't put my finger on it. 'Something's going down today, so watch your step, huh?' whispered Farouk as he sat to eat next to me.

'Yeah, I'm cool. Sit down and tell me what you been up to,' I said, not taking any notice of what was going on behind me.

Suddenly I felt a pain in my back. Damn, that hurt, I thought to myself. 'Hey Robbie, you've been stabbed,' Farouk shouted.

'What? Where man?' I shouted in fright.

'In your back, fool. Can't you feel the knife stuck in your back?' Farouk asked as he rolled his eyeballs around in his head dizzily.

'No. Pull it out of me, carefully. For God's sake don't twist the blade,' I said as I bit down on the table top to cushion the terrible pain shooting through my poor little body. Pulling the thing out of my back while two other prisoners helped hold my mouth down to the table, Farouk showed me a knife big enough to kill the average gorilla. 'Was that big bastard really stuck in my back?' I asked, still not realizing how close I was to death, and might still be for all I knew.

'I shit you not. That came out of your back,' Farouk assured me, with his hand shaking.

I took the knife quickly in my hands and looked around to see who might have thrown the knife in the mess hall. Everybody looked down into their plates or up to the ceiling like nothing had happened. Them dirty little bastards I thought, as my shirt was now soaking red. Still looking around, I ran my eyes over to Baby Louie's table. He was sitting two tables behind me, shaking his head around and around, singing some silly tune from the old country. I turned back to my table and asked Farouk if he thought that Baby Louie had thrown it.

'Does a bear shit in the woods?' Farouk answered, helping himself to my big bowl of mashed potatoes.

'Right. I'm gonna fix that bastard Baby Louie once and for all,' I shouted, not realizing how big that son of a bitch was. 'Well, I'm going now. You coming?' I asked Farouk.

'Do I have to?' he said with a weak smile, getting up slowly from the table. I got up bravely and turned around, looking straight over at Baby Louie who was waving me over with both hands and giving me a wink with his good eye. Farouk quickly pulled out his Girl Scout knife and shouted 'Let's go before I lose my nerve.'

We jumped up on the table behind us as most of the other prisoners ran for cover, grabbing their bowls of mashed potatoes. Begging me to keep on coming, Baby Louie started to move closer to us with his boys following behind. 'Get 'em,' he shouted as we ran at them and began to brawl all over the floor. I must admit, in all honesty, they gave Farouk and I a damn good beating as it was eight to one odds. I could hear the screams of Farouk calling for help and mercy as Big Louie, Baby Louie and the boys were stomping his ass ferociously. they finished me off quickly as I passed out from losing so much blood after taking more knife wounds in my chest, arms, and legs. I came around in my room. Well I call it my room as I am beginning to make a habit of ending up in hospital. Anyway, when I came to, I was bandaged from head to toe again. 'Hello Robbie. We gotta stop meeting this way or people will start to talk,' Nurse Maha said.

'Yeah, you're right about that. How's my friend Farouk? Is he doing all right?' I asked, hoping she'd say yes.

'Don't worry so much. He's a strong man. Just cuts all over his body and a few broken bones, that's all,' Nurse Maha said laughing, as she could only see my eyes between the slits of my bandages. 'When they brought you boys in here, they said you had been in an accident. That you two had got run over by a tractor in the potato fields. Is that right?' Nurse Maha asked gently resting her hand near my crotch in sympathy.

'Yeah, we got hit by a tractor. We got hit by a tractor named Baby Louie and boys,' I said as the bulge started to respond to her hand.

'I know what you mean. He's run over a lot of people lately, and they usually end up here,' she said, laughing and tightening her grip.

Poor Farouk and I were in hospital for four months recovering from the tractor, and it was great. Sweet Mama, Magic Pussy and Johnny Fuckerfaster from Canada came to see us most nights, bringing some kind of goodies stolen from the kitchen each time they visited us. You know, like steaks, chicken, wild rabbit, camel balls fried in garlic, candy, and sometimes even a drink of vodka distilled from the leftover rotten potatoes. Where did they get this, you may ask? Good question. They stole it all from the officers' mess, kitchen or storeroom. You remember Sergeant Socco's storeroom, huh? I mean that Johnny could get anything. He's truly Mr Fixit.

One night as Johnny, Magic Pussy and Sweet Mama sat with Farouk and I in our hospital room, Johnny asked me, 'What are you gonna do about Big Louie and Baby Louie?'

'I'm gonna take care of them first and then I'm making plans to bust out of here. I can't live this kind of life. It just doesn't suit my poor little old body. You can dig that can't you?' I answered.

'You know best, but like I said before, I will give you anything you need at any time. All you have to do is ask, old cock,' Johnny said, patting my thigh in friendship. (Well, I hope it's friendship.)

'Yeah, you know you can depend on us two girls also, but just don't ask for no pussy,' Magic Pussy said, laughing out loud with Sweet Mama.

'Now honey, we just ain't got nowhere to go. We got so used to this kind of life, shit, we wouldn't know what to do if we did get out of this hell-hole,' Sweet Mama said seriously and rather sadly. Seeing that everybody was going on a downer from the way I talked, I quickly changed the subject.

'Yeah you guys are right,' I said, 'Hell, why be crazy and leave all these men and all the food and drink you want for free? At least you don't have to pay no rent.'

'That's right, honey, there's plenty of big swinging dicks here. Lord knows them dicks are here and you couldn't eat 'em all in a hundred years, honey,' Magic said, and everybody joined him with a big falling-on-the-floor laugh. As the guys went on talking and telling jokes, I began to think about how I could escape before I died in this place.

About three days later, Sergeant Socco came into my room. 'Get up,' he said, 'Your resting days are over, Yank. We're gonna put your ass back to work, boy. Now don't you just love it?'

'Yeah, you know best, sergeant. Being a professional soldier and all,' I answered, very Uncle Tom-ish, trying to soften him up a little.

'I think you've learned your lesson after all, boy. Goddamn, I think we're gonna get along just great from now on,' the sergeant said, giving me a wink with his lying eyes. He took me back to the kitchen to work at my old job, peeling potatoes. 'Sweet Mama, here's your boy back. Now put this poor bastard to work before Baby Louie kills his ass and we gotta find another potato peeler,' Sergeant Socco said, smacking Mama on the ass and walking out the door smelling his hand, muttering 'Ooh la la, ooh la la, that bitch has sure got fire'.

'Glad to have you back home, Robbie,' Sweet Mama said, grabbing my hands.

'It's good to be back. Hey, where's Magic Pussy?' I asked as I looked around the kitchen.

'He's getting a present from the two of us for you,' remarked Sweet Mama, blushing with modesty.

Working in the kitchen like a dog in the heat, I stopped to wipe the sweat from my head when Magic walked up behind me and put his hands over my eyes to surprise me. 'Guess who, sweetie,' he said in a high pitched voice that reminded me of Tiny Tim.

'Elizabeth Taylor,' I said.

'Oh you beastly man, it's me, Magic Pussy. Anyway, I've got sweeter ass than that bitch and I'm thirty years younger, fool. Didn't your Mama tell you that the blacker the meat the sweeter it is?' And he threw his arms around me in joy.

'I know you're happy to see me, but for fuck's sake put me

down,' I pleaded, struggling to get my feet on the floor.

'Girl, you sure look good. Don't he look good, Sweet Mama?' Magic asked, rolling his eyes in the direction of my crotch.

'Magic Pussy, Sweet Mama, you girls are the greatest,' I said jokingly.

'Why hell, I know that,' Magic said, handing me my present with tears in her eyes.

'Now stop crying, Magic,' I said as I opened my gift wrapped in a red and blue paper with little yellow ducks on it.

'I just can't help crying when I'm so happy,' Magic whispered to Sweet Mama, who was also about to cry.

I opened the package after struggling with eight layers of wrapping, and found something that looked like an aeroplane wing, but with no fuselage. 'You like it? Isn't it nice? I asked Johnny to get it for you,' Magic said.

'It's lovely, I mean truly lovely and very sweet of you two to get it for me, but what the hell is it?' I asked, still looking curiously at the gift.

'You big dumb shit. It's a boomerang. You throw it and it comes back to you, or you can use it the way the aborigines do for hunting,' Magic said, explaining more about where it came from and what was the best way to use it, as he once knew how himself as a boy.

'That's all good and fine,' I said, 'But how am I gonna hunt behind these prison walls?'

'You don't, fool. You only hunt Baby Louie's big head. Got it? You catch him at the right time, and bingo upside his fucking head. Hit him once with this boomerang and it will mess up his brain for life. I know, we use this back home on big niggers like Baby Louie,' Magic said, laughing but still being as serious as cancer.

I gave it a try for a month, I practiced behind the arms factory late in the evening when all the prisoners and guards were gone. Farouk and one of Johnny's friends always acted as lookouts. After a while, I became such an expert at throwing the boomerang that Magic and Farouk began to call me 'The Boomerang Kid'. I could stand fifty yards away from Farouk and knock a potato off his head without touching him. Sometimes I would practice knocking birds out of the sky for our late night dinner for the guys back in the cell. After becoming so good with my new-found weapon, I began to keep and eye on Big Louie and Baby Louie.

One day as I was serving food in the chow line, Johnny came through and gave me a message to meet him in the exercise yard after the lunch session was over. After serving the session, I went out into the yard as Sergeant Socco always popped by for a quickie with Sweet Mama in the storeroom.

'Over here, darling,' Johnny called out, and went back to kissing Chellah. 'I know a good place where you can get Baby Louie without getting caught,' Johnny said.

'Where? Just tell me, man,' I said.

'I don't know if you know this or not, but baby Louie and his boys lift weights behind the old laundry building with his brother Big Bad Louie,' Johnny said. 'If you got on top of the canning factory when it starts to get dark, you could throw your boomerang and really split one of them bastard's heads, huh?'

'Right baby, I heard that loud and clear. I'll catch one if them bastards just right and disappear into the dark blue yonder,' I said, beaming with joy.

'Didn't I tell you old Johnny will take care of you? Now get out of here you sissy while I make love to my man,' Johnny said, taking my hand in an Arab handshake that seemed to to take an hour to finish. (You know what I mean – the handshake the black cats use in your local ghetto.)

I quickly ran back to the kitchen and started peeling carrots to look busy when Sergeant Socco came out of the storeroom with Sweet Mama. Socco tried to pretend that he was talking all this time about ordering more food for the camp to Sweet Mama. 'Yeah, I think a couple more bags of potatoes each week should make the mean happier,' he said to Sweet Mama.

'Anything you say, Sergeant Socco,' Mama answered, giving Magic and I a wink. As the sergeant was on his way out, he stopped and had a small conversation with me. 'Things have been nice and peaceful lately, and I want to keep it that way, Yank. You do understand that, don't you?' he asked, squeezing my arm very hard until it went numb.

'Yes, I understand,' I answered , rubbing my arm to make the numbness go away.

When he left, Sweet Mama explained he was only fooling. 'Good thing he was only fooling. If I thought that he meant it, I would have kicked his ass,' I said, beating my arm on a table to try to get the blood circulating again.

'What did Johnny have to say?' Magic Pussy asked. I explained everything to him and asked if he would like to come and watch me break a head that needed to be broke.

'Would I? Is the Pope a catholic? Is cock sucking fun?' said Magic Pussy.

I ran off to find Farouk and finally caught up with him washing the officers' cars in the motor pool section. Walking by a car that Farouk was wiping off, I made like I had dropped something on the ground and was looking for it. Down on my knees, I whispered to Farouk and asked did he want to come along tonight, and explained just what was going down.

'Would I wanta come? Is pig pussy pork?' he said, laughing out loud.

'Cool it, you cunt. You wanna get me in trouble carrying on like a silly girl?' I whispered and started back to the kitchen.

'Hey you, Yank, what are you doing so far from the kitchen?' a guard asked, walking over to me.

'I don't know, captain sir, I was daydreaming about home as I was walking and suddenly found myself in the motor pool. I guess I was dreaming about my old car at home,' I said in my most innocent way.

'You're the Yank with nine lives, aren't you? You're such a lying bastard a priest wouldn't believe you,' said the guard, motioning me to move off quickly. Boy, that was close, I thought to myself. After the late meal and all the dishes were washed, the mess sergeant ordered everybody to stay behind because he wanted to take inventory of all the stock in the kitchen and supply room. What luck I thought, now I've got the perfect alibi for where I've been.

'We can go now, Sweet Mama is going to cover for us while we're gone,' Magic Pussy said, shaking with excitement.

'You better stay here,' I said. 'I don't want to get you into any trouble on my account. The sergeant is gonna surely miss you, he knows how many cooks are on duty at all times, and he definitely knows your ass.'

'I'm not gonna miss this action, fool. And besides the mess sergeant is hot on Sweet Mama and is always chasing her. Tonight Sweet Mama's gonna let him catch her so we can do our little thing,' Magic Pussy said, snapping his fingers and dancing a little jig.

Running and zig-zagging through the little pathways between the buildings, we came upon Farouk standing in the dark near the canning factory. 'What's that black thing moving near the canning factory?' asked Magic.

'That's Farouk, stupid,' I answered.

'That nigger sure is black, ain't he. After serving him all these years and feeding him my best cooked pork chops, I never knew that nigger was that black. Did you?' asked Magic Pussy with a snicker, covering his mouth so as not to be heard.

'Forget how black that muthafucka is and help me across this fence,' I whispered.

After getting over the fence, Farouk saw us and came up to us. 'You're late, bitch. Where have you guys been dammit? I've been waiting for forty-five minutes.'

'I didn't have a thing to wear,' Magic said with a giggle.

'Now you two behave yourselves, man, this is some serious business,' I said. 'Now come on and help me get up on this roof before somebody comes along and fucks everything up.'

As Farouk was helping me to get up on top of the roof of the canning factory, Magic Pussy came over to give a helping hand. 'Don't feel my ass so much when you're giving me a boost up,' I said. Magic shouted back up at me, 'Fuck you, bitch. You girls are no fun at all.' When Magic said that in her girly voice, that damn Farouk began to laugh out loud and let my legs go, making me lose my grip on the edge of the roof. I came crashing to the ground, landing on my back and ass while Magic doubled up with laughter watching us rolling on the ground like schoolkids.

'If you girls don't hurry, Big Louie and his boys will be done gone in for the night, sweeties,' Magic said, reminding us that this was supposed to be a serious mission.

'OK, lets stop the bullshit and get on with what we started,' I whispered. After helping each other onto the roof, Magic motioned me over to the side where Baby Louie could be seen lifting weights under the courtyard lights.

There were eight of them down there, the two Louies and six of their goons. 'When are you going to throw it, Robbie?' asked Farouk, getting a little impatient.

'I don't know, but they'll do something wrong in a minute. We'll just have to wait patiently,' I answered.

'Isn't this exciting? I feel like I'm in the movies, don't you?' said Magic as she took out a candy bar.

'Give me a piece Magic,' said Farouk with his big mouth wide open and saliva running down the side of his jaws.

'No. I can't do that. I've only got five more bars left, fool,' answered Magic as he stuffed down a whole bar at once.

Looking down into the courtyard, I could see and hear an argument brewing between Big Louie and Baby Louie over who was the strongest. as this went on, the weights got heavier and heavier and heavier. This was gonna be a humdinger of a match, with me being the winner.

'Now. Get 'em lifting the heavy weights over their heads,' Magic begged.

'Why I do declare. Magic, you've got a mean streak in you girl,' I said as I unwrapped old Betsy Lou. (That's what I called my boomerang, Little Old Betsy Lou. I even wrote a song in the poetic style of a man I most admired, William Shakespeare. The name of the song was 'My Old Betsy Lou Is Gonna Fuck With You'.)

Anyway, I waited until the weights got really heavy and they were straining to lift them. 'Which one do you want to pay back first?' Farouk asked.

'I think that flash bastard Baby Louie. Yeah, he'll do for now,' I answered as it became Baby Louie's turn to life the bar. As he was straining to lift the weight once more with the veins in his head and arms about to pop out of his body, I finally let go my boomerang. Betsy Lou floated through the night sky like a bat out of hell. It made sweet music like an old English hummingbird chasing its mate. It went sweeping out over the air currents and came back down so sweetly upside that dumb fucker's head, making a hole the size of my fist. You should have seen it. It was a most holy sight, when them weights came down in slow motion upon his goddamned fat head, making Baby Louie yell out in a most unusual way as his ass settled into the ground like a newly planted tree.

Since I happen to be a trained doctor, remember, I can honestly and truly say that boy was totally fucked up.

'Where did this damn thing come from? I'll kill the son of a bitch for hurting my little brother!' shouted Big Louie as he lifted the weights off his little brother's bashed head. We made our way back to the kitchen quickly and congratulated ourselves on what a fine job we'd done reshaping poor little Baby Louie's head. 'Hurry and put on the whites before someone comes,' I shouted to Magic and Farouk, who were still talking about the skill I had in throwing Old Betsy Lou.

The prison siren went off and some of the prisoners ran to see what was going on. The mess sergeant, hearing the siren, ran out of the storeroom with Sweet Mama. 'What's going on out here?' he demanded.

'You tell us. We've been here all the time working our fingers to the bone,' Magic Pussy said, and then asked the sergeant, 'Have you been working your fingers to the bone also?'

'I don't know about his finger bone but I can testify under oath that this boy has been using another bone all night,' Sweet Mama bragged as the mess sergeant blushed.

'Alright, break this shit up. Where's that fuckin' Yank?' shouted Sergeant Socco, with Big Louie and Commandant Rashid following close behind.

'Here sir,' I said as I stepped forward from behind the serving counter. 'Where were you about half an hour ago? And don't you lie to me or I'll have your lying eyes burned out with a hot poker,' the commandant threatened me with his piercing bloodshot eyes.

'I was here sir, all night doing my work, which I love so well. If you don't believe me, ask the mess sergeant. He was with me every minute making me work hard,' I answered.

'Is that right? And you'd better not lie to me,' the commandant shouted angrily at the mess sergeant, who was now starting to shake in his old worn out boots.

'Yes sir, I was with him every second. He's the hardest working son of a bitch I ever saw in my whole life, why just look at the callouses on that boy's hands,' answered the mess sergeant.

'I know it was him. I know it was him. That son of a bitch lies like he breathes. He killed my little baby brother. My poor little baby brother. The Lord knows that no-good nigger murderer done it,' Big Louie shouted, falling to his knees, crying like a baby, just to impress the commandant. I could see that silly fucker peeping through his fingers when he was supposed to be crying and showing the grief for his lost brother.

Acting surprised, I said, 'Killed? You mean poor Baby Louie's dead? What a shame, he was such a nice guy when you really got to know him. He was so young to go, too. Wasn't he a really nice fellow, everybody?' Of course everybody that stood around us had to nod yes, as the poor no-good son of a bitch had just kicked the bucket, right?

'Yank if I thought just a little bit that you were involved in the killing, your black ass would be mincemeat, you got that, fuckhead?' the commandant shouted as he motioned everybody to leave.

'Yank, I'm going to watch you more closely from now on. I'm gonna be on you like steam on piss,' Sergeant Socco whispered to me as he followed the commandant out of the mess hall.

'You made me lie for you, you bastard Yank. I don't know what you did and I don't care, but just don't get me involved in nothing, or I'll have your ass first, you got that fuck head?' the mess sergeant shouted at me, shaking like a leaf on a tree as he took out a bottle of gin from under the sink that was nearby.

'Nothing ever happens around here,' Magic said, laughing and pouring me a drink from the newly opened bottle of gin.

'That was close. I ain't never been that frightened before. I almost lost my job, my life, and my army pension all because of some stupid Yank,' the mess sergeant kept repeating to himself.

'Stop fuckin' moanin'. He lied for you too. He could have said you were in the storeroom with me, and you know what Sergeant Socco would have done, don't you?' Sweet Mama said to the mess sergeant. The sergeant quickly turned and gave me a nod of thanks for saving his ass.

'Cheer up everybody. Let's have another drink before we all turn in for bed,' Magic suggested, pouring out some more of the mess sergeant's drinks.

On joining the line of inmates to be marched back to our cells, Farouk whispered to me as he passed that he had some good news for me, and would tell me later.

'There's been too much noise coming from these cells lately. I want it quiet tonight, dammit,' the sergeant of the guard shouted as he locked the cell doors. When the guard went back to his room and switched on his radio, that was playing 'Does Your Chewing Gum Lose It's Flavor On The Bed Post At Night', I asked Farouk what the good news was.

'Ssssh. Not so loud, stupid. I don't want the whole prison to hear ya,' he said, pulling me closer to him by my shirt collar.

'Sorry man, what's up?' I whispered.

'Tomorrow they are taking a bunch of volunteer prisoners to help sort out the lambs from the sheep herd, and there's to be a jail break,' Farouk whispered.

'How do you know this?' I asked.

'A friend of mine that was working in the commandant's office told me,' he answered.

'Why would anyone want to volunteer to sort out lambs in this heat? Volunteering, won't that look a little suspect?' I asked.

'No man, that's the beauty of it all. The reason many men volunteer is they get to fuck some of the sheep,' Farouk said laughing.

'Look man, I thought you were serious. Don't give me no

more bullshit. I want out of here man, so please don't play games about escaping,' I said to Farouk and was just about to pull away from his grip.

'I'm not joking man, I'm serious as cancer. Some of these Arabs here in prison used to be nomads and got to liking fucking sheep, man. It's simple, fool, everybody don't get a lot of pussy in Arab countries like you guys do in the west.'

'You mean to tell me that's why they volunteer?' I asked, a bit shocked that there were so many fags running about in this hell-hole.

'Well not everybody that goes on the trip fucks the sheep. Some guys just want to see what it looks like on the other side of the wall. Most of these old timers have forgotten what the outside world looks like. Now you can understand that, can't you, old cock? Anyway, the main thing is, do you want to make a break tomorrow at noon? Fessona, that's my friend, is a good organizer and I'm going myself because I trust him. I told him to count on one more coming. How about it, Robbie?' Farouk asked, hoping I would say yes.

'Does a bear shit in the woods?' I said.

'Only if he has to,' Farouk said, shaking my hand in joy and almost breaking it.

'You'd better get all the sleep you can get for the big day tomorrow,' he said, motioning me to keep everything to myself.

'Thanks for keeping me in mind, buddy,' I whispered, as the midget quietly moved over to unbutton Farouk's pants while I turned away to get some sleep.

The next morning as the sun came up, a guard came to our cell and shouted, 'OK dipshits, listen up. There's a truck downstairs waiting for volunteers to take to the sheep fields. All who's planning on going fall in line in front of me, on the double.'

'Get up quickly,' Farouk shouted to me, pushing me to make sure I was awake. When I got downstairs to the truck, it was packed out with some randy fuckers and had standing room only. Some of these guys were sitting on each others heads just to go. 'Anybody want these boots? If you do, raise your hand,' said a guard as just about everybody put up their hands.

'Put up your hand, Robbie,' Farouk whispered to me.

'Why? It's so damn hot.' I said, too innocent to know why.

'Take the damn boots, I'll explain later,' he shouted to me over all the other men who were grabbing for the boots. Moving out of the big wooden gates of the prison, I remembered that I hadn't said goodbye to Magic Pussy, Sweet Mama or Johnny Fuckerfaster. This made me sad because if I was successful in the escape, I might never see them again.

'Don't look so sad, they will understand. Look, you only found out you were coming on this trip last night, right?' Farouk said, trying to cheer me up.

'What are these boots for when it's so damn hot out here?' I asked.

'They are for putting the two hind legs of the sheep in so she can't move very much when you're fucking her,' he answered, showing me how it was done. I've heard a lot of things, but this shit beat it all.

'There they are men,' somebody yelled, and everyone pushed for the back of the truck. It was a field of about four thousand sheep, so I asked one prisoner, who was very excited, why was everyone rushing to get out of the trucks so fast?

'You don't want to get an ugly one, do you?' he said.

While most of the sheep were trying on their new boots, Farouk's friends were getting out their weapons, (not sexual) and waiting for the right time to attack the guards, who were also tucking a few hooves into their boots.

There were about fifteen guards who were fully armed, and four with only pistols who acted as the drivers. All in all, they had one jeep, a truck for the guards, a truck for the prisoners, and a small truck loaded with food and water. I almost forgot: and some extra rubber boots in case the guards wanted seconds. All the guards were in the fields, watching the men work at separating lambs or putting boots on the sheep. There's always one in every crowd – one stupid bastard was trying to fuck a ram. Meanwhile, nobody was watching the trucks except one guard, and he was sleeping as it was so damned hot. 'Just keep your cool and watch for Fessona's signal. He's hot shit at this game,' Farouk whispered while pretending to put his boots on a sexy looking lack sheep who had some wiggle in her ass when she walked.

Just as Farouk had mounted Black lady for some serious fucking, Fessona pulled a pistol from under his shirt and began to fire it like a madman, stampeding the sheep. The sheep ran wild and frantic with all that gunfire between the guards and some of Fessona's fucking fighting men. 'Get their guns. Kill 'em before they regroup,' Fessona shouted. Some of the dirty bastards that were trying to fuck the sheep ended up dead with hoof marks all over their asses.

All around me bullets were flying. 'Just keep your head down. Fessona's boys will have it under control in a minute,' Farouk shouted, firing his pistol at the same time. It was all over so quickly. Most of the guards had no bullets in their rifles. The war effort of fighting the White Army on the eastern border had left many of the Red Army soldiers and prison guards without any bullets for fighting. When the shooting started, most of the guards threw up their hands and surrendered without a fight or got stampeded by the sheep running around in their black Wellington boots. When some of the prisoners found out about the guards having no bullets, they fell to their knees and started to cry out of frustration. Just think, all these years those damn guards have been threatening to shoot us and they didn't have shit in their guns. The thought of it almost made me cry, too. 'You bastard. You knew all along that some of the guards didn't have bullets,' I shouted at Farouk as he was putting on a dead sergeant's uniform.

'No man, but I wish I had known. shit, I would have been unbearable to talk to on the way here,' he said, laughing.

'Now that the fighting is all over, how are we gonna get out of here?' I asked.

'I don't know, but you can bet Fessona has got it all planned. He's a genius, man, don't worry,' Farouk answered, motioning me to follow him over to the food truck. All the men gathered around Fessona, eating camel ball sandwiches taken from the food truck, and listened to Fessona's plan as he had done pretty good so far. His plan was to put on the dead guards' uniforms, take their trucks and pretend to be transporting war prisoners across the country to another prison camp.

'That's a fantastic plan, considering we have radios in the trucks,' I said to Farouk while changing into a dead guard's uniform.

'I told you, Robbie, I only hang with smart people. Of course that includes you too, old buddy,' Farouk remarked.

I knew things were going just a little too smooth with this plan, when all of a sudden I heard a shot fired from the other side of the trucks. 'He's in the grass, over to the right,' a prisoner shouted and hit the ground for cover. A tall lanky prisoner answered the shots with a quick burst of machine gun fire, cutting the grass and prison guard who had fired the shots to ribbons.

About the time Farouk and I got on the other side of the truck, it was too late. Fessona had been shot in the back by the prison guard who was hiding in the grass, as he was about to get into one of the trucks to use the radio. 'Move back and give him some air. I'm a doctor, let me check him out,' I shouted to the men who were standing around gawking and breathing in all the fresh air.

As I knelt down and opened Fessona's shirt to check his wounds, he drew his last breath and pulled my neck as if to try to tell me something.

'How is he?' asked a friend of his.

'I'm sorry, Fessona is dead,' I said as I closed his eyes.

'Now what are we gonna do?' I knew we should have stayed in prison.'

'How will we live?'

'Now we'll die like dogs under this sun.' These were some of the comments the men were shouting out in panic like little lost lambs. 'My friend Robbie Jones was a major in the White Revolutionary Army. I'm sure if you ask him nicely, he will led us to a final victory, or at least get our asses out of here alive,' Farouk shouted, urging support for his brilliant idea. Suddenly all the men joined him in clapping and cheering my name. 'Quiet men, quiet. I think we should let the major have a few words,' Farouk called out, and the men waited for my speech. I felt a strange urge in my thumb to assume command of the motley crew, and jumped up onto the hood of the jeep, which sank under my weight and made a huge dent. I then delivered a rabble-rousing, rip-roaring speech which would inspire the men to the utmost in order to achieve something or other.

'The first thing men, and I want to make this perfectly clear, is that I am not a major. I am a general now, and I demand the respect of a general,' I said, laughing and firing my pistol in the air like a real dip-shit.

'General Robbie, General Robbie, General Robbie,' the men chanted while firing bullets wildly in the air. After all the hoorah, hooray, ha ha, ho ho was over, I wondered how I was going to lead my little army of twenty-two men and how long we could last out in the middle of nowhere with very few bullets left. 'Let me take a walk for about five minutes and then you call the men together for a meeting,' I told Farouk.

After walking around alone for a while to clear my head, there were still some things I didn't understand. When I got back to camp the men were all sitting around in a circle waiting for me to come and make some plans. 'The first thing I would like to say men, is thanks very much for showing your confidence in me as a leader,' I said as I took some notes out of my pocket.

'The first question I want to ask you is, this whole area, is it a desert or not?'

'I see you have been talking to the prison doctor or one of the guards huh?' one of the men said.

'The guards just want you to think that all around the prison camp is desert so you won't try to escape. Why do you think they put a blindfold over your eyes and covered all the windows except one in the helicopter when they were delivering you to the prison camp for the first time?' one of the prisoners named Minkah explained.

'Yeah, I wondered why anybody would want to blindfold a prisoner when he's taken to a death hole, and one that has the reputation of never having an escaped prisoner gain his freedom,' I answered, scratching my head in bewilderment.

'Look around you,' the midget named little Loo-Loo explained while still holding a rather nice looking sheep and Farouk's thigh at the same time. (That damn midget sure loved to party.) 'All you see is green fields, yes? So to answer your question, the landscape is about half and half for about a three hundred mile radius. Most of the green areas are man-made for farming or growing trees for our paper industry in the south. It's an American idea first tried in Israel.'

'Thanks for explaining so intelligently to the general, Loo-Loo, I never knew you had it in you,' said a huge man from the back who looked like Jerry Garcia of the Grateful Dead. 'You in the back, what's your name?' I said.

'My name is Kala,' he answered with a voice as deep as the Grand Canyon.

'What did you do before the war here, Kala?'

'I was captain in the palace guard of the old president,' he answered.

'Well, you're a captain in my little army now, and I want you to carry yourself as one, OK?' I said, motioning him to sit down and be at ease.

'Men, this is my plan, so listen carefully. I won't repeat it again as we don't have the time,' I said, and went on to explain. 'We can't outrun the guards from the prison. They have helicopters, planes, and the whole of the Red Army to track us down and kill us slowly like dogs. Second, we don't have enough men or bullets to make a good fight of it. So if we can't fight and we can't run, what the hell can we do? I'll tell you, we can fight but not the way they think we will.'

The men cheered and fired more bullets in the air, forgetting that the bullets were in short supply already.

'First, we must make the guards think that we are gone and that we are trying to escape across the border. Second, after they begin to look for us along the borders and small towns, we'll attack the prison camp, freeing the other prisoners and holding the commandant and guards hostage for bargaining power later down the line. And the third point, and I want to make this perfectly clear, we will have a fort to protect us, food and water, guns, and a high powered radio transmitter to know when the Red Army are going to attack us.

'Are you still with me, men?' I shouted, throwing a bag of marshmallows in the air as our bullets were getting low. (Waste not, want not.)

'Yes my General, Lord knows yes, you are a genius, my General,' some of the men shouted in joy. One soldier got so excited he wanted to kiss my gun. I told him later.

'After we take the prison camp. let's kill the commandant and all the guards. Let's kill all the women and fuck all the men,' some smartass yelled from the back.

'No, no, my friends, we will need the commandant and some of the guards to bargain for our freedom, just like the general explained. Allah be praised,' Kala shouted in my defence.

'Thank you Kala,' I said, and went to explain the why's and why not's of the plan to the men. 'Are there any more questions?' I asked as no one spoke. 'OK men, this area is so flat with no place to hide, we'll just have to make a stand and fight. We'll have to pretend we're all dead when they send out a truckload of soldiers to find out what has happened to us.'

'But how can we fight so many men if we pretend we are dead?' asked the man from the back chewing on a half-eaten camel ball sandwich he had taken from a guard.

'When the soldiers move in close and see that everyone is dead, they will relax and lower their weapons. Then we will attack, killing them like dogs in our little ambush,' I told the camel ball eater. 'Let's quickly burn the trucks and spread all the guards' bodies on the ground. Then find yourselves a spot pretending to be dead and wait for my signal,' I shouted to the men as they ran to carry out my orders.

'Hey Farouk, you and Captain Kala go and tell some of the men to dig holes in the ground and hide in them.'

'Fuck off. You made Kala a captain. I ain't doing shit until I get something,' Farouk shouted, laughing.

'OK sissy, you're a captain too,' I said, motioning him to move quickly. 'Kala, tell everybody that after digging the holes in the ground to stay down in them until I give the signal to fire, OK?'

'Yes sir,' he answered and dashed away behind a huge rock where the midget was waiting for a quickie. As the men were spreading the bodies after going through all the dead soldiers' pockets and burning the trucks as I had ordered, I calmly walked over to the jeep which had a radio. 'General Robbie sir, I can't get anything on the radio about us being missing, whispered the radio operator as he tried to listen to some talking on the radio.

'Don't worry. It's still early yet,' I said, pointing to one of my men to bring over a captured prison guard.

'What time were you supposed to bring us back to camp tonight?' I asked the guard, who was shaking with fright.

'Eight o'clock, general. I swear to you I'm not lying.' And his lip quivered and he fell to his knees and begged me to spare his life.

'Take him away and keep a close eye on the other prison guards,' I ordered as some one on the radio called for the check-in password. The voice on the other end kept requesting that we acknowledge and give our password. 'What shall I do?' asked the radio operator, who was beginning to sweat and smell rather badly from all the pressure.

'Don't answer. Then they'll have to send somebody out here to check what's going on,' I answered like a true general. After our little stage-setting for the ambush was complete, Farouk and Kala reported back to me, buttoning their pants and followed by the midget Loo-Loo with a big grin on his face. 'Everything is as you wanted, sir,' Kala said as I was making sure the holes were dug just right around some of the positions I had ordered.

'OK, take out the radio from the jeep and burn it, and then take up your position in one of these holes. Lo-Loo, fuck off for a while. Find someone else and let these two do some fighting for a change,' I said. Loo-Loo offered to share my hole as Farouk and Kala saluted and disappeared into their separate holes. 'I love it when you talk dirty to me, general,' he said as I kicked him in the ass and motioned him to take a position behind a huge rock where four other big dicked boys were waiting for his services anxiously. 'Thank you again, my General,' Loo-Loo called from behind the rock with his mouth half-full with gratitude.

# 11

It had been more than three hours since the last radio call and the men were getting angry about staying in their fox holes as it was damned hot, with the afternoon sun beating down relentlessly. Just about the time when everyone was starting to complain restlessly and stirring from their cover holes, a message came over the radio. After taking down the message, the radio operator shouted to me, 'In forty seconds a plane will fly over this position, general. I just picked up the pilot's message back to headquarters.

'OK, thank you soldier. Everybody back in your damn holes. When that plane flies overhead, I don't want anybody or anything moving, and that's an order,' I shouted as everybody dashed back into their holes like frightened rats.

The plane flew over our position and made two passes before turning and making for home base. Once again the radio operator signaled to me. 'I have picked up anther message from the pilot to base command, sir. The pilot reported no movement and that the whole area was in complete destruction. He reported that in his honest opinion, everybody on the ground appeared to be dead, including the guards.'

After hearing the good news, I ordered the men out of their holes for a long overdue rest. 'That was great. Where did you learn that trick?' asked Farouk.

'Vietnam, old boy. That's where I learned everything I know and more,' I said, giving Farouk a wink and taking a long drink from my canteen as Farouk watched with envy.

'General, come quick. I think I have picked up something else here,' the radio operator yelled out.

'What is it?' I said trying to catch my breath after a short run.

'Two truckloads of soldiers are coming here to check out what has happened,' he answered. While the radio operator was going back into a sweaty shock, I could hear the camp's commandant shouting on the radio. He told his men to bring back all prisoners if any were still alive, so he could hang them in front of the other inmates as an example of what would happen to them if they attempted to escape in the future.

'Listen up, men. Back to your holes, this is the big one. Let 'em get close and wait for my signal. I repeat, wait for my signal and will have a victory over the soldier bastards,' I shouted as the men ran back to their holes.

Sure enough, ten minutes later two big transport trucks came out of a cloud of dust, heading in our direction slowly and cautiously. 'Stay down and don't shoot until you can see the whites of their eyes,' Farouk shouted. As the trucks pulled to a halt about fifty yards away from our position, half of its men got out and escorted the trucks by walking in front of them. After getting nearly on top of us and not seeing any movement but for the vultures starting to pick at the dead bodies, a captain told his men to put down their weapons, get some shovels and bury their dead comrades. I lifted the hatch that was covering my hole and saw to my surprise all the soldiers of the Red Army with shovels and stretchers, sweating in the hot baking sun as they buried their stinking, bullet ridden, dead comrades. Seeing this, I gave the almighty order. 'Kill 'em men! Kill 'em right now! Fight for freedom and victory! Freedom for the slaves!' I shouted as I let rip my Kellog's S-90 machine gun on two guards standing near a truck.

My men came out of their holes firing like maniacs. It was pure magic. Our bullets ripped into the soldiers so quickly, I don't think they could have fired more than ten times back at us before they fell. Some of the bastards were shot in their backs while running away from this good old boy fight, or shot as they tried to give themselves up peacefully. Some people just don't get any kick out of killing and will mess up all the fun, every time. This was a perfect ambush if I say so myself. Only two of my men were killed and they weren't important to the squad. My brave, fighting, sheep-fucking men pounced on the soldiers like a pack of flies on Mexican street meat. When it was all over, there were about six soldiers and their captain left alive. 'You don't fight fair, Yank,' shouted the captain while holding his right arm which was about to fall off.

'I guess you're right there, old buddy, but you'd better let me look at that arm before it gets any worse,' I said. After checking his arm, I gave him some good news and some bad news. 'What's the bad news?' he asked bravely. 'Your arm will have to come off now, and I mean this second,' I answered. 'What's the good news then?' he asked, 'You'll live. It's as simple as that,' I said, wiping a greasy machete on my sweaty shirt.

After taking the captain's right arm off from the shoulder,

which was a little more than necessary, I had a couple of men lay him in the back of a truck to rest. For saving the captain's life, he was most grateful, he wanted to pay back his debt by telling me where we could hide for a few weeks without the Red Army finding us. He had been a local farm boy and knew the area like the back of his right hand. I called the men together for a meeting after nightfall, and told them of the good news from the captain. As we sat around the campfire that night, and I had just finished explaining the plan, somebody yelled from the back with his mouth full of something that was brown and smelly, 'Yeah, but can you trust him?'

'We'll soon know when we get there, won't we, comrade?' I answered, not taking any notice of shit-mouth, and went on to explain a decent plan for survival.

'Anyway, we can't stay out in the open and we've got to hide for a while to make them look for us along the border. We were lucky today, as the soldiers we fought were untrained and old. But in the future you will be fighting front-line trained troops of the Red Army,' I said.

'You are the general. We go where you go, general. Won't we men?' shouted the faithful Kala. Once again the men gave out a loud cheer.

'There are some caves about twenty miles from here, due west. We've got to make it there tonight. Tomorrow will be too late . So let's hurry and move from this position now, before the commandant sends another plane and a fresh platoon of men to look for us,' I said, and motioned for the drivers to start the engines of the trucks.

'Move 'em out,' Farouk called to the drivers behind our truck. We travelled all through the night without running into the Red Army or any prison guards looking for us. Lucky for us there was a full moon and we could see where we were going without hitting rocks or sand hills. After reaching the foot of a hill, I stopped the truck and got out. 'What's wrong, Robbie?'

'I'm just checking to see if we got the right spot or if we gotta move on a bit,' I whispered to Farouk, not wanting the men to think I was lost or that I couldn't read the map I was holding in my hand.

'You stay here. I'm going up behind those rocks over there. I'll be back in a minute,' I ordered Farouk, and started to run up into the rocks at a strong healthy pace. After reaching the top of the rocks and watching the dawn of a new day, I looked down and saw the pass the captain had told me about. It was a well hidden pathway. It would be so easy to miss in the daytime or early morning. From the ground you would easily pass it by as the sun would shine directly in your face or the sun rays bouncing off the huge rocks would make too much of a light to look into. The only way you could see the secret pathway was by night or when flying over it. By night, if you didn't know what you were look- ing for it would be too dark anyway to see as there are no lights. So that only left the danger of somebody flying over the path through the huge rocks, and seeing everything. To hide here, we would need a lot of camouflage, which I knew about from my days in Vietnam. So I ran back and gave the men the good news. After telling everybody about it, I suddenly couldn't find the entrance now that I was on ground level again. 'You silly bastard. That's just like you. Go and ask the captured captain again to show off the entrance, fool,' Farouk shouted at me, laughing his head off. I ran to find the captain as the sun was now coming up and soon there would be patrols out looking for us. When I found the captain, I told him what had happened and he just smiled at me. 'Don't feel bad. It happens to everybody. Just always remem- ber, drive or walk to the rock that is shaped like an eagle's head and you can't be wrong. It will lead you to the cave further back into the rocks,' he explained, pointing with his good hand. 'Thanks once again, lefty,' I said as I ran off to lead my brave fighting men out of danger.

When I got back to the front of the rocks, a sentry called out in a high voice, 'There's a convoy of trucks coming this way and fast, sir.'

'Thanks soldier. I'll see that you get a medal for this. Everybody quickly follow the lead truck into the caves,' I ordered.

'Captain Kala, you take some men and cover our tracks going into the cave,' Farouk yelled.

'OK you got it,' Kala replied, running off to carry out his duties.

'Watch out for falling rocks and don't drive into the side walls,' I told the other drivers as Farouk was trying to drive through a narrow part of the passage. It took us about fifteen minutes to get everybody safely through the pass and up to the mouth of the cave, when a sentry yelled from the top of the rocks, 'They're right upon us, sir, but I don't think they've seen us yet.'

'Hell, what if they–'

'No if's, Farouk. Just let me handle this in my own way, man,' I said. I ran up the side of the rocks and joined the sentry who was on lookout. 'What's going on?' I asked.

'I don't know. They were going to pass right by here, but they suddenly stopped,' the sentry said.

'Pass me your field glasses for just a minute,' I whispered. Looking down into the Red Army truck convoy, I saw my old buddy Sergeant Killer Socco. He was beating two prisoners almost to death for changing a tire on the truck too slowly.

'What's going on out there? Have they seen us yet?' shouted Farouk impatiently.

'Just be quiet and everything will be alright,' I called back. Ten minutes later the trucks were on the move again without seeing the passage, headed for the sheep ranch we had left. I came back down to the cave entrance where Farouk had gathered the men to wait for my orders.

'OK men, I know you're very tired and want some sleep, but before anything you must clean the area and camouflage the trucks and cave entrance from the aeroplanes flying overhead. If we do that, then we know we're safe,' I yelled over groans of 'I'm too tired too work' or 'I wanna get some sleep' plus all the other bullshit too rude to print.

'Come on you lazy fuckers, this man is trying to save your stupid lives,' Kala shouted, giving me a wink. After the men had worked non-stop for three more hours, the place looked like paradise. 'Sir,' the radio operator called to me as I was shaving in an underground stream near the cave, 'I just picked up on the radio that Sergeant Socco and his men have found the bodies from last night's ambush.'

'Did Sergeant Socco report anything else?' I asked.

'No sir, but I'll keep you informed, sir,' the operator answered as he jammed his index finger up his nose to pull out today's dust and black funk.

After being in the cave for a week, the food was beginning to run low, but the men's spirits were high and they were ready for action of some sort. 'When are we gonna break out of here and free our friends back at the prison camp?' Captain Kala asked politely, 'It's not me, you understand. It's the men who want to know, sir.'

'Soon. You tell 'em I'll explain to them tonight over dinner, or after dinner, or maybe without any dinner, whichever is the case depending on the food supply,' I said, moving off to the rocks to think and finish off a leg of lamb by myself.

When the night came around, I went over to the radio operator in the cave before I joined the men. 'Are they still looking for us along the borders?' I asked. 'Yes sir, but there are still patrols moving through this area also, sir,' he replied as he glanced at my duffle bag, which smelled strongly of roast leg of lamb garnished with mint jelly.

'OK. Let me know if anything comes up while I'm talking to the men.'

'Excuse me, sir. Is that mint jelly on your duffle bag?' asked the radio operator with a smile.

'Hardly soldier. I eat the same dry rations as you do,' I answered angrily at his impertinence with lying eyes. Walking back to the men, I knew this was going to be the big one. How in the hell do I get myself into such shit all the time, I thought to myself as I walked to the middle of the circle to explain a plan which I did not have.

'I see most of you men want to fight, and some of you just want to go home, right? Well, we're gonna do both,' I yelled. The men liked that kind of pep talk and let out a loud cheer as I walked over to the fire. 'From tomorrow,' I announced, 'all you men will go into special training. You will learn how to kill with knife, how to use different types of guns, and how to make home-made bombs. After two weeks of learning to kill proficiently, we will move from here and give you a chance to use your new skills on Commandant Rashid and Sergeant Socco's men. How's that?' I asked. My brave men jumped to their feet and ran to pick me up on their shoulders, which split my pants rather badly from the back, and cheered once more. After all the cheering died down, I ordered Farouk to lead a group of men back to the sheep ranch to pick up some more lambs and goats as our food supplies were going down fast. 'Now look, asshole, don't get into any trouble on a simple job like this,' I ordered Farouk.

'Don't worry so much. I'm the one that picked you to be our leader, remember?' Farouk answered, giving me a friendly Arab handshake.

'You leave tonight and be back early tomorrow morning just to keep it safe. Oh, and keep an eye out for the Red Army truck convoys. They're still patrolling this area,' I said, and motioned him to leave quickly.

'What do you want me to do, sir?' asked Captain Kala.

'I want you to get some men and check how much ammunition and dynamite powder we have left to practice with,' I replied, offering him a drink of wine from a bottle I had found on a dead guard from the last battle.

'No thanks, sir, I'd better turn in as we've got a rough day coming up tomorrow,' Kala said.

'Yeah, see you tomorrow early,' I said, taking another drink of the wine.

The next morning, all was going well, with Farouk coming back safely and the rest of the men practising with the guns and bombs. 'I see you made the trip back safely. Did anything unusual happen out there?' I asked Farouk.

'Nothing happened out there, but I've got some news you might be interested in,' said Farouk, slapping me on the back.

'Tell it like it is, baby,' I said in a jive way.

'Well for one thing, the war's going bad for the Red Army. The whole Air Force consists of four old Mig jets from the early sixties. All their other planes have been destroyed along with most of the pilots.

'Any more good news like that?' I asked.

'There is a reward on your head, if that makes you feel important, sucker,' he added.

'How much? Don't bullshit me, man,' I said with a smile of confidence.

'It's only ten thousand dollars paid dead or alive, my little chickadee, so don't get your little drawers in a twist over it,' Farouk said, looking for the nearest coffee pot. Those cheap bastards, I thought to myself. 'Anyway,' said Farouk, 'Here's the really good news. Commandant Rashid is in the dog house with the President for letting you escape like he did. So the commandant is giving a party for some diplomats and other top officials to try to make some friends to save his red-neck self.'

'Are many people coming to the party? I mean anyone really big, like the President,' I asked, foaming at the mouth in anticipation.

'No, no, you were almost close though,' answered Farouk, playing coy.

'What?' I snapped.

'Hold on Robbie, what I mean to say is, no one really big will be coming because nobody wants to be around the commandant while the President is still angry at him and you're still running fancy free.'

'OK, well who's coming, Mr Smart Ass?'

'Only some top officers from around this area, and mostly the ones who hate the President's ass with a passion,' Farouk said, pouring himself some of my leftover wine.

'So when is this sweet little party?' I asked, as I took back my bottle from Farouk's greedy little hands.

'You won't believe this, but in two weeks time. I heard it on the radio last night as we were going to collect the lambs and goats from the ranch. Not bad for one night's work, huh?' Farouk said proudly.

'Not bad. Get some sleep now and I'll see you later tonight,' I said, pushing Farouk's hat down over his eyes.

I quickly went over to where most of the men were now learning how to use a knife on a man in the dark, and called everyone's attention to me. I explained to them about the party the commandant was having and how it was very bad manners that he didn't invite us, as we had been such good slaves and friends. This made the men real angry and obnoxious. Some of the men really thought that they should have been invited to this party to mix with the elite of the prison. For the next two weeks we trained the men from sunup to sundown, teaching them every way in the book, plus a few little extras I had picked up in Vietnam, on how to kill the enemy under every condition of war.

The two weeks of training the men to kill in combat went by very fast. The men were finally ready and were anxious for some action. The big day was tomorrow. Helicopters and long truck caravans were carrying food and drink to the commandant's party, the radio operator reported to me. 'Did they say anything else?' I asked.

'No, just that they wanted the helicopters checked and ready to fly first thing in the morning after the party,' he answered.

'It would be damn good if we could destroy the helicopters before they left the ground, wouldn't it?' I asked Kala.

'It would hurt them more than you think,' Kala said very seriously.

'What do you mean, soldier?' I asked. 'You're not fucking with me, are you?'

'No sir, I was still in the palace guards when the helicopters were ordered. There are only four in the whole country, sir. Two were destroyed early in the Revolution, and the other two that are coming to the party are all that's left. We hardly could afford to buy the four, with the economy being so bad and all. So I know the Red Army has no more to come. Not in this lifetime,' Kala remarked, scratching his ass and reaching for a flask of brandy, or at least it was brown liquid.

'Great news. So if we knock out these two helicopters, they won't have any more to send against us,' I said, and immediately called the men on a loudspeaker to gather around for a meeting.

'There are probably some big boys who are gonna be there tomorrow night, huh?' I asked Kala as we went to meet the men who were waiting for another rousing victory speech.

'I don't think the really big boys will be there. I think the President didn't want to come to the party because the commandant is in the dog house with him, but sent two of his private helicopters to deliver food and drinks because of the commandant's connections with the tribes in this part of the country,' Kala explained.

'You may be right, but the President is gonna be real angry when he finds out his two private helicopters are blown all to hell,' I said, giving Kala an Arab handshake. After all the men gathered around the rock that I was to speak from, I raised my hand in the air and called the men to order.

'Men. My brave fighting men. May Allah look down upon you and kiss you. Tomorrow night is the night I have been training you for. If you're not ready now, you'll never be ready. Don't let me down, you bastards. You will be divided into three groups. I will lead one, Captain Kala will lead one and Captain Farouk will lead the third bunch. If there are any stragglers and dipshits, Loo-Loo the midget will take care of you. The big party will be held in the officer's mess, but will end up on the outside of the prison gates in the whorehouse, fifty yards away,' I said, explaining on a map that was placed in front of the men, so that every swinging dick mutha could see. 'That whorehouse is my group's job. My men will take really good care of this position, I can personally testify to that.' With me saying that, the men all gave a big cheer and laughed. 'I know what you're thinking, boys, but we'll be too busy ducking bullets for that kind of horseplay,' I said. 'Now back to serious business. The whorehouse is where the commandant and the other top officers will be, and we will need most of them alive. You silly bastards would kill 'em all,' I said with a laugh.

'The second group, which will be led by Captain Kala, will blow up the arms factory as there's plenty of ammunition stored in the houses around the hospital and sergeants' quarters. By blowing up the arms factory, you will be diverting all the attention away from both groups. Your job is most important to our mission if we are going to succeed. Now after blowing up the factory, I want you to move quickly over to the guards' sleeping quarters, set up your machine guns and keep them busy until group three releases all the prisoners from their cells. Group three, you are responsible for releasing the inmates and then quickly rejoining group two to hold out until we arrive on the scene with the commandant's drunken officers, we hope, if all goes well. Are there any questions?'

One hand went up in the back. 'You in the back. What's your question?' I asked.

'What's gonna happen to all them pretty whores just going to waste while we are attacking?' he asked as the men fell about laughing.

'OK men. For the rest of the day just check all your supplies and equipment so as to be ready for tomorrow just like real soldiers do,' I said as I dismissed the men.

'This is exciting. I can't wait to see the commandant's face when we bust in on him,' Farouk said happily.

'You think that's gonna be funny, you just wait until Sweet Mama, Magic Pussy and Johnny see us stroll in with the commandant as our prisoner. That will really be something,' I said, searching for another bottle of stale wine.

'If we are lucky,' said Farouk, 'and I mean lucky and succeed in capturing the prison camp, what are we gonna do with it after we got it? I mean they are gonna throw everything at us but the kitchen sink. The President will make sure, personally, that his Red Army will destroy us one by one when he finds out it's you, old buddy, who's leading us.'

'Trust me. I'm the Yank with nine lives, remember? Everything will be all right, with a little luck. If, and I mean a big if, the prison camp has enough ammunition stored in the houses next to the hospital we will be looking good in any kind of fight. If not, then we would have lost anyway but at least we tried,' I said, trying to encourage Farouk to keep a civil tongue in his head.

'But the guards, at least some of them, didn't have enough bullets to fight us when we ambushed them at the sheep ranch. How do you expect to find enough ammo stored in the houses?'

'Maybe they don't have enough ammo to fight full strength for a long time, but they must have enough to fight for about three months or more, old chap,' I said, motioning him not to worry his little meat head about it.

Everybody turned in and was up early the next morning. 'Just be cool until the evening, men, and then we'll move out quickly. Oh, and check all your equipment once again just to be sure,' I told them. All that day the men sat around talking and playing cards until the sun went down, ignoring most of what I had said. 'You think it's alright to tell the men to get ready to move out now?' asked Farouk with impatience for some front-line action.

'Yeah, you give 'em the word now if it doesn't shake 'em up too much, and I'll be with you in a few minutes after I help the radio operator pack the radio in the jeep. He's a little too stupid to pack it by himself,' I said. After packing the radio and finishing off another roast leg of lamb behind some rocks by myself, I gave the command to move out. 'Hey Captain Kala, you take charge back here while I ride point,' I yelled from the middle of our little convoy before I moved up to the point. As we moved through the night, there was a full moon to light up the nearby fields and a gentle cool breeze hitting us in the face. The roads were empty as we moved through a wall of silence, with only our truck engines making a little roar. Boy, I felt just like General Montgomery going to meet Lawrence of Arabia.

'Sir, that's the prison up ahead where the lights are,' the driver assured me.

'Are you sure, soldier?'

'Yes sir, I wouldn't lie to you General Monty, I mean Robbie. They switch the red lights on so as all aircraft in the area can see them before running into the prison camp. It actually is a warning to keep away from the prison, sir. I think it's a rather marvellous idea, don't you agree sir?' (Ask any cab driver a simple question and you'll always get some smart ass answer.)

'I couldn't agree with you more, driver,' I said thinking this bastard had just taken some smart pills because yesterday this sucker couldn't speak English. 'OK slow down and let the others catch up with us,' I said looking back over my shoulder.

'It's kicking ass time now, boy, in a few minutes they're gonna get it,' Farouk said, trying to talk like a Yank.

'Yeah, but remember, you be cool and keep the men in line also, fool,' I said.

'Do we split up now, or move up a bit closer, sir?' Kala asked.

'We'll move up some more before we split up,' I said, motioning the convoy to move on cautiously. After moving up about two miles more, I stopped the jeep and took out my map rather aggressively from my back pocket just to show the men I meant business. Kala and Farouk got out of their trucks and ran over to me.

'OK, everybody set their watched to mine and we'll attack at three o'clock on the dot. Right?'

'What if –'

'No if's,' I butted in before Kala could finish talking. 'We must follow our plan to the T. At three o'clock we must all attack and I want no one to wait a second longer. This is most important if we are to be victorious tonight. You have your orders, so move out and good luck,' I said, shaking Farouk and Kala's hands.

'If I don't make it, it's been a pleasure knowing you, Robbie,' Farouk said before he ran back to his men.

'If you don't make it, don't bother to come back and tell me about it personally,' I shouted back at him.

I could hear the music playing in the prison camp as we split into three groups and went our own ways to carry out the plans. There weren't many guards on the walls, as most of them were attending the party, which made it easier to move around in the dark. 'Let's settle down behind the sand hills on the other side of the house, as we are a bit early,' I said softly to my men. The house was all in darkness because all the whores were entertaining the officers at the party over at the main prison camp. The shouts and the music were getting louder all the time. We waited and waited.

Eventually the big gates of the prison opened and out came the whores and officers. Whoever was driving was swerving all over the place like a crazy man, with the girls laughing in the back happily. After seeing the girls get out of the trucks with the officers and going into the house, my men became more alert instantly. 'Just keep cool,' I shouted to them as they were fighting over my field glasses to look into the windows. As they went into the house, all the lights went on with the music blasting in the night. They were playing some old Arabic tunes on the record player and giving out Tarzan yells as they chased each other throughout the house. To me the music sounded like shit, but I guess to them it was sweet music for loving or whatever.

My men were having fun too, by seeing the little side shows that were happening outside the house. One bitch came out of the house and gave a captain a blow job while he leaned against the wall, and another officer was fucking over in a sand hole. Everything was going according to plan, when suddenly another couple came out of the house and saw that the immediate area was crowded and decided to find somewhere else more private. Sure enough, they started to walk in our direction, holding hands and kissing passionately. 'Everybody, just keep your heads down and don't do any foolish,' I whispered as the couple continued to walk in our direction, feeling each other all over. They got right up on us and then stopped. My heart was almost in my mouth. I felt sure they were going to keep walking our way. When they stopped, the officer reached his hand underneath the girl's dress and began to feel her pussy, while she started to kiss and bite his neck hungrily. They were now standing about two yards away from where we were lying on the sand. After kissing and feeling her hairy snatch, and she stroking his cock vigorously, the guy suggested lying down on the sand to get it on good and proper. Oh shit, what's gonna happen now with all these horny men watching, I thought. Dropping to the sand, putting his cock into her, and moving like a true stud, he was just about to shoot his rocks when he looked into the eyes of about eight guys. You should have seen his face when I shouted, 'Get him, get him and the girl quick. Don't let 'em escape.' My men jumped on the girl and officer like stink on shit. Their training had come in mighty handy, for they slit their throats in a matter of seconds, and pulled the bodies over into our holes and out of sight.

'That was close,' one of the men said, wiping his knife on his shirt sleeve. Suddenly another officer yelled from the back door of the house, 'Hey Ali, Ali Musia, I know you're out there somewhere. Give me back my girl and go find your own.'

'Who's that bastard?' someone asked.

'Just be cool like before and everything will work out fine,' I whispered to the men as this officer asked another couple who were making love near the house, if they had seen Ali and his girl. The couple pointed over in our direction and he came running over fast like he was trying to surprise his friend Ali. When he got up close, he began to tiptoe very quietly to where we were waiting for his ass. 'Ali. Is that you?' he whispered as someone had made a movement. 'Yes, it's me. Come a little bit closer and see the hairy pussy on this young lady,' one of the men whispered back. when he came still closer after taking out his cock ready for action, WHAMMO. We all jumped on his ass like grease on fat. He had so many knife holes in him that in a matter of seconds he looked like a Swiss cheese.

About half an hour later, the other couples went back into the house and closed the door, thinking Ali and his friends would come back in after getting their rocks off. Anyway, the time had rolled around to five minutes before three o'clock. Most of the lights were switched off in the house and music was playing low so as not to disturb the guys getting their piece of ass upstairs. (I could be wrong, but that's my opinion. Anyway, it was time to go in and see, right?) 'OK. This is the big one. No more whores and fighting old men,' I said to my men as we closed in on the house. 'You four. Take the front of the house, and we'll take the back. I want everybody to put on your arm bands now, so we won't end up shooting each other in there,' I ordered. 'When we get in the house, my bunch will take upstairs, and you four take the down-stairs. We'll attack in two minutes from now. Good luck and shoot straight,' I said as I waited for the big hand on my watch to touch the twelve. This was it. My plan would be put to the test at last, I thought to myself, waiting for the explosion from the factory. I didn't have to wait long. As we burst through the back door, the explosion went off with such a bang that it blew out most of the windows of the house. As we ran through the house, there were screams of fright from the whores and shouts of 'We're being attacked!' from the soldiers lying on the beds and floors, all half drunk by now.

Glass and machine gun fire filled the downstairs rooms as well as the kitchen. 'Upstairs. Get upstairs before they come out of their rooms. Quickly,' I yelled. One of my men ran up the stairs but was met with a bullet fired by a colonel. I quickly let him have it with my machine gun. I knew I shouldn't have done that, but I panicked and just thought about getting out alive. I pulled myself together and ordered the men to follow me upstairs. when I got to the top, another officer jumped out of a room firing a pistol at me and hitting the hall light. I fell to the floor and put some rounds into his body. The bullets ripped into his chest and out again into the wall. Suddenly there were shouts of 'We surrender!' from one of the rooms. The downstairs was all quiet of shooting. 'Is everybody downstairs all right?' I shouted.

'Yes sir, we got 'em good. They're just like little babies, General Robbie,' one of my men yelled back upstairs.

'You two men. Check the rooms on the left and I'll get this room on the right,' I said to the men, motioning them to be care-ful. As I slowly opened the door on the right and looked in, guess what I found. It was Commandant Rashid standing behind a frightened whore, trying to hide in his underwear. 'Don't shoot. Please don't kill me. If it's money you want, look in my pants pocket. You can have it all and I've got some downstairs in a safe,' the commandant begged. 'Well, well, well, look what's popped up here. Why it's my old pal, Commandant Rashid,' I said as I stepped into the room and into the light. Old Rashid looked at me like he was seeing a ghost.

'Take him downstairs with the others and get on the radio and tell the guards in the prison to surrender on the commandant's orders,' I said, looking out the window and seeing a cloud of smoke and flame fill the sky around the prison camp.

'Sir, general, Sergeant Socco says he won't surrender until the commandant personally orders him to and not until.'

'Ah, you have failed, Yank. I knew Sergeant Socco wouldn't fall for your little stupid plan. The Red Army will be here and will destroy you soon enough,' he said sarcastically. I didn't say anything . I just slowly pulled my gun from its holster and pressed it up against the head of the commandant very gently. Feeling the barrel against his temple, the commandant slowly reached for the microphone and spoke into it. 'Sergeant Socco, you fool, surrender at once. That's an order. this maniac has a gun at my head. I repeat, surrender at once. This is your commandant speaking.' About ten minutes later the big prison gates opened and out drove Farouk in one of our jeeps, waving, and moving towards the house.

'Take our captives out to the trucks, drive them to the prison carefully, and lock 'em up until I get there,' I ordered my men, and thanked them for the good work they had done. 'Hey baby, we got lucky for once,' Farouk shouted, pitching me a bottle of whisky.

'Yeah, this time,' I said, giving him a hug.

'I hope I didn't do something stupid, but I only blew up the two helicopters that were in the prison courtyard. Was that all right?' he said, smiling from ear to ear.

'That's my boy. I clean forgot about them as I was so busy planning other things,' I said.

'Guess who's waiting to see you in the back courtyard. Sweet Mama, Magic Pussy and Johnny,' Farouk shouted. 'They couldn't believe it when I told them it was you who was leading us.'

'Come on. Let's not keep the sissies waiting much longer,' I said, picking up my bottle to leave for the prison.

When Farouk and I drove through the prison gates, the whole prison's inmates were out on the main courtyard to greet us with Sweet Mama, Magic Pussy and Johnny there leading them in a rousing song of freedom, or Swanee River, take your pick. 'You old son of a bitch, you old bastard, you. Honey, we thought we'd never see you again,' Magic Pussy shouted, throwing his arms around my shoulder, crying his eyes out with joy and the mascara running down his cheeks.

'I knew you sissies missed me, so I had to come back to say goodbye to you queens,' I said, hugging all three of my dear friends at the same time. 'Let me get to the office and organize this mess before we start to bullshit, huh? You guys know that when we get to talking you'll go on for hours telling me bout the big dicks that got away, OK fellows?' I said, moving off quickly before they could start talking again.

'Ooowee, that general shit has really gone to his head, baby. we ain't good enough for him now,' Sweet Mama called out to me while laughing with Magic Pussy and Johnny.

'Sir, all the prison guards are locked up in the cells. Is there anything else that needs to be done?' Captain Kala asked.

'Yeah. Call all the prison inmates together for me to talk to in about ten minutes time,' I ordered as I walked over to the main office. After setting up the radio and making sure my best man was operating it, I went back outside to speak to the men of my force and to the newly released inmates. While waiting for the men to assemble, I asked Sweet Mama and Johnny what had happened to Big Louie. Johnny said, 'Oh, I thought you had heard. he's dead. Dead as loose asshole muscles. A bunch of the inmates, seventy to be exact, caught 'em in the shower and had a knife cushion party. Everyone had a knife except Big Louie. Yours truly supplied the knives and I didn't even make a profit. Other than that, it's been a bit quiet around here. Anything else you want to know?'

'No, I guess that brings me up to date. Johnny, hold on a bit while I speak to all the men,' I said, mounting the hood of a jeep.

'Men, you are free men today. But this new freedom you have must be fought for. This time tomorrow the President and the main headquarters of the Red Army will have heard about this revolt here at the prison. And when that happens–' but before I could finish speaking a hand pulled on my coat and handed me a message. After reading the message, I continued to speak. 'Men, they've already found out about our little party. Lucky for us, they don't have any more aeroplanes to bomb this place. But you can bet they'll be here in two days with everything they've got. They're gonna make it really hot for you guys behind these walls when they do arrive, so if you can't take the heat get out of the kitchen now,' I said, trying to make the men angry and putting them in a fighting mood again. 'But have no fear, because I am here,' I said, pulling my pistol out from under my belt. We'll fight the bastards from sunup to sundown. We'll kick their big asses until our kneecaps fall off. We'll fight 'em on the east wall, we'll fight 'em on the west wall, we'll fight 'em–' Just then Johnny pulled at my pant leg and whispered, 'General, stop the shit and get on with the speech. You're over acting, bitch.'

'I think you're right, thanks,' I answered. 'Where was I, men… oh yes, men, my brave fighting men, we can win this fight if we only stick together. From tomorrow morning we'll set up barricades, teach you to shoot, to make bombs, and to cut a son of a bitch in the dark,' I shouted. The men cheered and clapped wildly at my stirring speech.

'Don't worry, just trust me. I want everybody to get some sleep now because we got a lot to do tomorrow. Break it up and get some sleep now,' I ordered, jumping down from the jeep hood as the men began to break up and leave to find a place to sleep. I went to talk to Sweet Mama, Johnny and Magic. 'Fellows, you don't mind if I turn in for the night do you?' I asked, yawning.

'Naw, you get some sleep and we'll see you tomorrow morning, sissy. That speech you made must have tired you out, it did me, ' Johnny said with a grin, pushing Magic and Sweet Mama away.

'That son of a bitch really takes that general shit seriously, don't he?' Magic whispered to Sweet Mama loud enough for me to hear, and then blew me a kiss goodnight.

The next morning everybody awakened to the sound of a crop-spraying aeroplane flying over the prison rooftops. 'Run for cover. Attack. Run for cover,' a peg-legged prisoner yelled out as he hopped for cover. All the inmates ran around the courtyard in a panic, with some tripping over the holes made by peg-leg. I jumped up and fired two shots in the air to get the inmates' attention.

'Stop running like fighting chickens with their heads cut off. That plane has no guns. It's only spying on us for the President's troops,' I shouted out, feeling very brave. The plane made one more low sweep, fired some machine gun rounds just to make me a liar, and turned for home. 'Sergeant,' I yelled. 'Who, me?' a small inmate said, looking around. 'Yeah you, you with the funny walk. You're now a sergeant. Call the men to order in the courtyard while I go and check on the radio reports,' I ordered.

'Yes sir. Thank you general for making me a sergeant,' he said, grinning from ear to ear and hopping off like Long John Silver at full speed. When I came back from the radio room, all the men were lined up in the courtyard, waiting for me to speak to them. 'Oh no, not another fucking speech. All this mother-fucking general seems to be doing is running from the radio room and back to the courtyard to make another fucking speech,' I overheard a scruffy inmate say to another while scratching his ass.

'Men, my original attack forces are well trained in the art of killing. They will now train you to be killing machines also. My two officers are Captain Kala and Captain Farouk. They will be in charge of all your training. Any questions you have, feel free to ask them and they will do their best to help you. The rest of the task force will be your instructors, so learn fast, learn it right, and learn it once. This training may just save your life,' I said continuing to explain.

'Everything will have to be learned fast, because tomorrow the Red Army is sure to be here. Without further talking, get to it,' I ordered.

'Mr Fancy Pants General, what do you want us to do while you he-men fight the war?' Sweet Mama asked while laughing with Magic Pussy.

'I just want you girls to boil some hot piss so we can throw it down from the walls onto the soldiers if they get past our first line of defence,' I said, laughing and falling to the ground on my knees, holding my stomach from laughing so much.

'Robbie, you're such a bitch,' Magic Pussy said.

'Seriously, fool, what do you want us to do?' Sweet Mama asked.

'OK girls, I want you to take some men with you to the building shed and bring all the tar you can find over to the kitchen and melt it down into big boiling pot,' I said.

'Shit. I knew my cooking was bad, but not so bad that I've got to mix some tar with it. What's the hot tar for?' Sweet Mama asked curiously.

'The same thing I wanted your hot piss for, fool,' I answered. 'Get going. Move your little asses quickly so I can come by later to check how you're doing,' I ordered.

'Toodly doo, goodbye to you, you big hunk of a general. Us girls are going now and get you your hot tar, honey,' Magic Pussy said as she and Sweet Mama skipped off towards the kitchen holding hands.

The whole day long the men were putting up barricades and training to kill the enemy. The only time that nothing of a killing nature was going on was when we stopped to feed the prison guards locked in our old cells.

'Sir, the prison commandant asked if he could have a few words with you,' Captain Kala announced.

'Yeah, take me to him,' I directed. As the commandant saw me walking along the corridor, I straightened up my shoulders and walked like a Canadian lumberjack. 'How's the food, gentlemen, is it to your liking? I'm doing he best I can to make you comfortable,' I said, smiling all over myself.

'You're going to pay with your life, Yank. You're not a bad fellow. You've got brains enough to know you can't win this foolish fight, so why don't you give up to me and my men and I'll spare your life. Is it a deal?' the commandant asked with a warm sincere smile.

'You must be losing your mind from having been locked up in this cell for so long, Commandant Rashid. Maybe you need another bowl of lumpy potato soup to clear your head. Guard, get the commandant some potato soup quickly. He seems to be going crazy,' I said as I left the cellblock calmly whistling 'Swanee River'. No, I tell a lie, it was 'Yankee Doodle Dandy'.

'May your mother suffer from giant piles in her ass, Yank, you mother fucker,' the commandant swore at me.

'Don't call me mother fucker unless you see my shoes under your mother's bed,' I yelled back as I closed the door. As I was leaving the cell block, and going down the stairs, Sweet Mama was coming up dressed in a silk dress and high heels. 'Where are you going Sweet Mama, looking so good with your bad self?' I asked.

'Robbie, please let me see Sergeant Socco. He's my lover and I miss him. I haven't seen him in so long it hurts. Please Robbie? Please let me talk to him for a few minutes,' he begged.

'Yeah, take your time, Sweet Mama. You know if I got it it's yours, right?' I said, running out the door to check the progress of the training and the barricades.

'Hey Farouk. Let's go and check all the positions and barricades in the camp,' I suggested. As we walked around the camp inspecting the various positions, I would stop and talk with some of the men and make little jokes with them. I must admit I was right proud of the men and how they were very disciplined under my command.

'I think they'll give a good account of themselves when the time comes to fight, don't you?' Farouk asked me as we walked up to the kitchen back door.

'Yeah, you and Kala have done a great job. I couldn't have asked for more from any man or army within the short space of time we have,' I remarked, and thanked Farouk at the same time. Walking into the kitchen and not seeing anyone, I called out, 'Hey Magic, Hey Sweet Mama. Anybody here?'

'Back over here. Just keep walking straight and you can't miss us girls,' Magic shouted. Walking down a small corridor to the point of Magic's voice, I could smell burnt tar in the air. 'Hey baby, you guys really are working hard, huh?' I said joking.

'Yeah, you bastard, your making us work harder than a nigger who stole the preacher's bull,' Magic pussy chided.

'Will it be ready in time for tomorrow?' I asked.

'Easily. When they come tomorrow, this hot tar will be ready for their asses,' Magic said, looking away.

'Where's Sweet Mama? Didn't she help you guys?' I asked, as Magic seemed to be looking for something.

'Oh, sure. Sweet Mama just left to see somebody a few minutes ago. Just a few seconds before you walked into be exact,' Magic Pussy said, lying his ass off.

'Where did he go?' I asked.

'I don't know. I'm not his daddy, you know,' he answered.

'Look, I'm your friend, remember? Just tell me the truth and everything will be cool. I don't care who's seeing Sweet Mama, as long as the tar is ready for tomorrow,' I explained.

'He's gone to see Sergeant Socco again. He was feeling very bad and down, so I told him to take off and I would finish off here. He's my best friend, Robbie, what can I say?' Magic said while putting more wood on the fire.

'It's all right with me. He's my friend also. After you guys finish up here, go get some rest for tomorrow. See you, Magic, tomorrow early OK?' I said before I went out the door.

# 12

It was a full moon and the whole courtyard was lit up while most of the men slept out in the open as the night was very hot and sticky. The whole place was in silence. All but the footsteps of the guards walking on the wooden ramps on the walls. Lying down in my blanket on the ground, and picking the sand from between my toes, Farouk whispered nervously, 'Do you really think they will come tomorrow Robbie?'

'Yeah, they gotta attack before we get organized. El Presidente never misses a trick when it comes to war and making people suffer. But don't worry. You just get some sleep for now, old chap,' I whispered so as not to disturb the other men or Loo-Loo the midget who was moving from guard to guard on the the walls giving his lip service.

Lying on my back and looking up at the stars, thinking about good old America, and how nice it would be to be back home, I was almost ready to close my poor tired eyes. Suddenly there were gunshots followed by loud shouts of attack. 'Escape attempt. The commandant's escaping.' Just as a guard called out the warning a bullet caught him in the back.

'Don't let 'em escape man. Block off the entrance to the main cell block,' I shouted, jumping up at the same time and firing my pistol into the cell block entrance. Luckily, Commandant Rashid's band of cuthroats never got past the entrance and were still trapped inside like rats.

'What's going on? I was sleeping with one of the whores and heard all kinds of noise out here. Will you tell me what's happening, sir?' Kala whispered to me as I was reloading.

'I thought you hated all whores, you bastard,' I reminded him.

'I used to, but not anymore,' Kala said smiling from ear to ear.

'Enough about your love life, captain, get some men and follow me,' I ordered. I ran through the big main doors of the cell block, firing my machine gun everywhere to make my cover. 'Give me some cover. I got the men you ordered,' Kala shouted.

'Go,' I yelled as I sprayed the whole hallway and walls with my machine gun fire as Kala and his men rushed through.

'You guys OK?' I whispered.

'Yeah, what's our next move, sir?' Kala asked.

'Just be cool and let me handle everything,' I said, then I shouted down the hallway, 'It's a shame you're gonna die in a cell block you once guarded, commandant. Even if your Red Army does kill us all, you won't be around to see us hanged, old boy. Just think. No more whisky and women, nothing. What do you say about giving yourself up. It's foolish to continue fighting in this manner, old cock.'

'We're not coming out, you black bastard. We can hold you off until our army rescues us tomorrow, Yankee dog. You bit off more than you bargained for, messing with a well trained Red Army officer, sucker,' the commandant yelled back, laughing at me.

'Sergeant Socco,' I called, 'Hey fat ass Socco, I know you can hear me. You don't want to die do you? You're just always gonna be a sergeant, but the commandant might get a promotion for his little deed if he lives. Now you'd better give up before I get angry,' I joked.

'Stick it, Yank. We've got you by the balls and you know it, sucker,' Sergeant Socco shouted back.

'Mr commandant, you and Sergeant Socco are too smart for a little old country boy like me. I admit you have me by the balls and I'm beaten. But because you have beaten me so bad and shamed me in front of my men, I'm gonna admit defeat.' Just then Kala and his men looked at me strangely thinking I was going mad in the head. 'Don't worry,' I whispered to Kala. 'Send a man to get me some kerosene. I'm gonna burn the bastards out,' I chuckled religiously.

'If you admit defeat, why don't you give up to me and I will spare your life. You have my word as an officer and a gentleman,' Commandant Rashid called out.

'Naw, I just feel so bad about letting you make a fool of me in front of my men, do you know what I'm gonna do to punish myself?' I said. There was a long silence as they were afraid to speak. 'What's the matter? Cat got your tongue? Listen up and I'm gonna tell you what I'm gonna do, Rashid. I'm gonna count to ten, and if you're not out by then, it's roast Arab and nigger's ass on the menu tonight. Burnt to a crisp, just like a good Texas steak,' I said laughing while my men poured kerosene all over the floor and walls and then sprayed a little bit of Grecian Formula 3 through the cell windows for good measure. The whole cell block smelled of kerosene with a pinch of eastern herbs from the kitchen by now.

'I'm counting now, commandant. Don't let your mouth spring a trap on your ass,' I shouted, and began the count. 'Ten, nine, eight, seven, six, five, I'm half way, sucker, don't be a fool if your nasty momma didn't raise one – four, three…'

'You don't scare us Yank, like you did the other stupid Arabs you've known. I know when to call a hand and when not to,' Rashid called out.

'Two, one. Goodbye Sergeant Socco and Commandant Rashid,' I shouted as Captain Kala threw a torch into the hallway, causing a huge explosion of flame that could match an oil well fire. Suddenly, most of the soldiers in their cells came out firing their guns and shouting hysterically, fools that they were. The flames went higher and higher as my men fired into the flames, hitting the burning soldiers and killing them as they staggered about.

'We surrender. Don't shoot. Please don't shoot. We're coming out with no weapons,' someone shouted. 'Come on out. If anyone tries any funny stuff, we'll shoot to kill,' Captain Kala shouted back. When the soldiers ran through the flames with their hands up, I noticed Sweet Mama coming out with them in her half-burned little silk dress and smouldering high heels. Then I understood the escape attempt. I felt really betrayed, as he had been a friend and I couldn't help him because all my men had seen him run out of the flames with the guards whom the men hated with a passion.

'What are you doing here with these losers, Sweet Mama?' I asked.

'I'm so sorry. I just couldn't help myself. Sergeant Socco is my life and I love him. What more can I say?' Sweet Mama said, looking down at the floor trying to avoid my eyes.

'Put them back in another cell block and this time double the guards,' I said walking over to the commandant.

'Sir, does that mean locking up Sweet Mama too?' asked Captain Kala.

'Yeah, but wait a minute. I want to have a quick word with the dumb commandant and Sergeant Socco,' I said. 'Rashid and Socco, you have tricked my best friend into helping you to escape. You shouldn't have done that, because I am going to make you pay dearly for that trick on him. Socco, you took advantage of Sweet Mama's love for you and caused him to betray me and the many friends he had. You dirty son of a bitch, you will pay for that,' I yelled into his face and motioned Captain Kala to remove the three of them along with the rest of the guards. Shit, what am I gonna tell Magic Pussy now, I thought to myself as I went back downstairs to the courtyard. As I entered the courtyard, the men cheered wildly, but I was in no mood for cheering now, as my best friend had just betrayed me. 'Break it up. Everybody back to your beds. The party's over. In a few hours, the Red Army will be knocking at the gates in front of you,' I announced.

The men stood and kept on cheering until Captain Kala fired a shot into the air and told the men that I was in a bad mood and felt ill. 'I hope you didn't mind me doing that, sir,' he said as the men made their way back to their beds and fighting positions.

'Naw, that's OK. I'll see you in the morning,' I said, feeling rather sad. As I lay in my bed, my mind stayed on poor old Sweet Mama. But I knew I had to get some sleep as it was pretty late already, and so I pulled out a bottle of whisky from under my pillow and downed it religiously. After gulping the whisky so fast, I fell off to sleep in seconds.

The next morning I woke up about ten o'clock to a bright sun shining into my gorgeous bloodshot eyes. Magic Pussy pulled my top blanket off my head. 'Wake up, you drunken bastard. You should be leading the charge, fool,' he said, laughing at me because my eyes looked like a set of mad dog's balls.

'I knew I could depend on you to wake me up. Is there anybody outside the walls yet?' I asked,

'Naw it's the same as it ever was. I'll be back in a minute. I'm going to make you some eggs and coffee OK?' Magic shouted as he ran away to the kitchen, not knowing Sweet Mama had been arrested for betraying me and the men. I got up and was about to wash my face when a man acting as lookout shouted, 'Sir, jeeps and trucks coming this way, and fast.'

'How many can you see?' I shouted back.

'I don't know. They're making so much dust on the move that I'll have to wait until they get a little closer, sir,' he yelled.

'OK, sound the alarm now and keep a sharp eye on them,' I ordered, forgetting about washing.

'Shall we move a few cannons up on the walls now, sir?' Captain Kala asked.

'Yeah, and if you see Captain Farouk, tell him I want to see him right away.'

The alarm went off and the men ran over to the walls and ladders like ants getting ready for the first big assault to take place. 'Sir, I can see the President's personal colors flying on one of the cars coming,' the lookout shouted down to me.

'Do you see anything else?' I asked.

'I think you'd better come up here and see for yourself, sir,' he advised. When I climbed up to the top and looked through my field glasses from the tower, I could see all around the prison camp for a radius of three miles. The President had come in style and force. Big field guns, small cannons, rocket launchers, and dressed as sharp as a country preacher in a shiny blue uniform covered with medals he had awarded himself. (A graduate of the same military school as Idi Amin of Uganda. They both majored in uniform design.) He must have had about two thousand fully armed men, dressed in cheaper versions of the same garish uniforms. They had surrounded the whole prison camp, blocking off all escape roads and pathways leading to or from the camp.

I knew that this was going to be a fight to the last man, but somehow I felt we could win without eight hundred men because we were fighting for freedom and we knew that God was on our side. Anyway, it is good to be positive, I thought to myself, after awakening from a short session of self-hypnosis.

After setting up camp and placing his guns in just the right strategic positions, the President sent a message by camel rider that he wanted to meet me on neutral ground to talk this little matter over before our slaughter. I went out the gate and over to a spot on my right about two hundred yards away from the prison camp under a date tree for our little meeting. The President stepped out of his car in his dazzling blue, two sizes too small, ass pinching, ball crushing uniform and walked over to me majestically. 'It seems like you are trying to make me kill you, Yank. I don't want to because you really are just a small fry, but you leave me no other alternative, nigger,' he said with a smile on his face, although really wanting to beat the shit out of me.

'Stop the bullshit. Did you come to surrender to me or not?' I shouted, spitting on his right boot top.

'You son of a bitch. I ought to shoot your black ass right now,' the President shouted angrily, and then quickly regained his composure with a smile on his face. 'Now look, you know you can't possibly win this fight. These men are my best rangers, trained in America, and we also outnumber you two to one as far as men go. So why don't you be sensible and give up like a good fellow and I will spare your life in the bargain. Is it a deal? Don't refuse because I won't make the offer again,' the President said, smiling and slapping his right boot with a whip made of human hair and skin.

'If I give up, what about my men behind the prison walls?' I asked.

'That's not your concern, old boy. We will let you live and see that you get to America safe and sound, my dear boy,' the President remarked, feeling sure that I would say yes to the deal.

'You have made a living off human suffering for the last time. I'm gonna put an end to you once and for good, old boy. So my answer to your question is eat shit, old boy,' I said laughing and looking at the expression on the President's face when I said no deal.

'I've never hated a bastard as much as I've hated you. I'm going to personally see that you hang with a mouthful of shit the next time we meet, Yank, and like they say in America, you can bet your sweet black ass on that, sucker,' the President shouted in rage, foaming at the mouth.

'Are you pissed off, Mr President?' I asked politely and all forgiving.

'You're damn right I'm pissed off,' he replied.

'Well it's better to be pissed off than to be pissed on, don't you think old cock?' I yelled to him as I walked off back to the prison camp.

'Smart assed nigger. I hate his ass with a passion,' I heard the President say to one of his men.

When I got back to the camp, Captain Kala, Farouk and Johnny Fuckerfaster ran over to me to ask what the President wanted. When I told them, they all fell about laughing. I guess when the men saw us laughing, their worries went away for the time being. 'Hey Kala, take over command here while I go get a cup of coffee in the kitchen, and call me if anything happens out there in the Red Army camp,' I said as I went off with Johnny and Magic Pussy.

While sitting down at a table having coffee and an anchovy sandwich, Magic asked me what was happening to Sweet Mama. 'I don't know. I'll let the men decide,' I answered.

'Let him be, Magic, he must be worried about saving all of us now, man. You'll be lucky if you get out of this alive yourself,' Johnny said to Magic in deadly seriousness.

'Yeah, I guess this wasn't the right time to bring it up. would you like a bit of roll to go with your coffee, Robbie? I just made them this morning,' Magic asked, trying to change the subject. Before I could ask for another anchovy sandwich instead of the roll, a field gun shell smashed into a building near us. 'Oh shit, they're starting the war now in the middle of my coffee break. What nerve.' I joked. 'See you later guys, I've got to go to work now. Keep your heads down and pray,' I said as I ran out into the courtyard. 'Everybody off the walls and into your fox holes. Leave only one brave man up there as lookout,' I yelled. The men ran down and jumped into the holes while shells landed all over the prison compound. For half an hour the shells kept on falling and burning most of the buildings. We can't take much of this shit, I thought to myself. Suddenly the shelling stopped. I guess they thought they had shown us enough of their firepower.

'Robbie, I mean general, they're coming at us on foot and full steam ahead,' Farouk shouted.

'Back to the walls, man, load the cannons and don't fire until I give the order,' I called. The men took their positions and waited for my orders to fire as the Red Army soldiers charged at us in their elegant blue uniforms which were now getting dusty on the legs. Lucky for us, they only made a charge at the front gate. I guess they were testing our firepower and how effective we were.

'Let 'em get real close before you fire, men, and remember, don't shoot till you see the whites of their eyes,' I ordered. Upon seeing the Red Army soldiers' eyes only about fifty yards away from our walls, I gave the almighty command to fire. Our bullets and cannon fire ripped into the bodies of the poor suckers with such force that it was like a Georgia duck shoot. The men of the Red Army fought hard and began to climb our walls with Ferguson F-69 folding ladders, the same type the CIA sold to the Egyptians to fight the six-day war with Israel. (Military experts agree that the sale shortened the war by several weeks.)

'Get the hot tar. Pour the boiling tar on their asses. Hurry men,' I called out. Screams of pain and agony came from the poor bastards trying to get over our walls. In most cases, the oil and tar was so hot that when it touched their bodies the flesh fell off their bones like tender barbecue. After this torture and ferocious ass kicking, a Red Army officer called out 'Retreat!' to his suffering men. It looked like a thousand Little Black Sambos running across the desert.

As the Red Army ran away with their tales between their legs, the men gave out a big cheer. 'We've done it. We beat 'em, didn't we. I just can't believe it,' Farouk shouted with joy.

'Yeah, but they'll be back harder the next time,' I answered.

'You really think so? Look how many we killed,' Farouk said, pointing.

'I know, but they will be back, so check out how many men we lost while I check on our other positions,' I ordered Farouk. Coming down from the wall, I saw Johnny standing over a body, crying uncontrollably. 'What's wrong, Johnny?' I asked. Johnny pointed to the ground where his lover was lying dead. 'I'm very sorry about him Johnny. I'll get some of the men to bury him and you can visit his grave later. But right now, I think you'd better come with me before you upset yourself more,' I said, putting my arm around Johnny and leading him away.

'Hey you, get some men to bury this man and report to me after you finish,' I ordered a guy who was resting on the ground looking at his swollen kneecap. I took Johnny to the kitchen and told Magic Pussy to stay with him while I went back to organize the men on the walls. 'Just leave the poor dear with me. I'll take good care of him, Robbie,' Magic said, wiping the tears from Johnny's eyes with her apron.

Just as I went back into the courtyard, rocket fire and shells from the big field guns of the Red Army ripped into the buildings around me, knocking everything flat as pancakes, and you know how flat that is. The men began to fall off the walls like flies, no, I tell a lie. Like brave fighting men. 'Everybody off the walls. everybody out of the buildings. For God's sake run and hide,' I shouted. 'Captain Kala, try to spread the word while I go to the other side of the camp to check damage,' I called out over the shells that were landing like raindrops.

After four hours of this shelling, we came out of our holes. A lot of my men were walking around senseless and in a state of shock. Seeing Farouk crawling out from an overturned jeep, I shouted 'Farouk, go get the whores and doctors out of their cells and bring them over to me on the double. Oh, bring two nurses also'.

Farouk came back to me ten minutes later and told me they had refused to come and were gonna stay in the cells. 'You mean you came back without them after seeing all these men in a state of shock and dying?' I asked, running off to their cell block. I ran in the door and pulled my pistol. 'All right sons of bitches, are you coming out of the cells or do I have to shoot you where you sit? Come out of those cells and let the doors hit you where the good Lord split you,' I said in a Shakespearian poetic way.

'He won't shoot. He's just bluffing,' a captain called out from an adjoining cell. I turned and shot him right between the eyes. As everyone watched him fall, I asked the same question again, 'Now are you coming, gentlemen and ladies of pleasure?' The two doctors and the whores quickly jumped to their feet, greeting me with big shit-eating smiles to signify 'Yes sir, boss nigger.'

'I saw that. You shot an unarmed officer, you rotten bastard. I wish I could get my hands on you, you sick killer,' the commandant yelled at me.

'Old man, you'd better be quiet. I haven't forgotten what you did to my friend, Sweet Mama, remember?' I snapped as I left the cell.

'How did you get them to come and help?' I couldn't make them budge no matter how much I pleaded,' Farouk said in surprise.

'I just went and asked them very nicely and appealed to their humanity that's all, just kindness,' I answered. 'Now you go with them and set up a hospital. Oh, and put a couple of guards in the hospital in case their kindness wears off,' I said, giving a small chuckle.

The night slowly rolled around and the shells had stopped falling for about two hours. As the men sat around our fires eating anchovy sandwiches, the Red Army men were probably doing the same thing around their campfires, only eating roast lamb with mint jelly. 'We took a bad beating tonight. We won't be able to take another one tomorrow this bad, sir,' Captain Kala advised me.

'Yeah I know, but don't tell the men that. Let me think of how to even the score first, huh?' I said, gnawing on a leg of lamb washed down with a left-over bottle of Dom Perignon 1953. 'What kind of guns were they? Whatever they were, they sure did kill our ass good today,' I whispered to Captain Kala as he watched me religiously finish the last drop of the French champagne.

'They are the very latest field guns from Russia. The old government ordered only six of them as they were so expensive,' Kala said laughing.

'I think the men know that it's the end tomorrow if I don't think of something fast,' I whispered.

'Nah, even if we all die tomorrow, they would rather die free men than die a prisoner in this place. That's why you don't hear anyone complaining, no?' Captain Kala remarked.

'I've got an idea. Come with me over to the radio room for a minute,' I asked Kala, whose stomach was by now growling like hell for want of food. After getting my hat, we walked over to the radio room and began to talk with one of the operators. 'Anything new soldier?' I asked.

'Naw. not really. Only they ordered some more shells for the big field guns. Other than that, it's just been your normal exchange of conversation,' the radio operator answered.

'How long will it take to move up some more shells here?' I asked, stifling a belch from so much cold champagne.

'About a week, because the Red Army is so disorganized and is still fighting a war on two fronts,' the radio operator remarked, eyeballing my shoulder bag which was showing the knuckle of my leg of lamb. 'That's just about right,' Captain Kala said, agreeing with the radio operator and also glancing at my shoulder bag. 'How many big guns do you think they have firing on us?' I asked Captain Kala.

'I'd say that by the way we have been taking a pounding, about four, sir,' he answered.

'That's it then. Why didn't I think of it before? The only way we can save ourselves is by going over behind enemy lines and blowing the guns sky high, baby,' I shouted with joy at my brilliant idea. 'We'll just get some men and do the job properly tonight while they're sleeping. How does that grab you, captain?' I asked.

'That's what I like about you, Robbie. You'll always find a way to make life exciting. That is a brilliant plan, my dear friend. By the way, is there any leg of lamb left in your bag?' Kala asked.

'Just a little, but I'm saving the bone for my dog. We've got other important things to do besides eating. Let's get started now on our mission. You'd better go and pick our best squad of men while I draw up a battle plan. I'll meet you in my office, or what's left of it, in about twenty minutes. Oh by the way pal, I do have an extra anchovy sandwich at the bottom of this bag,' I said, stirring through the dirty bag.

'I wouldn't mind that, sir, I haven't eaten today,' said Kala reaching for my hand.

'Oh damn, I forgot. I gave the sandwich to the dog also,' I said, turning away to take a quick nibble of the lamb leg.

'I'd like to kill that fucking dog,' Kala muttered under his breath.

'Captain do you want to come with me on this dangerous

mission?' I asked, wiping the grease from my mouth.

'Yes sir, you can depend on me, sir,' Kala said proudly but hungrily as he left the radio room to carry out my orders.

After about twenty minutes the captain knocked at my door. 'Sir, the men are ready for your inspection,' he announced.

'OK, but first step in here for just a second. Would you say the shells came from beyond the east wall?' I asked.

'Most definitely sir, I saw the guns in my field glasses today when they were setting them into position, sir,' Captain Kala replied.

'Then that's where we're gonna hit 'em tonight, old boy,' I shouted in happiness, and then walked out to the men. 'Hello my brave men,' I said, 'it's so good to see so many volunteers standing before me tonight for this heroic mission. The captain, I'm sure, has told you why we are going behind enemy lines, so I won't say any more than this. Be quiet and follow my orders and we'll all come back alive. How many men do we have coming with us captain?' I asked.

'About twenty-five sir, I picked the best that we have,' Captain Kala assured me.

'OK, move 'em out very quietly and I'll join you in a minute,' I ordered.

As the men moved off, Farouk and Johnny ran over to me. 'Hey, shithead, why didn't you invite us on your little night raid, sucker?' Johnny shouted.

'We might not make it back alive, so I thought it would be best to leave you two guys behind safely, old boy,' I answered.

'Come on Robbie, let me go with you. It will take my mind off my lover being killed. You know I'm a good fighter, so how about it?' Johnny asked very seriously.

'OK you can come, but you'd better not get into any trouble, is that understood?' I said looking him in the eye.

'You got it,' Johnny answered.

'And what about me? I can kick some ass too, you know,' Farouk said.

'You'd better stay this time. You'll be in command while I'm gone, so keep your eyes open and your ears down to the ground, old boy,' I ordered Farouk as I gave him an Arab handshake. Just as I was about to set off with Johnny to join the others, I heard the shout of a woman. I turned around to see four men trying to bring nurse Maha to me. She was still as fat as ever. 'Look what we found hiding in one of the houses behind the kitchen. We caught her trying to steal some food,' said one of the men. 'What shall we do with her, sir?'

'This fat bitch would make a great meal for a week,' another man joked.

'Take her back to the kitchen and feed her, then put her to work with the doctors until I get back. And don't harm her, she's my friend,' I ordered.

'Yes sir,' one of the men said as Johnny and I ran to join Captain Kala's squad of men.

'We're getting close now, be very quiet and obey all orders,' I whispered to the men as we climbed over some barbed wire and wooden fences that surrounded most of the Red Army camp. It was a full moon and most of the soldiers were asleep except for a few guards sitting around the campfires.

'There they are sir, right over there behind that big red tent,' one of my men whispered to me as I crawled on my belly through the sand. Sure enough, there they were, beautiful as ever. The big field guns stood side by side shining in the moonlight like trophies. It almost seemed a shame to blow up such beautiful guns, I thought to myself.

'Let's move a bit closer and then we'll take care of the guards,' I whispered. After moving over near the guns, and taking out our explosives, I motioned the men just to sit tight until I gave an order to move. 'How many guards do you see?' I asked Captain Kala.

'Two sir. It looks like they would never expect an attack in their own backyard,' he whispered to me.

'Get two of our best men with knives to take care of the guards before we make our move,' I ordered Kala.

'You got it,' he answered.

As the two guards walked past each other speaking a few words, four big hooked-style Arabic knives ripped into their backs, making them spit blood all down their dazzling blue shirts. 'Well done, Kala. Now you take Johnny and some of the men to fix some of the charges underneath those trucks and jeeps parked near the guns, while I attend to the field guns myself,' I directed Kala.

'OK sir, I'll meet you back here in about fifteen minutes,' Kala whispered as he went off with his men. Moving through the dark on our knees, we finally reached the beautiful blue steel guns. It was a pity to blow them up, but they stood in our path to freedom. My men stuffed the explosives down the mouths of the guns. 'OK, let's get out of here quickly before somebody comes along and discovers us,' I said, motioning everyone to retreat behind the fences.

When I got back to our original position, Captain Kala hadn't returned. What's taking him so long, I thought. Suddenly all hell broke loose. A big explosion went off, tearing the trucks and jeeps apart like paper. The explosion filled the sky with smoke, flames, and metal.

'Son of a bitch, I didn't give the signal to set off the charges,' I shouted angrily, throwing my cap in the sand. Just then Captain Kala staggered back across the fence with his clothing soaked in blood, and fell into my arms. 'What went wrong out there?' I asked.

'One of the men wired the explosive the wrong way round and blew himself up and set off the other charges in the process,' Kala answered, choking up blood with each word.

'Where's Johnny?' I asked.

'All the men are dead. I'm sorry general if I let you down,' Captain Kala whispered just before he died in my arms.

About this time, just about all the men from the Red Army dashed out of their tents and began to fire their guns at my men located near the fence. 'Light the fuse now, I shouted. As one brave man lit the fuse to blow up the big guns, the rest of us ran off into the dark while the Red Army soldiers continued to fire at the empty spaces that used to be occupied by my brave men and myself. 'Hurry men. Don't stop for nothing, just get back to the camp to fight another time,' I shouted. While running back to camp in the dark, another huge explosion ripped the air, blowing fire, hot steel, bodies, and sand everywhere like a Kansas tornado.

'I like it. Them no use big gun on us no more, no?' one of my men shouted to me in his broken English as we ran frantically.

'Not for a long time, baby, we hit 'em where it really hurts this time,' I replied.

'Open the gates. It's General Robbie out here,' I shouted to a guard walking along the wall. As the gates opened, Captain Farouk ran over to me and spoke. 'Now that was really something. The sky was a beautiful red when the explosives went off,' he said, shaking my hand. 'Where's Captain Kala and the rest of the men?' he asked, looking through the gates to see if anybody else was coming toward them.

'There was an accident back there. One of the men wired up the explosive wrong, killing Johnny and the rest of the men. Kala lived long enough to tell me what happened before dying in my arms. They never had chance, the poor bastards. What a goddamn waste of life,' I said sadly and walked away carrying this terrible burden.

'General sir, I have some more bad news to tell you. Something awful bad happened when you were gone sir,' Farouk said very formally. When Farouk said it was going to be bad news, I knew that he meant a catastrophe. So I asked him to explain slowly and carefully, all that had been going on lately, while I calmly braced myself, expecting the worst.

'I really did try to stop the men, sir. I fought nine of them off, but the other twenty overpowered me. It wasn't my fault, Robbie. Honest it wasn't,' he said, as his left leg began to twitch violently. He wasn't making any sense to me. 'Look Farouk, slow down and explain everything clearly so I can understand, whether it was your fault or not,' I ordered him.

'Well, while you were gone, the men found some whisky behind the cannon factory and started to drink heavily. I mean they put it away like a Baptist preacher from Evansville, as you Americans say. I didn't think much of it at the time, so I went to sleep, letting them have their fun as they have been under so much pressure lately. Well, to cut a long story short, they got drunk, angry, and downright mean. They went over to the prison, took out the guards and hung them one by one.' Farouk looked down at the ground, trying to avoid my angry eyes.

'You mean to tell me that you just let them stroll over to the cells and hang 'em just like that, one by one?' I shouted angrily, using all my strength to hold back my balled up, eyeblacking fist.

'No it wasn't like that at all. When I awakened from all the shouting and screaming, I rushed over to the men and tried to reason with them but it was just no use. Somebody threw a rock and hit me upside my head, knocking me out cold. When I came to, I was placed in your office as a prisoner myself, with two big guards standing outside. All I could do was to shout from your window telling them not to do it. You're a newcomer here and don't realize how bad the men hated the commandant and the guards,' Farouk explained, still looking at the ground.

'What about Sweet Mama. Did they hang him also?' I asked, trying to hold my left leg to keep from kicking him in the balls.

'Yeah, he was one of the first to go, it was a shame how they ripped off his dress, cut off his balls and stuffed them in his mouth,' Farouk answered weakly. As I was about to sit down on a stone wall from the shock of it all, Magic Pussy ran over in tears. 'Did you hear what they done to my friend Sweet Mama?' he asked.

'Yeah, and I'm sorry, Magic,' I said.

After sitting with Magic Pussy for about an hour talking and convincing him that he must go on living his life, I went and ordered some men to cut down the bodies and bury them. I then went over to the radio room to check the latest news.

'Sir, the President is angry with you for blowing up his guns,' the operator whispered to me as he continued listening to the talk on the radio.

'Any more news, other than the President being mad at me?' I joked.

'Yes, they are sending for another big gun and it will be here in about a week or so,' he answered.

'That's not to bad. I should have something going for us in that amount of time,' I said leaving the room.

'Sir, wait a minute please,' the radio operator called out, 'I just picked up the last part of a message being given to a field commander on the north side of the prison camp. They are planning to attack us tomorrow night at three in the morning, hoping to catch us asleep, the same way you caught them sleeping,' he said laughing, stuffing two marshmallows in his mouth.

'I feel we should be good hosts tomorrow night when they come, don't you?' I said.

'Yes sir, make it damn hot for them,' he said. As I went out the door, all the fatigue of battle caught up with me and I staggered to my bed. I slept through the next day until early evening. I ate a quick dinner and summoned Captain Farouk. 'Call the men together. I think they will want to meet our distinguished guests tonight,' I said coyly.

'Are we expecting some people tonight? Maybe a party, huh?' Farouk asked.

'Yeah, but not the kind you think, old boy,' I answered with a smile.

After Farouk had called all the men together in the courtyard as I had ordered, I spoke to them in a most serious tone. 'Men,' I said, 'you have done a very stupid thing by hanging all the prison guards while I was gone. That was real dumb. Now we don't have anything to trade with the Red Army to stop their attacks on us. So don't blame me if things get pretty rough from now on. Anyway, there's no use crying over spilled milk now, so let's move on to the task of staying alive tonight, OK?' With me saying that, the smiles came back on the men's faces and they were now cheering my name and clapping in excitement. 'Thank you men, thank you,' I said. 'Now calm down while I explain my plan to you, OK? I want all of you to understand that if we can hold off this attack tonight, with Allah's help, there will be no more big Red Army masters whipping and killing you from this night onward, this I promise you. I have a brilliant plan to put to you later if we can hold off this one big offensive.

'I want you men to rebuild your barricades, dig more fox holes, and stock up on more buckets of hot tar to throw over the walls. Also, supply yourselves with more ammunition, and last, build a safety wall here in the courtyard, four feet high out of sandbags. This is just in case the Red Army breaks through the main gates. The meeting is now over, so let's break it up and get to work fast. I want everything finished and ready for action by two o'clock in the morning. May Allah go with you in this fight to be free men.' And the men went off to their assigned duties.

'Robbie, is there anything special you want me to do, or just walk around and keep an eye on things?' Farouk asked, still feeling ashamed about letting Sweet Mama and all the guards go to their deaths while I was gone.

'I want you to check on all the positions in the prison and see that my orders are carried out to the fullest and then check back with me. Oh, and take along three other responsible men to help,' I said, patting him on the back to show that all was forgiven.

'Thank you Robbie, I won't let you down,' Farouk shouted as he ran off with his new self-confidence.

While walking over to the radio room, I stopped near a foot stool to re-lace my boots when Magic Pussy walked over to me and spoke. 'I wanna fight. I don't feel like cooking or hiding in the kitchen basement any more. Robbie, please let me fight. I know that I'm a bit of a girl, but I can still scratch some son of a bitch's eyes out, honey. Stop being a bitch and let me fight, huh? Please Robbie? My dear friend Sweet Mama is dead and gone. Most of my boyfriends are dead and I want to start a new life from now on. Be a pal, let me fight Robbie, please.'

Looking at Magic Pussy begging and almost about to cry if I said no, I agreed.

'Oh Robbie, honey, I just love you. Take out that dick and let me kiss it, you sweetie, you,' Magic shouted in joy as he picked me up in his arms off the ground and began to run in circles.

'Put me down! Put me down, you asshole, before some of my men see me acting like a fool with you,' I shouted repeatedly to my mad, mad, friend.

'I don't care who sees us, honey, I want everybody to know that I have a big dicked friend who is wonderful, kind, and I love him,' Magic said with tears of joy in his eyes as he continued to swing me around in his arms.

Suddenly the radio operator ran out into the courtyard and shouted 'General, the Red Army commanders have just given the orders to move their infantry troops over to the south wall.'

'Put me down, Magic. I've got work to do now. Not standing around fooling with a big fag all night,' I said as the radio operator stood looking in amazement at Magic Pussy holding me in his arms like a baby and me dodging his big wet lips that were trying to kiss me on my head, face, and hands. 'It takes a fag to know one, honey,' Magic shouted as I ran off to the radio room.

'Is the main attack still on for three o'clock in the morning?' I asked the radio operator who was fiddling with the knobs on the transmitter that was starting to give off little wisps of smoke.

'As far as I know sir, I haven't heard anything that indicates otherwise,' he answered.

'Well if you hear anything new, just call and I'll be somewhere in the courtyard with the men checking on last minute preparations.'

'Yes sir,' he answered as he turned back to the radio to try to get rid of the static and to put a cold cloth on the smoking transmitter. While walking out of the radio room into the courtyard, Farouk and Magic Pussy ran over to me in excitement. 'Robbie, you are a pure genius, I mean really the cat's whiskers,' Farouk said, shaking my hand vigorously.

'What do you mean, fool?' I asked.

'Why, your making Magic Pussy a captain for the brilliant idea he gave you about the dynamite.'

'And what brilliant idea was that?' I shouted, knowing this was going to be a real fuck up.

'Why, Magic ordered us to place dynamite all around the prison walls so that when you fired a bullet and hit one it would set off all the other charges next to each other in a chain reaction. Isn't that great?' Farouk said as Magic stood next to me blushing with pride.

'I must admit it's a great idea, Captain Pussy. But please don't do anything else without asking me first, you dumb shithead, you hear?' I remarked.

'You're such a bitch when you're angry, general, but it really turns me on, you beast,' Captain Pussy replied as the three of us went off to check the rest of the camp, laughing like schoolboys who had just played hookey from Sunday school. Like I had ordered earlier, the whole prison camp had been re-fortified at key positions and the men were in a god fighting mood. While standing on the wall near the main gate and looking out at the many Red Army campfires, Farouk spoke rather sadly and negatively, as usual. 'Robbie, I've got a feeling that this is gonna be our last battle together. Anybody can see that the Red Army got us outnumbered at least seven to one.'

'Yeah I know, but it's better to go down fighting like free man than as frightened chickens. Don't you agree old sport?' I asked.

'Yeah honey, I agree with you, Robbie,' Magic said and went on, 'Farouk, I think every man here knows he's gonna die tonight or sometime tomorrow, but you don't hear nobody bitching like a cry baby, do you?'

'I'm sorry, Robbie,' said Farouk, 'but we came so close to being free men and now it looks hopeless. I'm sorry for crying, but it's just the thought of dying a horrible death in the fighting tonight,'

'Now stop crying,' I said, 'Has old Robbie let you down yet? We still have one hour to think of something. Just trust me.'

'Sir. General Robbie. This nurse says that she's a friend of yours and demands to speak to you. What shall I do with her, sir?' a man that I had appointed to watch over nurse Maha and the doctors shouted up to me on the wall. I looked down and saw nurse Maha struggling with her guard and shouting, 'Please don't kill my brother, please general, don't let them kill my baby brother.'

'Let the nurse go and I'll be right down to sort this out,' I yelled as most of the men on the wall had now turned their attention to the nurse and the guard arguing like overgrown kids down below. After stepping off the ladder near the main gates, the guard ran over and began to explain to me what had happened. Apparently, nurse Maha had been hiding and feeding her brother in the canning and basket factory ever since the prison uprising when the guards were hanged savagely.

'Is it true what this man says about you?' I asked nurse Maha.

'Yes,' she cried. 'But he's my little baby brother. He's all I have left in this whole wide world. Don't kill him, please general,' nurse Maha begged, squirming on the ground, kicking her legs in the air with her eyes rolling counter clockwise, and finally beating her ample breast in anguish.

'Kill him. Kill him. he was one of the worst bastards in the whole prison camp. Let's hang him for the dirty dog he is,' some of the men called out in an angry rage after seeing nurse Maha do her overacting slave-momma Hollywood acting bit.

'General Robbie,' she said now, 'we have always been friends, yes? Well, if you spare my baby brother's life, I will show you a secret passage that will take you out about a hundred yards behind Red Army lines from the prison wall. How about that? Is it a deal? Please help me, Robbie, and I'll help you,' nurse Maha begged in desperation for her ugly baby brother's life.

'If you go and show Captain Farouk and some of my other men where the secret passage is, I'll spare your brother's life. If you lie, I'll let the men decide your brother's fate.Now go with the captain and show him the passage and come back to my office for further talks, OK?' I said, showing some compassion to an old friend who had helped me on many an occasion. (The hand massages, remember?)

'You give me your word as a true friend?' the nurse asked me as she started out the door with Farouk.

'You have my word as a true friend, nurse Maha. You have always been good to me with your hands, and now I would like to pay you back with the same kindness,' I answered, and a slight smile came over her round, sweating, tear-stained face.

'Are you gonna let that bitch's brother live after all the beatings and killings he's done to some of the inmates over the years?' Magic Pussy asked with some concern.

'Don't worry your pretty little head over such things. go over to the radio room and relay a message to President Ben Ali Hassan that we want to surrender and arrange for a time and a meeting place,' I ordered Magic Pussy, who was now standing and looking at me like I was a crazy man. 'Hurry fool, before it gets too late. I'll explain later, but for now just run and carry out my orders, OK?' I shouted to bring Magic out of his stupid looking trance.

'Yeah, what the fuck do I want to worry my pretty little head over men's talk for anyway?' Captain Pussy moaned as he danced out of the door pretending to be Snow White.

While I was looking over some maps and building plans for the prison in the filing room, Farouk and nurse Maha walked back into the office. Farouk said 'It's there, the secret passage is really there. This bitch wasn't lying after all.'

'I know. I have been looking at the prison building plans and spotted an old underground sewage drainage that was used when this place was a fighting fort in 1909,' I said, feeling very knowledgeable.

'I have lived up to my part of the bargain, now how about your part, general?' said nurse Maha.

'You and your brother are free to leave after I put my plan in action. Don't worry, just be cool for another day or two, and nothing is going to happen to you,OK?'

'Robbie,' said Magic Pussy, 'Robbie dearest. I gave your message to President Ben Ali Hassan, and he told me to tell you to meet him in front of the main gates in about twenty minutes, honey. Oh, and some of the men are outside waiting to speak to you about a little matter of surrendering,' said Magic as he blew a kiss at Farouk.

'Surrender? What kind of talk is that, Robbie? We can't do that,' Farouk shouted in anger, not knowing all the facts as usual.

'Calm down boys. Come with me outside while I explain to the men my new plan.' As I walked out the office door, some of the men were standing around moaning and looking very worried about the rumour of surrender that had spread across the prison camp like wildfire. 'Men, my brave fighting men who will follow me anywhere. We are not going to surrender to anybody. I just wanted the commanders of the Red Army to think that way so as to buy us some more time. We have just found a secret passage under the prison camp that comes out about a hundred yards behind the enemy's encampment. Isn't that great?' The men answered with a huge cheer as I continued to talk.

'We are going to kidnap President Ben Ali Hassan tonight while that bastard sleeps in his bed. he will be dreaming and thinking we are going to surrender to him tomorrow morning bright and early. Men, can you imagine his disappointment when we catch him with his pants down tonight. Now go back to your positions and think about going home as free men.' At this the men jumped to their feet screaming the cheers of coming victory.

As the cheering died down, one little freckle-faced man was waving his arm for attention. 'Speak up, soldier. You're among friends,' I said, forcing myself to smile, as I knew he was going top be a negative shit head.

'Sir, how is kidnapping President Ben Ali Hassan gonna help us get away from this prison camp without fighting?'

'Well, my little freckle-faced comrade in arms, Ben Ali Hassan will be our safe passage to Senegal. None of the Red Army soldiers would try to harm us and put the President's life in jeopardy if he's our prize hostage, old freckles – I mean old boy. Now move it quickly, men, before the President pays me a little friendly visit,' I ordered.

As the men dashed quickly back to their assigned positions, a guard on the wall called out, 'Sir, the President and his staff of top officers is approaching on horseback. Shall we open the gates?'

'No way, stupid, what you got in your head, rocks? I'll go and see the old fatso myself out the small doors on the side of the main gates,' I yelled back up to him.

'Hey Farouk, tell Magic Pussy to make sure that the men keep their guns silent unless something shitty happens out there while I'm talking, OK?' I ordered as I opened the small doors near the main gates to meet my old enemy, Ben Ali Hassan.

'Robbie, be careful my friend. That old bastard Ben Ali is a real slippery monkey, man,' Farouk called out as I passed through the doors.

'Yeah, but I got his number, man. I'm still the best in the west and can't lose the stuff I use and don't you forget it, captain,' I said, looking back and giving Farouk a big wink.

'That's right, honey. Talk that shit and bring me back a dick,' Captain Pussy called after me in his usual military manner.

# 13

While walking out slowly to meet Ben Ali, I could see him sitting on his big white Arabian stallion in the shimmering moonlight like some big proud Hitler, waiting for me to deliver my men to his proficient killing machine of slaves.

'That's far enough, Yank. I don't want you too close to me stinking and scaring my horse with your ugly face,' Ben Ali taunted as his men started to laugh at his unfunny joke.

'Yes sir, anything you say, Mr President,' I answered, trying to be obedient and humble like a beaten man.

'Now what's all this I hear about you wanting to surrender?' Ben Ali asked suspiciously.

'Yes sir, it's the honest to God truth. You have too much fire-power and my men have taken a terrible beating lately from your giant field guns. we have no more fight in us and I want to surrender to you, if you will spare my men's lives. I don't care about me, but please spare my men sir, I beg of you,' I said looking down to the ground all pitiful like.

A smile came upon the President's face as he looked down at me and saw a beaten man begging for mercy. 'What about Commandant Rashid, Sergeant Socco, and the prison staff. Are they still alive?' Ben Ali asked, staring me in the eyes to see if I would tell him a lie.

'Yes sir, they are being taken care of like prisoners of war. They are well fed and permitted to exercise twice a day behind the canning factory. All of your men are alive and well. I can assure you of this, Mr President,' I answered with all the sincerity of the Pope asking for a donation.

'Alright then, let my men go free and you surrender your rat-infested army of men to me this instant, and I'll let then live. But I'm going to make you suffer, boy. Allah knows your ass is going to suffer,' the President threatened and started foaming at the mouth again with the thought of kicking my ass royally.

'I can't do that, sir. First, I must have in writing that you will let my men live. Second, I must go back and convince them that no harm will come to them and that your word is as good as gold. And last of all, I must convince some of the prisoners not to carry on with this fighting and to let your guard staff go free unharmed. You must understand, Mr President, most of my men are very uneducated and undisciplined,' I explained as humbly as I could.

'Mr President sir, I told you he didn't want to surrender and that it was all a trick,' an advisor said to Ben Ali, who was fuming by now but said nothing.

'Mr President, I beg you to listen to me,' I pleaded, 'This is no trick but just common sense. Please be merciful,' I begged again as I fell to my knees pretending to cry, rolling over and over in the sand, kicking my legs in the air, and perhaps playing my greatest role since my boy scout summer cookie sales.

'Stop crying like a baby, and explain to me what you are trying to say, and stop all this mumbo-jumbo before I shoot you now like a dog, Yank,' the President said as he reached for the pistol in his holster. I quickly jumped to my feet and tried to explain sensibly, if that were possible.

'Sir, Mr President, who is loved by everyone. If you could give me until morning, I will personally guarantee the surrender of my men, the prison camp, and every last one of the staff of guards including Commandant Rashid and Sergeant Socco unharmed. If I lie, kill me in the most horrible death you can think of. I ask you to give me a little time and show mercy. Please Mr President. May the Lord bless you for your kindness,' I said as I again went into my act of rolling in the sand.

'Stop rolling on the ground like a mad man, Yank. You're overacting shit doesn't appeal to me or my horse,' shouted the President as he went on talking.

'I'm going to give you until morning to deliver my men, my prison camp, and your shitty little army of men to me right here on this spot. I know this is against my better judgement, but if this is some kind of trick,you will never live to tell about it. you understand Yank?' the President shouted down at me as I cowered in fear, and he turned his huge white stallion, who had left mountain of do-do next to me, to ride back to his men who were cheering as if they had won the World Cup.

'Oh thank you. Thank you, Mr President. You won't regret your decision. Thank you, Jesus. Oh Jesus thank you for letting the President show a little mercy and for the big present his horse left behind,' I yelled out to the President, his wonder horse, and his top staff officers as they rode off at a fast gallop. That stupid, fat muthafucka, I thought silently to myself as I ran back to the prison to tell the men the good news.

Before I could sit down to rest in the camp, Farouk ran over and asked 'What happened? Did they take the bait?'

'Yes, the hook, the bait, and the sinker, old boy,' I said feeling rather pleased with myself.

'Robbie, how did you do it?' Magic Pussy asked as he and others ran over to me.

'Oh it's really not that difficult for someone of superior intelligence and command ability,' I answered calmly like a real general.

'Honey, I knew you could pull it off, you're such a lying little bastard aren't you?' Magic teased, snapping his fingers in a be-bop style that went out with Lawrence Welk. No, I'm mistaken, Pat Boone.

'Farouk, get ten good men together for tonight's mission and meet me back at my office. Right now, I'm going to get me two hours of well deserved sleep, OK?'

'Yes sir, you got it,' Farouk answered.

'What do you want me to do, Robbie?' asked Captain Magic Fingersnapping Pussy.

'You just help keep an eye on things and check with the radio room while I get some shuteye. Oh, and tell the men the good news,' I said as I headed for my sack with my eyes begging me for permission to close.

While I was having a long overdue shave in my room, Farouk knocked on the door and entered. 'Robbie, it's time like you ordered, shall we get this little party going now?' he asked, looking like an overdressed mercenary ready for battle.

'Are you men ready to go?' I asked.

'Yes sir, ready and willing,' he assured me.

'Farouk, you had better stay behind and command the prison camp, while someone else comes with me and the men,' I ordered.

'Yes sir, but what about Magic Pussy? He wanted to come on this mission with you, sir,' said Farouk.

'Where is he now?'

'Still sleeping in his room. Shall I wake him?'

'No leave him be. I'll see him when I get back. Old Magic might get over there behind the enemy lines while all the fighting is going on and try to give away some pussy. You know he's such a bitch around a lot of big-dicked men,' I said making a joke of leaving him behind.

'Yes, I guess you're right, sir. Some of the men here could use his services badly,' Farouk said, adding his two cents to the matter.

'OK captain, tell the men to move out and follow me,' I ordered.

'Yes sir. OK you lazy lot. Let's move out,' Farouk ordered the men in a strong sergeant major voice.

While moving through the underground drainage passage with the men, a thought came to my mind: what if we fail? I think the men knew as well as I did that if we failed it would be our last mistake. As we moved through the cobwebs, flying bats, lizards and rats in the passage, we came to an opening at last.

'You men wait here while I go and check things out up ahead. Be quiet while I'm gone,' I ordered as I crawled on my knees as not to make too much noise. I slowly pulled away some sand that was blocking the exit with my hands and pulled myself out into the desert night sky and cool breeze. All was clear and I stood about a hundred yards behind the Red Army's encampment, just like the map was marked. With a feeling of the taste of victory and excitement, I ran back into the passage and gave the signal to the men to come on ahead by lighting three matches one at a time. The first man to step through the passage was old loud-mouthed, wet-lipped, Magic Pussy, much to my surprise. 'Magic, what the hell are you doing here? I thought you were back at the camp asleep, sissy,' I whispered, poking him in the ribs.

'Honey, you didn't think I was going to miss all the fun and big-dicked boys running around here, did you? Don't be such a bitch and let's get this shit on now, honey,' Magic Pussy said, blowing me a kiss.

'Hurry and get your ass out of the way and let the rest of the men pass, man,' I said.

After all of the men were out of the passage and standing around waiting for the next move, I explained to them the importance of team work and the element of surprise on the President's tent. This night was very cool and breezy, and a small sand storm was beginning to twist and turn like a tornado. Most of the Red Army men were asleep and their tents were in darkness while the campfires burned on in the night. This made it easier to find the big-partying President who took his fun in the night very seriously. Knowing the danger, we all set off to the big white tent with the national flag flying on top. The President's tent was about twenty yards away from the other smaller tents, underneath three tall date trees with four guards keeping watch. While we were crawling up slowly to the tents, a huge, greasy, fattish girl walked into the President's tent and suddenly the lights went out. I guess they were playing a game of hide and seek, with all the shouting and laughing that was coming out of the tent. 'What shall we do now?' asked a frightened soldier.

'We came here for the President, and the President we shall have, mate,' I whispered to the confused man. Moving in closer for the big moment, a small light came back on in the President's tent. 'Halt the men for a second, and let's see what is going on for a bit,' I ordered the men. With all the moaning and groaning coming from the President's tent, one guard began to peep into the tent, liked what he saw, and motioned the other guards to have a look. While the guards were looking in the tent, and giving themselves a deluxe hand job, I gave the signal for eight of my men to kill the guards as silently as possible. It was a pity to disturb those old boys doing the hand jive because they were really getting down. After killing the guards (one still had his dick in his hand) the rest of my men moved in closer to the President's tent with caution. About this time, my men also began to peek into the tent, and forgot all about the mission as I whispered repeatedly, 'Attack. Attack, you fools.' When my men did finally come to their senses, and entered the tent from all sides, we caught the President eating this huge fatso woman's private parts. She was too shocked to scream and fainted while the President had a big mouthful of hairy snatch. Quickly pulling the President's head back from his bad eating habits, one of my men stuffed the fat woman's drawers into the President's mouth and covered it with industrial adhesive tape to keep him from calling out for help.

'Looks like you have fucked up again, Mr President,' I whispered to Ben Ali who was now tied up on his knees like a dog begging for a bone.

'Hey you with the triple thick glasses, take the President out the back of the tent and make for the underground passage quickly before someone comes. I'll stay here with one of you and act as your rear guard,' I ordered.

'I wish you'd cover my rear, honey,' Magic Pussy joked, rubbing his fat ass.

'Oh, and four-eyes, take this silly fag with you before he gets us all killed,' I said.

'Come on Magic. Leave the general alone and let's get back to the passage like good little girls,' Four-eyes said to Magic, pulling him by the arm.

Sure enough, as Magic was being dragged out of the tent, he slipped and fell, firing off a round from his rifle. 'Oops a daisy, I think I've just made a boo-boo,' he said as he picked himself up off the ground slowly. 'Boo-boo shit, you just fucked up,' Four-eyes shouted, panicking with fright.

'Stop all the talking and move out while I fix up some dynamite with a trip wire attached to it, fools,' I shouted to Magic and the men, who were now standing scared stiff in the back. After seeing them run out into the dark desert for the underground passage, one of the men and I began to set dynamite around the entrance to the President's tent.

'Hurry man with the dynamite. Pretty soon Ben Ali's men

will be breathing down our necks like gorillas in heat,' I whispered to my slow-fingered man as the President's men piled out of their tents.

'The President is being attacked, save the President! Everybody to the President's tent!' a top ranking Red Army officer commanded as I peeped through a small slit in the tent.

'Oh shit. Let's get out of here right now man,' I shouted to my partner as we ran out the back of the tent into the dark. After running about twenty yards, a huge explosion went off, knocking us to the desert sand. In the Red soldier's haste to rescue the President, and to capture us, I guess someone just ran straight into the tent without noticing the trip wires attached to our lovely dynamite and spoiled the party – which was a blow-out anyway.

After picking ourselves up from the cold sand, and looking back to see nothing but a huge smoking hole big enough for an Olympic sized swimming pool and men trying to put out the surrounding tent fires, we made our way back to the old prison camp via the passage.

While walking across the courtyard with the man who had stayed behind to help me, I asked his name. 'Zagora Ali, sir,' he answered.

'Zagora, you are a good man. I want you to accept the rank of captain. Come with me and we'll see what's happened to our sexy little President,' I said.

'Thank you sir. I will serve you well, my general. Thank you sir, and may I kiss your gun?' Zagora said, shaking my hand and then kissing my shoulder gun in joy. When Zagora and I arrived back near the main gates where most of my men were gathered around a campfire chewing the fat, Farouk looked up and shouted

'What took you so long, general? You have been missing all the fun. Why, Mr President Ben Ali Hassan has been dancing for your brave and loyal troops.' I looked over near the fire and there stood President Ben Ali without his shiny uniform, which he loved so dearly, and dressed as a gypsy girl dancer.

'OK men, you've had your fun. Three of you take the President to a cell safely. He's our honored guest now. Zagora, I want you to take care of this little detail for me. Farouk, Magic, you two break up this little meeting and see that the men get some sleep and report to me first thing tomorrow morning,' I ordered.

'I knew old sour puss was gonna spoil all the fun with all that high and mighty general shit,' Magic said just loud enough for me to hear, while he hid behind Farouk.

'I think you've had enough fun for one night, shithead. Now do as I say and break up this shit meeting,' I shouted in anger as the men moved away quickly like frightened kids.

'Zagora, take away the tape from the President's mouth when you put him in the cell. We don't want our guest to be uncomfortable, do we?' I said giving the President an uptown wink and pinching his hooked nose.

'Yes sir,' Zagora answered as he took the President off to his cell.

'Before I turn in, Robbie, who's this Zagora guy? Don't tell me you made him a captain too,' Farouk said.

'Yes I did. Anymore damn smart talk from you?' I asked.

'No. No way man, you're the boss,' Farouk said, quickly moving away with Magic to their sleeping quarters.

The next morning bright and early, two high ranking officers came to the main gates and asked to speak to me. They wanted to try to work out some terms for the release of their beloved President. I did a slow John Wayne walk out the prison gates with a pistol tucked under my shirt and spoke to the two officers dressed in their shiny blue uniforms which were loaded down with gold-plated medals. 'Hello gentlemen, I'm the great General Robbie Jones. What can I do for you two old cocks?' I asked, continuing to pick my teeth with a wooden toothpick. A big, greasy, fat officer wearing a uniform two sizes too small spoke.

'I am General Petit, second in command only to President Ben Ali Hassan, and this is my assistant Major Youssef. We have come to offer you a free pardon of all crimes against the state and free passage back to America in return for the safe release of our beloved President Ben Ali Hassan. These are our terms, nothing more and nothing less. Is it a deal, General Robbie Jones?' he asked, whacking a small riding whip against his boots and knocking off his left heel that needed some repair done desperately. I just looked at the two officers with a smile on my face, then turned and started to walk away. General Petit called out, 'OK, I'm sorry, General Jones. Come back, my friend, and let's talk this delicate matter over like gentlemen. You must excuse my manners. I've been having some rather difficult personal problems lately. What do you say? Come back and let's talk, huh?'

'General, you came out here to bullshit the bull, man. I don't have time to talk nonsense with you. I've got much better things to be doing, old cock. Now if you want to talk seriously, let's talk. If not, I'll be on my way, old boy,' I insisted.

'I'm sorry. Please forgive me, but what do you want in exchange for the President's release? I'm ready to start the negotiations seriously, alright?' General Petit said, offering me a folding chair to sit in that a guard had quickly brought over. I sat and began to list my many demands.

'I want a jeep, five troop carrying trucks, one extra truck loaded with food and fresh water, a pardon for all the men in the prison camp who decide to stay behind, and last of all a truce between our armies until I and my men reach the Senegal border safely. Now in return for this truce and safe passage, I will release President Ben Ali Hassan as soon as my men and I reach the border. Now these are the terms and the only terms you are going to get from me, old boy. Take it or stuff it,' I said, pouring myself some iced tea that was sitting on a small table nearby.

'You drive a hard bargain, General Jones, and it will take a little time to get all the things you demand,' General Petit replied.

'How long?' I asked.

'Not long – by about two o'clock tomorrow afternoon all your demands will be met. Is it a deal then?' the general asked.

'It's a deal, but if you try any funny stuff the President will suffer. I don't think your military career would be worth shit if your government and your men found out that you could have saved the President but you blew it by being stupid, do you?' I asked.

'I agree with you, General Jones. You have my word nothing will go wrong and that we have a deal. I'll be here tomorrow at two o'clock with all your demands met. Until tomorrow then,' General Petit said, saluting me and then returning to his car with Major Youssef.

Walking back to the main prison gates, I was bursting with joy and full of pride. I had pulled this big beautiful deal off like a true general. I was going home at last with my men, some of whom were my dear friends. I was so happy, my walk turned into a jog and then a run. 'We did it. We did it. You're all free men, you are now free as a bird,' I called out to the men standing on the walls of the prison camp who were now waving and cheering like mad.

As I ran through the gates, it seemed like every man in the

prison camp was there to greet me with a smile and a friendly hug of joy. Farouk quickly picked me up on his shoulders, moved through the cheering men like a bouncer, and put me down on the top of an old burned out jeep so I could speak to the men. I pulled out my pistol and fired it into the air several times to get their attention and to make another of my rip-roaring victory speeches.

'Men. My brave fighting men. We have come a long way together and have fought many battles for our freedom. Lord knows this has not been an easy struggle, but now that's all behind us. You are now free men, free at last. I have gone to the mountain to speak to the Lord and he has told me to lead you to freedom,' I shouted, taking a quick sip of whisky from Magic Pussy's bottle. 'Tomorrow at this time there will be trucks loaded down with food and water, ready to take you to the promised land, the Senegal border. Praise Allah and the Lord, Jesus Christ for making this deliverance possible.'

I paused and raised my arms to receive the cheers, then had a larger sip of Magic's medicine, and continued my joyful speech:

'All of you men who wish to come along to the Promised Land that Allah has told me to lead you to, pack your bags and be ready to leave at noon tomorrow. The rest of you men that wish to stay in your native land to make your own Promised Land and good fortunes, you have been given a pardon for all of your crimes against the state by the government of Mauritania, signed by General Petit, who is now acting President. May Allah go with you in whatever you decide. May the burning tree that Moses saw on the mountain burn, burn, burn in your hearts with loving kindness,' I said, taking two more large swigs of Magic's whisky as some of the men began to cry huge tears that splashed on my dusty boots. By now some of the men were pressing close to touch my hand for healing and forgiveness of their sins. Some even tried to kiss my gun.

You may be wondering why some of the men would want to stay behind in the prison camp or this country, right? Well, I'll tell you. Most of these men couldn't read or write, had no opportunity of a good job, and no family. Since the start of the war they had gotten used to the prison way of life. How many times have you seen a guy come out of prison and promise to live a crime-free life, but ends up going back and forth to jail because he can't adjust to a normal way of life? One of the other main reasons for staying in prison is the love and comradeship between the inmates and a feeling of belonging to something, to maybe a place. (Many people join the Nazi party, the Ku Klux Klan, or the Dirty Bastards Club located at Sunset and Vine in Hollywood. Just to have the feeling of belonging when the rest of society won't accept them. I hear that each organization gives great Christmas parties.)

Anyway, as I stepped down from the burned out jeep, Farouk and Magic threw their arms around me, crying. 'Robbie, we are so proud of you. We never thought we would see the day when we would be free men again,' Farouk said.

'Now that I'm free, I don't know what to do with myself. What am I gonna do with my life, Robbie?' Magic asked sadly.

'Don't worry, I'll take you back to America with me if you will be a very good girl,'

'Hot shit. Would you, Robbie? You're not just saying that, are you?' Magic asked. I was joking originally, but seeing the joy on my dear friend's face and remembering all the good things he'd done for me, I said 'Yes,' with all sincerity.

'I'm sorry for crying so much, but I'm so happy Robbie. I'm going to pack my best dresses and shoes for tomorrow, OK? I'll see you later, honey pie,' Magic said, running off in a joyful world of his own.

'You really made him happy, Robbie,' Farouk said, feeling proud of my good deed.

'Yeah, he's a good girl. What are you gonna do now that you are a free man, Farouk?' I asked as we walked slowly over to my bombed out office.

'Oh, I think I'll go to Tangier to visit my uncle and then go on to study at one of the local universities to become a doctor like yourself,' he said, giving me a wink.

Just as I was about to enter my office, and Farouk was about to walk off to pack his belongings for tomorrow's trip, a voice called out from a cell window nearby. 'Hey general. This is nurse Maha. What about our little deal? I don't want no shit from you, you and your jive ass,' she shouted loud and common as a bar room whore.

'Tomorrow, you and your brother will be set free as I promised. You just relax until then, friend,' I answered back as I went into my office for a long overdue rest.

After waking up from a short rest of three hours, I got up out of bed and walked over to the main cell blocks to speak with President Ben Ali Hassan about the good news. 'Hello Mr President. Have you heard the news?' I asked.

'Yeah, I heard. But you won't get away from me that easily, Yank. Somewhere down the line you will make a slip, and then my men will make you pay with your life,' he said, with a lot of fight still in him.

'You may be right, but I don't think so. Anyway, I'm not going to kill you. You will be released as soon as we reach the Senegal border. Oh, and one other thing. I may not kill you, but if you try to escape or cause me any trouble whatsoever, I'll beat the living shit out of you. Now even you can understand that, can't you?' I asked.

'You're gonna get yours soon, boy. Real soon,' he answered as I turned and walked away singing, 'Oh How I Love My Red Hobnail Boots'.

The night was warm and peaceful, and the men danced and sang old folk songs happily around the many campfires. I guess one of the most popular songs that night was, 'Don't Step On My Blue Suede Hobnail Boot'. Magic pussy was dressed as a big tit girl, dancing around one of the big campfires as the men clapped and demanded he showed a bit of skinny leg or hairy ass. Farouk walked over to me and spoke. 'Magic is in his dream world tonight, huh? You know he's not wearing any drawers under that thin dress, don't you?'

'Yeah, and he's as happy as a dildo in a sex shop tonight,' I said.

'You think everything will go according to plan tomorrow, Robbie? It all seems like a dream to me, I mean going free and all,' Farouk said, still feeling a bit nervous as Magic let out a loud whoop and fell to the ground into a soldier's waiting arms.

'You worry too much, man. Go join the singing and dancing and have a good time. Or get Loo-Loo the midget to give you a blow job. Have some fun and I'll see you first thing in the morning, OK?' I said, moving away quickly from all the negative vibes that Farouk was giving out.

Around one o'clock in the morning most of the men began to wander away from the fires to their beds for some sleep or whatever. Magic Pussy, drunk as a country preacher, continued to dance well into the morning. It was always difficult for Magic to leave a crowd of big dicked men, especially when he was pissed.

When morning rolled around, I was awakened by loud singing and cheering from the men under my window. I got up and walked over to the window, looked out and saw them singing and waving signs saying 'We Love You Robbie'. I was choked up with emotion and was about to wipe my eyes with my shirt and tail, when someone called out loudly, 'The trucks are here. We're going home at last. Praise Allah!' I quickly put on my pants and ran down into the courtyard to sort things out with the men.

'Calm down everybody. Calm down. While Captain Zagora and I go out the gates and check our travel arrangements,' I shouted over the laughter of the men. 'Farouk, you sort out the ones who want to go with us to the border and the ones who want to stay behind, right?' I ordered.

'You got it, Robbie. Just get out there and make sure we can get the hell out of here, like fast man,' he said smiling and feeling a bit more confident about my plans now.

I walked out of the gates without my shirt or shoes with Captain Zagora to meet with General Petit.

'Hello General Jones. I have delivered all your demands. Would you like to check them?' General Petit asked.

'Yeah, I'd better. Zagora, check the trucks while I finish talking with the general,' I ordered.

'Yes sir,' he answered as he walked off to check the merchandise.

'Oh, by the way, General Jones, it wasn't in our bargain, but what's happened to the prison guards you captured?' General Petit asked curiously.

'Oh, you mean Commandant Rashid and his men, right? Well my dear general, your heavy field guns fired a direct hit into the section of the cell block where they were being held hostage and killed them all instantly. It's a shame to lose such fine soldiers in the prime of their careers, don't you agree sir?' I asked, pretending to be sad.

'They knew the dangers of being a soldier and I hope they died like the brave men they were,' the general said looking at me, not believing a word I had said. (I wonder why. I only told a small black lie.)

While the general was still talking some off the wall politics to me, Captain Zagora walked over and spoke. 'Robbie, it's all there, just like you wanted. Even the trucks are filled with gasoline,' he assured me.

'I've lived up to my part of the bargain, now it's your turn to show good faith on your part, General Jones,' General Petit said, not really trusting me.

'Like I said before. The President will be released when we

reach the border town of Podor. We will drop him off at the local police station unharmed. Oh, and I don't want any of your men following us too closely or my men might get the wrong idea and hurt the President. You understand that, don't you,' I said, giving the general a wise wink as I motioned my drivers to come and drive away our newly acquired trucks loaded down with goodies.

'I will keep an eye on you, Yank, but at a safe distance. So until we meet at the town of Podor, may Allah be with you and peace around you for always,' he said as he walked off with the major, back to his waiting chauffeur driven car.

'May Allah piss on you too,' one of my Christian drivers called out to the general, who was now sitting in his car sipping a cold Martini.

'OK men, take care and drive these trucks back to camp safely,' I ordered the drivers who were waiting, as I jumped up in the back of the lead truck. It took us about an hour and a half to load up the trucks with weapons, luggage, men, and the little food we had left after dividing it with those who were staying behind in the prison camp. I made damn sure we wouldn't be the ones who went hungry and starved to death. (Nothing personal, you understand.) After ordering Zagora to take President Ben Ali to the lead truck and to wait for me, I jumped up on the hood of a nearby truck and spoke to the remaining men for the last time.

'Men, my brave fighting men, we have been friends for a long time and have fought many battles shoulder to shoulder and arm in arm to gain this new freedom we have today. I hope in the choice you have made to stay behind, you will go on to better lives and will prosper with the help of Allah. Goodbye and may Allah be with you in everything you do and hope to be,' I called out, feeling sad to leave so many brave and nice guys behind. The men cheered and fired their weapons in the air when Farouk ran over and asked,

'Robbie, what about nurse Maha and her brother? Shall we bring them along with us?'

'Yeah, put them in the back of one of the trucks. I made a promise to nurse Maha and I want to keep it. Oh, and make a last minute check on Magic Pussy and see if he's alright and is in one of the trucks, OK?' I ordered Farouk as I went off to start the convoy moving. While sitting in the lead truck with President Ben Ali Hassan and the driver, Farouk called on the radio to say that everything was alright with the convoy, so I motioned my driver to move out slowly but surely. The moment the driver started the engine and slowly moved off into the desert is a moment in my life that I'll never forget. It seemed like the gates of heaven lay just over the horizon. I was free at last. I was on my way home to America, the playground of the world. Finally the nightmare of Mauritania was behind me. No more beatings or having someone locking me up like an animal and screaming obscenities at me. (You know I wasn't used to that shit.)

This was a great feeling, and I rode in the truck for the first twenty miles without saying a word but with a huge smile on my face. I felt like a big dick teenager coming back from his first visit to a Nevada whorehouse. (Some of you fellows out there know that feeling, don't you.)

In the midst of my daydream of freedom, Ben Ali Hassan said to me sarcastically, 'I knew you were stupid, but I never for a minute thought you were this stupid. You really think you're going to get away, don't you?' I was so wrapped up in thought at the time, I just ignored his remarks and continued to daydream about America and the big-tit women I wanted to service when I got home safely. While still daydreaming about six black Amazon girls breaking into my Beverly hills home, wanting to ravish, be downright dirty, and take advantage of my poor little body, Farouk called me on the radio,

'Robbie, two of the trucks have flat tyres. Can we stop and fix them now?' he asked.

'Yeh, we'll stop for a few hours and then get back to the journey. Get Magic and his boys to serve up some food while we're stopping too, OK?' I said.

'Can I get out of this truck to stretch my legs also?' Ben Ali asked.

'Sure old buddy. Just as long as you are a good boy, anything is possible,' I answered taking a piss against the back tyres of the truck. While sitting in the shade of the trucks eating with Farouk, Magic, and the President, a twin engined plane flew over our position twice before turning away.

I could see this unsettled the men terribly, so I called out, 'Don't worry about that old crop dusting plane. It belongs to the Red Army and it's part of the deal that they can monitor our position up to the border of Senegal. Now finish your meal and let's think about going home. I felt better myself seeing the men smile and laugh about how nervous they had been over a little plane flying by.

'You talk so much shit that it comes out of your ears, Yank. You know my men are going to cream your ass somewhere between here and the border, sucker,' Ben Ali bragged as he chomped on a mouthful of mashed potatoes.

'Is he telling the truth, Robbie? Are his men waiting out there somewhere in the desert to kill us?' Magic Pussy asked, now unsure of me or anything else. Seeing Farouk and Magic both being rattled by what President Ben Ali had to say, I spoke calmly but like a true General.

'Look you two sissies, he's in a very tight spot. He's afraid to die. He's lost his men, country, and he is losing the war badly. He will say anything to save his neck. Now who do you believe, him or me?'

'Oh you, darling. I know you're telling the truth because your lip doesn't quiver and your eyes have that gorgeous, Errol Flynn look,' Magic said grabbing me by the arm.

'Yeah, I was only checking to be sure myself, Robbie,' Farouk said, rather weakly and still unsure.

'Farouk, you and Captain Zagora go and see that the men are ready to move out in twenty minutes. We have a time schedule to keep to, old boy,' I ordered.

'You got it, Robbie,' he said, as Magic went off with him, still nervous about the future. The next five days went along beautifully, like clockwork. The men were well fed, happy, and were looking forward to going to their new homes and lives in a new country. They had even gotten used to the crop dusting plane flying over every after noon to check our position as we got near the Senegal border.

Meanwhile, unknown to me, the acting President Petit had called together all the top diplomats and high ranking officers of the county to decide if it was better to save President Ben Ali Hassan or to choose someone else to take his place in office.

Well you know how that goes, right? When the cat's away, the mice will play. So their decision was to replace President Ben Ali Hassan, and award the office of President to General Petit. His orders were to stop the war from going from bad to worse, and to crush my small army of escaped prisoners at all costs before we reached the Senegal border.

Anyway, after reaching the town of Podor which was now bombed out, deserted and flat as a pancake, I gave the order to keep on moving as we were only about forty miles away from the Senegal border. The men felt a bit shaky after seeing the town flattened, but kept their heads as they saw I was determined to get them to the border safely like I'd promised. After passing the town, there was a silence among the men for about a mile and a half, then the men forgot all about the past and started to sing songs of going home and a chorus or two of 'Don't Step On My Blue Suede Hobnail Boots'.

'What's going to happen to me, Yank? You were supposed to let me go free when we got to the town of Podor. Is this the way you keep your word?' Ben Ali asked.

'You sit tight, fathead. Your people don't want you back. You always treated your officers and men like shit, so why would they want your nasty ass back in power?' I asked calmly.

'You're loving this, aren't you. But you will soon feel the might of my army when they come to rescue me, then your ass is mine. Yes sir, I'm going to beat all the black off your ass,' Ben Ali threatened.

'Shut up, nobody's coming to rescue you. Let's be honest with one another. Would you in your right mind risk being killed to rescue a mean, fat overbearing son of a bitch like you? I'll answer that for you – hell no,' I said to Ben Ali as I motioned the driver to stop the truck.

'Hey driver, radio Farouk and tell him it's eating time and to tell the men one hour only,' I ordered as the President was beginning to worry over what I had said. While the driver was calling Farouk, I spoke once more to the President. 'Cheer up, old cock. Let's get out of the truck and stretch our legs. Life is never as bad as you think it is, let's get a bite to eat and you'll feel better. The worst that can happen to you is ending up in Senegal broke and working as a camel boy,' I said, laughing and pulling Ben Ali's favorite cap down over his eyes as if he were the local dipshit in high school. After eating some sandwiches that Magic Pussy had fixed, washed down with some exotic wine from Tangiers, I ordered the men back in the trucks so we could finish driving the last twenty miles to the border and freedom. Five miles down the road, which was rough as an Indian corn cob, we began to see road signs directing us to the Senegal border. Boy, was this a sight for bloodshot eyes and aching asses. The men began to sing louder and I became so happy, I started to sing the song 'Lucille' by Little Richard, which annoyed the President greatly. Suddenly, four fully armed crop dusting planes made a low flying pass over the convoy, scaring the hell out of everybody and turning a lot of the men's pants from green to brown instantly.

'Are those planes from Senegal?' the driver asked rather nervously.

'No way. They wouldn't use old beat up crop dusting planes to check us out. If they come back this way, we've got problems, driver,' I answered, wishing I'd brought along an extra pair of brown pants, as the ones I was wearing were taking a beating. Lo and behold, the planes turned into the gleaming sunlight and started back towards the convoy firing their machine guns. The President became over excited and shouted in my ear like a cunt, almost damaging my eardrum,

'I told you. I've got you now, Mr Big Shot Nigger. Your ass is grass and I'm your lawnmower, sucker. My men have come to rescue me at last. Free at last. Free at last. Thank God I'm free at last,' the President sang as he clapped his hands with joy.

'Like hell they did. They came to kill your nasty ass with the rest of us, fool. Why do you think they're shooting and bombing the trucks, to take you to a ball?' I said, as the planes swept over shooting and bombing the trucks like maniacs. I quickly jumped up on the fender on my side of the truck, and motioned my men to get out of the trucks and run into the desert. This was even worse as there was only a giant open space of sand with nowhere to hide.

After the planes had made about six passes over the convoy, their bombing and machine gun fire had totally destroyed the trucks. They now turned their attention to the men scattered in the open desert. Looking over at the burning trucks and many of my men lying dead in the sand, I called out to the remaining men who were running across the desert in a panic. 'Don't run, men, stand and fire your guns at the planes as they attack us. Don't run for Godsakes. Do you hear me you scared mother fuckers?'

The men paid no attention to me, with not even a kiss my ass or a goodbye as they continued to run further into the desert with me chasing after them calling them all kinds of sons of bitches that I could think of. Running after my brave men and screaming obscenities at the top of my lungs, and not looking where I was stepping, I tripped over a piece of wood that was buried in the sand. Cursing myself like a drunken preacher for falling, I grabbed the piece of wood that was under my foot and began to kick the hell out of it when suddenly I noticed it was a sign reading, 'Stop. Danger. This area is a minefield. Property of the Royal Army of Mauritania'. I quickly jumped up and ran into the mine-field, forgetting about my own safety and well-being, calling out to my brave men, 'Minefield! This is a minefield, you assholes! Come back you dumb bastards! For God's sake come back!'

All my shouting was in vain. They were too busy running and shooting at the attacking planes to pay any attention to their brave general risking his life for them. Between the planes firing their machine guns from the air, and mines exploding under their feet, it was only a matter of time before my men and I would be lying dead in this hot desert with huge vultures picking the flesh off our bones. I knew this would be the last battle I would fight in this lifetime as I fired my rifle at the low-flying planes and silently prayed to God at the same time.

Just as I ran into a cloud of smoke to protect myself from some on-coming machine gun fire, I ran into Farouk, almost knocking him down.

'Robbie, save me. I don't want to die. I don't want to die so close to freedom,' he shouted in terror grabbing at my arms. Farouk was in a state of shock. He wanted to live and enjoy his new freedom so badly, he didn't realize he had lost his right arm in the battle.

'Don't worry Farouk, I'll get you out of this mess,' I said, trying to assure my dear friend that everything was going to be alright, but knowing that Old Man Death was waiting for both of us. I put Farouk on my back and started to run back towards the trucks to get out of the minefield when Farouk screamed in terror.

'Robbie, Robbie. I've lost my arm. My right arm is gone!' Farouk started to cry, struggle, and scream like a madman as I tried to run and keep him from falling off my back at the same time. Believe me, it was a bitch of a job. While running a zig-zag pattern through the clouds of smoke and sand to avoid the machine gun fire, a plane made a low pass on my right side, firing its blazing guns.

'I'm hit. Oh God, I'm hit,' I called out as I hit the hot desert sand, losing my grip on Farouk's body. After the plane passed over, I slowly turned over on my side to see if Farouk was alright and saw him start to crawl away from me on his hands and knees. I made a move to stop him, but the pain in my back and hip was too much to bear so I called out frantically,

'Farouk. Farouk, My dear friend. Come back. You'll never make it. Watch out for the –' but before I could get the word 'mines' out of my mouth, Farouk had crawled upon one, setting off a chain reaction of five more around us. After the first explosion, and seeing my friend Farouk blown to pieces before my very eyes, everything went completely blank. I guess I must have passed out, because I don't remember a thing after that terrible moment.

# 14

When I did finally come round, I opened my eyes and saw Magic Pussy dressed in a red chiffon blouse over his prison uniform pants, eating a leg of southern fried chicken. I knew at that moment that I'd failed to live by the rules of God and the Ten Commandments, and therefore I was surely in hell. I quickly closed my eyes again, and thought how nice it would have been if I'd lived a Christian life and had gone to heaven to be with my dear mother and friends, when Magic broke the dream by whispering in my ear, his breath heavy with garlic from the salad, 'Hi there, honey. would you like some of my chicken? Or a bit of little old gorgeous me? Robbie, it's me. Magic.' I couldn't bring myself to open my eyes and see hell again, so I pretended not to hear Magic, hoping that he would go away.

'Robbie, you old son of a bitch, you ain't dead, fool. You'd better open your damn eyes before I piss into a jug and throw it all over your head, bitch,' Magic threatened jokingly. Knowing that Magic can get very crazy at times, I opened my eyes and saw him getting ready to piss in a clay bottle that was sitting on a table near me.

'All right you big fag, don't start no shit,' I said, still feeling very weak and unable to move.

'Robbie, I'm so glad you're back with me, darling, for a while I thought you were a goner. You were hurt pretty bad, and in a coma when I first brought you here. I have been praying every day for the last two months to the Almighty God to make you well again, and to give you back to me,' said Magic, tears of joy running down his face, and ruining his purple mascara.

'Two months? Is that how long I've been here?' I asked taking a sip of water from a glass on my bedside table.

'That's right, old cock. I have been singing and talking in your ears for eight hours a day, every day, trying to bring you out of your coma. The Lord knows I've tried,' Magic said, smiling and feeling very proud of his deed.

'Damn. No wonder I woke up. All that horrible singing must have been too much for my brain to take,' I said, trying to smile in spite of all the pain shooting through my back and legs. Forgetting about my battle wounds, I asked Magic about President Ben Ali Hassan and what had happened to my men back in the desert.

Apparently Magic was smart enough to dig himself a hole in the desert sand to hide and then pulled a dead body over him for cover while all the fighting was going on. When the planes flew away and all the bombing and machine gun fire had stopped, he pushed the dead man off the top of him and crawled out of his hole. He went on to explain that while searching through all the dead bodies for me, he came upon President Ben Ali Hassan's body lying face down in the sand with a bullet hole the size of a baseball in the back of his head. As for my men, the bombing, the machine gun fire, and the minefield proved to be all too much for them. Not one of my brave fighting comrades survived this all important battle to reach freedom, other than Magic.

Magic went on to say that after searching for my body for about half an hour with no success, he figured I was dead like the others. He was just about to give up and had started to walk back toward the burnt out trucks to look for something to help him survive in the desert, when low and behold he suddenly heard a funny sound and saw a slight movement from under a small sand hill that resembled a shallow grave. He quickly ran over and started to dig away the sand with his hands, finding me just barely alive and shot up all to hell.

In a way Farouk had helped save my life also. When Farouk was killed by a mine, he set off five more near us, right? Well I guess most of the sand from the explosions was what was covering me when Magic Pussy found me. Anyway Magic pulled me out of the sun and into the shade of a burned out truck, and cared for me the best he could for one day before moving on towards the border. Seeing that I was getting worse and had passed out again, Magic put me on his back and started walking across the hot desert desperate to save my life.

To make a very long story short, while Magic was walking he met some desert nomads who saw I was badly hurt and that Magic was almost dying of thirst and exhaustion. They put us into a wagon and brought us to the palace of a rich Arab merchant and slave owner who offered to care for us for a price. As soon as Magic finished explaining to me what had happened, I thanked him again for saving my life, but wanted to ask him a few more questions to satisfy my curiosity.

'Something smells a bit funny, man, you said something about a price before. Now what's this price shit?' I asked.

'Oh the price, that's nothing, honey. I promised Mr Jerez that if he cared for you real nice like then delivered you across the border of Senegal to the town of Dogona safely, that I would stay behind and be a devoted slave. Now don't you upset yourself, honey, you just get better fast and everything will be alright, babykins,' Magic said cheerfully, as if nothing was wrong with the price.

'I don't care what kind of deal you made, you big stupid fag. You are coming back to America with me as a free man. You silly big—' before I could say the word 'fag', my eyes became heavy and my voice weak and I fell asleep.

'Ooh la la. I love it when you're fighting mad, Robbie,' Magic said, laughing and pulling the covers up to my shoulders. After two weeks of being wheeled around in a wheelchair by Magic, who didn't have a driver's license, a doctor came to see me. After looking at my X-rays he reported that I would never be able to walk again unless I had a special operation on my spine done by a top surgeon. Anyway as soon as the doctor left the palace half-drunk after drinking some wine with Magic and I, Magic tried everything to cheer me up. Even resorting to making funny faces and doing his silly dancing walks with his finger stuck in his asshole. After he settled down, Magic spoke again. 'Don't worry, Robbie honey, when you get back to America, and you're gonna get back as sure as my name is Pussy Galore, you can have that silly operation and you'll be as good as new,' and he started to dance again, building up to the wildest frenzy. Although I had felt bad about the news the doctor had given me earlier, now I was just glad to be alive, and changed the subject away from sickness and my disability.

'Captain Pussy, my dear friend, what are the women like around this place. Have they got any big tit girls around loose who are begging for it?' I joked.

'Me honey, I'm asking for it and you can have all you can handle, baby,' Magic said, pulling down his baggy pants to show me his big hairy ass.

'I don't want no fag's hairy ass, fool. I'm talking about real girls. The kind that are split up the front instead of the back,' I said, laughing again as Magic did another dance making his funny faces.

'Oh, you mean that kind of ass. Boy, are you kinky. Well, the mistress of this house is fantastic. She's black, big assed, got big tits, and a smile that will make you cream in your pants. Is that the kind of woman you want?'

Before I could answer, an Arab walked into the garden accompanied by two huge, big fisted, black guards.

'Hello. I see that you are looking well and are up and about these days. My name is Mohammed Ram Jerez. I am the master of this humble house,' he said, shaking my hand. This humble house he was talking about was a beautiful palace of Moorish architecture that most millionaires would never dream of owning in a lifetime.

'My name I Robbie Jones, and I thank you for saving the lives of my friend and I, but I think the price you are making my friend Magic pay is a bit high,' I said, not caring what would happen to me. Master Jerez's mouth fell open from the shock of me talking to him in the manner that I did. Then a smile came on his pimpled face as he spoke.

'You two are very lucky to have such friendship. I want the two of you to come and have dinner tonight with my wives and me. I have a surprise for you, Mr Jones, that will appeal to your race and background. Does that please you?' he asked.

'Why Master Jerez, that is most kind of you. Magic and I would love to attend a dinner with you and your wives and any worthy young lady you can find who is lonely for American company and hospitality. Until tonight then,' I said, wondering what surprise he had in store for little old me.

Still smiling, he turned and motioned his two bodyguards to make way for him and left us feeling a bit confused.

'What do you think he's up to, Robbie?' Magic asked.

'I don't know, but we'll find out tonight, won't we,' I answered, scratching my head.

That was a night I'll remember for the rest of my life. I tell you no lie. When Magic wheeled me down a long hall up to the big shining dining room doors trimmed in gold coins, we heard loud Arabic music playing and thought the palace was jumping like a party back home in the States. 'I hope he's got some handsome big dicked men in there waiting for me,' Magic said, pushing his dick to one side of his pants to make it stand out and look bigger than the average bear's.

'Yeah, and I hope he's got some big assed women in there ready to ravish my body when I look into their eyes, also baby,' I whispered to Magic, rubbing my hands together in excitement.

'OK Magic, let's go in there and give 'em hell. Open up and open wide, so this big dicked boy can see inside,' I said, looking up at Magic and smiling as I motioned him to open up the doors.

Magic wheeled me into the dining room and I immediately noticed that there were no women in the joint. Not even a fat ugly one. I figured that we were a little bit too early and the master's wives with my surprise big tit lady would be along later to deal with me royally.

'Come right in, gentlemen. You're right on time. I like men who arrive on time. It spoils the meal otherwise,' Master Jerez said, motioning to Magic to wheel me over to a seat next to him. As Magic pushed my squeaky wheelchair slowly over to a place at the table, he had a big, gleaming, dick-sucking smile on his face. I guess he couldn't help himself after seeing all those big, black, muscled bodyguards in the room. After leaving me, Magic went to his place at the table and almost broke the chair trying to sit down and look sexily at the bodyguards at the same time, like an idiot.

It seemed as if Magic went wild. He was smiling at all the guards, moving nervously in his chair as if he had a thousand ants in his pants, and smacking his lips loudly to give the guards a clue that he needed something in his mouth. Preferably a big, black dick looking over big hairy balls. 'Mr Jones, you have a very interesting friend there. I've never seen a happier man in my life. Is he always this happy?' Master Jerez asked, referring to old wet lips Magic Pussy who was now blushing shyly.

'Yeah, he's a real firecracker when he gets going,' I answered, wanting to crawl under the table with embarrassment.

'That's right honey, I'm ready for a big dick Freddy and I'm looser than the average goose,' Magic said, laughing and downing his glass of wine in one gulp.

I hope Magic doesn't get totally pissed tonight and turn out the joint, I thought to myself as Master Jerez spoke: 'Would you like dinner now?' Before I could answer, Magic butted in.

'Honey we are ready for anything. You show it to us and well find something to do with it,' and he leered at the youngest of the guards. Old Jerez didn't really know what to think about his wine guzzling fag guest, whether he was joking or being serious. I think Magic was beginning to completely piss him off.

Anyway, the servants brought in the food and some more wine while I tried to cheer up Master Jerez by telling him how nice the palace was, and Magic continued to drink heavily and flirt with the bodyguards who by now were starting to get a bit pissed off themselves. 'Eat, my friends. This is one of Mauritania's best known dishes,' Master Jerez boasted as he took a napkin from the table to wipe away the pus from a burst boil on his neck. Struggling to retain my composure from the nasty scenes on both sides of me, I asked 'What is this delicious dish?'

'This dish is called lamb cous-cous. Try it, and you'll like it, pal,' Jerez assured me. Before trying the cous-cous, I asked Jerez where his many wives were and why they had not joined us in this wonderful feast. 'Oh I'm terribly sorry, Mr Jones, but my wives went into town for some shopping and decided to stay another day. Anyway, we can talk man's talk while they are away, huh?' Master Jerez said, with a wide Creole, boot-licking grin that made me wonder what was really going on.

I hope this mother isn't a closet queen, I thought to myself as I took the first fork full of cous-cous into my mouth. When the cous-cous hit my taste buds, which had been used to potato soup garnished with a rotten onion ring, I felt as if a volcano was going to blow out of the top of my head. God damn this shit is hot, I thought to myself as I looked over into Magic Pussy's eyes which were now going counter-clockwise, steam coming from his ears. 'Is that hot enough for you smart assed boys?' Master Jerez asked sarcastically.

'Well sir, I've got nothing against your cook, good as he may be, but I think he used too many hot spices in this doush-doush dinner,' I said, not wanting to piss Master Jerez off, whose face was looking meaner and meaner now.

'First of all Mr Jones, as stupid as you are, the dish you are eating is called cous-cous and not doush-doush. Secondly just for your information, we did overdo the hot spices just for you and your stupid faggy friend,' Jerez said, his voice becoming harder with each word. Just like old times, getting the shit beat out of you over a nice meal, I thought to myself as Master Jerez moved over to me and sat his ass on the top of the table next to my plate.

'Now you boys have been smarting off at the mouth lately, and have lost your respect for your master. You must be taught again who's the boss around here and who are the no-good slaves. Now eat that really nice cous-cous my chef prepared, before I get really mad,' Jerez shouted, looking angry as ever.

I took another small mouthful of cous-cous and spit it out on the table, splashing over Jerez's right hand. As Jerez wiped his hand on my napkin, a big fisted bodyguard smacked me across the face and hoped I would say something smart about his mother so he could hit me again and again. 'That's enough for now, Boola. we don't want to spoil Mr Jones' meal, do we,' Master Jerez called out to his mean looking bodyguard, who was about to draw back his hand to give me another blow. While checking my head to see if it was still on my shoulders intact, Magic spoke up in a temper. 'What the hell is going on here, Goddamnit? Master Jerez, you promised me that you would treat my friend with kindness and see that he gets to Senegal safely if I stayed behind as one of your slaves. What's happened to our little bargain?' Magic said, walking over to me and checking to see that I had not been hurt badly.

'Boy, you had better not use that tone of voice again when you're talking to me, but I will tell you what's going on,' Master Jerez said, pouring himself another glass of wine and continuing to talk, the boot-licking grin back on his face. 'I have decided to sell both of you to a dear friend of mine, and make a nice profit. You two being such loyal friends, I didn't want to break up the set. Now you can't fault a man who's looking after his own business can you?' Jerez said, smiling as kindly as he could.

'No, I can't fault you, but I want you to know you are a low life, red faced, rat mouthed muthafucka. Now you can't fault me for feeling that way about you can you?' I said, calmly pouring myself a glass of Master Jerez' high class wine from Pico Rivera, California. (You can't picture the quality of these vineyards.)

Jerez jumped up from the table, said something in Arabic to his main bodyguard, Boola, and then spoke in English to us. 'Well gentlemen, it's getting late and I must get some beauty sleep. I'll leave Boola and his friends to entertain you while I'm gone. It's been a lovely meal and I hope you will come again sometime. Ciao, bambini,' he said in a nice, warm tone before leaving the room.

As soon as Jerez left, his six huge, black bodyguards walked over to Magic and I, surrounding us with fists clenched like sledge hammers. 'What do you think they're gonna do to us?' Magic asked, hoping they would snatch him out of his chair and make love to him in a most brutal and savage way.

'Oh, I think they'll sit down with us, drink a little wine to be sociable, and tell some dirty jokes to keep us entertained,' I said, hoping that there was no rough stuff coming up for dessert.

Just as I said that, Big Fist Boola drew back his arm like a baseball pitcher, and let it go like he was throwing towards home plate in an all important World Series game against the Yankees, hitting me upside my damn head so hard, that I saw red and white stars. After finding my head half way down my back, I looked up at this big, smiling, overgrown nigger and tried to reason with him the best I could, because this nigger hit harder than Paul Bunyan on an off day. 'Now look, Big Boola, we are both black. You wouldn't hit a black brother in a wheelchair again would you?' I asked, forcing a big watermelon-eating smile and looking as humble as I could. (It's hard to be humble when you're as cool as I am.)

Big Boola returned a bigger watermelon eating smile, and then went wild as a madman, beating the living shit out of me. (Pain, pain, pain, and more pain. This nigger may not have known about watermelons, but he sure knew how to hurt me.)

'Stop that. Stop that, you beast. If you want to beat on somebody, honey, beat on my ass. I'm ready for some pain, all you can dish out, you big ugly muthafucka,' Magic Pussy shouted, not knowing how hard this big nigger was punching me over my head. As quick as lightning, five other bodyguards surrounded Magic and started to beat the hell out of him. They beat poor Magic's ass like they were trying to beat the black off him.

This fight was worse than the Battle of Little Big Horn, with General Custer and the Indians in the starring role. As I was wheeling my chair around the table dodging the many heavy punches thrown by Big Fist Boola, I saw Magic taking a right royal ass-kicking for free, out of the corner of my eye. 'Alright dammit, I'm not gonna take this shit much longer. If you mutha fuckas don't stop pinching me so hard and so fast, I'm gonna really get mad,' Magic Pussy was shouting in a high pitched voice, as the bodyguards continued to stomp his ass unmercifully.

Anyway, after the massacre, with Magic claiming that the bodyguards never laid a glove on him, Big Boola wheeled us, bleeding badly on the newly laid carpets, down to some smelly cells in a rusty wheelbarrow that was meant to haul horseshit from the stables.

When the morning came, Magic and I looked as if we were

auditioning for a part in a play called 'The Ugly Monster', and our bodies felt as if two hundred Sherman tanks had run over us. I know you're gonna think I'm lying, but when I looked into a small mirror that was hanging on the wall, it broke. A mirror can take just so much ugliness, if you see what I mean.

Around noon, a doctor came to bandage our wounds. He put so many bandages all over our bodies that we looked like two Egyptian mummies, all dressed up to go nowhere. After taking care of us he went to speak to Master Jerez and advise him that some light work out in the garden would do us the world of good. I guess he figured the fresh air would help our wounds heal faster, and that we wouldn't be stinking so bad either.

After working in the palace gardens for two weeks doing light work, like pouring horse shit over the rosebeds and pulling weeds from around the palace tennis court, our luck finally changed for the better. The way our luck was going before, if we didn't have any bad luck, we wouldn't have had no luck at all.

Anyway, one sunny day with the sky filled with puffy clouds and the birds singing joyfully in the trees, Magic and I were working on our knees among the honey bees behind master Jerez' wives quarters, when a woman dressed all in black and wearing a small veil over her face walked into the garden with her three chubby, overfed children. They took no notice of us, working our fingers to the bone, and started to play with a soccer ball, sometimes speaking in English.

'Did you hear that? She spoke to her kids in English and they answered her back in English,' Magic said, looking over at the playful kids and the woman.

'Look you, keep your mind on your work before you scare the kids with all the bandages on your face and get us into trouble,' I said, not even looking over at the woman bending over and showing her pink panties, black seamless stockings, and a pink garter trimmed in silver on her right thigh, just above a small mole. As the woman continued to play with her two little girls and the boy, the naughty little bastard of a boy, who was wearing his mother's high heeled shoes, got angry and kicked the ball near where we were working. The smallest girl began to cry, fell to the ground, and began to curse like a drunken sailor from the ship of Captain Ahab. 'Don't cry baby, Mommie will get your ball for you. Now stop crying like a good little girl,' the woman said to the little girl nicely.

'I don't want the fucking ball now,' the little girl shouted back in anger, and turned and blew her nose on her new pink chiffon dress.

'Now don't talk like that, Jazzmenaco, I'll get your ball for you dear,' the woman said, and turned and walked in our direction to retrieve it. 'Talks just like her fucking father,' she muttered as she kicked a clod of grass out of the lawn. As the woman reached down to pick up the ball, she spoke to us with such a sexy velvet flavor. 'I'm sorry to disturb your men in your work, as I know you do it terribly well, I'll just pick up the ball and be out of your way. As she noticed the bandages covering our heads like mummies, and me still in the wheelchair holding my crotch, she enquired, 'Aren't you the two young men my husband said were run over by our prize bull in the west pasture?'

'You're very close, lady. We got run over by some men who were full of bull and wanted to give my friend and I inexpensive plastic surgery to re-arrange our faces,' I said, as I checked to see if my brakes on the wheelchair were working properly.

'Oh I see,' she said laughing, then started to walk away.

'Excuse me madam, I hate to bother you, but where did you get that ring on your right index finger?' I asked. Magic looked over at me as if I were going crazy, and motioned me with his hands to shut the fuck up.

'Oh, you mean this ring. I've had this ring for a long time. It hurts to talk about it, and anyway I don't want to get you into trouble so I had better go now, before another heavy-fisted bull gets loose and runs over you again,' she said with a smile and a wink. 'But why did you ask about this particular ring, anyway?' she asked, looking around to see where her children were.

'I gave a ring just like the one you're wearing to my wife in America many years ago, when I was a lad at Stanford University. She had greenish eyes, so I bought her a green emerald ring set in diamonds to match them,' I said, and thought of my beloved Shilee.

'That was very nice of you. What was your wife's name, may I ask, or is it too painful to talk about?' she asked, as her kids ran over to her grabbing for the ball which was held tightly between her legs.

'No, I can talk about it. Shilee has been dead for a while now,' I said, and was about to continue to speak when the woman butted in quickly.

'Did you say your wife's name was Shilee?' she asked, with excitement in her voice.

'Yes I did, and she was from a well-to-do family in this country,' I answered.

'Is your name Robbie, by any chance?' she asked, looking at all the bandages covering my face.

'Yes. My name is Robbie Jones. How did you know that?' I asked, as her little boy pulled down his little riding pants, ripped off his little underwear and calmly pissed on Magic Pussy's favorite little rose bush. The woman stood in silence for a moment, the tears began to roll from her eyes as she spoke to me in a shaky voice filled with sadness and joy.

'Robbie. Robbie, my love. It's me, Shilee. The wife you thought was dead. I have prayed to Allah all these years just to let me see you again before I die.'

Shilee ran and knelt down before me as I sat in my wheelchair choked with emotion. The words just would not leave my mouth. 'Robbie, I won't let anybody ever hurt you again, my love,' Shilee said to me, as we hugged each other in joy and excitement. The little girl, seeing Magic's displeasure over his pissed-on rose bush, suddenly kicked him in the shin and said, 'Piss on your old rose bush, you big pervert. My daddy told me about you.'

'Robbie honey, you have really done it now. Man, don't you know that's Master Jerez' *wife* you are holding and smacking your lips all over, fool?' What if he comes out here and sees you two horsing around like a couple of lovesick kids?' Magic said nervously, looking around to see if anybody was coming and stepping on the little boy's hand that was busy trying to untie his shoelace. The little boy screamed, and ran to show the swollen hand to his mother.

Trying to change the subject, and divert attention away from the boy, I said, 'Don't worry Magic, this is my life too. Let me introduce you two nice people. Magic Pussy, meet my former wife Shilee. Shilee, meet my dear friend Magic Pussy. He's the jivest mutha you ever want to meet,' I said, trying to pat the little boy on the head. Shilee, feeling very proud of her children, introduced her son Toma, the eldest of the girls Jamela, and the baby Jazzmenaco, named after the music Shilee loved so dearly.

'How do you like my little family?' she asked overflowing with joy.

'You have a wonderful family, all but that damn mean husband of yours,' I answered.

'He's a pussycat when I'm around, so don't worry about him

anymore. Robbie, I thought you were dead after the plane crash, and that's the only reason I married again. You do believe me, don't you? Rather than have something bad happen to me or be sold into slavery, I married Master Jerez. Anyway, he's not so bad when you get to know him and he treats me well,' she said, giving me a kiss on my cheek.

'I understand, Shilee, whatever happens from now on, we'll still always be the best of friends and love one another. I know you can't leave your family and friends to come away with me now, but I will ask you one big favor. And you know I wouldn't ask unless I needed something badly,' I said, giving Shilee a kiss on the forehead.

'What is it? You know all you have to do is ask,' she said.

'I want you to help my friend Magic Pussy and I to escape across the border to Senegal. Then we can make our way back to America with a bit of luck,' I pleaded.

'You don't have to escape from here. I'll talk to my husband and explain everything. Before you know it, you and Magic will be flying back to America in style. How's that for service, my darling?' she asked, grabbing my hand and putting it to her face.

'Just do what you can without getting yourself into trouble with your husband,' I said, feeling numb with excitement.

'Look honey, just help us get out of this place as quickly as possible, before that son of a bitch of a husband of yours takes a notion to kill us. And that's without the bullshit, honey,' Magic Pussy said, grabbing my other hand and putting it to his face also.

'Magic behave yourself. Shilee, don't mind him. He's just trying to look after me,' I said.

'That's alright, Robbie, I understand. He's funny and cute,' Shilee said, laughing.

'I want the two of you to join my family and I for dinner tonight, and Robbie, you can tell me all the things you've been up to since we separated after the plane crash. I will send my private maid to bring you to the palace later. Right now, I'm going to give my babies a bath,' Shilee said, giving her kids a hug and a kiss.

'Watch it Robbie, you remember the last time we went to dinner in the palace. We had knuckle sandwiches served to us,' Magic said, pointing to his bandaged head.

'What does he mean, Robbie?' Shilee asked curiously. Before I could answer, Master Jerez ran into the garden, screaming abuse at me and hurting my feelings.

'You stupid shit, how dare you look at and speak to my wife?

I'm going to beat the shit out of you for this,' he shouted as he began to kick out the spokes of the wheels on my wheelchair and pound my sore, aching, bandaged head.

'Stop that my husband, you big bully. Shame on you for beating this poor man in his wheelchair,' Shilee shouted as Master Jerez grabbed a nearby shovel and started to smack me over the head royally.

'This man and his friend are no good pieces of shit. I'm going to sell their asses just as soon as the bandages come off their fucking heads,' he shouted back angrily to Shilee.

'Well the way you are beating them, they'll be here for years. These two men are my dear friends, especially the one in the wheelchair,' Shilee said, motioning for a servant to come and take away the kids, in case Master Jerez wanted to spill some more of my blood. (Wasn't that thoughtful? She protected her children from the sight of blood.)

'You mean this bigheaded nigger in the wheelchair is a friend of yours, dear wife of mine? Since when?' Master Jerez asked as Magic tried to hide behind me and my wheelchair.

'Since many years ago. Now put down that shovel down before you hurt somebody, and come into the palace while I explain everything to you in the sauna,' Shilee said to Master Jerez, giving me a wink to let me know that she was taking care of business, the old fashioned way. Old Jerez smacked Magic upside his fat bandaged head with his fist, threw down the heavy shovel on my right foot, almost crushing my toes, and then called me a horse-faced, gap-mouthed bastard before walking away like a spoiled kid with Shilee to the palace, arm in arm.

As Jerez' bodyguards led Magic and I back to our cells, we passed near an open window and heard Master Jerez plead with Shilee and call out, 'Please, no. Say·you were married to anybody but this nigger. Oh, I know. It's a joke, isn't it?'

Laughing between us, we reached the cells and then later, Magic started being his old negative self, as usual. 'Now look what you got us into. I told you not to get mixed up with the master's wife. I told you stupid,' he said, over and over again like a broken record.

'Sit on it, Magic. Just sit on it. I know what I'm doing,' I said, wondering if Shilee could really help us.

'Honey, you give me something to sit on that's long and hard and I will with pleasure, bitch,' Magic said sarcastically.

After about six hours of sleep, Master Jerez woke us up as he and his main bodyguard Boola came into our cell. Big Boola handed us two bowls of potato soup, garnished with an onion ring, and Master Jerez spoke to us as we ate.

'I'm sorry, my dear boys, but you will have to miss the roast lamb dinner my wife is serving in the main dining room tonight. Anyway, we can finish our little business right here once and for all, don't you agree?' he said, spitting at a fly that was walking up the wall minding its own business.

'Anything you say, Master Jerez. By the way, can Magic and I get another bowl of this delicious potato soup? It may not be roast lamb with garlic and lemon juice surrounded with boiled potatoes and peas with butter, but this damn soup is good,' I said, trying my best to brown-nose old Jerez as Magic quickly snatched the onion ring from my soup and swallowed it whole.

Master Jerez smiled, and motioned Big Boola to go and get us some more of the shitty potato soup, without the onion ring. While Boola was gone, Master Jerez sat down with us and started to talk in a nicer tone of voice. 'I am sorry about what has happened to you in my country and how I've treated you two during your short stay here – but that's life. Anyway, Shilee has explained everything to me and I'm willing to forget the whole matter and help you get to America as free men,' Master Jerez said calmly, at the same time watching to see our reaction.

'Thank you very much sir, the past is the past. Right now, Magic and I just want to get safely to America as soon as possible. Anything you can do to help us will be appreciated, Master Jerez,' I said, still not trusting this old bastard one bit.

'What about you? How do you feel about my offer?' Jerez asked Magic, who had moved behind the wheelchair just in case some heavy blows were coming up on the menu again.

'Honey, I don't like violence. The Lord knows I detest it. I just want to leave this place as soon as possible. Shit, I've had more fun at a hanging,' Magic said, putting his arm around my shoulder.

'OK, it's all settled then. I promised my wife that I would release you unharmed and help you get back to America. In return, she promised me never to see, speak, write, or even telephone you, Mr Jones, as long as we are man and wife. I think that's a good deal, don't you?' Master Jerez asked me.

'Yes, it's fine by me. The past is the past,' I said, not wanting this old boy to change his mind at the last minute.

'Now that we understand each other, gentlemen, here's what I'm going to do for you from the goodness of my heart, praise

Allah. I am going to see a top diplomat tonight after dinner to arrange for two passports and some other necessary papers for your friend Magic to get into America. There should be no problems, as this man and I once served together in the army. Anyway, he's a dear friend of the family.

'Well gentlemen,' he went on, 'it looks like you will be on your way to America tomorrow morning. There is just one little point I would like to make, as this will be the last time we meet, hopefully. Tomorrow morning Boola will drive you two across the Senegal border, then to the airport 15 miles outside the city of Dakar. I don't want you to get any funny ideas about coming back for anything, because if you do, and I catch you, I will kill you in a most horrible way. Do I make myself clear?' Master Jerez said, shaking my hand and getting up from the cell floor.

'Loud and clear. You won't have any trouble from us after tomorrow, sir. If you catch me back in your country at any time, I want you to kick my ass,' I said, feeling good vibes from Master Jerez' handshake.

'Honey, you have made my day, talking sweet like that to Robbie,' Magic said, giving old Jerez a wink.

As Master Jerez was going our the cell door, he turned and commented, 'I hate your faggy friend, Mr Jones.' He smiled at me, and walked towards the palace.

'Honey pie, did you hear that? Why that little no-dick son of a bitch,' Magic said, laughing and spinning my wheelchair around in joyful circles.

All that night I laid on the cold cell floor thinking about Shilee and how hopeless it was to try to see her again before I left for America, when Big Boola and three other guards opened our cell door. Boola walked in first and motioned to two of the guards to grab Magic and I. 'Master Jerez told me to give you your two typhus injections required for your American visas tonight, so that we won't have to waste time tomorrow. Just relax, it won't hurt,' Bog Boola said, moving towards Magic Pussy with a big smile on his mush.

'I don't need no damn shot, honey. I'm cleaner than the average bitch. You better take it your damn self,' Magic said, struggling with the guards, trying to scratch their eyes out with his long painted fingernails.

'It's alright, Magic. You'll need the injection before you'll be allowed into the United States. Don't worry, I'm having one myself,' I said, trying to reassure him that everything was kosher.

'You see, your friend Robbie is a brave man. Hold still. It won't hurt one little bit,' Big Boola said, smiling at Magic.

'OK, but don't bruise my skin, honey. One of them big handsome American boys might want to kiss this arm,' Magic said with a weak smile, fainting when the needle went into his arm.

'What a big sissy,' one of the guards commented as Big Boola moved toward me to give me my injection. After giving me the shot, Big Boola smiled and said sarcastically, 'I hope you have a good trip, stupid.' As my head started to feel heavy and dizzy, I could hear Boola say to the other guards before going out the cell door, 'That will fix 'em good. They won't wake up for a long time. I bet when we drop the bastards off tomorrow in Dakar, they will be really shocked and surprised at where we left them.'

As I tried to wheel my chair over to Magic to check that he was alright, I guess I must have passed out from the phony injection, because everything went black, and I don't remember a single thing after that moment.

# 15

The next morning when the sun came up, I awoke to the sound of birds singing in the trees and the humming of bees swarming around a blossoming orange tree against a dazzling blue sky. And here I was nestled in a trash dump with my wheelchair crushed as if a tank had hit it lying in a heap nearby. I slowly raised the top half of my body up, looked around, and started calling out for Magic Pussy to come and help me.

Suddenly from underneath a pile of garbage and boxes nearby, Magic's head popped out and shouted, 'Robbie, is that you? What kind of shit is this? My head feels terrible. I thought we were going home in style, not ending up on some trash dump like a couple of bums.'

'Stop moaning, sissy, and come over here and help me,' I said, swiping at the huge flies swarming around my head and face. Magic got up and started to remove the garbage that was covering my body and said, 'Robbie, what are we going to do now? We don't even know where we are'

'Don't worry, old man, I always think of something to get us out of trouble, don't I?' I said.

'Yeah, that's what worries me, you thinking up some other brilliant plan, fool,' Magic said laughing after looking at my smashed up wheelchair.

'Hey Magic, look, there's a big white building over there on your right. Maybe if we go over there, we can find out where we are. Come on. Pick me up and let's get over there fast.'

Magic picked me up and carried me on his back through the trash dump and onto some nicely cut grass, when suddenly a voice called out. 'Hey you damn bums, don't walk on the fucking grass. Can't you read the signs all around here?'

We saw an old black man running towards us, chewing tobacco and spitting about every five steps that he took. Magic laid me down on the grass and sat himself down for a rest as the old man came closer and said, 'Damn, you boys must be new around here, huh? Don't you know this is the American Embassy grounds? And that you can't just walk on the grass when you feel like being silly. You boys look pretty fucked up in the head for my liking.'

'Look, old man, calm down a bit. We are new around here and didn't know this was the American Embassy grounds. My friend and I are very sorry for walking across your nice grass and garden. Will you forgive us, friend?' I said, trying to be friendly.

'Well, I don't know. You boys look mighty fucked up and are probably up to no good. I can tell, you know. I can tell by looking in your friend's bloodshot eyes that something is wrong here,' the old man said, spitting a big wad of tobacco juice near Magic's foot.

'Watch that spitting, honey. The next time you gotta spit, you had better point your mutha fuckin' jaws in another direction. You don't know me that well to be spitting on me, honey. I ain't cheap, and I don't take that shit from my mother let alone a rag and bone man like you,' Magic said angrily, rolling his eyes at the man.

'You see? I told you there was something funny about you two boys. You there boy, with the red fingernails and false eyelashes. The devil has put a curse on you, judging by the way you act. You act just like an old boy back home in my tribal land who used to put on dresses and suck all the big dicked men whenever there was a full moon. The Lord knows the devil was in that poor boy. How else could he be that low down and just no good?' the man said, backing away from Magic as if he had the black plague.

'Well honeychild, I must be the big bad devil himself, because I don't need no full moon to suck no big dicks. Speaking of dicks, how's that big boy in your pants?' Magic said las the old man looked at him in disgust.

'Magic, please be nice to the old man. Behave yourself and be serious for a while, dammit,' I said to Magic, then turned to the old man to speak of matters that were of more importance. 'Old man, where are we and what country is this?' I asked.

'You are in Senegal, and where you are at this moment is Dakar. yes my boy, you are in the beautiful city of Dakar and in the American Embassy grounds talking to its proud groundskeeper, who wishes that you would fuck off and stop asking so damn many questions. You can quote me on that, if you wish,' he said as he put another big wad of tobacco in his mouth.

'OK, old man. Just one more question before we leave. What time does the American Embassy open?' I asked, still swiping at the flies buzzing around my head.

'10am every day but Saturday, Sunday, and holidays. Now can I get back to my damn work? You boys ask a lot of questions for bums. You two are the craziest niggers I ever met in my life. Shit,' he said, turning to walk away, picking his nose.

'Is the embassy open today?' I called out.

'No. It's a holiday today. The embassy won't be open until Tuesday, tomorrow,' the old man shouted back, putting a green slimy bogie in his mouth along with the tobacco.

'Now what are we gonna do? We've got no money, nowhere to stay tonight, we're both starving, and here we are stranded in a city we don't know anything about,' I shouted in frustration.

'Now look who's bitching like a sissy. Don't worry, Robbie, I'm used to this kind of shit. I'll take care of you, but first we gotta get some new clothes if we want to come back here and speak to someone in the embassy tomorrow. You don't want to look like a bum, do you?' Magic said, helping me to my feet and up onto his back.

While wandering through the busy streets of Dakar with me being carried on Magic's back, many of the people stopped and stared and made funny jokes. This didn't really worry Magic and I. What did bother us was passing by the many shop windows with all that food on display and our stomachs telling us that it was time to eat.

Anyway, trying to ignore the food displays in the shops and markets, Magic finally found a Turkish bath located above a shoe shop just off a street named Merindes. Magic sat me down on the stairs in the hall passage and went alone to talk with the manager. I don't know what he said, or what he did, as it could have been a thousand things, knowing Magic the way I do, but anyway the manager came back with Magic in arm and helped me up the stairs to the locker room, all friendly like.

'You boys just relax and enjoy your baths. If there's anything you need, and I mean anything within reason, just push this button to the side of the door and I'll send someone to tend to your wishes,' the manager said, smiling all over himself closing the bath door.

'What did you say to get us in here for free?' I asked Magic, noticing a bit of cock juice in his hair.

'Nothing. You worry too much, honey. Just relax like the man said and let's enjoy the bath,' Magic answered as three well dressed gentlemen walked into the locker room speaking in German and began to undress. While Magic and I were undressing over in our corner, the three men looked over and started to laugh at us, as we were dressed worse than your average rag and bone man.

'Let 'em laugh, honey, we'll see who has the last laugh later,' Magic said as he saw how hurt I was. He picked me up and carried me into a cold shower and then into the hot Turkish bath, where we sat and talked about old times for about fifteen minutes. While the other three men sat in the opposite corner to us, laughing and talking merrily in German, Magic whispered to me, 'Let's go. Now is the time to get some new clothes. You understand my meaning, Robbie?'

'Yeah, let's go. We'll show them bastards how real men are supposed to dress,' I said. After changing into their new tailor-made clothes, that we had so kindly been lent by our German hosts, Magic and I looked sharper than a tack and sleeker than a nail. We were dressed to kill. Why, we must have been the cleanest niggers in town. 'Let's go before the manager comes,' said Magic helping me up onto his back. Magic tip-toed down the main stairs and ran out the door, across the street, and hid behind a telephone repair truck.

'Why don't we keep on running instead of waiting around here?' I asked Magic, who was now peeping from behind a truck with me still on his back.

'I thought you might like to see the faces of the three bastards who were laughing at us when they climbed down the stairs wearing our gear,' Magic said.

'Fuck them guys. Let's go on and see if we can eat some food. I'm hungry, shit,' I said pulling him by the shirt collar.

'Watch the shirt, sucker. I didn't steal this shirt for you to be fucking with it. I gotta look good for the men folk around here, you understand that, don't you?' said Magic.

While Magic was standing there with me on his back talking bullshit, I happened to look through the inside pocket of the coat and found a wallet that belonged to one of the Germans. 'Hey Magic, look through this wallet I found in the pocket and see what's in there we can use,' I said.

'Alright baby, now we're getting somewhere, Robbie,' Magic said as he turned the wallet inside out frantically, finding nothing but German credit cards and half a pack of condoms. 'Those fucking shit Germans, why don't the bastards carry paper money with them?' Magic shouted in anger.

'Come on. Let's use the credit cards to get something to eat in a nice restaurant for a change. it doesn't matter,' I said, trying to calm Magic down as people were starting to gather around us and stare.

About six blocks away from the Turkish bath, we found a really nice little restaurant called the Harem Gardens, just across the street from a public park. As we were about to enter the restaurant, a shoe shine boy working near the entrance asked Magic if he would like a shoe shine. Since Magic was wearing leather and alligator shoes, he replied 'I'm terribly sorry, son, I wish I could help you in your hour of need. Maybe tomorrow I'll need a shine.'

'You need one today, you big fucking fag, and give that poor monkey on your back a banana, too,' the boy said laughing as he took off down the street.

'Did you hear that honey? He called you a monkey. What a cheek,' Magic said.

'He called you a fag. So what,' I answered.

As Magic walked through the restaurant with me on his back, most of the clientele looked on in disgust and began to complain to waiters. I guess we looked a bit weird at that. Anyway the manger ran out of his office and over to us and started to manhandle Magic, which was definitely a mistake, little did he know.

'Honey, take your hands off me. you don't know me that well

to be fucking with me. I ain't cheap,' Magic shouted loudly. I quickly butted in on this classy discussion before Magic could put a beating on this poor bastard's head, and explained to the manager why I was up on Magic's back. After all was said and done, thanks to me, the manager invited Magic and I over to the bar for a drink until a table became available for us to partake in a little dinner.

A handsome bartender in a Senegal national costume walked over and asked what we would like to order. He had a hump on his back and a pleasant smile on his face. Other than that, he seemed like a rather nice fellow who enjoyed his work. And that's more than you can say about a lot of hump-backed bartenders nowadays. Magic asked 'How much is a shot of whisky?' The bartender answered 'Twenty dollars, sir.'

'Damn, that's awful high,' Magic shouted out loud as common as shit.

'I know. It's the inflation of the economy, my boy,' said the bartender, giving me a wink.

'Well how much is a shot of vodka then?' Magic asked, watering at the mouth now for a drink of anything. The bartender answered calmly and with a civil tongue in his mouth, 'That will be only fifteen dollars in American money, sir.'

'Fifteen dollars? Damn, man, that's still as high as hell,' said Magic, becoming more upset and more thirsty.

'Yeah, but I only work here and I don't make the rules, my friend,' said the bartender, now polishing a shot glass.

'Now look, I'm really getting mad. How much is a shot of gin, dammit?' Magic said, leaning across the bar in the bartender's face with his breath smelling like do-do.

'Now that will only be five dollars a shot, sir,' said the bartender with a great deal of patience.

'Then give my friend and I a shot of gin. That's still as high as hell, you know,' Magic snapped.

The bartender went away and came back with a large bottle of cheap Russian gin, poured us a shot each, and then moved to the other end of the bar. While Magic and I were enjoying our gin, sipping it slowly, the bartender began scratching the hump on his back and said aloud, 'This damn hump is itching like hell. Excuse me if I scratch it in front of you two gentlemen.'

Magic Pussy being a quick witted type of guy, looked up at the bartender and said, 'Hump. I thought that was your ass. Everything else is so high in this joint.'

While Magic and I were laughing, falling all over the bar at the expression on the bartender's face, the head waiter came over and showed us to our table. Boy, we were ready to grease.

As soon as we sat down, the people sitting at the next table got up and left rather quickly as Magic began to make funny duck noises with his mouth. 'Magic, please, no more. I can't take any more of your silly jokes,' I said, holding my stomach from the pain of laughter.

'Honey, I'll run all these silly stuck up fuckers out of here. They don't know who they're messing with,' Magic joked as he picked up the menu.

In the middle of our nice meal of roast duck, potatoes, and peas with mushrooms, the head waiter came over to our table and asked how we would like to settle our bill. 'We'll pay using our National Allied Credit Card, sir,' I answered, stuffing a juicy piece of duck into my mouth and chewing on its tender texture.

'May I see your card, sir?' the head waiter asked, smoothing the lapel of his dinner jacket that was stained with mushroom gravy and mustard.

'Look, bitch. Can't you wait until my friend and I have finished eating? What kind of shit is this anyway? My damn duck is getting cold, sucker,' Magic shouted at the shaky head waiter.

'I'm terribly sorry sir, but I must see your card. It's a house rule,' the head waiter said with a polite smile that said nothing.

'It's alright, Magic, the man is only doing his job. Show him our card,' I said, wiping the duck and mushroom juice from my chin. Magic took out the German credit card from his top coat pocket and put it into the head waiter's outstretched hand. 'This son of a bitch doesn't believe we can pay, Robbie. Shall I scratch his damn eyes out?' he asked.

'Cool it, man. Let the man do his job,' I said.

The head waiter looked at the card, then at the two of us, then back at the card, then back at us before speaking. 'Which of you is Mr Hans Von Strauser?' he asked.

Both Magic and I pointed at each other at the same time and shouted together like two idiots, 'He is.'

'The both of you can't be him,' said the head waiter, starting to look a little bothered about the bill. With Magic and myself trying to think fast to answer the head waiter's question, again we pointed to each other at the same time and shouted together as if singing a duet, 'He is.'

The head waiter handed the card back to Magic and looked at

the two of us in disgust, shaking his head as he walked away from the table.

'Don't come back over here asking no silly-assed questions, unless you got some more food with you, sucker,' Magic called out across the restaurant to the head waiter who was still shaking his head in disgust at our rude behavior. (Little did he know that Magic was just getting started.) Magic turned back to me and we both fell back in our chairs laughing like two schoolboys who had just stolen the rabbi's Mogen-David wine from behind the refrigerator. 'Boy, did we fuck up tonight,' I said, laughing.

'We? Where did you get that "we" shit from? You fucked up. From now on let me do all the talking, Mr Fancy General,' Magic said as he reached over and took a spoonfull of my mushroom sauce reeking with garlic.

Anyway, after finishing the meal and ordering four more bottles of L'Orangerie cheapo French wine, this old restaurant didn't seem so bad after all. We became louder and louder, and the restaurant started to empty before the manager came over and warned us about our strange behavior. As the manager walked back to his office, I whispered to Magic, 'I think we had better leave now before someone calls the police.'

'Fuck the police. Fuck the manager and all the other on-looking mutha fuckas,' Magic shouted loudly.

Just then the manager rushed back out of his office and whispered something into a skinny-headed waiter's ear, and then went back in the office. The head waiter then called all the other waiters around him and instructed them to guard all the exits. I guess they wanted to make sure the bill was paid. Anyway, I was having fun and was having fun and was too drunk to care to think straight about the whole matter at the time. Magic and I were having a ball laughing, joking and screaming at the top of our voices, when suddenly I heard the sounds of police sirens moving nearer and nearer.

'Magic. Do you hear what I hear?' I shouted.

'What? All I hear is a ringing in my ears. Let's have another fucking drink. we can afford it, shit,' Magic said, pissed as your average bear.

'That ringing in your ears is the police, fool, and they're coming for us right now. if we don't get out of here quickly, it's back to jail again for a long time, nigger,' I said, trying to make Magic understand this delicate situation, as the waiters all had big shit-eating smiles on their faces at our dilemma.

'How in the hell are we gonna get out of here? Those damn waiters have all the doors guarded,' Magic said as the sirens got closer. I had to think quickly. Suddenly a brilliant thought came to my genius mind. Jump through the huge plate glass window right before you, dummy.

'That's it. We have to jump through the window, ' I whispered.

'You and what fool? I know I'm drunk, but I ain't crazy,' Magic said, laughing and making funny faces at me.

'You see how you're stretching your face to make it funny? Well, if the police catch us wearing stolen clothes and carrying a stolen credit card, they're gonna stretch our asses, sucker,' I said as the sound of the sirens stopped in the parking lot.

'Promises, promises. All you do is make promises. Come on, let's get out of here, you big sissy,' Magic said, quickly helping me onto his back. 'Are you ready Robbie? Just cover your head and eyes and be ready to go when I say 'Geronimo',' Magic whispered as the waiters watched us intently.

'Let's go. Let's go before –' Before I could finish speaking, Magic ran towards the plate glass window and shouted 'Geronimo!' as we crashed through the huge window onto the ground outside.

'Get up, muthafucka, the cops are right behind us,' I shouted as Magic rolled on the ground laughing his head off. He quickly picked me up and ran into the nearby park and hid behind some bushes. I thought it was strange that the police didn't give chase. They just stood talking to the manager, looking at the broken window, and occasionally shining a flashlight into the park. We later found out why they didn't give chase the hard way. The name of this particular park was the Rochester Public Park, named after the first English Viceroy of Senegal, General 'Rocky' Rochester. This park was famous for its highly professionalized muggings. The muggers in this neck of the woods knew how to put an old fashioned beating on your ass in a royal manner. This was the only place in the city of Dakar where you got your ass kicked and robbed of your worldly goods with the muggers thanking you for your contribution and inviting you back any time.

Anyway, Magic and I didn't know all this good stuff then and we went further on up to the darkest part of the park to hide. 'This will do for now, Robbie. Shit, I'm tired of carrying your heavy ass. Let's sleep here for the night,' Magic said as he lowered me to the ground carefully, not wanting me to wrinkle my suit too badly.

'Yeah, this will do. It's dark enough and no one should be passing by here this time of night. I think it's pretty safe, don't you?' I said. Magic was now making a pillow for me out of his suit coat.

'Yeah, you're right. Let's get some sleep so we can get up early tomorrow and get to the embassy, OK?' he whispered.

'Yeah, goodnight Magic. And I want to thank you for helping me like you have. I'm really grateful,' I said, swiping at a mosquito buzzing around my ear.

'Forget it, sissy, and get some sleep,' said Magic, quickly falling into a deep sleep, snoring like a hibernating bear. I turned over and fell to sleep immediately, dreaming of a successful operation on my spinal cord and the big tit women that wanted to ravish my body royally.

The next morning Magic woke me up screaming, in a state of panic. 'Robbie, wake up! Some son of a bitch has stolen our clothes right off our backs.'

'Magic, calm down. Keep a civil tongue in your head. It's not so bad,' I said, looking up at Magic standing in front of me naked as a jaybird.

'Oh it's not so bad, huh? Well just take a good look at yourself, fool,' Magic said, smiling and scratching his nuts.

I looked down at my poor body and noticed that all of my clothes were gone also and shouted, 'Hey man, some bastard has stolen mine too. At least they could have left our nasty drawers. Now what are we going to do?'

Magic spoke laughingly, 'It's not so bad after all. The people who stole our clothes right off our backs must have been real professionals and gentlemen, because they left behind their fine stylish rags.'

'What do you mean? I asked.

'Why, these fine stylish rags over here,' Magic said, picking up two large pieces of rag that looked like potato sacks.

'What's that shit, man? That shit looks like two potato sacks sewed together with holes cut out for the arms and legs,' I said, now realizing that I might have to wear one of them.

'That's exactly right, old cock, now stop bitching and put this one on and let's get to the American Embassy quickly, fool,' Magic said, and throwing one suit of potato sack rag over to me.

'When is this fucking nightmare going to end? Just tell me

when, just tell me when,' I shouted in a fit of temper.

'Don't let it get you down, honey, things could be worse, you know. Here, let me help you with that,' Magic said, helping with my potato sack.

'Man we can't go to the embassy looking like a couple of bums, why they'll just laugh us out the place. Can you imagine the expression on the Marine Guard's faces when they see us walking up the steps dressed in potato sacks?' I asked Magic, who thought he looked much slimmer in his sack.

'Robbie honey, I don't see a damn thing wrong with these pretty little sacks. You look cute in yours. It shows your lovely knees.' Magic walked out of the park and through the many back streets to reach the embassy, so not to draw too much attention to him carrying me up on his back and letting the people in the market place see us both dressed in our new tailor-made potato sacks.

As we went up the embassy steps a marine guard called out, 'What do you boys want? The garbage dump is at the back.'

'Look man, we don't want no garbage dump, our damn clothes were stolen last night. You think we go around dressed like this all the time? We came here to speak to someone to help us get back to the United States,' I snapped.

'I'm terribly sorry sir, I thought you was one of the local niggers and up to no good. Why, back home in Montgomery, Alabama we had niggers –' Before the stupid marine could finish speaking about his red-necked daddy, Magic moved off toward the embassy doors madder than an unpaid whore leaving the guard talking to himself.

'Are all white people like that back in America?' Magic asked as we went into the lobby.

'No, they're not all like that, just in parts of America like the South, the Midwest, the West Coast, the East, and the North. Other than that, it's OK,' I said, motioning him over to the information desk.

'Oh that's OK then. I thought all of America might be like that,' Magic said as we approached the desk.

'Can I help you two nig... gentlemen?' asked a pretty blonde, blue eyed, red-necked secretary sitting behind the information desk with her dress pulled up to her meaty thighs.

'Yes ma'am. I would like to speak to the ambassador or a high ranking official to help my friend and I. It's an emergency,' I said, still sitting on Magic Pussy's back.

'Yes, I can see what you mean,' she said, smiling after checking our fashionable potato sacks. 'Are you American citizens?' she asked.

'Yes we are,' I said, lying about Magic.

'Could you and your friend find a seat, and the ambassador will see you as soon as possible. Oh by the way, what are your names please?' she asked.

'Mr Jones and Mr Johnson,' I answered, looking down between her meaty thighs. As she began to write down our names on a pad, Magic carried me over to some nearby seats next to the water fountain.

After sitting and waiting to speak to the ambassador for about three hours, he finally arrived wearing an old Robert Hall suit that was two sizes too small with a very shiny seat, and motioned us to come into his immaculate office. Magic lowered me onto a chair, from where I began to explain everything in the most minute detail. I became so dramatic that tears were running down my cheeks. The ambassador meanwhile, sat discreetly holding his nose from the odor of our bodies and clothes. Every five minutes he would get up and go to the window for fresh air, saying 'Damn, I needed that air. What kind of cologne are you boys using, white beans?'

'Well sir, now you have the whole story. We were just wondering if you could help us,' I said, trying to be humble and only telling a little white lie here and there to make the story as interesting as possible. (If this story sells, I'll take up writing seriously.)

'Can I be perfectly honest and frank with you two boys?' the ambassador asked, looking at us very suspiciously.

'You can be Frank, Bill, Charlie, or anybody you want to be honey. I think you're cute, myself,' Magic said, giving the ambassador a wink of the eye and rolling his tongue around his lips.

'You niggers come in here with some cock and bull story and expect me to believe it, don't you? For a start, the faggy nigger with you, Mr Jones, is not an American citizen. He talks like he still has a dick in his mouth. Secondly, I don't give a shit what happens to you, Mr Jones. Anyway boy, you ain't got no damn business over here messing with these fine people. you should be back home on some old boy's plantation picking cotton, or fishing on the banks of the Ohio river and eating watermelon. Speaking of watermelons, would you two boys like a piece now?' the ambassador asked, lighting a huge Cuban cigar.

'Mr Ambassador, things have been really bad, honestly. Can

you find it in your heart to help us? I beg you to show a little compassion and mercy in your decision about helping us. I beg you,' I said in all seriousness.

'Now isn't that just like a nigger? Begging and crying after he's done fucked up. I'll tell you old boys what I'm gonna do for you. You bring me two thousand American dollars and I'll fix everything so that you two can enter the States legally,' said the ambassador, moving over to the window again for some more fresh air.

'Is the two thousand dollars for our passports, sir?' Magic asked, as I was too ashamed and hurt after begging the big, fat, red-necked fucker to help us in our hour of need.

'Boy, your papers will be in order. You have my word on it. Now that two thousand dollars you boys are going to give me, out of the kindness of your poor little hearts, is my business for whatever it's for. You understand? Anyway boy, you'd better learn fast not to question a white man,' he shouted.

'Come on Robbie, I think we'd better be going now,' Magic said, helping me on his back.

'Yeah we'd better, before I say something I may regret later,' I said.

'You boys come back when you got that money, ya hear? Oh, and anytime you want a piece of nice fresh watermelon just go around to the back of the embassy, to the back door and tell old nigger Jake that I said you could have a piece. The Lord knows I don't like to see nobody suffer, and I can see that you two boys have suffered for too long. Y'all come back now, ya hear?' the ambassador said, closing his office door behind us.

After giving the ambassador's private secretary all the information she required for making up the new passports, Magic helped me up onto his back once again and started to walk across the lobby toward the exit doors when I suddenly noticed a shiny new Westinghouse wheel chair parked outside the gentlemen's toilet.

'Hey Magic, stop. Do you see what I see?' I said, turning his face in the direction of the chair.

'Kiss my ass, honey. Robbie, I'm gonna take that chair for you. I'm tired of carrying your heavy ass, honey,' Magic said, helping me down from his back onto a wooden chair in the corner. Magic ran quickly over to the wheelchair and wheeled it back over to me. 'You going my way honey child?' he asked jokingly, helping me into the shiny new wheelchair. 'Now I hope that feels better. For a while I felt like a horse carrying your heavy ass on my back,'

Magic said, wheeling me through the embassy main doors past the marine guards, and down a ramp onto the sidewalk. 'Stop bitching and push, sucker, while I try to think of how to get two thousand dollars to get home,' I said, still feeling ashamed of having to beg that fat red-neck ambassador who was a fellow American for help.

'Stop worrying so much. I'll think of a way to get the money. What can you do anyway? First let's find a place to stay tonight, safely this time, and then we'll worry about how we're going to get the money,' Magic said, pushing the wheelchair down the sidewalk and making the noise of the car engine revving with his mouth. Magic wheeled me half way across the city into the worst part of the Old Casbah, and I mean this son of a bitch was old. I'll bet Moses had an apartment here. Have you ever heard the saying 'Take me to the Casbah' in the movies? Well, most people think it's a romantic place to fantasize about. let me tell you honestly what it is really like, in four easy words. It's a shit house. Most casbahs are dirty, nasty, and are full of undesirables such as pimps, prostitutes, beggars, homosexuals, pickpockets, dope sellers, and the likes. While being wheeled down one of the main streets of the Casbah, I suddenly noticed from the corner of my eye a middle-aged man following us.

'Hey Magic, there's a man following us. He's been trailing us for the last two blocks.'

'I know honey, I can't help it if he finds me charming and irresistible. You wait here while I go and have a word with the poor man. Now don't you move until I get back. You understand Robbie?' Magic said, running off toward the smiling man.

'Don't go, Magic. Come back here. That man could be dangerous and do your ass in,' I called out. I was too late. Magic was halfway across the street when I called out to him. He went into a side alley next to a coffee shop arm in arm with the man and came out about twenty minutes later, spitting some white stuff to the ground. He then kissed the man passionately, had a quick feel of the man's cock and balls, and then ran across the street toward me, waving bye to the middle-aged man who now seemed most grateful and a few pounds lighter. 'What did that guy want? You could have been killed running off with a strange man like that, fool,' I said, with some concern for Magic's safety.

'Don't be silly, Robbie, that was such a nice man. He thought I was one of his old army buddies from his home town. You always think the worst of everything. Now let's go and find somewhere to stay tonight and get something to eat,' Magic said.

'Well, wipe that cock juice from your moustache before you wheel me anywhere,' I said, dropping the subject. Magic continued to wheel me down the many side streets of the Casbah for about an hour before coming to a bar called the Hercules Palace, which was next door to a gym, that had the most notorious shower room in the city. Those boys would whip your ass for a bit of head and sometimes whip your head for a bit of ass. I thought it might be a normal bar at first glance, with all the tourists and their cameras, but after having a couple of free beers from the owner of the bar who was sweet on Magic, I noticed that most of the clientele was gay and wore leather jackets like the ones that the American rockers and bikers wore in the fifties. The rest of the costume consisted of blue jeans with handkerchiefs hanging out of the back pocket, each of a different color which signalled the particular type of deviation the wearer was into. The red for wanting top be beaten, the blue for wanting to beat the reds, the green for wanting someone to shit on them, especially if he was an Ex-Lax lover, and yellow signified the desire for a pissy shower on your head, if you could aim straight.

Anyway, Magic left me at the table along with a beer and said that he'd be back shortly and not to leave. Where could I go anyway in this wheelchair, dummy, I thought to myself. While sitting at the table drinking my beer and minding my own business, two big muscular gay fellows walked in and sat at the table next to me talking in loud voices. 'Honey, I bought a big black dildo from that new sex shop on Moobah street today,' said the bigger of the two guys, running his fingers through his curly blonde hair on the side of his head.

His friend smiled and said 'Oh that's nice. Did you have it gift wrapped?'

'No, I just ate it right there,' said the first guy, laughing and giving his friend a kiss on the cheek.

Just as Magic walked through the bar doors, the gay couple turned their attention to me. The biggest of the two, who was wearing a toupee which covered the bald spot down the centre of his head, spoke to me. 'Hi there, handsome. What are you doing later? You want to come back to my house for some fun and games, huh?' As soon as he said that, Magic walked over to the table and caught the last part of the conversation. 'Look bitch, if you want some fun and games later, the fun part will be kicking your ass so hard that your nose will bleed. The game part, honey, will be how many times I can flush your toilet before that shitty wig you're wearing so badly will go down the hole. Now piss off before I really lose my temper. The fucking cheek, trying to pick up my best friend. Anyway suckers, Robbie likes pussy,' Magic shouted to the big guy in anger, giving me a wink.

The couple moved away from the table quickly as Magic started to explain what he had been up to during his absence. 'Honey, I found the cutest little place to stay and a job to go along with it. How's that for service?' Magic asked looking all excited.

'Where is this place?' I asked.

'Stop asking so many questions and let me take you over there. Come on, Robbie, let's go,' he said.

'OK, but don't leave me alone again in a fucking queer bar. I just might give some dick away,' I said jokingly.

'You should be so lucky,' Magic said as he wheeled me out of the bar.

Magic was singing in his raspy soprano voice and doing a little dance step as he pushed my wheelchair down the side streets, and finally into a barn that smelled of camel shit. 'What is this? Don't tell me this is the place you found for us to stay,' I complained.

'Stop bitching. The owner said we could stay in a room upstairs for free, if we only help out with some of the work around here,' Magic said proudly.

'What kind of work does he want us to do?' I asked, a little pissed off.

'Well you can work in the front house behind a nice desk checking in and out the camels to the tourists, and I can clean out the barn and feed the bastards,' Magic explained.

'And how much is the owner going to pay us for our work?' I asked.

'Twenty dollars each month. That's what it comes to if you figure it out in American money. I like a nice round figure, don't you?' Magic said, helping me out of my wheelchair and up the stairs to our room, if you could call it that. (I must sound pissed off. Well it's true. But this was really the Hilton Pits.)

'See, it ain't so bad, huh?' Magic said as he carried me into the room almost slipping on some not so dry camel shit.

'It's a shit hole. It's a real shitty shit hole,' I shouted in a rage, wanting to crush a grape in fierce anger.

'Not when you put a woman's touch to it. Why honey, this will be like a place when I get through with it,' Magic said, holding me in his arms and giving me a big wet kiss on my forehead.

The room was small and had a camping stove in the corner to do all the cooking. The toilet, which had no running water, was right next to the cooking facilities. This place was the almighty pits. It was dirty, had smeared camel shit all over the floor, huge rat holes in the wall, and the ceiling had holes in it and was starting to cave in on our heads. I know you think I might be lying about my next statement, but I swear on my grandmother's life that I saw a cockroach kick a rat's ass and take the cheese from its mouth. That's the kind of neighborhood we were moving in to. Well anyway, this was to be our home for a while, at least until we could scrape together the two thousand dollars to get home.

For two months Magic and I worked and lived upstairs above the barn, and we were still no closer to having the two thousand dollars than when we first started. The old man who owned the camel riding school worked our asses long and hard. We worked from six in the morning to five in the evening, and boy it was a bitch. Sometimes after work, Magic and I would go down to the beach and buy some fresh fish from the fishermen who couldn't sell all their catch of the day.

One day after buying some fresh shark meat from a woman named Boobalina, Magic wheeled me along the beach where I just happened to mention our crazy dilemma. 'Magic, we gotta do something. I don't know what, but we gotta get ourselves out of this shit somehow,' I said.

'Yeah I know, just let me think of something while I'm pushing you along the beach. I always think better in the sea air,' Magic said, stopping the wheelchair and sitting down in the sand. While sitting in my wheelchair and letting the sea breeze wash my face, I realized what a good friend Magic Pussy was, even though he was also a pain in the ass. (I don't mean that literally. I like pussy, remember.) Why, Magic had so many opportunities to leave me flat broke, in a wheelchair, and in a country I know nothing about, to go off with a wealthy tourist somewhere and not worry about me. You see, Magic stood about six feet ten inches, was well built, and was naturally good looking with a head full of black curly hair. Why, he was like a big black gladiator, and the men would fall over themselves sometimes, just to speak to him. Of course Magic loved this, but he would never, but never, desert me in my hour of need. He was a true friend of mine, no matter what he did. For Magic probably loved me more than I loved myself. While reflecting on all this, and watching the

waves pound on the rocks, a shout from Magic broke the spell.
'Robbie, I got it. I can get a job working in a club as a male dancer.'

'Male dancer? Who wants to see a male shaking his ass on
stage?' I asked.

'You'd be surprised, honey. There's a club on Spartel street in
the Casbah that's looking for a female impersonator to join the
cast. I can get a job there. The owner has already asked me if I was
interested, honey.'

'When did you speak to the owner?' I asked.

'Two days ago when I came to the beach alone to pick up the
fish. You remember I got home late? Why honey, I walked into
the club swinging my hips and drove the owner wild. I had his
tongue hanging out he wanted me so bad. You can understand
that, can't you?' Magic said, laughing and grabbing my chair and
making it spin in circles.

'Yes Magic, I can understand that, but won't it be dangerous
working in a place like that?' I asked.

'Baby, I'll be queen of the place. Now you tell me who's gonna
be foolish enough to mess with me when all the men in the club
are in love with yours truly? You tell me, honey. Just look at this
handsome face and body,' Magic joked, pushing me along the
beach with the sea breeze hitting me in the face.

'Magic, I appreciate what you're trying to do and I'm grateful.
Lord knows I'm grateful for your kindness and devotion, but I
don't want you to get into any trouble on my account, so I think
you'd better forget it,' I said, worrying about Magic's safety and
well-being.

'Shut up, sissy, I'm gonna do it. Anyway, you're gonna be
there to keep an eye on me so that I won't get into any trouble,'
Magic said, patting me on the shoulder.

'What do you mean? I can't work in the club while I'm in this
wheelchair,' I said.

'Oh yes you can. You are going to be my light man. You know,
work the lights while I'm doing my act? All the big stars carry
their own light men and you're mine. I've already spoken to the
owner of the club about you, sweetie. It was having you and I
working together or nothing at all. You see how momma takes
care of you? Now stop bitching and let's go home and cook this
shark garnished with mushrooms. I'm hungry, shit,' Magic said,
laughing and doing an outrageous little dance in the sand.

'OK sissy, let's go,' I said feeling much better about the whole
matter.

Well, Magic got the job just as he promised, and got me a job working the lights for the whole show. It was a nice job for my part. I'd sit upstairs in the lighting booth and work the lights from eight o'clock in the evening until two o'clock the next morning. The pay wasn't bad for this part of the world, either. Magic made two hundred dollars a month and I made one hundred dollars a month. We moved from upstairs over the camel riding school to a nice little apartment around the corner from the club, paying about one hundred dollars a month, American. For a change, everything was going great. Magic was the talk of the city and people came from all over Dakar to see him perform his act dressed as Cleopatra. Every night it was standing room only, and the men's eyes would almost pop out of their heads when Magic made his entrance. Some nights the people in the club would give Magic a standing ovation when he quoted his favorite saying while sitting on the knee of the man he had brought up on stage.

'What's that in your pants so big and hard that I'm sitting on, honey, a baseball bat? Oooh, you're awful, but I like it.' This would bring the house down every time and the owner loved every minute of it.

Me, I wasn't doing badly myself. I was going out with an American white chick named Connie Loulabelle Robins from New York City. She was a hippie type and was working her way across North Africa to Marrakech, the mecca for far-out dope heads. Anyway, Connie was a nice sort and worked in he club as a waitress part-time, and I mean very part-time. During the day she would go down to the beach and sell marijuana to the many German tourists, or just hang out smoking shit with me. No use wasting good marijuana, is there. Connie also had some of the best pussy I ever poked. Sometimes when she really wanted to show me who was boss and make my poor body suffer, she'd raise her body up off the bed with me lying on top of her fucking like pussy was going out of style, jam her right index finger into my ass while talking dirty to me at the same time and fuck the hell out of me.

I confessed more things to that lady that I ever told my priest. That bitch brought out the cave man in me, mean muthafucka that I was. Her pussy got so good at times, that I honestly didn't know whether to beat it or eat it. Seriously folks, I think I had better get back to the story, because I know you people out there don't want to hear how Connie made my cock into a black banana split by putting whipped cream, cherries, fresh cut orange slices dripping with juice, and a few raisins all over it before jamming into her greedy, luscious, dick-loving mouth. Now you know that I must have had the sweetest dick in town with this kind of shit going on.

# 16

Like I said, things were really going well for Magic and me, at least until one night. While working at the club testing the lights before it opened, a stranger walked up behind me and tapped me on the shoulder. I slowly turned my wheelchair around and looked up at this mountain of a man and said, 'Can I help you in any way?'

'Are you Robbie Jones?' he asked.

'Yeah, what's left of him,' I joked.

'My name is Koroba. Connie's ex-boyfriend. I want you to tell her that I'm looking for her and want her back,' he said, smiling.

'You tell her yourself, man, I ain't her daddy. I'm just fucking her,' I said with a religious smile that would have made Billy Graham blush.

WHAALUPP, upside my head. This big muthafucka hit me so hard, he almost knocked my dick string loose.

'Look nigger, I'm joking. You tell her that if she wants to keep her pretty face, she'd better come home before I get really nasty. As for you, you no-legged bastard, I'd better not see you around her any more if you know what's good for you.Do you know what's good for you nigger?' he asked, balling up his fist again and making it sell to the size of a cantaloupe.

'I know that I don't want you to hit me upside my head no more, if that's what you mean,' I said, sliding down into my wheelchair.

'That's good. Now you can laugh on the other side of your face, nigger boy,' big Karoba said, walking away and making the floor shake with the sheer weight of his body.

Just then Magic walked in the club, accompanied by two middle-aged admirers. 'Hey Robbie, how's everything going?' he shouted to me up in the lighting box.

'Just let me find my head before I answer that question,' I called back. Magic ran quickly upstairs to see what was going on and shouted in his best girlie voice which was ear piercing. 'Damn honey, what's happened to your eye? Don't tell me Connie beat the shit out of you last night when I didn't come home?'

'Nope. You're almost right, though. Her ex-boyfriend did it about a minute or two before you walked in the club so smugly with your two tricks,' I said, holding my eye.

'Come on, let me take you downstairs and put some ice on that eye before it gets bigger, and you can tell me all about it then,' Magic said.

While sitting in Magic's dressing room having the ice applied to my eye, and explaining to Magic what went down, Connie walked in to the dressing room and said, 'What happened to your eye honey?'

'Your ex-boyfriend is back in town,' I answered.

'Did he do that to you? That big, stupid ass,' she snapped.

'Yeah, I would have kicked his ass, but he ran away too quick,' I said, showing how brave I was, pounding the armrest on my wheelchair with my fist dangerously.

'Don't worry about him again. He's just mad because he went away and left me for another girl and I found you, you handsome devil. I'll go and see that son of a bitch now and tell him a thing or two about fucking with you. I'll see you later about one o'clock. Don't worry about me, I can handle myself, honey,' Connie said as she rushed out the door.

'You tell him that the next time he comes around here, I'll cut his balls off or do something worse,' I called out.

'Boy, that's a tough little momma you got there, Robbie,' Magic said, smiling and starting to put on his make-up in front of the mirror.

'Yeah, she's alright,' I answered, taking a sip of Magic's Tab Bola Beer.

The club opened and was packed within a few minutes, standing room only. The show was going well and Magic sent me up a bottle of whisky to keep me company until Connie arrived. Boy this was living. About two hours later, Connie came up the stairs dressed in a low-cut black dress that showed off her tits, and walked over behind me, putting her hands over my eyes and saying in a sexy voice, 'Guess who?'

'Do you like black banana splits?' I asked.

'Yes,' she answered softly in my ear.

'Do you have red hair around your pussy? I asked.

'Yes, and lots of it,' she whispered in my ear, one again sliding her hand down to my crotch.

'Then you must be Old Rag Mouth Frieda from Indiana,' I said, joking.

'You silly boy,' she said, giving me a playful smack across my jaw. 'How's that eye?' she said, kissing it tenderly.

'It's alright now. just sit down on my knee and give me some loving, baby,' I said as she grabbed my cock-a-rooney, then sat down on my knee giving me another kiss on my greedy lips.

'Did you see Karoba and get everything straightened out, before I kill his ass?' I whispered into Connie's ear as the cabaret music was so loud.

'Yes, you don't have to worry about him anymore. I told him to fuck off because I love you and that we are going back to the States to be married,' she answered.

'What did he do?' I asked.

'He cried, as usual, and begged me on his knees not to leave him. But it was no use. I still told him that I loved you, honey,' Connie said, giving me a hug. I guess it pays to have a sweet dick in your pants, I thought to myself.

While watching the show and sipping on a long, cold whisky, Connie asked to be excused to go to the ladies room which was on the other side of the club. 'Robbie honey, I gotta take a piss. I'll be back in a minute and don't talk to my strange men,' she joked.

'Hurry back. Magic will be going on soon,' I called out to her as she went, and then I turned my attention back to the stage where a woman was being fucked by a snorting donkey, who obviously enjoyed his work, and was the surprise attraction of the evening during dinner.

As I sat watching this big dicked donkey put a mean fuck into the smiling woman, and the cheering men shout, 'Shoot it into her, big donkey, shoot it into her,' two guys ran up behind me and started pushing my wheelchair toward the stairs at a fast pace.

'What the hell's going on here? Who in the fuck are you guys?' I shouted, trying to reach for the brake handle on my chair.

'Karoba warned you, but you wouldn't listen, black boy,' one of the men said, laughing and rolling his eyes like Groucho Marx. Before I could call out for help, I felt myself and the wheelchair flying through the air and down the stairs. I felt like Peter Pan until I hit the floor. As soon as I hit the floor, the wheelchair came crashing down upon my head seconds later, causing me a great deal of pain. the people around the staircase began to scream in terror, frightening the donkey on stage who was now biting and kicking anyone who dared to come near it not wearing a dress. I guess the woman on stage getting the fucking thought the donkey was really getting excited because I could hear her shout to it, 'Is it good to you honey? Is it good to ya?' The stage hands rushed onto the stage and tried to drag the woman away from the donkey as she was now beginning to talk very dirty to it. Me, why the people left my ass on the floor bleeding profusely from a deep scalp wound until dear Connie came to my rescue. I heard one smart ass from the crowd say, 'That nigger fucked up the show. Why couldn't he walk down the stairs like everyone else instead of trying to ride his tricycle down 'em?'

Hearing all the noise and commotion, Magic rushed from his dressing room and called out 'Robbie, Robbie, where are you?'

'I'm down here on the floor in the middle of the crowd,' I shouted as Connie tried top push the people back a bit so I could get some air. Magic pushed his way through the crowd, picked me up in his arms, and carried me out of the club to our apartment around the corner. After laying me down on the front room sofa, he spoke with some concern about my safety. 'What happened Robbie? Are you alright?'

'I think I'm alright. I'm just glad I didn't break my neck or something worse,' I said, feeling myself all over, checking to be sure. About this time Connie walked into the apartment wheeling my slightly bent wheelchair. 'Thanks for bringing my chair,' I said, while holding the right side of my head.

'Robbie, I think that bastard Karoba had something to do with pushing you down the stairs,' Connie said, checking my head at the same time. 'Yeah, you're right. I heard one of the men mention his name and say something about 'I had been warned to keep away from you'.' Who is this Karoba fellow anyway, and what's his damn game?' I asked, thinking there was more to this than meets the eye.

'OK, you have a right to know now, after taking a beating like you did tonight, honey,' Connie said, and went on to explain. 'Karoba wants me to sell dope for him and to work in his casino as a prostitute fucking the rich, fat, Arab oil men. He runs a crooked gambling joint on the west side of town. You know the kind of place I mean.'

'You mean fixed roulette tables, loaded dice, and other things of that nature?' I asked.

'Yeah, the whole bit and much more that I don't want to lie about in this book. He's got his hand in everything that's dishonest and makes a lot of money in this city conning the poor stupid customers.'

'Well, our friend has made me suffer, so I think it's time he suffered a little bit, don't you agree Magic? I asked, giving Magic a wink.

'I'm game if you are, Robbie,' Magic said smiling.

'What do you two mean?' asked Connie, with a worried look on here face.

'Just this. Does Karoba make a lot of money each week and where does he hide it?' I asked Connie.

'Man, he makes a lot of money each week and I do know where he hides it. I used to help count the money and then put it in the wall safe every Sunday night after the casino closed. How's that for service?' Connie said, smiling for revenge.

'Where's the safe located?' I asked.

'Right behind the picture of Mona Lisa in his bedroom over his waterbed,' she answered.

'Well, we'll just have to pay him a little nighttime visit and rob his safe, won't we?' I said, wanting to laugh but for the terrible pain in my head.

'You'll never make it to his bedroom. He has two guards outside his door every night and his apartment is on the sixth floor over the casino. There's no way you can get to the safe,' Connie warned us.

'Are there any burglar alarms anywhere?' Magic asked, filing his fingernails calmly.

'No, not yet. But he's planning to have one installed later this month. I know that because before I ran away he was talking about getting one,' she answered.

'Well, we'll just have to rob his safe next Sunday night sometime, right?' I said, looking up at Magic.

'Look you fools, the only way you can get to that safe is to climb up the outside walls of the casino, which you two can't possibly do. The other problem is, even if you do manage to get into the apartment, you won't know the numbers to open the safe and I sure a shell don't know them. So what then?' Connie asked, becoming more worried than ever over our safety and well-being.

'Don't worry your poor little head, honey, I'm a master safe cracker and cat burglar. It's the only trade I know, other than sell-ing Pussy,' Magic commented.

'You see Connie, you have nothing to worry about, love, Magic went to prison for cracking some of the best safes all along the Ivory Coast of Africa and Mauritania. There's nothing about cracks that Magic doesn't know like, for example, cracks in another man's ass, cracks in pussys, and cracking safes,' I said.

'Honey, I'm the best in the west when it comes to safe crack-ing and I'm hell when I'm well, and I'm loose when I'm full of juice, that's a little Shakespeare if you want to quote it, darling,' Magic said, talking his jive talk he had picked up from the Master, me. While Magic stood there talking his jive and bullshit to Connie, my head began to spin and everything went black and I passed out on the couch.

When I woke up the next morning to the sound of the radio playing, Connie spoke. 'Are you sure you're alright, honey? What happened to you last night?'

'I guess I must have passed out, but I'm alright now. You want to fix me some scrambled eggs, please baby?' I asked.

'OK, you just lay back and take things easy while I go and fix your eggs, Robbie,' she said, giving me a kiss on my greedy lips.

Just then Magic came into the room and shouted to Connie to fix him some eggs also, and then sat down to talk with me. While sitting and discussing the plan of how to rob Karoba's safe, Connie walked back into the room with some food. 'We got it all figured out now, Connie, Magic will drive a stolen car to the casino, climb up the walls, enter the bedroom and rob the safe, while I stay in the car acting as lookout. If anyone comes, I'll light a cigarette to give warning. Magic being as good as he is, should be out in no time,' I explained.

'What about me? What do you want me to do?' Connie asked, not wanting to miss out on the action.

'I was coming to that, darling. I want you to go back to Karoba and pretend you are sorry for leaving him. Tell him you'll never run away again. Tell him anything. Just make sure he's not suspi-cious of anything and that he trusts you. Now that shouldn't be too hard for a sweet-pussy girl like you, should it?' I said.

'I'll have him eating out of my hand,' Connie replied.

'It's better him eating your pussy, honey, it tastes sweeter,' Magic joked.

'How do you know, Magic, you haven't tasted it,' Connie shot back.

'Robbie told me, honey, that boy's toothbrush is full of hair every morning, sweetie,' Magic said with a whoop of laughter.

'Stop it you two. Let me finish explaining the master plan. We can talk about who is eating who and how good it is afterward. Now Connie, this is very, very, important to the plan if it is to succeed. Next Sunday night, after counting all that luscious green money from the week's take, and putting it into Karoba's safe, you must get him to take you out to a restaurant, dancing, and then for a walk on the beach. Anything but to the bedroom where the safe is, stuffed with all that luscious green, hard crackling paper money waiting for us,' I explained carefully.

'Yeah, but what time?' she asked, absently scratching her crotch.

'What time do you usually finish counting the money?' I asked, absently watching her scratch.

'Around one o'clock, most nights,' she answered.

'OK then. Magic will hit the safe at one thirty sharp. Is that OK with you, Magic?' I asked.

'Anytime is the right time for me, honey. What kind of safe is it?' Magic asked Connie like a real pro.

'It's a heavy duty Sorbonne XK .67 Reverse Special,' Connie answered taking the dirty dishes back to the kitchen for the cat's tongue to wash.

'Will that be a problem for you, Magic?' I asked like the amateur I am.

'No way, baby, I'll crack it with my eyes closed. I can be in and out of his apartment in about ten minutes. The hard part is climbing up the casino walls, I just know I'll ruin my manicure, but it will be all right once I get myself into shape, Robbie, don't worry,' Magic said, walking off to the toilet for a piss. As Connie put on her coat and walked over to the door, she turned and said 'Where should I meet you and Magic the day after the robbery and at what time, lover?'

'Meet us at one o'clock in the afternoon inside the old mosque on Roman Street, just opposite the new post office. OK honey?' I said, blowing her a kiss.

'It's a bitch going back to that bastard. I really hate going back to him, but I'll do as you say. By the way, what happens after I meet you with the money in the mosque? I hope you don't plan on staying around here long. Karoba will turn this city upside down looking for us. There's no place in Dakar for us to hide safely. Have you got a plan for leaving the country?' Connie asked as she walked back over to me and gave me a kiss on my greedy, waiting lips.

'You don't think I'm that stupid, do you, not to have a getaway plan, huh? Magic will come in the mosque and meet you, then bring you to the car where I'll be waiting, and drive us to the air[port. Now you must not be late getting to the mosque, because we've got a plane to catch at two o'clock going to the good old USA. Now how's that for planning?' I said, rubbing my hands underneath Connie's dress and up between her meaty thighs.

'Oooh Robbie, you are awful, but I like it, baby,' she said, giving me a big wet kiss and quickly walking over to the door before she started to cry at the thought of leaving her meat man. 'Watch yourself and I'll see you next Monday at one o'clock as planned,' I said, blowing a kiss to her as she went out the door. Magic quickly ran into the room and shouted, 'I'll see you next week, Connie.'

'OK Magic. Don't do anything I wouldn't do while I'm gone,' Connie shouted back while walking down the hall passage.

'That was a long piss you had,' I said to Magic.

'I wanted to leave you two alone to talk a bit before coming back into the room. Anyway, you ain't my daddy to be telling me how long I can take a piss, bitch,' Magic joked.

'Magic, can you make me a cup of coffee and call the airport on the phone downstairs to reserve three tickets for us to fly to the States on Monday afternoon at two o'clock. Any airline will do, but I prefer Pan American,' I said, lighting a cigarette and wishing that it was a joint of you know what.

'I'll do that right now.' Magic said, going out the door humming a few bars of the song, 'If It Don't Fit, Don't Be Shitty And Force It'. While Magic was downstairs on the phone making the reservations and trying to sweet-talk the guy on the other end of the line, I became dizzy in the head and passed out in my wheelchair. Meanwhile, Magic continued to rap on the phone for another twenty minutes before seeing a cloud of smoke coming from underneath our apartment door. He then threw down the phone, ran upstairs, kicked in the door, and saved me by wheeling me through the fire and smoke in the hallway to an open balcony window.

While Magic was trying to revive me, some of the neighbors from downstairs came up to our apartment and put out the fire in the front room. I guess my cigarette had fallen to the carpet when I passed out and started the fire. Once again my dear friend

Magic had saved my life and I was grateful.

'What happened Robbie, did you fall asleep with your cigarette in your hand?' he asked, opening the kitchen door too let
some of the smoke and smell out.

'No man, I passed out again. I don't know what's wrong, but
sometimes I get these dizzy spells and just pass out with no
warning at all. I shit you not,' I said, rubbing my knee.

'Lucky I saw the smoke coming from the apartment, or you
would be one dead nigger by now. I can't take my eyes off you for
one damn minute without you getting into some kind of trouble,'
Magic said jokingly.

'I know, but what can I do? Trouble is my middle name,' I said
trying to smile, but knowing that something was very wrong
with me.

'Seriously Robbie, that's the second time you've passed out.
When did these dizzy spells start?' Magic asked.

'Just after Karoba's men pushed me down the stairs. Yeah,
that's it,' I said remembering the nightmare clearly.

'Well I'll tell you what, old boy, this robbery had better go
right next Sunday night, because you need help badly before
your dizzy spells become worse. Lucky that we are going to
America next week where you can get the best doctors available
to check you out,' Magic said, cleaning up the mess made by the
fire, like the good girl that he was.

'Did you make the reservations for our tickets?' I asked.

'Yeah, it's all set for two o'clock Monday on Pan American
Airlines, and guess what? I also got a date with the desk clerk for
tonight. Oooh, that man drove me wild talking dirty on the
phone. Why, I almost creamed in my britches,' Magic said,
running quickly to take a shower before his date with his newest
unknown lover, Carson P. Carson.

All that week it seemed like every other day I was passing out
from my dizzy spells. Why, Magic must have spent his whole
week's salary paying the doctors to come to our apartment to
tend to me. I was losing weight from not eating and I felt just
awful. Many times I wanted to end it all and take the easy way
out by committing suicide, but the thought of going home to
America kept me from doing it. Anyway the big day was finally
here, it was Sunday and the day of the robbery as well as my
chance to get even with Karoba.

About eight o'clock that night Magic came up the stairs to the
apartment and shouted, 'OK Robbie baby, I got the stolen car.

Now let's get to work. It's a case of shit or wipe now. Are you ready for the big night? Why tomorrow honey, we're gonna be on a plane bound for America and flying in style,' Magic said in excitement.

'I'm ready, let me give the ambassador a call and tell him to meet us at the airport with our passports tomorrow at fifteen minutes before two, just to be sure that nothing goes wrong,' I said.

'You think he will?' Magic asked.

'He'd better. We are paying the bastard two thousand dollars, shit,' I answered as I dialled. After talking to the ambassador and agreeing to pay him an additional one thousand dollars for his personal service, I motioned to Magic that it was time to leave for the casino.

'That son of a bitch of an ambassador is a crook. What kind of shit is he playing on us?' Magic asked angrily, wanting to squeeze a grape to death.

'Don't mind him. He knows that we need his ass right now. We'll get even with him later,' I said, closing the apartment front door. Magic wheeled me down top the car, drove to the casino and parked along the seafront under a full moon shimmering on the water.

While sitting in the car passing the time as we were a little early, and watching people walk in and out of the casino dressed in evening gowns and tuxedos, I said to Magic, 'Hey, do you know where I can get a small deadly snake by tomorrow noon?'

'Yes, why do you ask?' he answered, keeping an eye on the casino entrance.

'I want to give the ambassador a little present tomorrow when he opens our briefcase to count the money,' I said with my most evil smile.

'I'll get the snake after we pull the job tonight, OK?' Magic whispered as a drunken couple lurched past our car, then stopped as the man took time to piss on the front wheel of our car before stumbling on down the street with his hired date.

After waiting for three long hours in the car, the casino began to empty as the gamblers and the musicians of the cabaret made it to their cars and drove off moments later. The lights went out and the casino staff walked out the doors shortly after, said their goodbyes to one another and went their separate ways.

'You see that light up on the second floor? It's probably where Connie and Karoba are counting all that beautiful money,' Magic said, pointing to the window.

'Yeah, it shouldn't be long now before they leave, providing Connie doesn't give him a little quick head,' I said. The front of the casino and parking lots were now deserted.

'You want another cigarette?' Magic asked, searching the glove compartment for another butt.

'Naw, be cool. Here comes a cop from behind the bushes,' I whispered.

The policeman slowly walked up to the car swinging his billy club and said, 'What are you two doing here? The casino is closed.'

'We are just waiting for my wife. She's a bit late getting off work tonight, officer,' I answered.

'Where does she work this late at night? I hope she ain't selling no pussy along my beat, because I'll kick that bitches ass,' the officer said as he rapped his club on the window for emphasis.

'No sir, officer, she works in he casino as a cook,' Magic quickly answered.

'Well don't hang around here for too long. This can be a very dangerous place at night. See that you're gone when I come back this way later. All right?' the officer said, shining his light in the car and then walking off across the street toward the casino, humming a few bars of 'Old Folks At Home'.

'Boy that was close. I'm glad he didn't check to see if the car was stolen,' I said to Magic, who was keeping an eye on the lit window.

Suddenly a light came on in Karoba's bedroom for about ten minutes and then went off again. 'That's it baby, the room is on the sixth floor and facing the sea, just like Connie said,' Magic whispered.

'OK. Get ready. They should be coming out of the casino in a few minutes,' I answered.

'Don't be nervous. It will be a piece of cake pulling this job, honey,' Magic joked. Just as he said that, the casino's main doors opened and out walked Connie and Karoba, with two of his bodyguards following closely.

They walked down the stairs, got into Karoba's Rolls-Royce, and drove off toward the city center. 'Alright you big sissy. Do your job and be careful. Remember that if you see a light in the car, that means someone is coming so watch yourself. OK?' I said as Magic picked up his bag of equipment and got out of the car, walking like a swishy John Wayne.

'Look man, I told you before. You're dealing with a real professional. I've done this more times than you've had hot dinners, sweetheart,' Magic said as he ran from the car to the casino across the street. It was a beautiful sight watching my pal Magic Pussy scale up the walls with his equipment like a human fly and into Karoba's bedroom window. He was in the bedroom for about twenty minutes before coming out and starting down his rope to the ground. Just as Magic was halfway down the wall, and old guard with a pot belly and his huge guard dog walked around the corner of the casino, then stopped to light a cigarette. (Actually it was a joint, just to make the lie more interesting.)

I quickly lit a match to give Magic a warning of danger, but Magic didn't see the signal and continued down the swaying rope like a stormtrooper bucking for a promotion. When Magic Pussy hit the ground, the guard saw him running across the lawn and called out. 'Halt! Halt you bastard before I let my dog loose. Halt, nigger!'

Magic looked around at the guard and his huge dog, and started to haul ass toward the car with his equipment and two big bags of money. I quickly opened the front car door and shouted to Magic. 'Hurry. The dog is gaining on you. Hurry for Godsakes!' As Magic ran around the rose bush, the dog slid around the rose bush. As Magic ran around a big oak tree in the garden of the casino, the dog slid around the oak tree. As Magic ran across the street, puffing and blowing, the dog slid across the street. 'Oh my God. That son of a bitch has got me and he won't let go,' Magic yelled as the dog bit down harder, pulling on his blood-soaked left hand.

Seeing the guard pull a huge pistol, big enough to kill an elephant, and that he was about to cross the street, I shouted to Magic 'Move back, Move your head and shoulders back towards the headrest on your seat so I can take a swing at the dog with this hammer I found under the seat.'

'Stop talking and hit the bastard. He's biting the shit out of my hand,' Magic called out in a great deal of pain and with agony on his face. As the guard fired his pistol twice into the car at us, I quickly let the dog have it over his wolf-shaped head with my hammer as hard as I possibly could. I was trying to do some very serious damage to that mutt's head. The dog's eyes suddenly went counter-clockwise, his balls fell below his knees, and all four of his legs collapsed at the same time, letting his belly drop to the ground, and a very strange expression come over his face as he looked up at me as if to say, 'Why me? I'm only doing my job, nigger.'

'What about the money? It's lying in the street. When the dog bit me I had to let it go,' Magic shouted in panic as he started the car engine.

'Damn the money. That crazy guard is trying to kill us, fool,' I said as the old guard ran nearer the car shouting filthy obscenities in regard to our dear, beloved mothers, God bless their souls. Magic quickly drove off leaving the two sacks of money behind and the guard now standing in the middle of the street firing his pistol at the back of our speeding car.

'You bastard. What didn't you ask Connie about the guard and his dog? I could have been killed, shit,' Magic snapped, shaking like a leaf on a tree.

'I'm sorry about that Magic,' I said apologetically, giving him my handkerchief to wrap around his bleeding hand. To change the subject, I said in fun, 'Magic, you done real well tonight. Why everytime you ran round something in the casino, that damn dog would slide around it. If that dog had been chasing me, I think I would have shit on myself,'

'Shit on yourself, why do you think that dog was sliding so much, fool,' Magic said, finally able to laugh about it and causing an awful smell in the car. 'Look, we'd better not go back to the apartment tonight. Let's drive into the countryside and sleep in the car,' Magic suggested, nervously squirming in his seat.

'You think Karoba might put two and two together and come looking for us?' I asked, holding my nose because of the smell from Magic's shitty pants.

'Maybe. Let's play it safe just in case,' said Magic, turning the car into a small dirt road and driving up into some nearby hills, the land where Moses might well have roamed preaching the word of God Almighty. After reaching a nice secluded spot near a small lake and switching off the engine, I spoke to Magic as he tended his wounded hand. 'Well, we can kiss America goodbye for now. Just think of all that lovely money we let slip through our hands tonight. Son of a bitch, and kiss my old boots,' I shouted in anger as Magic knelt by the side of a small lake and started to undress and wash out his underwear and pants that were shittier than the average bear's. Magic looked over at me while scrubbing another hole in his underwear, smiled, and then said rather calmly, 'Honey, we may have lost the money bags, but we didn't lose everything. I'm a professional, remember sweetheart,' he said in his best Humphrey Bogart voice as he stood on one leg to slip back into his wet undies.

'What do you mean by that?' I asked, thinking that all had been lost. Magic reached into his wet pants pocket with his right hand and pulled out a diamond ring set in gold and silver, then started to wave it in front of my face while singing 'Na Na Na, Na Na Na.'

'Where did you get that from, pal? It's beautiful,' I said in excitement.

'I took it from Karoba's safe along with the two money bags. I couldn't help myself, I guess the devil made me do it. I bet it's worth seven or eight thousand dollars on the black market in town. Don't you think?' Magic asked, rolling his big eyes like Groucho Marx at the lovely jewel and knowing he had saved our poor asses once again.

'Yeah, I believe you're right, pal. Do you know anyone who would give us a good price for it on such short notice?' I asked admiring the ring and then trying it on for size.

'No problem. I know a Jewish closet queen who owns the antique shop in the Casbah who will give me a fair price. But still, you have to be very careful with a Jewish fag, wherever you find her. We'll go to see him early in the morning and see what he can give us for the ring. On the way into town, we'll pick up a couple of skull caps just to show our good faith in his judgement,' Magic said, taking the ring back and trying it on for himself.

'What about the snake I wanted you to get for me?' I asked, trying to find a comfortable position to sleep in on the the small front seat of the car.

'I'll get it for you tomorrow after selling the ring,' Magic said as he jumped over the front seat and into the back. Have you ever seen a black two hundred and twenty-five pound sardine in a leather can? that was Magic as he curled up to sleep.

'OK, let's get some sleep no. Oh, and thanks for everything,' I said.

'Yeah, you sissy, now let me get some sleep too, please,' said Magic, falling asleep instantly.

The next morning bright and early, Magic drove the car with me still fast asleep to the Casbah and parked in front of his friend's antique shop that was already crowded with tourists and shoppers. You must forgive me, but if you call lots of broken toilet seats, bath tubs, and old rocking chairs without the armrests and with the backs missing, 'antiques', then I guess my uncle George was in the antique business also. Only back home we would call this a junk shop – plain and simple without some fancy Hungarian name. Anyway, Magic went into the broken-down shop while I stayed in the car keeping watch for any unusual persons. In about twenty minutes Magic ran from the shop screaming as if the devil himself had showed him his private parts with the intention of violating his body. 'Move over. we've gotta get the hell out of here, and stop looking at me like I'm crazy, fool.'

I quickly moved back over to the passenger's side of the car as Magic started the engine and drove of like a bat out of hell down a lot of side streets knocking down several pushcarts that got in the way. 'What happened in the shop?' I asked as Magic Pussy turned into an alley and parked the car behind a department store.

'What happened? I'll tell you what happened. The ring was a fake, that's what happened,' he answered, shaking all over as if he had a bad case of the heebie-jeebies and the rocking pneumonia.

'Fake? How do you know that?' I asked, seeing America slip away once again.

'Do you remember me telling you that I knew the owner of the shop? Well, his name is Bergota. Anyway, to make a long story longer, Bergota reached under the counter, pulling out a little green box with the prettiest embroidery on it, and showed me twenty-five other rings that were identical to mine, and you know what pissed me off, honey? That son of a bitch also told me that Karoba's men had forced all the jewellers and antique shop owners in the city to sell the rings to the tourists on a regular basis or risk a broken head,' Magic explained.

'OK. Now what made you run out of the shop the way you did?' I asked, as the story was getting more and more cloudy.

'I asked him how much he could give me for the fake ring.'

'And then what happened?' I asked, waiting for the juicy bits.

'Well, honey chile, Bergota took off his skull cap to show me that he meant business, and offered me a hundred American dollars, and then had the nerve to laugh at me as if I were some kind of fool. While that bastard was laughing and bending over to put the phony rings back under the counter, I quickly grabbed a clay model of a dildo and smashed him over the head with it as hard as I could. Honey chile, blood went everywhere. I hope I didn't kill his cheating ass,' Magic said, still shaking with fright.

'Did he have much cash lying around?' I asked, expecting the worst.

'I looked in his cash register, but found nothing. Then I remembered from my last love session with him, how he told me that he always carries his money around his waist in a money belt. So I opened his shirt and there it was, honey. Just waiting for me to take it,' Magic said, showing me his new money belt.

'How much did you get?' I asked, admiring the black and silver studded belt.

'How much? Feast your eyes on this, Robbie. Five thousand, two hundred and fifty two sweet American dollars. Now ain't that a sight to behold?' Magic showed me the money in his outstretched hands.

'That's great, Magic. You've saved our asses again. Let's hurry now and pick up that snake you told me About, and then we'll get Connie from the mosque before something else goes wrong,' I said, handing the money back to him. Magic started the car engine and drove to beautiful downtown Dakar to a specialist pet shop. He bought a deadly asp snake for two hundred dollars and then drove towards the mosque located on the opposite side of the city.

I guess Connie must have had all kinds of crazy thought passing though her pretty little head thinking about our safety, or the possibility that we would take the money and keep on going like most of the people she had been used to dealing with. If she only knew what had happened to us today. As the car swerved around a corner just two blocks from the mosque, the snake box fell off the seat onto the floor, immediately getting all of my attention. 'Hey Magic. You made the damn snake box fall on the floor, driving like a mad man. Can that damn snake get out of the box and bite one of us?' I asked, sliding in my brown pants.

'Naw. Stop being a sissy. That snake ain't gonna fuck with you, unless you fuck with it.'

'Slow down man, there's the mosque up ahead. be cool now,' I said, looking out for danger. As we pulled up in front of the mosque and parked, I noticed that everything was too quiet for my liking. 'Magic, keep the air engine running. I can feel something wrong here, but I just can't put my finger on it,' I said.

'You worry too much. Ain't nothing wrong here, sissy, I'll just run in the mosque, pick up Connie and then dash back to the car in a jiffy. Now are you pleased daddy, or is it mommy, now that you're bitching like an old queen?' Magic said, walking off towards the mosque entrance

'Magic, I ain't fooling. Watch yourself in there,' I shouted. Walking at a quick pace, Magic was just about twenty yards away form the huge gold plated mosque doors, when suddenly the doors opened and out ran Connie, her dress covered in blood and screaming her lungs out.

'Go back. Go back, Magic Pussy. They're gonna kill you.' As she screamed her warning Karoba and two of his henchmen stepped out from behind the huge doors and began to fire their pistols at Magic Pussy, who had turned and was hauling ass back to the car faster than Jesse Owens. As the two henchmen continued to fire at Magic, Karoba slowly walked over to Connie, who had tripped and fallen to the ground trying to warn Magic, aimed his gun at her head and fired the deadly bullets of revenge while showing no emotion on his face.

The anger inside of me was too much to hold back as I saw Karoba pull the trigger and blow away half of poor Connie's face as her limp body fell to the ground. 'You stupid murdering bastard, I hope your shit mother rots in hell,' I shouted in anger and frustration at not being able to do anything to stop this mad killer. Poor Magic, now scared shitless, jumped into the car and drove off like a man possessed by the devil himself, almost knocking over an old woman selling ass on a nearby street corner.

'That's the second time today things have gone wrong. Shit, I could have been killed. It seems like everybody is trying to kill my ass. Where to now, Robbie?' Magic said, driving at breakneck speed wile looking in his rear view mirror to see if Karoba's men were giving chase.

'Just drive to the airport,' I said sadly and nervously as I looked at the speedometer.

'Robbie, I'm terribly sorry about what happened to poor Connie back there. I wish there were more I could have done to help her. She saved my life, you know. If it weren't for her warning I'd be dead by now,' he said as he wiped the tears from his cheeks.

'Yeah, it's a wicked world. It always seems like the good die young. Try not to upset yourself by thinking about it and let's hurry to the airport before the ambassador thinks we aren't coming,' I said, giving Magic another one of my handkerchiefs to wipe away the purple mascara running from his eyes.

After arriving at the airport and parking our stolen car in a dark corner of the underground car park, I asked Magic Pussy if he had brought along the briefcase, as I had requested two days earlier.

'Yeah, it's locked in the trunk of the car. You want me to get it?' he asked, helping me out of the car and into my wheelchair.

'Yeah, but put the snake in the briefcase first, then pile the money over it so the greedy bastard of an ambassador won't notice the little surprise that we have in store for him,' I said with an evil smile.

'You got it. I bought the meanest and most deadly snake to be found in this part of the country,' Magic said, taking the snake from its box and gently putting it into the bottom of the briefcase all comfortable like.

'Now cover the snake with the money like a green blanket to keep it warm. By the way pal, are you sure this snake is really deadly? It looks awful small to me,' I asked, not knowing much about snakes.

'Yeah man, stop worrying. This snake may not be very big, but it's as deadly as hell. It's the same kind of snake Cleopatra used to kill herself with. One bite from this little bastard will knock your dick string loose, and I mean forever,' Magic said, covering the asp with the money.

I took the case and put it on my lap as Magic wheeled me from the car park into the airport lounge where the ambassador was waiting near the electric doors leading into the cafeteria.

'Well hi there, boys. I thought you boys wasn't gonna show up. Have you got my money?' the red-necked ambassador asked as he handed us our passports.

'The money is in the case that I am holding in my hand, sir. You want me to give it to you right here in the open where everyone can see the transaction?' I asked, as it wasn't like the Humphrey Bogart movies I had seen.

'It's the best way, son. That way nobody's gonna think anything bad about our little meeting. Why, anybody watching would just think you nigger boys just wanted to talk to your master. Now give me that money boy, I've got an appointment with the Senegal president in about half an hour and I don't want to be late,' the ambassador said, smiling from ear to ear, like the good old boy that he was.

I handed the briefcase to the ambassador with my most courteous smile and said 'Thanks for helping us. Maybe we'll see you again in the States sometime and get together for dinner in one of Washington's finest restaurants.'

'Not if I can help it,' he said, quickly opening and closing the briefcase to check the money was really there as the airport was now crowded with people walking about near us. 'You boys are alright. I hope you have learned your lesson and will stay home in future. You are the kind of boys that will give home-grown niggers a bad name. Bye, and have a good trip, ya hear?' the ambassador said, walking toward the men's toilet and going inside humming a few bars of his favorite song 'My Brother Wears A Red Dress on Sundays'.

'I guess that big-lipped muthafucka is gonna count our money while he's having a shit,' I said to Magic, who was now waiting for something exciting to happen. Magic turned to me and said, 'I hope that snake bites him dead in his ass,' then chuckled to himself as he wheeled me over to some nearby seats where we sat and waited for the big moment.

About ten minutes later, a huge fat man came running out of the men's toilet screaming his lungs out. 'Help. Help, somebody please help. There's a man in the toilet dying form a snake bite.'

Two airport guards who were standing near the information desk talking and watching the girl's asses go by, quickly ran over. They calmed him down, proceeded to have a few words with him and then rushed into the toilet. They found the red-necked, short-dicked ambassador slumped over on his toilet seat surrounded by the three thousand dollars which had fallen from the briefcase onto the floor with our little pet snake who had done his job so well.

Seconds later, the men's toilet opened and one of the guards, holding his nose from the funky smell, called out to a janitor who was cleaning the stairs leading up to the departure lounge, to come and remove the deadly snake which was ready to bit anyone who came near it without purple mascara on. As the big-eyed janitor slowly walked into the toilet to remove our little asp, the guard ran to phone for an ambulance to remove the dead body of our dear cheating friend, the ambassador.

'Well, that's the end of that. That son of a bitch won't be conning any more poor people out of their worldly goods,' I said as I motioned Magic to wheel me to the ticket desk.

'Robbie, you're great. A pure general and a genius if I must say so myself,' Magic said, laughing as he wheeled me across the airport lounge. Seconds after receiving our tickets and our boarding passes from the desk clerk, an announcement was made over the loudspeakers that our flight was now boarding.

'That's it, Magic. America, here we come,' I said in excitement, shaking Magic's hand in gratitude.

'Yep, America is gonna love this queen, honey,' Magic said laughing and wheeling me down the twisting, turning corridors to the boarding gate. As the plane took off from the runway and lifted up into the air with Magic Pussy and I looking out the windows, the thought of Shilee and the many dead friends I had left behind flashed across my mind and brought a sadness to my heart. To close my mind to the nightmares that had happened, the loss of friendships, and the betrayals, I kept repeating to myself over and over, that's the way God planned it. Who am I to try to change the plan of the Almighty? You win a few, you lose a few, I thought to myself to ease the pain in my heart and mind. Magic Pussy, who was still looking out the window, leaned back in his seat and tried to cheer me up as he noticed that I was on a downer and sinking fast. 'Hey Robbie, let's have a nice bottle of champagne to celebrate your return to America,' he said, all wide-eyed and happy as a lark.

'Yeah, that sounds like a great idea. Tell the steward to bring us one, pal,' I said in a cheerful voice as I didn't want Magic to start to feel sad and go on a downer also. Magic Pussy looked around, motioned the tall blonde steward over to our seats to take our order, and then started to flirt with him. 'What would you like sir?' the steward asked.

'I'd like you if you're free later, honey. I can make you feel loose as a goose and free you of your juice, sailor,' answered Magic, giving the steward a big wink.

'Honey, I'm already married to a well-hung black man, but if there's something else you want, just push the button on the side of your armrest and one of the other girls will be most happy to serve you,' said the steward, starting to walk away.

'Hey, bring my friend and I the best bottle of champagne you got, honey,' Magic shouted to the girly steward who was now walking down the aisle as if he had a dick in his ass.

'That bitch is too smart for my liking,' Magic said jokingly.

After the champagne arrived, we sat drinking and talking about old times. All of a sudden I started to feel sick and dizzy in the head. 'Are you alright? You look terrible all of a sudden,' Magic said, wiping the sweat from my forehead.

'Yeah, I'm alright. You're just saying that about me so that I'll give you my share of the champagne, you little sneaky bastard.' As soon as I said that, my arms and hands went numb, letting my glass fall to the floor, and I passed out in Magic Pussy's arms, forgetting everything from that moment on.

When I did finally awaken, while being wheeled on a stretcher through the airport lobby at Los Angeles International, I was looking at a group of Hari Krishna freaks trying to sell everyone a plastic rose and a book for ten dollars. The ambulance attendants who had picked us up cleared Magic and I through customs quickly with the help of the special agent in charge of the station. They then drove us directly to Cedars-Sinai Hospital. We were brought up on the back elevator directly to the contagious disease ward in case we had carried some ferocious sickness with us. I was then put in Room 109, and Magic was released six hours later, after getting a clean bill of health, except for a small gonorrhea infection in the asshole, possibly from the steward in flight. He came up to my room to check on me. We talked awhile and then I gave him an address in downtown Los Angeles in the Mexican section where he could stay with some friends of mine for a month or two. That was the last time I saw Magic, but he still calls me at least once a week. Old Magic Pussy is doing fine. He lives in San Francisco with a Japanese sumo wrestler and is planning to get married and settle down to being a normal housewife, at least as normal as Magic can be.

As for me, I'll be alright. I'm lying here in bed with a half bottle of gin, telling you my life story, and just waiting patiently for my operation which will take place this coming Tuesday at three o'clock in the afternoon.

Wish me luck and may your God go with you.

# Epilogue

The practice of slavery in Mauritania as depicted in this book has been a way of life that has existed for hundreds of years and continues to this day virtually unnoticed by the civilised world. Nor is Mauritania the only country where this is true. It will require the active participation of the United Nations to put an end to this suffering and inhumanity.

*Geno Washington*
*Fall, 1998*

# New titles from The Do-Not Press:

## Ken Bruen: A WHITE ARREST Bloodlines
*1 899344 41 1 – B-format paperback original, £6.50*

Galway-born Ken Bruen's most accomplished and darkest crime noir novel to date is a police-procedural, but this is no well-ordered 87th Precinct romp. Centred around the corrupt and seedy worlds of Detective Sergeant Brant and Chief Inspector Roberts, A White Arrest concerns itself with the search for The Umpire, a cricket-obsessed serial killer that is wiping out the England team. And to add insult to injury a group of vigilantes appear to to doing the police's job for them by stringing up drug-dealers… and the police like it even less than the victims. This first novel in an original and thought provoking new series from the author of whom Books in Ireland said: "If Martin Amis was writing crime novels, this is what he would hope to write."

## Mark Sanderson: AUDACIOUS PERVERSION Bloodlines
*1 899344 32 2 – B-format paperback original, £6.50*

Martin Rudrum, good-looking, young media-mover, has a massive chip on his shoulder. A chip so large it leads him to commit a series of murders in which the medium very much becomes the message. A fast-moving and intelligent thriller, described by one leading Channel 4 TV producer as "Barbara Pym meets Bret Easton Ellis".

## Jerry Sykes (ed): MEAN TIME Bloodlines
*1 899344 40 3 – B-format paperback original, £6.50*

Sixteen original and thought-provoking stories for the Millennium from some of the finest crime writers from the USA and Britain, including **Ian Rankin** (current holder of the Crime Writers' Association Gold Dagger for Best Novel) **Ed Gorman, John Harvey, Lauren Henderson, Colin Bateman, Nicholas Blincoe, Paul Charles, Dennis Lehane, Maxim Jakubowski** and **John Foster**.

## Jenny Fabian: A CHEMICAL ROMANCE
*1 899344 42 X – B-format paperback original, £6.50*

Jenny Fabian's first book, Groupie first appeared in 1969 and was republished last year to inter-national acclaim. A roman à clef from 1971, A Chemical Romance concerns itself with the infa-mous celebrity status Groupie bestowed on Fabian. Expected to maintain the sex and drugs lifestyle she had proclaimed 'cool', she flits from bed to mattress to bed, travelling from London to Munich, New York, LA and finally to the hippy enclave of Ibiza, in an attempt to find some kind of meaning to her life. As Time Out said at the time: "Fabian's portraits are lightning silhou-ettes cut by a master with a very sharp pair of scissors."

## Maxim Jakubowski: THE STATE OF MONTANA
*1 899344 43 8 half-C-format paperback original £5*

Despite the title, as the novels opening line proclaims: 'Montana had never been to Montana". An unusual and erotic portrait of a woman from the "King of the erotic thriller" (Crime Time magazine).

# New titles from The Do-Not Press:

## Miles Gibson: KINGDOM SWANN
*1 899344 34 9 – B-format paperback, £6.50*

Kingdom Swann, Victorian master of the epic nude painting turns to photography and finds himself recording the erotic fantasies of a generation through the eye of the camera. A disgraceful tale of murky morals and unbridled matrons in a world of Suffragettes, flying machines and the shadow of war.

"Gibson has few equals among his contemporaries" —Time Out

"Gibson writes with a nervous versatility that is often very funny and never lacks a life of its own, speaking the language of our times as convincingly as aerosol graffiti" —The Guardian

## Miles Gibson: VINEGAR SOUP
*1 899344 33 0 – B-format paperback, £6.50*

Gilbert Firestone, fat and fifty, works in the kitchen of the Hercules Café and dreams of travel and adventure. When his wife drowns in a pan of soup he abandons the kitchen and takes his family to start a new life in a jungle hotel in Africa. But rain, pygmies and crazy chickens start to turn his dreams into nightmares. And then the enormous Charlotte arrives with her brothel on wheels. An epic romance of true love, travel and food...

"I was tremendously cheered to find a book as original and refreshing as this one. Required reading..." —The Literary Review

## Paul Charles: FOUNTAIN OF SORROW   Bloodlines
*1 899344 38 1– demy 8vo casebound, £15.00*
*1 899344 39 X – B-format paperback original, £6.50*

Third in the increasingly popular Detective Inspector Christy Kennedy mystery series, set in the fashionable Camden Town and Primrose Hill area of north London. Two men are killed in bizarre circumstances; is there a connection between their deaths and.if so, what is it? It's up to DI Kennedy and his team to discover the truth and stop to a dangerous killer. The suspects are many and varied: a traditional jobbing criminal, a successful rock group manager, and the mysterious Miss Black Lipstick, to name but three. As BBC Radio's Talking Music programme avowed: "If you enjoy Morse, you'll enjoy Kennedy."

## Ray Lowry: INK
*1 899344 21 7 – Metric demy-quarto paperback original, £9*

A unique collection of strips, single frame cartoons and word-play from well-known rock 'n' roll cartoonist Lowry, drawn from a career spanning 30 years of contributions to periodicals as diverse as Oz, The Observer, Punch, The Guardian, The Big Issue, The Times, The Face and NME. Each section is introduced by the author, recognised as one of Britain's most original, trenchant and uncompromising satirists, and many contributions are original and unpublished.

## Also available from The Do-Not Press

### The Hackman Blues by Ken Bruen
ISBN 1899344 22 5 — C-format paperback original, £7
"If Martin Amis was writing crime novels, this is what he would hope to write."
— Books in Ireland
A job of pure simplicity. Find a white girl in Brixton. Piece of cake. What I should have done is doubled my medication and lit a candle to St Jude — maybe a lot of candles."
Add to the mixture a lethal ex-con, an Irish builder obsessed with Gene Hackman, the biggest funeral Brixton has ever seen, and what you get is the Blues like they've never been sung before. Ken Bruen's powerful second novel is a gritty and grainy mix of crime noir and Urban Blues that greets you like a mugger stays with you like a razor-scar.

### Smalltime by Jerry Raine
ISBN 1 899344 13 6 — C-format paperback original, £5.99
Smalltime is a taut, psychological crime thriller, set among the seedy world of petty criminals and no-hopers. In this remarkable début, Jerry Raine shows just how easily curiosity can turn into fear amid the horrors, despair and despondency of life lived a little too near the edge.
"The first British contemporary crime novel featuring an underclass which no one wants. Absolutely authentic and quite possibly important."— Philip Oakes, Literary Review.

### That Angel Look by Mike Ripley
"The outrageous, rip-roarious Mr Ripley is an abiding delight…" — Colin Dexter
1 899344 23 3 — C-format paperback original, £8
A chance encounter (in a pub, of course) lands street-wise, cab-driving Angel the ideal job as an all-purpose assistant to a trio of young and very sexy fashion designers.
But things are nowhere near as straightforward as they should be and it soon becomes apparent that no-one is telling the truth — least of all Angel!

### It's Not A Runner Bean by Mark Steel
ISBN 1 899344 12 8 — C-format paperback original, £5.99
'I've never liked Mark Steel and I thoroughly resent the high quality of this book.' — Jack Dee
The life of a Slightly Successful Comedian can include a night spent on bare floorboards next to a pyromaniac squatter in Newcastle, followed by a day in Chichester with someone so aristocratic, they speak without ever moving their lips.
From his standpoint behind the microphone, Mark Steel is in the perfect position to view all human existence. Which is why this book — like his act, broadcasts and series' — is opinionated, passionate, and extremely funny. It even gets around to explaining the line (screamed at him by an Eighties yuppy): 'It's not a runner bean…' — which is another story.
'A terrific book. I have never read any other book about comedy written by someone with a sense of humour.' — Jeremy Hardy, Socialist Review.

**Also available from The Do-Not Press**

## Charlie's Choice: The First Charlie Muffin Omnibus by Brian Freemantle – Charlie Muffin; Clap Hands, Here Comes Charlie; The Inscrutable Charlie Muffin

ISBN 1 899344 26 8, C-format paperback, £9

Charlie Muffin is not everybody's idea of the ideal espionage agent. Dishevelled, cantankerous and disrespectful, he refuses to play by the Establishment's rules. Charlie's axiom is to screw anyone from anywhere to avoid it happening to him. But it's not long before he finds himself offered up as an unwilling sacrifice by a disgraced Department, desperate to win points in a ruthless Cold War. Now for the first time, the first three Charlie Muffin books are collected together in one volume. 'Charlie is a marvellous creation' – Daily Mail

## Song of the Suburbs by Simon Skinner

ISBN 1 899 344 37 3 – B-format paperback original, £5

Born in a suburban English New Town and with a family constantly on the move (Essex to Kent to New York to the South of France to Surrey), who can wonder that Slim Manti feels rootless with a burning desire to take fun where he can find it? His solution is to keep on moving. And move he does: from girl to girl, town to town and country to country. He criss-crosses Europe looking for inspiration, circumnavigates America searching for a girl and drives to Tintagel for Arthur's Stone... Sometimes brutal, often hilarious, Song of the Suburbs is a Road Novel with a difference.

## Head Injuries by Conrad Williams

ISBN 1 899 344 36 5 – B-format paperback original, £5

It's winter and the English seaside town of Morecambe is dead. David knows exactly how it feels. Empty for as long as he can remember, he depends too much on a past filled with the excitements of drink, drugs and cold sex. The friends that sustained him then – Helen and Seamus – are here now and together they aim to pinpoint the source of the violence that has suddenly exploded into their lives. Soon to be a major film.

## The Long Snake Tattoo by Frank Downes

ISBN 1 899 344 35 7 – B-format paperback original, £5

Ted Hamilton's new job as night porter at the down-at-heel Eagle Hotel propels him into a world of seedy nocturnal goings-on and bizarre characters. These range from the pompous and near-efficient Mr Butterthwaite to bigoted old soldier Harry, via Claudia the harassed chambermaid and Alf Speed, a removals man with a penchant for uninvited naps in strange beds.

But then Ted begins to notice that something sinister is lurking beneath the surface

**BLOODLINES the cutting-edge crime and mystery imprint...**

## Hellbent on Homicide by Gary Lovisi

ISBN 1 899344 18 7 — C-format paperback original, £7

"This isn't a first novel, this is a book written by a craftsman who learned his business from the masters, and in HELLBENT ON HOMICIDE, that education rings loud and long." —Eugene Izzi

1962, a sweet, innocent time in America... after McCarthy, before Vietnam. A time of peace and trust, when girls hitch-hiked without a care. But for an ice-hearted killer, a time of easy pickings. "A wonderful throwback to the glory days of hardboiled American crime fiction. In my considered literary judgement, if you pass up HELLBENT ON HOMICIDE, you're a stone chump." —Andrew Vachss

Brooklyn-based Gary Lovisi's powerhouse début novel is a major contribution to the hardboiled school, a roller-coaster of sex, violence and suspense, evocative of past masters like Jim Thompson, Carroll John Daly and Ross Macdonald.

## Fresh Blood II edited by Mike Ripley & Maxim Jakubowski

ISBN 1 899 344 20 9 — C-format paperback original, £8.

Follow-up to the highly-acclaimed original volume (see below), featuring short stories from John Baker, Christopher Brookmyre, Ken Bruen, Carol Anne Davis, Christine Green, Lauren Henderson, Charles Higson, Maxim Jakubowski, Phil Lovesey, Mike Ripley, Iain Sinclair, John Tilsley, John Williams, and RD Wingfield (Inspector Frost)

## Fresh Blood edited by Mike Ripley & Maxim Jakubowski

ISBN 1 899344 03 9 — C-format paperback original, £6.99

Featuring the cream of the British New Wave of crime writers including John Harvey, Mark Timlin, Chaz Brenchley, Russell James, Stella Duffy, Ian Rankin, Nicholas Blincoe, Joe Canzius, Denise Danks, John B Spencer, Graeme Gordon, and a previously unpublished extract from the late Derek Raymond. Includes an introduction from each author explaining their views on crime fiction in the '90s and a comprehensive foreword on the genre from Angel-creator, Mike Ripley.

## Shrouded by Carol Anne Davis

ISBN 1 899344 17 9 — C-format paperback original, £7

Douglas likes women —— quiet women; the kind he deals with at the mortuary where he works. Douglas meets Marjorie, unemployed, gaining weight and losing confidence. She talks and laughs a lot to cover up her shyness, but what Douglas really needs is a lover who'll stay still —— deadly still. Driven by lust and fear, Douglas finds a way to make girls remain excitingly silent and inert. But then he is forced to blank out the details of their unplanned deaths.

Perhaps only Marjorie can fulfil his growing sexual hunger. If he could just get her into a state of limbo. Douglas studies his textbooks to find a way...

**BLOODLINES the cutting-edge crime and mystery imprint...**

**BLOODLINES the cutting-edge crime and mystery imprint…**

## Tooth & Nail by John B Spencer
ISBN 1 899344 31 4 — C-format paperback original, £7

The long-awaited new noir thriller from the author of Perhaps She'll Die. A dark, Rackmanesque tale of avarice and malice-aforethought from one of Britain's most exciting and accomplished writers. "Spencer offers yet another demonstration that our crime writers can hold their own with the best of their American counterparts when it comes to snappy dialogue and criminal energy. Recommended." — Time Out

## Perhaps She'll Die! by John B Spencer
ISBN 1 899344 14 4 — C-format paperback original, £5.99

Giles could never say 'no' to a woman… any woman. But when he tangled with Celeste, he made a mistake… A bad mistake.

Celeste was married to Harry, and Harry walked a dark side of the street that Giles — with his comfortable lifestyle and fashionable media job — could only imagine in his worst nightmares. And when Harry got involved in nightmares, people had a habit of getting hurt. Set against the boom and gloom of eighties Britain, Perhaps She'll Die! is classic noir with a centre as hard as toughened diamond.

## Last Boat To Camden Town by Paul Charles
Hardback: ISBN 1 899344 29 2 — C-format original, £15
Paperback: ISBN 1 899344 30 6 — C-format paperback, £7

The second enthralling Detective Inspector Christy Kennedy mystery. The body of Dr Edmund Godfrey Berry is discovered at the bottom of the Regent's Canal, in the heart of Kennedy's "patch" of Camden Town, north London. But the question is, Did he jump, or was he pushed? Last Boat to Camden Town combines Whodunnit? Howdunnit? and love story with Paul Charles' trademark unique-method-of-murder to produce one of the best detective stories of the year. "If you enjoy Morse, you'll enjoy Kennedy" — Talking Music, BBC Radio 2

## I Love The Sound of Breaking Glass by Paul Charles
ISBN 1 899344 16 0 — C-format paperback original, £7

First outing for Irish-born Detective Inspector Christy Kennedy whose beat is Camden Town, north London. Peter O'Browne, managing director of Camden Town Records, is missing. Is his disappearance connected with a mysterious fire that ravages his north London home? And just who was using his credit card in darkest Dorset? Although up to his neck in other cases, Detective Inspector Christy Kennedy and his team investigate, plumbing the hidden depths of London's music industry, turning up murder, chart-rigging scams, blackmail and worse. I Love The Sound of Breaking Glass is a detective story with a difference. Part whodunnit, part howdunnit and part love story, it features a unique method of murder, a plot with more twists and turns than the road from Kingsmarkham to St Mary Mead.

# The Do-Not Press
## Fiercely Independent Publishing

Keep in touch with what's happening at the cutting edge of independent British publishing.

Join The Do-Not Press Information Service and receive advance information of all our new titles, as well as news of events and launches in your area, and the occasional free gift and special offer.

Simply send your name and address to:
The Do-Not Press (Dept. BB)
PO Box 4215
London
SE23 2QD
or email us: thedonotpress@zoo.co.uk

There is no obligation to purchase and no salesman will call.

Visit our regularly-updated web site:
http://www.thedonotpress.co.uk

---

## Mail Order

All our titles are available from good bookshops, or (in case of difficulty) direct from The Do-Not Press at the address above. There is no charge for post and packing.

**(NB: A postman may call.)**